JUDGES' CITATION
FOR THE 2022 RESTLESS BOOKS PRIZE
FOR NEW IMMIGRANT WRITING

An intricate international thriller, *Between This World and the Next* tells the story of Fearless, a burned-out British war photographer, and Song, a Cambodian woman who has been physically and psychologically marked by the violence in her country. When Song disappears, leaving only a mysterious videotape behind, Fearless must navigate a dangerous network of power brokers, transnational kingpins, sex traffickers, and arms dealers, uncovering a sprawling network of criminality and corruption in a newly post-Soviet world. Praveen Herat challenges our own complicity as passive observers when exposed to a constant stream of media depicting suffering across the world and asks what we truly know about anyone, even those we hold dearest. And yet, riven by dark acts, the book is uplifted by love—love between sisters, love of the bereaved, and a remarkable platonic love between Fearless and Song.

This propulsive, page-turning novel is a passionate exploration of power, poverty, and greed. With its sharp new perspective, *Between This World and the Next* pushes the boundaries of what a literary thriller can achieve.

PRIZE JUDGES TIPHANIE YANIQUE,
DEEPAK UNNIKRISHNAN, AND ILAN STAVANS

Praise for

BETWEEN THIS WORLD AND THE NEXT

"Captivating, immersive, and arrestingly beautiful, *Between This World and the Next* holds you in its grip as it effortlessly navigates the complexities of our modern world."

— SALEEM HADDAD, author of *Guapa*

"A hauntingly beautiful story of loss and war and the lives we build around them. Herat's rendering of Cambodia is vivid, dark, and heartbreaking, as three-dimensional as any character. With echoes of Lawrence Osborne and Graham Greene, *Between This World and the Next* brutally and wrenchingly captures the consequences of modern amorality and the sacrifices we make for redemption. A tale that's determined not to let you go."

— I. S. BERRY, author of *The Peacock and the Sparrow*

"After a chance encounter, Song and Fearless, each burdened with trauma, each with grief, set off on an extraordinary journey. First through the Cambodian underworld to uncover the mastermind behind a brutal criminal ring, then across Asia, Africa, and Europe to find and save each other, and finally through a mazy wilderness of arms dealers, spies, ordinary citizens, and corrupt, powerful bureaucrats to see if even in this fallen world, they might retain their fundamental humanity and, just possibly, also find the one true reason to live: love. Thrilling, terrifying, and complex, endowed with unforgettable characters and imbued with great beauty, *Between This World and the Next* is a terrific, gorgeous novel."

— PAUL GRINER, author of *The Book of Otto and Liam*

"Set in Cambodia, *Between This World and the Next* is a tender yet clear-eyed thriller, enlivened by a large cast of succinctly drawn characters led by haunted war photographer, Fearless, and Song—a local young woman who has just about mastered how to keep her nightmares at bay. Elevated by a subtle hum of near-poetic prose, *Between This World and the Next* is a compelling debut by a novelist who clearly enjoys his storytelling, but also cares about enduring human questions of love and rage, witness and action, and what it means to be good."

— NII AYIKWEI PARKES, author of *Tail of the Blue Bird* and *Azúcar*

BETWEEN
THIS WORLD
AND THE NEXT

BETWEEN THIS WORLD AND THE NEXT

PRAVEEN HERAT

RESTLESS BOOKS

NEW YORK • AMHERST

First Restless Books hardcover edition June 2024

Hardcover ISBN: 9781632063670
Library of Congress Control Number: 2023945865

This book is supported in part by an award from the National Endowment for the Arts.

Cover illustration by Sukutangan
Cover design by Keenan
Text designed and set in Monotype Dante by Tetragon, London

Printed in the United States of America

1 3 5 7 9 10 8 6 4 2

RESTLESS BOOKS
NEW YORK • AMHERST

www.restlessbooks.org

For my mother
—and in memory of my father

BETWEEN THIS WORLD AND THE NEXT

Open your eyes. Empty your mind. What's happening in the present will pass. This is what Song tells herself.

It's dark and hot and the middle of the night. Through the light that comes from the open door, she sees a bead of sweat on the tip of his nose.

He's kind to have given her fruit juice. How long since she's tasted juice like that. Fresh from Pursat oranges, so sharp, so sweet, the little flakes of pulp floating on her tongue.

But no one has touched her in a very long time. So many hands for so many years and then weeks and months of not being touched at all.

He holds her head down, twists it to her good side.

Images circle in her mind. Her old home. The starlight on the floor. Her golden bear under the crook of her arm.

Don't follow those thoughts, Song tells herself. *You're eighteen, not twelve.* Her body goes limp. The bead of sweat finally falls—a drop on her cheek that runs away like a tear.

When they want to imagine someone else, they close their eyes. But his eyes are open, roving her face with a kind of hunger she isn't familiar with. He gasps, tenses, stays completely still.

When she looks again, he is standing in the corner of the room. His back is turned and his shoulders are hunched.

"Orkun charan," he says to the back of the door. *Thank you very much.* As if she'd had a choice.

She listens to his feet slap down the stairs, then gets up and crosses the courtyard via the walkway.

In the guest apartment she hurries to the wet room. She will wash it away and it will flow to the river. Dissolve into the endless tides of the sea.

After she is clean, she wraps herself in her sampot and winds her krama around her head so the burned side is covered. Down in the building's entrance hall she lights the incense sticks in the spirit house. She checks the small blue and white saucer of lychee and smells the jasmine.

"Respect the spirits but don't think they give a damn about your sister," Mr. Thom makes a point of telling her. "Just accept the truth. She's as good as dead."

But Sovanna will find her. And then anything and everything will be possible.

An army truck thunders along the street. Song blows out the match and ducks into the shadows, crouching between the scooters that are parked inside the hall. Through the metal concertina gate she sees soldiers in the truck bed. People are unhappy with the results of the elections and the men will make sure they keep their objections to themselves.

Up above, she hears Thom slamming the door of the Naga Bar; the drunken muttering of the last barang as they lurch into the street and hail their motodops. The power goes out suddenly: no more karaoke, no streetlight. After the sound of the engines have faded, there is only a barking dog and the noodle boy tapping his woodblock. Toc-Toc. Toc. Toc-Toc. Toc.

Back in her room, she looks down at the trio of men on the street corner, bathed in the light of the almost full moon: the tire repairer, asleep within a fort of inner tubes; the cyclo driver curled in his passenger seat like a house cat; the motodop lying flat on his back, his feet crossed casually on the handlebars of his Daelim. She knows each man well, his temperament, his mien, their grumbles and quarrels and laughs. She knows the people who dwell in the dark apartments above—their thoughtfulness at sunset, when they emerge onto their balconies to gaze east to the river in the rose-colored light. But none of them know her. Three rainy seasons have passed since Song has stepped outside. This building—this labyrinth of dank stairwells and partitioned boxes where bong thoms and drunken sexpats get their kicks—is her prison.

Once Sovanna has found her, they will go back to Battambang—to the days of playing tag under the stilts of the family home, the chickens squawking and scattering at their feet. In the heat of the midday sun, they will gather under the shade tree, listening to the sounds of the vast, silent country, sensing the year's turning through the harvests of fruits and vegetables.

At the end of their working nights in Phnom Penh, they would lie together and list those harvests as a way of remembering:

"Rice," she would say, resting her head in Sovanna's lap.

"Mango," Sovanna would reply.

"Coconut."

"Cassava."

"Potato."

"Papaya."

"The flooded fields of lotus and lilies."

Song imagines she is helping Ma, chopping the greens for the evening meal: grilled buffalo, a special treat that proves their parents do their best, even in times of hardship, even in the midst of war. Ma tells her to call Sovanna and Pa. And when she shouts *bong*—big sister—Sovanna answers *oun*—little one—just as she has always done, even though she is only ten minutes older. Then she walks steadily across the field and Song sees her beautiful face in the twilight—a face to which Song's had once been completely identical.

When she remembers that face, and feels the radiance that comes from it, Song forgets what she has suffered, alone in Phnom Penh these years.

Empty your mind, she tells herself again as she waits for sleep. It's okay. Even what just happened. You can put it in a space outside the story. She will not remember. He never came. For what circumstances would bring it back, what conjunction of the stars?

PART 1

"Only part of us is sane: only part of us loves pleasure and the longer day of happiness, wants to live to our nineties and die in peace, in a house that we built, that shall shelter those who come after us. The other half of us is nearly mad . . . and wants to die in a catastrophe that will set back life to its beginnings and leave nothing of our house save its blackened foundations. Our bright natures fight in us with this yeasty darkness, and neither part is commonly quite victorious, for we are divided against ourselves and will not let either part be destroyed."

REBECCA WEST
from *Black Lamb and Grey Falcon*

"If only it were all so simple! If only there were evil people somewhere insidiously committing evil deeds, and it were necessary only to separate them from the rest of us and destroy them. But the line dividing good and evil cuts through the heart of every human being . . . it is after all only because of the way things worked out that they were the executioners and we weren't."

ALEXANDER SOLZHENITSYN
from *The Gulag Archipelago*

1

"Nairobi. Kenya. Dar es Salaam. Tanzania." Song practiced the names as she cleaned the Naga Bar, clearing its tabletops of glasses and ashtrays, sweeping up tissue balls and cigarette butts and chicken bones, wiping down the sticky leatherette of the armchairs, bagging up the cans of Angkor and Anchor, gathering the towels that were wet with sweat and come and blood. Every day, this was what she loved to do in secret: listen to the World Service while she got through her chores, trying to learn of the world beyond these walls. She enjoyed the shapes the foreign names made on her tongue. How jealous she and Sovanna had been of Chamroeun in the village when he was allowed to go to the wat to read and write! When they escaped, that's what they'd do. Go home and learn for the sake of learning.

There had been bombs, the announcer said, two weeks ago, on August seventh. American embassies attacked. Two hundred dead. Four thousand injured. She placed the newly clean glasses on the shelves of the bar and polished the beng wood of the seven-headed Naga sculpture. In the VIP room, she stopped mopping and stood still for a moment; there was a discussion between several men with words she didn't understand. She was trying to decipher it when Thom burst in, growling.

"What the hell, bitch! I told you only yesterday! Get the apartment cleaned. The guest will arrive in an hour."

He was bare-chested, his sampot hitched above his knees, the corners of his eyes and lips tightly clenched.

Before she could say a word, he swatted her with his newspaper. As she cowered, he kicked at her legs, then flurried her with slaps and punches, half of them landing, half grazing the wall. Her krama came loose and fell when he yanked at it.

"No, please!" she cried. There was no point in saying that he had never mentioned cleaning the apartment.

"What? You don't like it? Come then! Let's go."

Gripping her by the upper arm, Thom pulled her down the stairs, hustling her across the foyer and up to the street gate.

"Here! You go, then. Let's see what you do."

He hauled open the concertina.

"Come on. No one's keeping you."

It was true. No one shackled Song or bolted her door at nightfall. The only thing that imprisoned her in the Naga was her shame. Not the shame of how her face looked but the shame of what it said to people. For only someone bad in some fundamental way—deeper than even their thoughts or feelings—could deserve to be punished in such a horrible manner.

"Beam kador khnom," Thom muttered as he tramped up the stairs. "And don't forget to bring in the deliveries."

No matter how hard Song toiled, Thom would find fault. But it didn't bother her now. She was beyond hating him: his stale milk smell and his prahok breath and the big mole on his cheek whose hairs he loved to preen. She had learned something from him. To *not* be like him. To never be unjust, to never feel so weak that only someone else's misery might make you stronger. Everything else he did, she could wipe from her memory, along with the other men that had loomed over her life: men like the hundreds of johns from their days in The Sunflower, the "five-star" bar she and Sovanna once worked in; men with wide-eyed stares and silent cries during the years when she had come to despise her own beauty. Oh to be ugly, to be undesirable. The irony of that wish now.

Once Thom had entered his room and slammed the door, Song hurried back to reclaim her krama. As she bent over to tuck it into a knot around her head, something caught her eye: a fragment of plaster, crumbled from the wall—no doubt a casualty of one of Thom's stray kicks. It revealed a cable, thinner than normal electrical cord, that she had never noticed during all her mopping and sweeping. She reached down and prodded it as if it were a small, still animal.

But there was no time to investigate. She swept and mopped the guest apartment, made both beds, and opened the door to the balcony for air. Just as she did, the drinks truck arrived and she hurried up and down the stairs, hauling beer crates and jangling boxes of vodka.

As she stepped outside with bottles of water to stock the guest apartment, the heavens suddenly opened, unleashing the monsoon. Something unbidden rose in her stomach. She rushed to the toilet and threw up violently, the sound of splashing overwhelming all her senses: her puke in the bowl, flushing water, thundering rain.

She didn't hear the street gate opening or footsteps hurrying into the building's foyer. Only until they turned the last flight of steps did she register that two men were on their way up. As she sprinted to the door she heard one asking in English:

"And what time will my friend Mr. Federenko get here?"

2

"Mr. Federenko come soon," the driver said, lugging Fearless's duffel up the stairs.

Above, on the landing, he saw a blur of pattering feet and a cowled figure disappearing through a door. The rain was disorienting, hammering on the skylight like a million masonry nails tossed from above. Fearless's work as a war photographer had taken him nearly everywhere except Asia, so the sheer speed and volume of the monsoon surprised him. When the driver led him through the open door of a whitewashed apartment, he was stunned to look out from its balcony and see the water reaching pedestrians' knees, the thoroughfares now canals traversed by cars and tuk-tuks that left parabolas of foam rippling in their wake. Clothes stuck to people's skin. Ropes of water twisted from awnings.

Cambodia at last. How long his life had been this way, disappearing in one location and resurfacing in another, consistent only in its utter inconsistency.

Quae mundi plaga?

That was his perennial question on waking: which country, which place, which time zone, which bed? Often, the light from the crack in the curtains would show fruit slices under cling film or rectangles of Lipton tea, a whirring ceiling fan that signified *hotel*. If he were luckier, he'd see Laure's hair tumbling across the pillow, the constellation of moles on the nape of her neck, the cornflower blue sheets of their bed in the cottage.

"But Cambodia. Really!" Conrad had muttered when he'd revealed that Alyosha had offered him the trip.

"I go now," the driver said, putting Fearless's duffel down by the sofa.

"Remind me of your name." He liked the man's gentle smile and thick wedge of hair.

"My nem Bun Thim." The *bun* rhymed with the *un* in *wunderbar*; the *h* in *Thim* was barely detectable.

"Thank you, Bun Thim." When Fearless reached to shake the man's hands he noticed that they were ridged with horrible burns, the skin behind the knuckles pulled tight, knotted and warped.

He watched Bun Thim's Toyota crest through the waters and join the sporadic traffic back on the riverside. Fearless wandered slowly around the apartment. There were two bedrooms, one internal and one giving onto the street. He would let Alyosha decide who would have which.

Then came a kerfuffle outside on the stairs—an ostentatious stamping of wet feet on concrete.

"Bacha! You're here!" Alyosha cried, striding in, his arms spread wide.

Fearless hardly had a chance to take him in before Alyosha hugged him, but he could tell his friend had changed. This gentleman in a suit, hair trimmed and freshly Brylcreemed, was nothing like the scruff he'd met six years ago. There was weight around Alyosha's cheeks, now pressed firmly against his: the signifier of a new prosperity.

"Mon frère," Alyosha whispered—the greeting he always reserved for Fearless.

"Mon frère," Fearless replied, returning the embrace.

Alyosha patted Fearless's back several times before a series of hiccups seized his chest.

"Oh, Laure!" Alyosha murmured. Images spiraled through Fearless's mind. Her red hatchback flipping end over end. Firefighters wrestling hoses on a carriageway dotted with wreckage. The contents of her handbag strewn on the tarmac: the plane tickets for their last holiday before the baby was born; the hospital form with all the details of how she would give birth. They would listen to *The Köln Concert* and *Spirit of Eden*, she had decided.

Alyosha emitted another hiccup. "It seems like only yesterday I was talking to her on the phone."

"You spoke to Laure recently?"

"It was strange," he said, gripping Fearless's upper arms. "She called and said she urgently needed my advice. And I gave her a time to call back and waited. And waited. And then—I heard the reason why."

He stifled another sob and hugged Fearless again.

"How was the funeral?"

"Fine," Fearless said.

But it had been dreadful. There had been demons in the vaulted ceiling of the cathedral, curling their tails around the ornamental bosses and cackling. Laure would have hated it. A Church of England service. Congregation, save for Fearless, all dressed in black.

"They brought the baby," Fearless said. "In a little white coffin." He pressed his eyes into his friend's pinstriped shoulder; the paramedics had performed an emergency C-section at the scene.

Alyosha cupped Fearless's head in both hands and brought it down till their foreheads pressed together.

Everything about the funeral had been wrong, so wrong, but he hadn't dared argue with Laure's father, brother, and sister, their backs lined up on the pew in front of his. Laure had wanted a cremation with her ashes scattered in the Channel. "Afterwards, everyone can add a stone to the cairn in the garden," she had said. "They can watch the sun set. Drink some cognac if they like." It was a professional quirk to muse about such things—in hotel rooms, at bars, under curfews and gunfire.

"I'm so glad you're here, bacha," Alyosha said, wiping his eyes. "I figured you need a change. Get away from that cottage."

"I've barely been back there."

"What?"

"There's too much shit."

"All her papers."

"All her papers and files piled everywhere. Foreign Reporter of the Year. She was in the running, apparently."

"Let Conrad and Lucy take care of it—what is family for?"

Alyosha was right. His surrogate father and surrogate sister; there was no one else on earth who would now lay claim to him.

He dug out a pack of cigarettes and held it out to Alyosha.

"No. I've given up."

"What? Jesus. No."

"I have to keep these clean," said Alyosha, drawing back his lips.

"Oh my," Fearless said: Alyosha's teeth, mangled in his Red Army days in Afghanistan, had been replaced by a set of gleaming implants.

"I have a dentist in Tel Aviv. And look," Alyosha said, lifting his arm to reveal a golden Rolex. "Like Paul Newman. Thirty-six thousand vibrations per second."

Fearless smiled. The acquisitiveness he would have sneered at in any Western friend he forgave in someone who had lived through Brezhnev's gody zastoya. Alyosha had queued for toilet roll in subzero temperatures. Supermarkets, salami, and chewing gum were magical to him.

"See. These little subdials—that's what they call them—have block markers. These tiny squares on the very thin sticks."

"But Cambodia. I can't believe it. What the hell are we doing here?"

"I have clients to entertain for a few days in Phnom Penh. But we'll take a trip to Angkor Wat. Visit the orphanage I'm helping."

"Do people come to Phnom Penh for entertainment these days?"

"My boss has investments here. When I met him, it spoke to me. Because I've always felt a connection to the country through your father." Alyosha clapped his hand on Fearless's shoulder. "You know how much I believe in destiny."

"But also that we're all the masters of our fates."

"Well, destiny exists, bacha, but our fates are not decided. The invisible hand puts us down on the board, but *we* are the ones who choose when and where we move. And after this deal is done in Cambodia, I'm going back to Russia. No one will be bossing me."

Alyosha's certainty never ceased to amaze Fearless; it was why Fearless—for whom belief was always provisional, always tempered with the duty to see the other side—adored him.

Alyosha held up his finger and thumb and moved them slowly closer together. "Once this deal is done, I'll have new apartment in Moscow. I don't care if they are saying gold rush is over. Or a Stalinka. No—a house! Yes. A palace in Rublevka!"

"And Odesa?"

"What? No no. Forget about Odesa."

"What about Vera?"

Alyosha shrugged. "Things happen."

"You should have told me. What?" Fearless put his hand on his head and kept it there. "This is big," he added.

"No, not big. No no. She has the Siemens washing machine she is always dreaming of. Come—you know what Khrushchev said. About the wet hen."

An exceptionally tall Black man came through the door. His torso was broad and impressively tapered, his black T-shirt tucked into loose, black slacks. He carried a hard-shell Samsonite attaché case.

"Ah, you're back," said Alyosha. "Fearless, this is Amos. Amos, Fearless. Did you manage that job?"

Amos nodded and raised the case.

Despite his imposing build, Amos was no tough, Fearless saw. There was something about his short dreads that softened the first impression. And he had to be trustworthy—that much was certain—for Alyosha was rarely happy delegating any task.

"Back in Bosnia and Chechnya, Amos, I was Fearless's fixer. He gave me a job when I had nothing. I never forget this."

"He showed me your p-pictures," Amos said in a South London accent.

"Of the bombings in Nairobi," Alyosha added. "Fearless is always the same. The right man, in the wrong place."

It was pure coincidence, Fearless wanted to tell them. He had gone to Nairobi with Luke to visit Jimmy—a "high school reunion," Luke had dubbed it, though they had known each other longer, since the age of twelve. That night, he had passed out on Jimmy's sofa, still fully dressed, before the first explosion made him sit up in a daze. The second explosion—the real bomb—shattered the windows of Jimmy's apartment, the hail of a million fragments bouncing off Fearless's back as he crouched down and huddled, the thunderclap rattling his windpipe.

"The scale of the destruction," said Alyosha, "is hard to imagine."

"You don't have to," said Fearless. "It was just like Grozny." In Grozny they had learned that concrete can melt like marshmallows or even float in the breeze in papery strips.

The seven stories of the building next to the U.S. embassy in Nairobi were pancakes; a crater had been ripped from the asphalt in front. Fearless had grabbed his camera on autopilot, tripped down the stairs, sprinting then stopping and crouching in the street: making himself a stone in a river of panic as commuters fled in the opposite direction. He kept their grimacing mouths and eyes in the foreground, blocking out the dust and heat and screams, focusing on the essentials—light, aperture, shutter speed. On Haile Selassie Avenue, a blast of fire had engulfed the street, incinerating anything within a hundred-yard radius. He shot the side of a bus peeled back like the lid from a tin of sardines. Every pane of glass in every building was obliterated. Heading directly into the sulfurous cloud above the ruins, he stumbled on a moraine of smoldering rubble, bruising his knees and searing his hands. Through the haze, three soot-covered ghosts emerged in front of him, each heaving the limb of a body bathed in vermilion.

All these memories had been swept from his mind, the space on its table taken up by what had happened the next day, when he returned to England.

"You got close," said Alyosha.

"You know me," said Fearless, as he remembered stumbling out of the wreckage to find Jimmy somehow there—in his blue and white pajamas, his whole body quivering in shock.

"This is normal," Fearless wanted to tell him. "Our ability to exterminate makes us who we are." He wanted to share his mantra with Jimmy, and Luke too, who was now huffing up behind him: *I will not feel. I will not feel until I have to.* They had smoked their first cigarettes together, listened to *White Light/White Heat* on repeat, started their own tribute band, drunk till they chundered, copied each other's answers, crashed and burned with girls too pretty for them, but they had never shared a catastrophe like this—the stock-in-trade subject matter that had become his vocation. He wanted to know if they felt the same thrill when they saw the dead: the thrill that it wasn't you; the thrill that they weren't yours.

Alyosha knew the feeling intimately. They had lived through it together, so many times.

But there was something Fearless wanted to confess to Alyosha: if he had caught the right flight back to England from Nairobi, if he hadn't stayed to photograph what unfolded that day, then Laure wouldn't have been on that motorway alone. She might still be alive. If there was anyone he could say that to, it was surely Alyosha. Fearless could lay out all of his guilt; he could tell him about the ring he'd bought for Laure in Nairobi that now he would never have the chance to give.

"You know," Fearless said, pushing away the thought, "the bombing—it never occurred to me it was Islamists."

"After our time with Khattab—our old friend Samir Saleh Abdullah al-Suwailim—it is obvious, Fearless. They have seventy-two virgins! Waiting in paradise!"

"They attacked an idea, though, not a country."

"Pah. This is the world in 1998."

Alyosha's pocket started to chirrup and he held his hand up and turned away to take the call, wandering over to the entranceway of the apartment, with Amos taking up a position nearby. Hunched over, Alyosha was silent for a moment before he shouted into the receiver in a language that sounded Slavic.

"You want needles!" he finally spat in English. "What the fuck? There is not enough time for this bullshit, I tell you."

When the rain stopped, Fearless went onto the balcony. The sun hesitated, then reignited. People in the shop buildings opposite ventured out from the cover of porches and parasols. The riverside grew more crowded, with scooters buzzing around cars. On the bank, a circle of men played keepie uppie with a shuttlecock. "Sir, you buy scarf from me!" a ragged girl shrieked at a middle-aged traveler. "One for tree dollar! Two for fie!"

Alyosha was returning the phone to his pocket and speaking to Amos when Fearless stepped inside.

"Problem?" Fearless called out.

"Don't worry, bacha. It's just a big act! For negotiating you must know the red lines, yes? The lines the other person will not cross. Once you know what is impossible—everything follows."

"What does that have to do with pretending to be angry?"

"The lines they think *you* do not cross are crucial also. This is the act, bacha. The greatest weapon. This and complexity—making things so complex, so . . . baroque—yes, baroque is the better word. For the design is there, Fearless, but only we see it. Anyway, all this means I must leave you now. How do you say it? See a man about a dog."

"Okay. I'll unpack and take a shower. Which bedroom will I take?"

"Whichever you want. I'm putting you here, Fearless, but I stay somewhere else. There's a reason I have Amos, apart from his piloting skills; even honest men must have protection in this world. With you I won't take risks. And this place, you know, is much, much better than any hotel. Everything on your doorstep—bars, wats, the river."

Fearless laughed. Even Alyosha was going to leave him.

But then Alyosha, hiccupping again, produced a photo from his jacket pocket. "For you," he said. "Because you were always on the other side of the camera."

In the photo, Fearless and Laure are sitting at a table, his shirt unbuttoned, her hair in a chopsticked bun. They smile at the camera, not on demand or in response to something, but from a deep contentment shared with each other.

Alyosha was right: he had always hated shooting the people he loved. He had wanted to look at Laure with his own eyes only. A sob started to tremble on the edge of his lips.

"Let me give you something, bacha. Did you sleep on the flight?"

"Not a wink."

"Then here." Alyosha produced a silver snuffbox. "Be sure to hold these under your tongue, okay?" He pressed four blue pills into Fearless's palm. He also produced a candy-striped bag, the kind one might find in an English sweet shop. "To take away the taste," he said, catching Fearless's eye and winking. "Get a few hours' sleep and meet me later at the Naga Bar. It's just next door. We'll have some drinks. Then you'll feel it."

"Feel what?"

"The feeling of being far away from your troubles."

"I don't know if I want that."

"You can be different here in Cambodia. Everything is possible."

Undressing, Fearless caught sight of himself in a mirror, still bruised and scratched from what had happened in Nairobi. His ribs were on show; he'd barely eaten in weeks. After a shower, he rummaged for his clippers in his duffel and buzzed his head in long, practiced strokes until his scalp had only the shortest stubble.

In the mirror, his face bent and snapped back into shape. Even as the pills were taking effect, he was experiencing a kind of emotional come-down—not just from his grief but from the nerve-shredding adrenaline that had made his working life a constant state of emergency.

When he lay down, the Valium fell over him like a blanket over the cage of a fretful hawk. The mattress sighed and took on the shape of his body; he let himself relax under the spell of the ceiling fan, which cantered and creaked and wobbled on its axis.

He had been here, his father—here in Phnom Penh. Twenty years earlier, Cambodia—or Kampuchea, as his father would have called it—was a paradise, a realm of dreams made material.

"The world's last great hope!" the ten-year-old Fearless had heard him cry: the conclusion of a speech to a hall of rapt enthusiasts, his voice crescendoing, his fist pounding an invisible door. He was an important man, Fearless had learned then. Now he tried to remember what else he had said. He must have railed against imperialism, warned of nuclear Armageddon. He must have sung the praises of Asia's liberation movements. The Khmer Rouge were forging "a new covenant between men." They had handpicked him to visit their miracle in person; the next week, he would embark on a ten-day tour. There were murmurs of approval, hushed excitement, scattered applause.

"He was my age now," Fearless whispered to himself, his eyelids resting on little, hard tears. And he had died, in this city, before his time.

At the edge of Fearless's vision, a gecko fishtailed along the wall, disappearing into a crack. He wanted to go with him, he decided. No, no. He wanted to *be* him.

3

For a half hour after Bun Thim had brought the barang to the guest apartment, Song heard people and voices on the stairs. Then, the concertina gate opened and crashed shut in the signature rhythm of Thom going out, and an eerie quiet descended on the building, so quiet she could hear faint snoring from the guest apartment.

All the while, the wire that Song had discovered in the VIP room called to her.

Down on all fours, she observed how the plaster had been chipped out and carefully filled over again in bright new grout.

Outside the room, the trail grew cold. No one had tampered with the tiled corners of the bar. But out in the corridor, she picked it up again: slightly raised plaster running along a wall, turning the corner and disappearing into Thom's room.

In the event he happened to return, she set up the ironing board and laid a shirt over it as an alibi. Then she paced out the distance to where the wire ought to emerge, somewhere behind his old rattan closet. When she juddered the closet away from the wall, she saw that the wire converged with another from a plug, the two cables entering a drilled hole in the backboard.

Pinpricks of sweat broke out on her forehead. She repositioned the closet and opened its doors, wincing at the whining creak of their hinges. At the bottom, a colorful blanket covered something hard and cuboid: a big steel box with a hasp and heavy padlock.

As she bent down to examine it, she heard sandals slap up the concrete staircase. Thom. And someone with a high, nasal voice. Terrified, she jumped into the closet to hide.

"Let me count it," Thom said, entering the room.

A bag rustled. She could hear the other man suck his teeth.

Through razor cuts of light in the weave of the rattan door, the pair came into focus, backs turned, heads bent. She was aware of empty coat hangers dangling, which would tinkle if she made the slightest movement.

As he raised his head she noticed the other man's hair, an excelsior of black and glistening curls. She'd seen girls with a similar style plying their trade in the Naga and young brides done up for their weddings on the street—but never in her life a Khmer man with a perm.

Thom carried on rustling in his plastic bag. "Twenty thousand. Thirty thousand. Forty thousand. Fifty thousand." While he counted, the man with the curls began to turn.

Every fiber inside Song recoiled when she saw his face. A cry stabbed her ears. A motorbike keened. A dark colder than the darkness in the closet. Rain splashing everywhere—hot, stinging rain. "Close the window!" someone was shouting. "Just get it closed!"

She shut her eyes so tightly that the corners burned. The hasp of the padlock pressed into her calf.

The man—he was barely more than a boy—turned his gaze fully onto the closet doors. She'd thought she had wiped that face from her mind, its spit and venom, its demented glee.

His eyes narrowed. Had he heard her breathe?

"It's all here. Let's go. You're going to be late," said Thom.

The men turned and moved toward the door. Then, a few seconds later, footsteps hurried back. A drawer was pulled open. She could see Thom rooting around, then heard a ripping sound as he removed a plastic bag covered with tape. Hurriedly he stuffed the wad of cash into it, re-taped it, stashed it, and dashed back out and down the stairs.

Once the street gate clattered again, Song tore down the corridor, bursting into the toilet to vomit a mix of panic and the remains of the bobor she'd had for breakfast. But the memory—of that night, the boy's snarling face, the roar of engines—was back, acid rain tumbling all around.

When she heard the minivan pull up outside and its door sliding open on its runners, she tied her krama and hurried down, grateful for the children's laughter spilling onto the street. How could they always be so happy? Whenever she saw them, it was impossible not to smile too—even when smiling made her scars sting and smart. Bopha, Samnang, Rathana, and Dara rushed into the hall, hurling themselves upon her, helping her to forget whatever she'd just faced. They were the age she and Sovanna were when their lives had been whole, long before they had been taken to Phnom Penh.

"Let's eat our rice now!" Rathana shouted, squeezing her hand.

"Wash first," Song said, running her fingers through his matted hair. She pointed to his feet, all black and grazed and cut.

"Ot tee!" said Rathana, stamping his heel.

"Jaa, jaa," said Bopha, pressing herself against Song's legs. From behind her back, the girl magicked two lotus flowers, their closed buds bleeding orange and peach and purple.

"Where'd you get these?" Song shouted as the children ran to the yard, kicking off their flip-flops and stripping their clothes. Hurrying after them, she rushed to take down the washing as they began to run the tap into the big red bucket. "Wait till I take the clothes down, please!"

But Rathana was already scooping up water with a plastic cup and pouring it over himself and Samnang and Bopha. It was their game to lift the cups as high as they could and let the water arc, the streams crossing and guttering. The yard became a riot of splattering water, with Song snatching clothes and towels off the line, plastic pegs tumbling and bouncing off the concrete.

"Not too loud! Don't shout. There's a barang up there sleeping." But not even that could dampen their spirits.

Rainbow soap bubbles made an orrery around the children as they lathered themselves into creatures of white foam, then sloshed and rinsed till they were glistening brown seals.

"You wash with us today, *srey sa'art*? Come come, pretty lady."

Song laughed and shook her head. She couldn't imagine revealing herself to them.

"Blow the snot from your nose, will you, Rathana."

"So cooool!" cried Samnang, squeezing the bar of soap to send it rocketing high into the air. Rathana and Bopha scrabbled to chase it across the floor, the yard echoing with their cries and laughter.

"My turn!"

"No, me!"

"I'm bigger than you."

"Liar!"

Dara hung back, dressed in his oversize men's shirt. He was the smallest and shyest—watchful, like Song. When she looked at Dara watching Rathana, she could see how she once must have been, watching Sovanna, yearning so much to be like her, racing after her in the morning sun through the shimmering green of the paddy. Sovanna would get too close to the uncultivated land, where the landmines might be, and Song would scream "Chop!" while Sovanna would laugh, caught up in the thrill of being alive.

As the others dried off, Song took Dara and washed him, his face pointed up as she soaped and rinsed his hair, eyes firmly closed, mouth set in a pout. When she smoothed his hair behind his ears, he opened his eyes, and she saw something in his gaze she couldn't quite put her finger on. She felt the urge to scoop him up in her arms and open the gate and run into the street and keep on running forever.

"They're not so dirty," Dara said to her as she checked his nails. "I wear my rubber gloves and boots when I climb on the mountain."

She told herself not to love him or any of these kids. Her job was just to wash them and feed them and dress them and make them ready for what happened next—that thing she didn't want to think about. She ought to treat them coldly and just get it over and done with. But they were so like her, owning nothing save the will to survive; having no clothes save the ones that were soaking in her tub; no parents; no hope that a future could be shaped and not just suffered.

Later, after she had done her best to attend to their cuts and grazes—cursing the fact that her antiseptic had run out—and they had quietly eaten their meal sitting in their underwear, she took their plates and helped them dress in the clothes that had been laid out for them.

"It's you, the srey sa'art now," she said to Bopha as she tied the spaghetti straps of her sundress into a bow. "And you—my bong thoms!" she joked, as she parted the boys' hair.

Then she led them to the room off the back of the bar. They were silent now. There were some toys for them there, which Dara and Samnang fell upon, and a handful of magazines with colorful pictures and words that neither they nor Song would ever be able to read.

Satisfied they were settled—and with no sign of life from the guest apartment—Song went down to wash in the courtyard. Afterwards, she rubbed tiger balm onto her tender stomach and got dressed again in her other set of clothes.

Outside, the heat of the day had relented and the street was starting to bustle with life. The apartment children played flip-flop games on a strip of dirt. Motos and cars rolled back and forth, turning down all the roads on which Bun Thim had once driven them. She knew much of the city back in those days. But she should be grateful, she told herself: what other person in her position could ever dream of having a job or shelter?

Then the street gate rattled.

"Oun!" came a frail voice, quavering from the bottom of the stairs.

"Yes pu!" she answered. "I'm on my way." She bound her krama around her head once again.

When she reached the lobby, she brought her palms together at her nose and murmured, "Chom reap sor."

Dressed in his crisp white shirt, the Chief stood in front of her, leaning on his wooden cane. He nodded almost undiscernibly, half of his face almost kind, the other paralyzed and marked by its vertical scar.

Slowed by creaking bones, he picked up the tiny rattan chair that lived in the lobby and placed it in the doorway. Then he lowered himself into it, adopting an expression of quizzical interest as he observed the street. The smell of prahok drifted from a food seller's stall; a metal spoon clattered in a wok.

The Chief raised his eyebrows and let out a deep sigh. "Sing 'Kom Nirk Oun Eiy,'" he said after a time. "Like that night at The Sunflower. Do you remember? It feels so long ago."

Song turned and walked back up the steps, taking her place in the shadow on the mezzanine. When she sang in this spot, her voice would resonate in the stairwell. It might disturb the barang in his guest apartment, and Mr. Thom would certainly resent it—but there was nothing he could do: the Chief's pity—and guilt—kept Song safe. She hated the old man, but at least he knew her. For the working girls in the Naga, she was just a scar-faced cleaner, but he, at least, understood she was something more.

She took a moment to set and compose herself, her mind running ahead through the lines of the song. Pa had taught her these old-time tunes. He had seen Ros Sothea herself sing in the early days of her career, long before the King had dubbed her Preah Rheich Teany Somlang Meas: an experience so memorable he took her name for his daughter. Sometimes she forgot: her real name was Sothea.

Song opened her mouth and a voice poured out, spring-water-clear and free of worry, into the stairwell, through the lobby and over the street:

I look to the sky, the sky's so far.
I look to the stars, the stars are as far.
Water's waves crash and swirl.
I reminisce. I feel a sadness.
A sadness that makes my heart burst.

The street kids playing flip-flop games stopped for a moment as the voice spread above them through the colors of the sunset—scarlet and blood orange, pink and ether blue.

I remember the hand you used to hold.
I'll miss you. Our love has melted away.
We will part; I'll miss you. Don't miss me, baby.
All right my baby, my pretty baby.
Karma is forcing us to part.

As her voice echoed through the stairwell, Song thought of Sovanna and then of the wire in the VIP room. She imagined freeing it from the plaster and following it along corridors, through walls, into the street, across rooftops, along telegraph poles, over the country, through rice field and jungle and mountain, past borders, across whatever landscape she'd need to take to get there, to wherever Sovanna might be. But that was stupid. Impossible. It was Sovanna who would save her—and she already knew exactly where the wire led.

This life and the next, my baby.
I'll wish for you. Hopefully, I'll get what I wished for:
That I'll meet you in every life after this.

As the last note faded from Song's breath, night fell, the same way it always does in Cambodia—like a shop shutter clattering down on the day.

The old man raised his hand and she left him to his thoughts, moving up the stairs, deeper into the dark.

4

Fearless could have sworn he was woken by singing, a melody so full of longing that it flooded the stairwell outside. But by the time he groggily swung his legs off the bed, pulled on his trousers, and looked out onto the dark landing, there was no one around save a scuttling cockroach.

In the next building, Fearless located the Naga Bar at the top of a set of steep, dank stairs. He rapped hard on a solid metal door whose surface buzzed with distorted bass notes.

Bolts were drawn, grating in their barrels, and then music erupted in a cloud of cigarette smoke. A little Khmer girl in a halter top beamed up at him.

"Hello Sir you're welcome!" she cried in a high-speed, high-frequency singsong, the sequins on her top equally bedazzling. "My name Lucky! I'm Khmer. Only Khmer girls here! No Vietnam!" Her tiny hand yanked Fearless into a space not much bigger than a boxing ring, packed with men dappled in pink and purple light. "No Vietnam girls!" she repeated as she dragged him into the fray.

The clientele in the Naga were exclusively white and male, aged twenty to sixty, with other girls like Lucky fawning over them. Girls in boob tubes and miniskirts and high-heeled sandals. Girls so thin you could snap them like breadsticks, cooing and smiling and pouting and flirting in the way only people paid to do it can muster. Perched on knees, they massaged hairy thighs and ran their perfect fingernails along sunburned forearms.

Fearless surveyed the faces in the crowd, but the only one he recognized across the bar was Amos, who met his eyes for an instant before he was abruptly jostled to one side. Clearly, Fearless had arrived at a celebratory moment. Bottles banged in rhythm on tables, faster and faster as a cheer surged through the crowd. A spray of liquid arced above everyone's heads, droplets anointing his shoulders and cheeks.

"Za vashe zdorovye!"

"What you want drink?" Lucky shouted in his ear.

"I'll have a beer—but I can get it myself."

Seeing rows of bottles on a shelf in the corner, he worked his way crabwise through backs and shoulders.

Fearless knew these men at once from the way they carried themselves: he had photographed them back in Moscow in '94. There, in Yelena and Levin's tiny flat in a typical Soviet khrushchyovka over cold red borscht and warm black tea and the contraband Marlboros Fearless had smuggled through customs, Yelena, with her big brown eyes and pageboy haircut, had explained their world and how they moved in it.

The Russian state didn't exist—that was her first lesson. "My only lesson!" she shouted, raising her finger.

It was a void, she said, an emptiness into which prospectors and prostitutes and pillagers were scrambling—just as they'd done in America's Wild West. Those men, she told him, *were* the state.

"Impossible for you to understand! For you, state is buildings. Laws, courts, police. But here, it is actions of men. The will of whoever takes power."

"Tsepochka!" said Levin.

"He says it's a chain."

Levin took over, tugging on his forelock. He explained how the men— local toughs bedecked in gold jewelry and Adidas tracksuits who offered protection to traders and extorted tributes—had evolved from running street markets to more ambitious operations. Brawls and street fights were replaced by civilized meetings where organizations settled disputes by negotiating percentage points. There was still violence, yes, but only 'disappearances' that the police would investigate and conveniently forget.

"What these men do," said Yelena, "is provide services. Enforcement. Justice. Protection of property and contracts. The tributes are taxes but really much cheaper. You get more for your money because competitors are everywhere. They are like your"—Levin tried the English word—"'corporations.'" His finger then danced across a Moscow map pinned to the wallpaper of faded sunflowers, sketching out networks and territories, past and present: the Shvonder's Brigade, the Herat Association, the Solntsevskaya Bratva, the Orekhovskaya gang. "And don't forget KGB are also in such groups! Alpha. Vympel. All are there." Twenty thousand or more had been discharged by the security services or had willingly left to join the entrepreneurs. And to make it more confusing, there were active KGB in the gangs, infiltrators who promoted the "real" state's agendas, making it impossible to distinguish which man belonged to which organization, let alone what his individual motives might be.

Yelena and Levin doubted Fearless would get photographs. But as soon as Fearless met their first group of contacts he realized there was something they hadn't appreciated: these men were not only vain, they cultivated their vanity; they were the ripest fruit a photographer could pick. Kachki: guys who loved to work out, who were proud to have Fearless accompany them to the gym, snapping their beetroot grimaces as they toiled in the power rack.

From his position at the bar, Fearless scanned the same genre of faces, hoping to pick out Alyosha. Through the sun-fried expats, proud libertines, and two spotty boys who had the air of Mormon missionaries, his eye alighted upon a colossal wooden carving: seven giant snake heads rearing over a wooden booth, occupied by a man who was obviously the boss. Around him sat three heavies with sausage fingers, their neck rolls bulging over their collars. The man himself had the girth of a hippo, the edge of the table pressing into his gut. In one hand he held a folded handkerchief that he dabbed against his temples as he sat watching his crew pass back and forth with the girls, swishing the beaded curtain into a neon-lit passageway.

When Fearless turned back, he spotted Amos again, closer this time. "Can I get you a drink?" he shouted. "Vodka, is it?"

Amos raised and tilted his glass. "Water," he said.

"Do you know where Alyosha—"

A voice growled from the other direction, cutting him off. "No camera here! You take your fucking camera and go outside!"

When he turned to look, Fearless's mouth opened wide. Six years had passed since he'd seen Wish in Bosnia. He had dyed his hair a shocking, peroxide blond, but the piercing gaze was unmistakable. How the hell had he ended up in Cambodia?

"I haven't got my camera," Fearless replied meekly.

Alyosha must have brought Wish here—that was the only explanation.

"And I've given up photography," Fearless added. After Laure's funeral, he had sat on his old bed in Conrad's house and disassembled his first love, his scuffed-up Rolleiflex, scooping its parts into a Sainsbury's bag.

But Wish ignored him and moved away into the crowd.

"He likes you," said Amos.

Fearless laughed—just once. "Funnily enough, he used to. I knew him when he was a sniper. He was only nineteen. The best with an M48 in Sarajevo. William Tell and 'White Death' combined, people said."

As he took another draft of beer, Fearless's time with Wish came back to him, high up in the abandoned tower block, his camera trained upon Wish as he, in turn, trained his sniper rifle on the street. There had been an instant rapport between the two of them, innocent beginners trying to prove themselves, hoping to catch people unawares. After several days together, Wish had beckoned Fearless closer and invited him to look through the sight of his gun: "See! There. This one is clever."

When he pulled the trigger, a blond girl on the corner raced across the road, dashing past the sign reading PAZI, SNAJPER! The girl had counted each of his five rounds and worked out the time it took to reload.

"When I shoot the fifth, see, there she goes. This is why I love her the best."

Every day it was the same. Wish would see her approach and shoot off every round save for his last; that way he could maximize his time for spying on her.

To Fearless's left, a portal of light opened across the Naga bar. Finally—Alyosha! Men rushed to greet him. They clasped his arm and patted him on the back as if he were a politician flush from an improbable election victory. He accepted the plaudits with a beaming grin, gripping each man's hands in both of his. The atmosphere rose like a swell in the sea. There was more applause. Another cheer. A man climbed onto his chair, blowing kisses and cackling.

Fearless felt a sense of pride observing Alyosha working his way through the well-wishers. Avuncular yet stern, understanding what each of them needed: an arm around the shoulder, a clip on the ear, a glance, a wink, a back-slapping embrace.

"What's Alyosha pulled off?" Fearless turned to ask Amos, but he too had disappeared into the crowd.

When Alyosha reached Fearless, he punched him playfully on the upper arm. "I'm embarrassed to have you here, bacha! But these guys prefer these . . . 'facilities.' And you know, we must not judge. Here, brothels are normal. The ancient king of Angkor kept a beauty in a tower and had to visit her every night; otherwise, he would receive her curses and die. You see the wooden carving over the booth there? That's what the woman becomes after the king has had his way. The naga, the serpent with its seven angry heads."

"You make whoring sound poetic."

"Oh, it's money, I know. They say brothels make more than entire budget of the Cambodian state. Other nations have oil and gas and grain. Financial services. Diamonds. But they have their people. Girls like this. Little babies they put to adopt."

Alyosha gave a sidelong glance and leaned in further, his breath in Fearless's ear warm and moist.

"Have a drink, yes. But don't waste your time with these guys. Once my deal is done I'll be in a new league. Today, we need lawyers, strategists, systematic thinkers. Not these nonliquid types stinking of aftershave and jockstraps."

Fearless wanted to ask him about Wish, but Alyosha was gesturing to the old man in the booth.

"Here, bacha. I need to have a tête-à-tête with my associate. But take this. Enjoy yourself." He pushed a fold of dollars and a plastic square into Fearless's palm. "The girls' tubes are tied but here is highest AIDS rate in Asia—thanks to our generous friends in the UN."

When Alyosha turned to go, Fearless slid the condom under an ashtray. But he didn't hate the gesture. Alyosha had a different way of looking at things, which was, after all, why Fearless loved him.

While his friend sat in conference with the fat man under the heads of the naga, Fearless got himself into a game at the nearby pool table, making friends using a mix of pidgin English and Russian with Vadim and Timur and Subkhan and Pavel, the alcohol softening his consonants and adding a delay between the words he thought and those that came out of his mouth. Fearless gleaned that most of the men came from the same army regiment.

"The pride of Pridnestrovie!" said Vadim, pointing to the booth. "Over there you see our Colonel Vasiliev."

After Vadim won a best of five, Fearless went down onto the street for some air. The scooter taxi guys roused themselves when he appeared but slouched back when he raised a cigarette to his lips.

He was about to head back when Bun Thim's Camry pulled up. A red-faced man dressed in an orange Hawaiian shirt got out and hurried around to the other rear door. The man dived into the vehicle and dragged a white girl onto the street, her miniskirt riding up her long, slender legs.

"Nyet!" shouted the girl, flailing at the man with her handbag as one of her high heels tumbled into the gutter.

As the man hustled the girl into and up the stairwell, Fearless went over to retrieve the shoe, but by the time he had reentered the bar she was disappearing behind the curtain—a shock of platinum bob behind swaying beads. Alyosha too had vanished.

"They bring the girl Larissa from big hotel," said Vadim, tapping him on the shoulder as he turned the high heel in his hands. "The Cambodiana. Down on riverside over there."

"She's Russian?"

"Wish only fucks white girls. No Chinks. He's . . ."

"Fussy."

"He thinks Cambodians are dirty. The girls, they take yama tablets."

Fearless frowned.

"Horse medicine," said Vadim. "Crazy pills."

"Are there many white prostitutes, here, in Cambodia?"

"Of course. The rich Cambodian, the Thai. They pay ten times. And Wish pay too. He call this girl every fucking night." Vadim put his hand around his own throat and mimed choking. "Forget this. Come—let us play more pool."

The girl came back through the curtain alone as Vadim was racking up their second frame. She carried one high heel, dangling from its strap. As she nudged her way through the crowd of men, Fearless imagined the grit and cigarette butts that were no doubt sticking to the soles of her feet. Her mascara was smudged and her face slightly puffy. Nevertheless, her obvious beauty remained undimmed—her features sharp yet delicate, eyes blue and strikingly light.

As she neared the exit, Fearless held out the other shoe. But at the moment the girl's hand closed around its heel and her gaze met his, a sharp pain stabbed Fearless's temple. He'd been struck but had somehow stayed on his feet. When he turned, clutching his head, Wish was next to him, pushing the girl back with his arm across her chest.

"What d'you say?" he snarled. "What d'you tell her about me?"

When Wish came at him again, Fearless was ready. He braced his left leg and planted his right foot squarely on Wish's advancing knee. The contact was light but enough for Wish to topple, his leg buckling under him.

Whatever Wish had done with the girl, it hadn't quelled his anger—he sprang up again, emitting a guttural roar. But just as he leapt, his body snapped back, as if he were a dog at the end of its choke chain: Amos had intervened, taking hold of Wish and disabling him with a firm full nelson.

"Get out! No one wants you here, motherfucker!" Wish shouted, struggling, his feet dangling uselessly in the air.

"I'm a guest."

"Some guest—they keep you in the whorehouse!" A spume of spit escaped from Wish's mouth.

One of the other men—a brute with a bulbous shaved head—put his arm around Fearless's shoulder and guided him through the crowd. By the time Fearless was pushed into a seat next to Colonel Vasiliev, a huddle of men at the bar were calming Wish down, one of them watering a semicircle of shot glasses.

"The Chechen is back," announced one of Vasiliev's men.

The others turned to look as Alyosha reentered the Naga.

"You call him the Chechen?"

"Alyosha—get our friend here another drink!" shouted Vasiliev.

Fearless rubbed his eyes and tried to focus. Was the grogginess too many beers or the effect of Wish's sucker punch?

Vasiliev threw his heavy arm around Fearless's shoulders. "He has a temper, that Wish. Alyosha's little guard dog. He believes he can train him. Make him do tricks."

"I'm Fearless," said Fearless.

"Alyosha showed me your photographs."

"Did you like them?"

Vasiliev shrugged.

"And what do you do?"

"Me?" Vasiliev laughed. "I'm a cow farmer. I milk cows!"

His goons, taking their cue, guffawed in unison.

Vasiliev's smile wrinkled his whole face for an instant. But then his expression grew stony again. "No no no. We don't talk business. We are here to forget. There are no killings in Cambodia. Not like Moscow these days. Fifteen, twenty, thirty people every day. Here, the police . . ."—he leaned in—"are friends."

Emerging from the huddle of men around Wish, Alyosha arrived with a bottle of vodka and a highball glass. "Gin tonic," he said, sliding the glass in front of Fearless.

"Za vashe zdorovye!" Vasiliev boomed. "I like a man who can keep his cool in a fight."

Vasiliev clapped his hand on Fearless's head and jiggled it, as if he were checking a stick shift in neutral. There was yet another buoyant swell of laughter and merriment.

"I don't fight," said Fearless, "but I can defend myself if I have to." But no one heard him above the hubbub.

Fearless was glad when Alyosha sat down beside him.

"Why is Wish here?" he asked. "He was itching to pick a fight with me."

"There's good in Wish. He's troubled, but there's good."

"You're always trying to convert people, Alyosha."

Alyosha put his arm around him. "With you, this is true."

As he pulled him close, Fearless felt the riot of the bar fade and his mind tuning in to Alyosha's frequency. After a while, he found himself beginning to relax, warm in the cocoon of his friend's concern, Alyosha giving him space to talk and even admit what he had struggled to admit to himself.

"I missed the ultrasound." Laure had stuck the picture on the fridge: a black-and-white bean curled in a cake slice of static.

"It happens."

"It happens, Alyosha, because I make it happen. I missed it because I didn't want to accept the baby was coming. I mean, I did want children, but not right now. You know our jobs. How would you cope with the pressure of having to stay alive for someone else?"

Alyosha pursed his lips and nodded slowly.

Fearless shut his eyes, wondering if he was being honest. He made it sound so noble—when he was driven by self-interest. What child would benefit from a father who resented it and regretted the life he hadn't been able to live? That would have been a more revealing question to ask. Or why not leave the child completely out of it? I want to do what I want, I want to live how I live, and have no obligation to anyone else. There.

The day the doctor confirmed her pregnancy, Laure had brought champagne and taken him to bed—but his mind was not with her, even when he came. When he collapsed and rolled over, he saw his father in Port-au-Prince, sitting on the veranda of the Hotel Oloffson with his copy of *The Black Jacobins* open in front of him, the shadow of the young waitress—his mother—falling across the page.

How could he put all this into words, even to Alyosha?

"Did you say any of this to Laure?"

"No—not a word."

"But that's good. You're always too hard on yourself, bacha. This is why Laure loved you—don't you know? There are situations where it isn't right to tell the truth. And this happens even more when we find ourselves in love." Alyosha gave a half smile.

"You mean you're in love too?"

"Well. Maybe." Alyosha placed his hand over Fearless's and squeezed. "Lyubov zla, polyubish i kozla, as we are saying."

"It's time you went," shouted Vasiliev, leaning over the table. He tapped on his watch—a gleaming Rolex like Alyosha's.

"Yes?"

"Any moment our friend is landing."

As he rose, Alyosha put his hand on Fearless's shoulder and raised his voice to address the table in Russian. Fearless managed to catch the drift. He was telling them of the *dolg* that he owed to Fearless, and how Fearless had earned his name by saving Alyosha's life. It was quaint, this idea of bearing a life debt; Fearless had intervened miraculously in Alyosha's timeline and therefore everything he lived was owed to Fearless.

"In short, he's something you bastards wouldn't understand," Alyosha concluded.

"What's that?" asked one of the goons, raising his eyebrows.

"A good man," Alyosha deadpanned. "I tell you—a Buddhist. He wouldn't step on an ant if he could possibly avoid it." He looked down at Fearless and gently kneaded his neck. "I need to meet someone from the NGO we are helping. Take them to their hotel. No time for another drink."

Then he was gone again, accompanied by two of Vasiliev's men, and Fearless was left with a pang of guilt at his thoughtlessness, for admitting he had doubts about fatherhood to his friend who had desperately tried and failed to have kids.

Fearless drained his glass. The men were unimpressed by Alyosha's tall tale of derring-do. Alyosha had been unconscious when Fearless had dragged him from the flames; he had no idea what had actually happened. Fearless decided to head back to the apartment.

But when he stood up to leave, it was as if the wire between his brain and limbs had been snipped. On his ass once again, he felt drunker than he'd ever felt—a colorful, hallucinatory, interdimensional drunkenness.

More shot glasses were chinked. Wasn't that *his* hand that was holding one? Yes, there was the ring—the one Laure had bought him in the souk in Essaouira. He remembered whirling Gnawa dancers in long black robes, the clashing tbal drums and rippling garagab. He glimpsed Amos again in the distance and raised his glass, his vision momentarily blinded by purple-pink ice cubes—but when the glass was lowered Amos was gone.

The desire to cheer and celebrate now surged through his body. He *could* forget everything here. No one knew what had happened to him.

"More vodka!" someone yelled. It was his voice. Yes, it was him. Sweat was pouring from him, great beads of it rolling freely across his temples.

Now that they knew he was English, his companions had a new toast. "From Russia with love!" they cheered, their thick laughter enveloping him. They drank to Russia, to the British Empire, to the Kingdom of Cambodia. To Margaret Thatcher and Yuri Gagarin and the spirit of Lenin. Fearless was good at getting drunk with other men; he'd perfected it at checkpoints and outposts in Bosnia, where the surliest fighters would soften when you sat down and toasted each other in the dugouts. They would produce rakija bottles filled with slivovitz and the little lab flasks they called čokanji-čokanjčići—and then you'd be shouting "Živeli! Živeli!"

Someone raised a song now. They put their arms around each other.

"Komsomol youth . . . Our mighty friendship is our strength!"

They swayed in their chairs till he tipped onto the floor.

An arm came around him and lifted him to his feet.

"To the glorious armies! To the heroes of the 14th!"

The room was a carousel—speeding up, slowing down. Words became difficult—both speaking and listening. Fearless caught only random snatches of conversation: Gulf Stream, someone was saying across the table. They were talking about the weather, then. No—a private jet: a Gulfstream that had once been owned by the Cardinals. None of it made sense. More vodka! To hell with it. He'd always reined himself in because he had always been scared: his father's revolutionary fervor was a loss of control, a giving-in to a seductive, addictive power. But what did anything matter anymore? He'd go as far as he damn well pleased.

But then a heavy door closed on the whirling world and he was alone, in a white room, on a simple wooden chair. On the wall hung a triptych of half-naked girls, the middle one veiled by a transparent negligee hanging like mist around her torso. She stood in a turquoise pool. Water lapped at her thighs.

Her hand touched his shoulder. A leg swung around to straddle him. Sequins glittered in front of his eyes in pink, soft-edged hexagons. Up close, he could see a pattern of stitching—diamonds of elastic that expanded and folded to reveal two soft mounds of flesh, sinking into his face. The scent of honey, of skin the color of honey, filled his senses; hair, long black hair, curtained his eyes. Hands took his head and tilted it back, his mouth gaping open, gasping for air.

He wanted oblivion. He was ready. Let it come.

And then the whiteness of the ceiling blinded him, resounding in his head like a mightily struck gong. He saw tiny watch hammers, little ticking hands, before everything capsized—and all that was left was black.

When he came round he was bathed in the gray light of the moon. There were steps in front of him, to the left and right, running up, running down: an Escher painting of infinite staircases. His legs were rubber, but his feet limped along a walkway. Someone was holding him up and pushing him along: a stranger with a cowled face, breathing hard under his weight.

"I want to go home. But I don't know where home is," he said. He was pleased with the way those words came out.

Then a wave of pressure surged in his stomach, curled in upon itself, and tumbled from his mouth. He was on his knees, bile flowing over his tongue, his stomach contracting so hard he thought his ribs might snap.

"No no! You walk!" said a voice. "Get up and move!"

BETWEEN THIS WORLD AND THE NEXT

They came to a doorway. There was light and a bed—it was the bed in his apartment, wasn't it? He wanted to go to it but instead he was being turned and lowered onto a hard, cold floor. He was naked, he realized. How long had he been naked? Ropes of icy water lacerated his flesh and danced on the tiles around his head.

He was mesmerized by the geometric patterns of those tiles—an infinity of tessellated shapes and stipples.

"I killed her," he said. "By not being there. But it's the same. I killed Laure and the baby. Our child."

5

Bopha was the first to push herself up from the mat, her eyes squinting in the yellow light from the hall. "What is it?"

"Come, all of you," Song said. "I need your help."

Rathana sat up and rubbed his eyes while Bopha got to her knees to shake the other two awake.

Song led them to the guest apartment, into its bathroom. A naked, wet barang was lying splayed on the tiles.

"Who's this?"

"I don't know," said Song. "Is he one of them? I think he is with the Russians but he mostly speaks English."

The children stayed silent.

"Is he one of them, children?"

"No. He is not," Bopha said.

Song grabbed one of the man's arms and legs. "Then we should get him to the bed. Support his head, Bopha. Rathana—this arm. Dara and Samnang, take his other leg."

The children weren't much help, but Song was surprised by the strength she had, by the muscles in her back and shoulders that all the days of laboring had given her. Navigating the narrow doorway and the step down into the bedroom, they almost let his body drop, but with a cry—*Now heave!*—they manhandled him onto the mattress.

"Bopha, find some underwear in his bag," Song said, as she pulled his body onto its side and propped the pillows behind his back.

The child turned out the duffel bag and sifted through the contents.

Song yanked the boxer shorts up the man's legs, snapping the elastic onto the top of his thighs as Bopha returned the contents to the duffel, pausing for a moment to examine a little velvet-covered box.

As Song covered the man with the sheet, Bopha climbed up and, laying her hand upon his chest, said with a serious look, "I'll make sure that he's breathing, bong."

"Okay, keep an eye. Come get me if anything's wrong."

Song got a mop and headed back to the walkway where she had found the barang—a lurching, naked, frothing-at-the-mouth zombie. He had been standing in the moonlight, moaning strangely, his penis dangling flaccidly between his legs. The way his eyes rolled back had struck her particularly: the man wasn't just drunk or high, it seemed to her; he'd been pushed to the brink of death, his toes curled on its edge.

Still, she would have been happy to leave him to his own devices until he collapsed on all fours and vomited everywhere, his hands reaching out and muddling the sick. Once he had made a mess, it was her responsibility. She tried to help him to his feet but only succeeded in making him vomit again, his necklace—a plastic letter on a string—swinging back and forth below his chin.

Men! she cursed, as she mopped up now. She had spent her life cleaning up after them. Or servicing them—which was often the same thing. Button cocks, bent cocks, fat stubby red cocks. Flaccid, rearing, undecided, priapic. How many she'd seen. How many wide eyes and open mouths. How many bleated baas and yeses and ouis.

Men. How easily they believed what they wanted to believe. She had seen other girls—Sovanna included—accept their fate. Men fell in love with Sovanna and never with Song because they couldn't fool themselves into thinking that Song belonged to them. They knew Song was splitting herself, compartmentalizing what her body did and where her spirit dwelt in the hope it might remain undimmed and untouched.

When Song got back to the apartment, the children were still watching over the barang.

"He sleeps a bit," said Rathana, "but then he wakes up and starts saying things."

"In English, I think."

"Yes. It's English, not French or Russian."

Bopha lifted up the man's forearm and turned it toward Song. "Look."

On its inside, running from wrist to elbow, was a series of straight-line scars, between one and three inches long. Sometimes the lines were parallel, sometimes they crossed.

"Old scars," Song said, leaning over to examine them.

The next time he stirred, the man vomited again. But this time they were prepared: Song had readied a bowl and flannel. Not long afterward, he reared up and began to rant, but fell calm when they pushed him down and laid their hands upon him. Later, when Song began to sing, he seemed to relax. She leaned in and murmured gently into his ears, so softly the high notes disappeared on her lips.

"Beautiful," he whispered in a moment of lucidity, his eyes flickering open, meeting hers for an instant. Then his breathing slowed. His color seemed to return.

There was something powerful about the way they were touching him, each of them joined to the other through him. Song had a memory of being with Pa, Ma, and Sovanna, doing the same—but when was that? They were laying their hands on the flanks of an animal—their buffalo, it must have been, sleeping peacefully on the ground.

6

At dawn, after she had prepared the rice for the priests, Song carried a tray to the guest apartment, nudging the door gently open with her elbow.

In his sleep, in the smoked-glass dark of the room, the barang's face was now relaxed and peaceful.

Why help him? She had cleaned him up and made sure he was safe—why should she do anything more?

But somehow, to her he seemed different from the others. He spoke English, not Russian. The children were not wary of him. It was stupid, but the scars on his arm made her wonder if he might be like her. At first glance, he seemed to be a white man. But when you saw the texture of the stubble on his head or the darker color of his penis, you knew he was something more complicated than that.

She put the tray beside the bed and went to the window. Lifting the curtain to check the street, she glimpsed orange parasols bobbing in their direction. Under the rails and display cases that the shopkeepers had moved onto the sidewalk, she could see golden robes and bare feet covered in dust: her cue to get the bigger pan of rice for the daily almsgiving.

Kneeling at the opening of the concertina gate downstairs, she positioned the rice in front of her, the serving spoon ready, conscious of the tension that had seized her neck and back ever since she'd seen Sokha's face again.

As the priests approached, she shifted the rice pot into the doorway. Raising her palms to her eyes, she gave the sampeah, then doled out a ladle when the first bowl appeared, then a second and a third, never raising her head. Words of blessing were muttered in response as she did this, in an intricate language that no one understood.

On the fifth and last bowl, the rice stuck to the spoon and she tapped it against the pot to dislodge the sticky grains.

"I saw your sister," a voice said.

She glanced up to see a monk—a novice not much older than she—staring back.

The words put their hands around her throat and squeezed.

"I thought it was you," the novice said. "But then, when I looked, I saw the difference."

"My sister?" she mumbled.

The boy glanced sideways. "We were with a dying man, chanting for his soul. And I saw her in the garden of the next-door villa. I saw her on the third day and I saw her on the seventh."

The senior monk, who was leading the group to the neighboring building, stopped and turned to see what was going on.

"What villa?" said Song. "That can't be true."

"Behind number 20, Street 334. Between Street 57 and—"

"Novice! Come along!"

Behind Song, Mr. Thom now came down the stairs. The boy's face mirrored the panic on her own. "Next time sweet cucumber," he mumbled, conscious that Thom was now close enough to hear. Then, in an instant, he rejoined the line of parasols.

Thom pushed Song aside and peered into the street. "Lok sang akrork," he spat. "*Asking* for food! As if we're some kind of restaurant!"

Trasak paem. Sweet cucumber? What did he mean?

Her eyes filled with water. Surely it couldn't be true. Sovanna was here? Thom was wrong, then: she *wasn't* dead. She was in Phnom Penh. But for how long? She had to be a prisoner. And she must have been told that Song was gone. Otherwise Sovanna would have done everything she could to find her. The Naga would have been one of the first places she'd look.

Then it came to her: the monk meant Sweet Cucumber Street, the nickname people had for Street 63.

Something hard and vicious clipped the side of her head, snapping her out of her racing thoughts.

"Don't just stand there, cunt! Start cleaning the bar." Thom turned and clomped back up the stairs, pulling his T-shirt above his nipples and idly scratching his belly.

As she walked behind him, Song sensed something inside her, stirring and stretching after a long hibernation. It didn't matter that she was too ashamed to risk going outside and being seen. It didn't matter that even if she managed to get to this villa it would be next to impossible to free Sovanna if she were a prisoner. Air was flowing into her lungs. Her spine began to straighten. She looked at the pot and had the urge to raise it. It was plastic but hard enough to do some damage. She could leap up and bring it down on the flat of Thom's crown and beat him till his brain was soft as bobor.

But at the top of the stairs, his legs went in the other direction. So what: Sovanna was no longer a ghost. She was crossing back over the water. Stepping onto the bank. Finally retaking human form.

PART 2

7

When Fearless's eyes flickered, he saw a curtain backlit by sunshine, wafting in from the window on a breeze. For a while, drifting on the sea between sleep and wakefulness, he watched the fabric inhale and exhale. Laure, of course, was standing right behind it. As long as he lay still, she would remain watching over him, casting a golden veil around the space. There, just there, alive, complete. Then a dirt bike turned onto the street with a belching roar and the dream was punctured; there was no getting it back.

On his other side, he heard a snap and then a clacking. He turned to see a little Cambodian girl, sitting on a stool and swinging her legs. The clacking was the sound of a gobstopper in her mouth; the snapping, the box he had bought in Nairobi. Quickly, she reached out and handed him the velvet-covered cube.

Taking it, he blinked several times and unglued his tongue from his palate. "Engagement ring," he said in a hoarse, whispering voice. He opened the lid to take a look at it himself. "Speak English? I bought this for a lady."

"Pretty lady," the little girl said.

He sat up slowly, running a hand across his stomach and wincing through gritted teeth.

Holding up the ring in the space between them, he let the light play across its dark blue stone. He remembered the shtick from the dealer in Nairobi: "In this light, sir, you will see all the tanzanite's colors: blue, pink, and even red. The Maasai chiefs give this stone to their wives. It is to celebrate the successful birth of their babies." That had appealed to Fearless: giving Laure an ancient symbol of new life.

Breaking his reverie, the girl reached into her mouth and produced the gobstopper, also holding it up for him to see. She had reached a blue layer, beneath which was green.

He tried to swallow but couldn't. "The whole wide world," he said. "You win."

She popped the sweet back in and pointed to the bedside table, on which sat a covered saucepan bound in a tea towel, a china bowl of rice, and a big steel spoon.

"Who are you, little one? What's your name?"

"My nem Bopha."

"Hello Bopha. My name is—" He had the urge to say "Joseph," but then followed the groove of habit: "Fearless."

When he lifted the pan's lid, the steam from a golden broth surrounded them and hunger stirred inside him for the first time in weeks.

"Do you know what happened to me, Bopha? I don't remember."

She didn't understand or didn't want to answer. Instead, with great care, she took a spoon, served the soup and poured him a fresh glass of water from a jug.

Fearless removed his string necklace so it wouldn't dangle in the food. The first spoonful was delicious, the broth meaty yet light: the perfect antidote to whatever the hell he'd drunk or snorted.

"Wish," he murmured. Yes. Wish had taken his opportunity for revenge. He had been standing at the bar with Alyosha, hadn't he? He had slipped something into his drink without being seen.

As he ate, Bopha took his string necklace and held it up, twisting the plastic letter *s* that hung from it back and forth.

"You like?"

"Sa'aht," she said to herself.

"You have it," he said. "I don't want."

She drew in her chin.

"Sa'aht," said Fearless, mimicking her. "It's for you. Take it. Go on. It's no problem."

When she had hung it around her neck and placed her palms together, Fearless opened his hand and waggled his fingers. "Only one dollar!" he said—a joke that made her smile. He was good with kids; any photojournalist had to be. They were instant pathos. Innocence. Blamelessness. Hope. The letter had fallen off a grave marker in the Lion Cemetery in Sarajevo when a funeral he'd been covering had come under shelling.

A young woman hurried into the room and cried out. She carried a soft-haired broom in one hand, and her head was wrapped in a gingham cloth as if to protect her from clouds of dust. There was something familiar about her, but he couldn't work out what. Immediately, she put herself between him and the child. Seeing the necklace, she ordered the girl to take it off.

"No no—it's my gift," said Fearless.

"She does not want presents."

"It's nothing. Let her have it."

Bopha scurried away.

"What's your name?"

"Song."

"I'm Fearless. Is it you that left this soup?"

But the girl bowed her head and quickly hurried after Bopha.

Someone else now appeared: a young Khmer man whose eyes opened wide when he saw Fearless. Another young man jostled up behind, peering over the first one's shoulder inquisitively.

"Sua s'day," Fearless said, his throat crackling around the words.

Alyosha's voice barked and the men stepped back.

"Ah—thank God! I heard you were drunk as zyuzya."

"I'm fine," Fearless said. "I think I threw up everything."

"Fucking shit," Alyosha exclaimed. His bare ankle had brushed a mosquito coil. He dusted off its ash, hopping on one foot, and scowled. "So you're okay, bacha?"

"I've had hangovers," Fearless said—though he knew that what had happened was something quite different. Not just what he'd ingested but the feeling he had had—the desire for oblivion, for giving up on life.

"That's good. Okay. But something's come up. I cannot spend this day with you after all."

If Fearless's mind hadn't been so focused on piecing the previous night together, he might have been more disappointed at this news. But he was connecting the mosquito coil to the cleaning girl to the wet room. There was a beaded curtain. A dazzle of sequins.

As Alyosha made his excuses and took his leave, Fearless's eyes fell on the rice pot on the nightstand. Yes. Returning it would be a perfect pretext for finding her.

When he was dressed, he went around the other floors in the building, knocking on locked doors but receiving no responses. Returning, he found a doorway that led to an external walkway from which staircases ascended and descended to a courtyard below. Over the railing, he saw a clothesline, a cluster of plastic bowls, and a bucket.

Along the walkway, he heard movement behind another door. When he nudged it an inch, he saw her foot. A little farther: the fraying edge of a royal blue sampot. Another inch and he could see her fully, side on and deep in thought, slowly and steadily brushing her hair: a long black curtain swept to the right. But, as he took a step into the room, she tilted her head and flipped the hair over, making him draw in his breath and shrink back. The other side of her head appeared to be missing; it was a large patch of scalp, the skin of it rippled and ridged, her right ear shriveled as if its cartilage was melted wax. For a split second, the sight brought the fire back to his mind and he was stumbling through the nursing home in Bosnia, walls collapsing, the old people trapped and suffocating behind glass.

He must have made a noise, because the girl cried out and scrambled for a cloth to cover herself.

"I'm sorry," Fearless said, pushing the door open fully. "I came to say thank you and return this pot."

The girl tied a knot in her scarf and held herself still—an animal realizing its predator is too close to flee.

"What happened to your head? Who did that to you?" Fearless blurted—words he rued the moment they left his lips. But before he could apologize, the girl fired back:

"Who did this?" She tapped her left forearm.

"Sorry?"

She meant the scars that he always covered up with long sleeves.

"I did," he said—once again without thinking.

She looked up at him, then down, then up again with narrower eyes.

Why hadn't he made his usual excuse? The old story about his arm being caught in barbed wire—the story he had told every woman he'd ever slept with.

"I did it when I was young and messed up and in pain."

The first time, in his teens, it had been an accident: a scratch from a coat hanger as he was reaching for a shirt. But then he had done it on purpose a week later. And again. For month after month after month. Doing it made him feel like he was achieving something, that—somehow, in some way he couldn't begin to verbalize—he was making everything that had gone wrong right again.

He looked away from her and scanned the room, trying to get a grip on the world the girl inhabited. To call it a cell would have been far too generous. An old beer crate next to the door contained a scattering of possessions. Apart from that, there was nothing save a tub with two lotus flowers and the thin mat on the floor on which she sat. Light fell across her through the bars of a window grill that in its ornate flourishes suggested better times. But that would have been long before she took up residence.

"What can I do to thank you for helping me?" He reached into his pocket. "Maybe you could use this?"

The moment he offered her money he regretted it.

"No no," she said.

"Please. Take it."

"No!"

He put the rice pot down and turned to take his leave.

"Wait. Sir."

"Yes?"

"You can do something. Please. I need to go in taxi car somewhere."

"Okay."

"A taxi car and driver. Tonight. When it is dark. But don't tell anyone. Not your friend. It's secret."

"You mean . . . Mr. Federenko?"

She met his eyes. The fierceness of her gaze caught him off guard.

In the West, even among the well traveled and well read, any Russian-sounding name could arouse a frisson of suspicion, making Alyosha an instant cliché: KGB agent, scar-faced mobster, rogue scientist, criminal mastermind. These stereotypes had given birth to some bizarre contradictions. The Russian is state-controlled and cannot think for himself—because he does not see the world as it truly is. And yet he is also manipulative and deeply devious, driven by insatiable material greed. Maybe Song's dislike of Alyosha was part of this web. Which was ridiculous, for Alyosha was not in fact ethnically Russian. But that was the thing about prejudice, Fearless knew; he had experienced it himself for as long as he could remember.

Song told him the time and place to wait, and Fearless left her quietly and walked the streets, waving away the scooter taxis that beckoned at every junction, trying to remember the last time he'd been anywhere without a project. Interests, pastimes, hobbies, occupations: he'd had nothing else in his life except for photography. Images from a book he had loved as a child—*What Do People Do All Day?*—floated through his mind: dogs and rabbits sawing tree trunks into logs, grading ground for roads, mining coal and tin. He could picture his father reading the book out loud to him, the two of them squeezed onto his single bed. He's turning the last page. It's time to turn out the lights. *I love you, little man:* there were not many men who would say that—not of his father's generation and class. "You must always remember, Jojo," he had told Fearless more than once, "that people are good at heart, even when they don't seem to be."

The simple taxi ride now loomed large in his mind. Throughout his career, he had always strived not to intervene in any situation. If he intervened in something, he couldn't capture it on film. Not getting involved helped everything remain the same. But now, without his camera, maybe he could *do* instead of observe. Not like before, and not like his father, who himself had been a passive observer in Cambodia.

On his father's visit, every last detail had been stage-managed: the places they went, the people they spoke to, the designated times for eating and sleeping. Fearless knew this from a detailed report, published by a Swedish journalist not long afterward. Along the roads the visitors had traveled in their chauffeur-driven Mercedes, Cambodians had lined up, dressed in new clothes, like Catholic children awaiting a papal motorcade. They had been on their best behavior wherever the party arrived: fishing cooperatives and engineering schools, pig farms and pharmaceutical plants, cutting-edge irrigation projects, gleaming new rubber factories, during meals in communal halls in well-maintained villages that manifested the perfect society Khmer Rouge rationality had produced. At night, the visitors were returned to Phnom Penh, directly to their lodgings on Monivong Boulevard, where supplies of gin and cigarettes were laid on.

Fearless now entered a bustling market, which offered some respite from the heat of the day but overwhelmed him with the aromas of spices, meat, and sweat. He stumbled into a white man—"Sorry, so sorry!"—haggling at a hardware stall over an electric iron. Exiting onto a street of shop houses and blinding light, he suddenly found himself back on the riverside, not knowing whether to head to the left or right. The rush hour was in full swing, motorbikes and tuk-tuks everywhere. Streets that had been deserted two hours ago were alive with people heading home to their families.

His father must have known that he hadn't seen ordinary Cambodian life. Fearless suspected the thought might even have tickled him. So what if it was PR? What government on earth doesn't do it? And the Khmer Rouge had liberated Cambodia from a more pernicious farce: the CIA-backed sham of the Lon Nol government. How could rallying their people to put on a show be worse than the Americans and their carpet bombs and chemical sprays?

At first, Fearless thought it was a hallucination—in the distance, an elephant floating toward him, drifting through the mass of riverside traffic. It was as if, in the middle of all the bustle and turmoil, the restaurants and bars, the workers and beggars, the privileged and the dispossessed, there was a still, silent center: a heart of peace that went at its own pace, that was always open and forever forgiving. Slowly, the giant emerged from the haze of heat, motorbikes weaving around it with nonchalant ease as it lolloped along the tea-colored river.

Fearless decided to follow it, watching from a distance, hoping it would somehow take him home. Instead, it led him to a vast hotel that was a mishmash of modern and ancient Khmer styles: the Cambodiana. Where had he heard that name before? Here, at least, he would be able to arrange a car and driver and take Song wherever she wanted to go.

8

"Did you tell him?" Song said, as she slid onto the back seat.

"Did I tell my friend? No," Fearless replied. "Not a word."

Without glancing at him, she gave the driver the destination.

"Where are we going?"

"It won't take long time."

Song told herself she ought to hide her anxiety, to relax her fists and uncurl her toes. As far as he was concerned, this might be a simple errand. But could it really be true? Could Sovanna be there? And even if she was, what would she do when she arrived? If Sovanna was somehow captive, she could hardly knock on the door. And the shock of seeing Song alive might itself be hard to handle.

She looked away from Fearless and scanned the city streets, which for so many months had been nothing but distant sounds to her: car horns, restaurant chatter, voices over karaoke machines. The facades of the buildings were big blocks of pale moonlight, the narrow streets below cast into shadow. They passed rows of shuttered shops; construction sites crosshatched with concrete columns, their stick-thin rebars needling the stars. Rhombuses of gold along the street announced beer gardens, around which motodops congregated like geckos.

In her mind, she called up a map of the city—its grid of streets edged by the blue band of the Tonlé Sap and topped by the teardrop of Boeung Kak Lake. Here: left on 144. Now: crossing Norodom.

"I want to thank you again for helping me," Fearless said.

What was she meant to say to that?

As they drove into the heart of Boeung Keng Kang 1, an area of large residences, apartment buildings, and embassies, she recognized a villa that Sovanna and she had "visited"—the love child of an '80s office block and a colonial-style house, with mirrored glass windows and elaborate pediments. As soon as she caught sight of it, she tried to push it from her mind; the man there had wanted to pinch and slap and spit on them. When Bun Thim had seen what he'd done to Sovanna, he reached for the machete he kept under his seat. They'd had to talk him down—it would have been the death of all of them. "You're welcome," she remembered. "Please come again." That was what the Chief had always taught them to say afterward.

Sovanna had taken the brunt of that man's punishment. From their earliest days, she had acted as Song's protector. While Song had worked in the house beside Ma, Sovanna toiled in the field with Pa, shoveling dung or threshing rice: she had always been tougher. Even on the night they had "lost their happiness," she had pushed herself in front of Song and taken the lead.

"Got me an eager beaver!" the john had exclaimed, pushing her onto her knees and sniggering to himself. He was a barang that the Chief called Mr. UNTAC. Skinny from dying—you could see it in his sunken cheeks, the line of his pelvis, the way his skull flexed beneath his paper-thin scalp.

When the six years that followed tumbled through Song's mind—from the first months at The Sunflower with the twelve-hour shifts to the "home visits" that ultimately became their principal job to the night that changed everything and led her to the Naga—she was glad that fate had brought Fearless to accompany her. When she had thought about taking this journey, she'd anticipated only the horror of being seen and not the terror of being assailed by ghosts of the past.

"You're welcome," she said, turning to face Fearless for the first time.

After rolling past the illuminated signs of Sihanouk Boulevard, the taxi slowed, pulled right onto Trasak Paem, and then entered a stretch of imposing houses—the homes of samdechs, ayudoms—the rich, government men.

"Okay. I go," she said after telling the driver to stop.

"We'll wait?"

"You give me money you say you give." She had realized she would surely need it if Sovanna was alive.

Fearless reached into his pocket and drew out two ten-dollar notes. They had no idea how much this amount of money could buy, she thought—how long you could survive on what to them was loose change.

On foot, she turned the corner onto Street 57, hurrying from the darkness under one tree to the next. All the while, she told herself not to hope. More likely than not, the novice had been mistaken.

Here it was: house number 32, a broad, two-floor villa, with a vast pitched roof and portico—the kind of rich man's palace she had worked in many times. It was surrounded on all sides by a lush garden of trees: tamarind, jacaranda, longan, sugar palm. She walked around the block. Over the wall she could see the gleam of a four-wheel drive and a spacious balcony draped with tumbling bougainvillea. Around the corner, two men in army shirts stood guard.

Pulling the krama tighter under her neck, she made a pass, turning onto the other side of the block. The walls of the villa were high—with shards of glass as big as one's palm along the tops—but the wall of the house that backed onto it, where the priests had chanted for the dead man, was much lower, with a jack tree that spread over both gardens. And in the dead man's house there was no sign of life, only a night guard asleep on a folding chair cocooned in the hazy silk of a mosquito net.

Returning to Street 322, she hid behind a tree and waited. From her vantage point, she could see the guards entering their hut. When the angle of their heads and jerking hands told her they were immersed in a card game, she scurried back and hauled herself over the neighbor's wall, landing in a dense but soft thicket of ginger plants. Giving thanks to the cicadas, she hid under the leaves: the insects' shimmering wall of electricity was even louder than the singing of the blood in her ears.

The guard would have appeared by now if he'd heard any disturbance. And the jack tree was only ten feet away, strung with its heavy, pendulous fruit. In the shadows she could make out a network of branches she could use to plot a route over the wall.

She crawled through the ginger, pulled herself onto the lowest branch, side-footed along, and then pulled herself up again. Sweat trickled down the small of her back; she tried to quiet her breathing. But when she looked back, within touching distance of the wall, there was no light or sign that anything had been detected.

Save for a window casting an oblong of light, Sovanna's villa—if indeed it was hers—was quiet. Craning her neck, Song could make out a lamp-shade in the lit room.

After five minutes more, her ears pricked up. She heard music pumping out: American pop. With the branch between her legs, she edged herself along, now crossing the boundary of the wall below.

Then a strident voice blared across the rooftops—a sharp metallic sound that phased in and out. A sound truck blasting a political message. Combined with the pop music and the shrill of the cicadas, it was the perfect cover. Now or never, she told herself.

She landed in a cluster of gardenia bushes, the jack branch rebounding and shaking up and down. The bushes were gray in the dark, but she knew the flowers were yellow. Maybe the true nature of things could always be sensed, no matter the light or context or surface.

The pop music roared; from the way the light flickered, just thirty feet away, she guessed it was coming from a television. But she could see no one inside—just the standing lamp and a Chinese closet, golden dragons winding across its facade.

And then a girl's arms appeared, held high above her head. Sovanna. Oh, it *was* her. The boy priest had been right. She was alive. Complete. She glided past the window—turning, dancing. Someone near her started clapping with meaty hands.

"Come on. Let's dance!"

It was her voice! Sovanna's voice!

"Come on. Why why? You no fun."

She drifted into view again, eyes closed, body naked save for a gleaming necklace with a flashing blue stone. Then she lowered herself and disappeared. The clapping man stopped clapping and sighed a long, overblown sigh.

Song resisted the urge to call out for her sister. A bead of sweat ran into her open mouth.

What would she do? There was no way back up the jack tree. But a large, dense longan grew on the other side of the lawn. She would have to make a break across a lake of moonlight and leap into another garden. She stayed where she was, hiding in the leaves.

Then the TV stopped and a door creaked on its hinges and, in that moment, the jack tree released its fruit. One, two, three of them came tumbling, two of them crashing onto foliage, the last even worse, booming on something hard and metal. Song threw herself flat, the moist earth in her nose. She must have shaken the fruit loose when she leapt from the tree!

Song heard a rattle of bolt and whine of hinge. A flashlight came on and bobbed around the corner. "Who's there?"

She could see the outline of a peaked cap and shoulders; a pool of light trembled over the long-leaved grass. The light settled on the wall and began to track across it as the arm of the silhouette reached for its holster. Grim irony: that in the very moment of finding something to live for, she now faced the prospect of meeting her death. *I exist!*—that was what she wanted to shout. When Sovanna had been dead, her life had become unreal, because no one else had been there to witness or know it.

Inch by inch, the oval of light panned across the wall.

Then the window of the room opened and a white man appeared, his balloon of a belly pressing against the curlicues of the iron grill. "What is this?" he said in English. It was the voice of Colonel Vasiliev.

The guard held his hand up and Vasiliev shrunk back as he raised the flashlight higher into the branches of the jack tree. Song dug her toes deep into the earth.

At the moment the guard's colleague came around the corner to join him, he turned his head for a moment and she took her chance. In an instant, she was on the grass, fully exposed in the moonlight, every twitching muscle hell-bent on reaching the longan. A shout went up and the air cracked like a whip and then there was a clap from the direction she was running in. Then she was knee deep in leaves and leaping for a branch and the glass shards on the wall were bursting into fragments.

Something tore at her as she fell into thorns, her head and shoulders and elbow throbbing. No time to stop: another stretch of grass, another towering tree, a fence tipped with arrowheads. There were shouts, lights going on in houses. She swung her legs over, arched her body inward. She was falling, the ground rushing up to meet her, her krama ripped from her head, snagged on an iron barb.

Knifepoints stabbed at her ankle. Blood was trickling down her face and arm. She hobbled to the first corner she could find and took it. Restaurants, bars, motodops, a car. Up ahead, a boulevard shimmering with yellow lights. Dirt bikes revved in the direction she had come from; one of the guards sprinted around the corner on foot.

Which way was the taxi that the barang had brought her in?

The guard saw her and shouted. She headed for the boulevard—it had to be Monivong—and bolted straight into the throng of motos and tuk-tuks. Horns howled and wailed in unison. The smell of burning rubber mixed with the taste of sweat and blood. She didn't look back to see if the guard was following as she jumped the median and made it to the other side. She hadn't stolen anything—he must have been able to see that. She was nothing, no one—there was no reason to follow her.

As soon as she left the boulevard, she found herself on another side street where, as quickly as the light and traffic had assailed her, she was once again enfolded in silence and dark. This street was lined with modest houses. She panted, limping, taking the first narrow turning, a dead end where she came upon a ditch covered in undergrowth, well out of the sight of the nearby dwellings. She crawled into the culvert and made herself small.

There was no sound or movement; no flashlight panning the area. Soon, she told herself, she would double back to the car. In the meantime, she bound the cut on her arm with the remnant of her krama, tightening it by pulling the end with her teeth.

Her mind teemed with questions. How would she get Sovanna out of there? And if she could, where would they escape to? Battambang? But how?

Over the next five minutes, her body felt heavy. The sleep she had lost saving Fearless laid claim to her. After weeks of vomiting, she was suddenly ravenous.

Just a moment more—then "home" and food, sleep and plan. But then sleep took her before she could resist it, rocking her tenderly in its soft, supple arms.

9

Fearless knew the sound of a gunshot when he heard one. He told the driver to wait and headed in the direction in which Song had disappeared. But when he turned the corner, the street was deserted. Then he heard a volley of shouts, which he followed onto another road. Here, a security guard—his trousers tucked into his boots—was calling out and hailing another guard in the distance. At the same moment, Vasiliev came out of one of the houses, doing up the buttons of a capacious short-sleeved shirt.

When he saw Alyosha's boss, Fearless stepped back—how would he explain his presence in this place? He watched Vasiliev berate the Cambodian guards, clipping one sharply around the back of the head before he walked into the little booth outside the house's entrance, came out with a deck of cards, and threw them into the street.

It couldn't be a coincidence that they were here. But why did Song need it to be a secret?

Back at the car, he waited for her to return, reassuring the driver that he would be paid for his time. For a while, they leaned against the car, smoking in silence. Then Fearless began to pace up and down the stretch of sidewalk, watching the motos roll by in twos and threes, the black hair of the riders flowing in the breeze.

Minutes stretched to half an hour. He remembered his adoptive father Conrad's oft-repeated advice: "War is hanging around. Have a history book in your bag. Use the time to learn. Read Rebecca West on Yugoslavia. Find stuff that actively contradicts your own opinion. That was your father's blind spot. Before he left for Cambodia, I tried to give him the Ponchaud book and he pushed it away."

Fearless had no book now. And what opinions did he have? What was he doing, standing here on a street in Phnom Penh?

The hour mark came up. He began to feel irritated. When taking photographs, he could happily wait days for the decisive moment, but waiting for someone out of obligation was infuriating. The irony that making others wait was his modus operandi shamed him, which only made his irritation grow. That was why Laure had driven alone to the airport: he had made her wait and pushed her past her limits. He should have left Nairobi and been at the wheel.

"You have no consideration," Jimmy had said the night before, when he'd shared his big plans to Jimmy and Luke over dinner. He would propose to Laure, and then they would move with the baby to Israel. He'd have a staff position; no more funding his own work—and no more living hand to mouth. He'd root himself in one place and photograph subjects over time. All those partings and returns with Laure—a braided cord of longing and resentment—snipped. And when the baby was bigger, Laure would resume work; Israel was a node in her investigations into Russian money laundering.

"But have you asked Laure what *she* thinks?" Luke added, skeptically.

"Sometimes," Jimmy said, "you're in your own little bubble."

But why pick on him? Laure was hardly a saint.

In their last argument about work, he had grabbed her folders angrily. "You say you want me home but then spend all your time on these!"

"Put them down, Joe."

The doctor had advised her to rest. But she had just traveled to Moscow. Fact-checking, she said, more work-obsessed than him, determined to push back against the tide of quantity over quality and bite-size tidbits over long-form analysis. She was switching away from reporting to investigative work.

He opened a file and grabbed a handful of sheets; as Laure rushed toward him, paper sailed everywhere.

"You idiot. You deserve to be hit in the fucking face!"

Those were her words as she stormed out of the room. The exact words she knew would hurt him most.

But then she came back and made things better. "I mean *this* time. I mean you deserve it, this time."

When two hours of waiting on the street had passed, Fearless shook his head and conceded defeat.

Back at the Naga, he headed straight to Song's cell in the hope that somehow she had already returned. Alone there, he was struck again by her lack of possessions. The only decoration was a newspaper cutting on the wall: a pretty Khmer woman with bouffant hair, holding a microphone to her lips and smiling enigmatically.

Throughout the night, Fearless went back—at two a.m., three a.m., and 5:30—but the room was always empty.

When sleep finally came, he was a child again, in the hall of his parents' house. He could see the orchid on the shelf above the pot where they kept the keys. And the suitcase. He was walking toward that suitcase again, reaching out: there was a letter there for him. Then the dream was broken by a rifle. The sound was like someone slamming dustbin lids together: bam. Bam-bam-bam. Bam. Bam-bam-bam-bam. His eyes flicked open and he sucked in a mighty gulp of air.

The curtains had just been swished.

"Rise and shine!" cried Alyosha. "My God—you look even worse than you did yesterday."

"What the . . . ? What time is it?"

"Midday. Time for R & R. Let's go to the Cambodiana. Bring your trunks and your sun lotion. Look here—I remembered my table tennis bats."

Fearless's expression must have spoken for itself.

"No swimming pool? Okay. But what shall we do? Go to a field like the other tourists and blow up cows with RPGs?"

Fearless hesitated. He was going to ask whether Song had returned—after all, Alyosha might help him find her—but then he remembered the promise he had made. "No—let's go to the school," he said instead.

"What school?"

"The Genocide Museum. What's the name of it? S-something."

"S-21. Tuol Sleng? Bacha, you are joking me. Come on! Doctor Alyosha is prescribing massages and margaritas!"

"Listen, Lyosha. The night before, I was dying. I mean it. I wasn't drunk. Not drunk like normal. It felt like . . . a kind of . . . annihilation. And now I want to do what I came here for. You said it yourself when you suggested this trip. I've talked about it before and can't leave it undone. Return to the place that's tied up with my father. Make peace with it. What do I have left to lose? Your words."

Alyosha exhaled slowly.

"Don't worry, then," Fearless said. "I'll go on my own."

"Oh, for God's sake. Amos—go and tell Bun Thim to bring the car."

"No cars. Let's get bikes and ride there—like the old days." Fearless pointed across the road. "You can hire them over there. What do you say, Lyoshenka? Or are you a big fat chicken?"

10

In the culvert, Song slept through the call of a distant rooster. Even the clanging of a gate as someone left for work didn't penetrate the heavy, wet wool of her slumber.

She was dreaming that she was walking along a bridge between their houses.

"We'll have two houses," Sovanna would say as she stroked Song's hair at the end of the day, combing it from root to tip with her fingers. "We'll build one exactly the same, right next to the old house, and make a bridge between the first floors so our children run back and forth."

"We'll have children?"

"But no husbands."

"I'll have my children and you'll have yours."

It took rain to make Song rouse herself from this dreamworld—an unusual morning storm that forced drips through the branches above. For a while, she lay motionless, her eyes squinting in the light, before she became conscious of her cuts and bruises.

"Ot tee," she muttered. Dawn was long gone and Thom would be up, making sure she had completed her morning tasks. Then she remembered that her krama had been ripped from her head and she had used what was left of it to bind her injured arm. Gingerly unpeeling the blood-soaked fabric, she was relieved to see the wound wasn't as bad as she feared.

Peering over the top of the culvert, she spotted a line of washing in a nearby yard: white pillowcases and towels soaked by unexpected rain. She darted out, little pebbles pricking the soles of her feet, and thrust her arm through the fence, her fingertips just tipping the hem of a towel, making it sway once, then twice, until it swung into her grasp. As soon as she'd snatched it, she began to run, wringing it out and binding it around her head.

As she turned the first corner, the world rushed at her in its vivid glory, compelling her to respond, demanding she laugh or scream or weep. How long had it been since she had moved fifty feet in a straight line in daylight! Just to feel the sun and air, the breath in her lungs, sent electric shivers across her chest. And not only that—she had a goal to live for now. Her mind was frantic, calculating, triangulating.

This much she knew: Sovanna was still a slave after all these years. Even if she could somehow pass her a message, let her know she was alive, Sovanna would be helpless. And any attempt to contact her would put them both at risk. If she were caught, they would not just throw her out of the Naga. They would do what they did with anyone who made trouble for them. Like the street performers who had once been brought to perform at the Sunflower, they would take her by the neck like a snake or chicken, hold her up, drop her into a box, and make her disappear. For so long she had dreamed of Sovanna freeing *her*, but now Song would have to assume the mantle of savior.

That's what she was going to do. Set them free. Get them home.

11

Fearless paid at the booth and stepped into the compound. Before him lay a broad lawn, a stand of coconut palms, and a wide, gray, three-story rectangle that had once been a school in 1960s Phnom Penh. Alyosha gestured for Fearless to go ahead, positioning himself in the shade cast by the nearest outbuilding. He fanned himself lazily with a handkerchief, Amos stationed by his side.

The only visitor, Fearless wandered the building's corridors. This is where the enemies of the Khmer Rouge were brought—the rich, the intellectuals, the teachers who'd once taught at this school, for imprisonment, torture, confession, and death. When the hoped-for rice harvests never came to pass—with so many skilled technicians and managers killed—the regional bosses allocated their yields for export. The result was internal famine, which the leadership blamed on counterrevolutionaries—which, just like rice, had to be manufactured. What had happened here, Fearless knew, was a kind of alchemy: any type of person could be brought through the gates and transformed into a wicked, rebellious traitor. The Khmer Rouge said that these people must be "solved"—as if all people were problems whose answer was zero.

The first rooms Fearless walked into were empty shells that once held row upon row of desks. Attentive faces would have looked up from *cahiers*. The teacher's desk would have been stacked with *bulletins scolaires*. Standing there, he could almost imagine it was *les grandes vacances*—that the room was just waiting for the summer to end. But further along, other spaces shattered the fantasy. Here was a hall that had been divided into small wooden holding cells, each no bigger than a Victorian outhouse.

Then came the notorious torture rooms, empty save for the rusted frame of a bed—an iron grid upon which thousands had suffered. Here, old and young, women and men, had been strung up, waterboarded, raped, electrocuted, whipped, flayed, and experimented upon, the blood sucked from their veins, forced to swallow their own excrement. In time, even the torturers themselves were found guilty of one charge or another and tortured by their successors.

On a board outside the room, the camp regulations were posted: *You must immediately answer my questions without wasting time to reflect. While getting lashes or electrification you must not cry at all.*

His chest felt tight. Wasn't that his own mantra? "I will not feel. I will not feel until I have to."

In the last block, Fearless came to a long narrow room filled with black-and-white photographs: thousands of faces staring at the camera. Just as the Russians had done before the Great Purge, the Khmer Rouge had photographed their victims in their final moments. It was as if they supposed that their administrative excellence could make senselessness logical and evil sane.

Each photo was overpowering. Did they know what was about to happen? Did they understand there was no escape? Didn't that one look like Song? No, the eyes were different.

Cruelest of all were the children under ten—who, if they'd lived, would be his age. While he was struggling with his first long divisions, they were being beaten, strangled and garroted. No matter how long mankind lived, no matter how much kindness it practiced, there was no making up for what had happened here.

"You here? Are you here?" he started to whisper.

His searching of the headshots grew frantic now. There was someone he was looking for, someone connected to his story. Fearless's breathing was heavy, his back streaming with sweat. The mosquito bites that riddled his body pulsed in constellations.

He could hear Amos and Alyosha talking quietly through the open window—the most he'd heard Amos say since he'd met him:

"Why ask him? I could have taken it."

"Come now. You? Your mother's faith rubbed off on you."

"I don't think he knows anything. I r-really don't."

"I know you're here." Fearless was speaking out loud now. "Show yourself. Let me see you. Let's see where you are." His gaze darted across eyes and mouths, faces whirling around him until he was blinded by their blur. And into this centrifuge came yet more flickering images: the bitter grin of Wish; long black hair hanging over him; the swinging legs of Bopha, gobstopper clacking between her teeth. The eyes had to be there. The last eyes to see his father.

Then he was stumbling into the sunlight as if he'd jumped from a moving train. Doubled over, swaying, mouth too dry to spit.

Amos reached down and locked forearms with him. Fearless gripped back, his thumb pressing a tattoo of a caduceus.

"Are you okay, bacha?" Alyosha asked.

"I was looking for his killers. They were arrested and brought here. Did I ever tell you about that, Lyosha?"

"There can be no way of knowing."

"They're here. I'm sure."

Alyosha took him by the shoulders. "I told you we should go to the hotel and drink cocktails. Let's get something to eat. We're all hungry, no?"

"Okay. But then we go on."

"Where?"

"To the Killing Fields."

"What the hell."

"Just humor me."

Alyosha shook his head. "It's lucky we have bikes. Bun Thim would never agree to go there."

The rumble of the engine and his long shadow in front of him as the setting sun lit up the road to Phnom Penh allowed Fearless to clear his mind for a moment. He shifted the bike into fifth and throttled hard, the ends of his unbuttoned shirt flaring out behind him. Alyosha and Amos pulled alongside out of necessity; if they lagged behind they would choke on his dust cloud.

When Fearless turned to look at him, Alyosha was grinning at the thrill of the ride, leaning in as their bikes hummed in tandem. He shouted something out, nodded, shouted again.

"What?"

Alyosha pointed down the road.

In three hundred yards they would come to an intersection, on each side of which was a roadside shack; approaching on the perpendicular was a giant dump truck. At their current pace, they would be obliged to slow down, stop, and give way to its massive hulk at the crossroads. But at full speed they would most likely beat it by seconds. Alyosha was issuing a friendly challenge.

"Yeehaaaa!" Alyosha yanked on his handlebars, pulling a wheelie. At the same instant, Fearless's rear wheel juddered in a pothole and he fell behind as Amos caught up to Alyosha, a hundred yards from the crossroads and two hundred from the truck.

Just as Alyosha and Amos reached the intersection, a Land Cruiser appeared from behind the truck, a speeding two-ton block of burgundy and gold, and there was no time to do anything but yelp in surprise. As Fearless slammed on both his foot brake and hand brakes, the Land Cruiser hit Alyosha's front wheel and sent him flying, the bike ricocheting away like a fragment of shrapnel, dominoing into Amos, who was thrown to the ground, his machine careering away beneath him. Debris exploded into the air. The Land Cruiser axeled through 540 degrees, the truck veering off the road and plowing into the fields, raising massive clouds of dust that swallowed everything. Fearless was completely subsumed by the thunderhead as he struggled to control his skid and keep his bike upright.

Maybe it was the dust and the black smoke engulfing them, but in a matter of seconds darkness had fallen. Fearless dropped his bike and tried to orient himself, shielding his face with his forearm, choking on grit. A door slammed and someone let out an animalistic cry. He rushed toward the scream.

Then he stumbled over someone: Amos sitting in the dirt, holding one of his arms and trying to speak.

"Sh—, Fff . . . Fffff . . . Fuckingpopmyshoulder!"

The smoke parted and he saw a man—a white man—leaning back and dragging Alyosha's body. A scowling face. A snarl of effort. It was the man he'd seen in the market in Phnom Penh, the one who'd been bargaining at the household goods stall; he remembered the deep vertical furrows on his cheeks. He was heaving Alyosha into the back of the Land Cruiser.

"Popmyarrrrm! Ge . . . Ge . . ."

A door slammed. The engine revved and wheels began to spin and the man and Alyosha were lost in dust, and they were choking all over again, Amos's cry of pain piercing the dark and echoing over the fields.

12

After the relief of finding Thom gone, Song discovered a fold of dollars under her sleeping mat, enclosed in a piece of paper with a tiny pencil sketch: a man with a shaved head, flat nose, and full lips. She recognized Fearless's face at once.

He puzzled and intrigued her. The way he had confided in her, both drunk and sober: saying he had killed his wife, telling her he had harmed himself. She had listened to so many men over the years, heard so many lies, stories, excuses, and justifications, but she had rarely experienced someone confessing to something she felt certain he *hadn't* done, let alone revealing a weakness few would admit. But then she remembered him gasping when he saw her scars. He *was* like everyone else: obsessed with the visible, regardless of their gods and the temples they built to them.

This extra money would allow her and Sovanna to improvise. It might pay for unplanned nights in unexpected places if they had to throw people off their scent. Again, she ran through the plan she had devised. They would approach Battambang from a counterclockwise direction, stopping off in Kampong Cham or Kampong Thom, rather than taking the direct route through Kampong Chhnang and Moung Ruessei.

She and Sovanna had escaped The Sunflower only once. That day, when they were fifteen, they had made it as far as the bus station, where they wriggled onto the crowded flatbed of a Battambang-bound truck, hiding among ankles, knees, and elbows. But mere seconds after the driver had turned the ignition, the Chief's men roared up, waving and shouting. They hauled them off the truck by their hair, dragged them through the dust, with Sovanna swearing and spitting and kicking.

When they got back to The Sunflower, Song braced herself for a beating, but the Chief had no intention of damaging his assets. *Stupid girls. In three years, you would have been back home. Getting married, having a family. But now your debt must go back to zero.*

Oh the lies! Song had thought. But he divided her and Sovanna. "You and your big ideas," Sovanna started to mutter. To this day, she was working off the debt Song had accrued.

Below, she heard the minivan in the street and the children's chattering voices. Quickly, she slid Fearless's fold of dollars under her mat again.

What she felt when she saw them jumping down took her by surprise. It was like the urge she'd had to smash Thom's head with the rice pot: the sensation that she no longer needed to accept life as it was. She could open up a vein to the anger she held on their behalf, a reservoir deep inside her which she had always sealed up. She could tap it, let its contents surge up and erupt.

"Hey, bong—let us in!"

Rathana was the first to rattle the gate. Bopha followed after, the letter necklace dancing on her stomach. The usual raucous hubbub began. Here was Rathana demanding his dinner before they washed, Samnang stripping off her clothes and falling over her shorts. There was Dara, hanging back, giving her that funny look he always saved for her.

"Is he here?"

"No—Thom's been out all day, Dara," she told him: up to something with his metal box; meeting with . . . why not say his name? Sokha. Yes. "Sokha," she said out loud as the children raced past to the yard, not listening.

Soon, the naked mischief-makers were running water into the bucket, scooping it in their cups and splashing it around. This might be the last time she'd hear the joyful laughter that, in her darkest days, had been her only reason for living.

"Rice."

"Mango."

"Coconut."

"Cassava."

"Potato."

"Papaya."

"The flooded fields of lotus and lilies."

"You wash with us today, pretty lady?" Rathana shouted, and, this time, feeling love rising up like the song in a bird's breast, Song pulled up the plastic washing stool and offered herself to them, taking off her shirt and wrapping her sampot around her.

For a moment, the children were abashed, and then Dara stepped forward. When the others saw Song was happy to allow it, they helped him unwind her krama, their boisterousness forgotten. When the fabric was loose and her hair fell freely around her shoulders, Bopha folded the krama and left it to one side.

Then Rathana reached for the soap and delicately began to lather and rub it into and along her hair. The last time someone washed her, it had been frantic and terrifying, Bun Thim splashing her in the mud of the Tonle Sap, desperately trying to neutralize what Sokha had thrown on her. Other little hands now joined Rathana's. They were gentle and tender, reaching all over her, sweetly, curiously, not pretending they didn't notice but neither scared nor disgusted by her burns and grafts.

"Srey sa-art," said Bopha in a whisper to herself.

When the soaping and shampooing had been done to their satisfaction, Samnang dipped her bowl into the bucket of water, bringing it up perfectly full to the brim. She poured it reverently, the water running through Song's hair and across her face and over her covered breasts and stomach and thighs, washing away the smarting and stinging of her grazes. Again and again the water flowed, refracting the sunlight in white arcs and stripes. She cried as it came down, keeping a straight face so they wouldn't notice, her tears becoming part of the flow of water that flowed from them.

Afterward, when she had dressed and settled them as usual, she began to work through her list. In the bar, behind the beer barrels, she found an old, transparent plastic tube; blowing sharply into it forced out a web of dust and debris. Then she took a crate, filled it with empty Stolichnaya bottles, grabbed the claw hammer that was kept on a nearby shelf, and hurried down to the entrance foyer where the motos were parked.

She closed her eyes for a moment, giving thanks to her father. It had been his crazy idea to keep a petrol bomb ever ready in their house. "What a waste!" Ma had said. "What if the *yuon* were to ransack this place?" She summoned her memories of the bike shop mechanics. How had they done it as she watched them from her window? Open the petrol tank. Submerge one end of the tube in the petrol. Make the tube into a U shape, ensuring the bottom of the U was always lower than the level of the tank.

Now all she had to do was raise the free end to her lips. A quick suck and the golden-brown liquid emerged, settling in the arc of the bottom of the U. After that, it was easy to fill the bottles halfway, screwing the lids tight and resealing the motos' petrol tanks. When she was finished, she hid the bottles in the darkness of the broom cupboard, under an old bucket, covered with rags.

Back in the room, she pulled her picture of Ros Sothea off the wall and fashioned it into a kind of envelope. "What can I do to thank you?" she repeated under her breath.

Sitting at the window, she saw Thom return and head for the bar. Now all she needed was for darkness to arrive; everything else could be done at the last minute. She willed the sky to fade from bleached blue to gray to indigo. The owner of the bike shop mirrored her impatience, it seemed. He was pacing back and forth across the sidewalk. When his wife called him in, he hawked betel juice into the gutter. "Choi may!" he shouted, smacking his hands together.

Finally, when the sun set, she headed for Thom's room, opened his top drawer, and ripped out the plastic bag of cash, stuffing the wad of money inside her waistband. She would do what she could for the children. Breaking the padlock on the box in the closet would be impossible; even if she had the strength, the clanging would draw too much attention. Using the claw hammer, she levered up the lid, finding exactly what she had expected inside—a video machine connected to the end of the wire. She ejected the tape and slid it into the envelope made from the picture of Ros Serey Sothea. Then, as she turned to leave, another idea came to her. She took the pillow from Thom's bed and ripped it apart, spreading handfuls of polyester stuffing around. She turned out his drawers, tossing clothes and papers behind her, throwing any valuables—his alarm clock, a pair of fake Ray-Bans—into the plastic bag that had held his money. Then, in Fearless's apartment, she did the same, tipping out his duffel bag and scattering the contents. It was a strange and strangely guilty pleasure for her: creating chaos for somebody else to clean up. Satisfied that the mess looked realistic, she slid the videotape under Fearless's pillow.

Back in her room, she fashioned a sling out of her kramas, including the bloodstained half she hadn't had time to wash. Once she had wrapped and folded the Stoli bottles into it, she shifted the bundle onto her back and knotted the ends around her chest, tucking the claw hammer into the folds of fabric. She squatted up and down to ensure the bottles didn't clink, conscious of her breasts, which seemed swollen and more sensitive after the beating she'd had from Thom. Then she slipped onto the mezzanine and down to the next landing, the only sound the thumping of her pulse in her head.

At the bottom of the stairs, she wrought one final piece of havoc. Offering up a silent prayer of forgiveness, she placed her foot on the supporting post of the spirit house. As it crashed to the floor and its finial and balustrade cracked, a hot flush began to spread across her body. It was Thom who had always made a point with the observances, who presented one face to the world and pulled another behind closed doors. What came crashing to the ground was not the spirit house or the spirits, but his hypocrisy and venality and evil heart. Let them come, spirits of the ground, who were older and wiser and truer than the people who walked all over them. Let them no longer be falsely at peace in this place and rise up in anger, spiral up the staircase, into the Naga, down every corridor and fuck-room, howling, petrifying everyone in their way. She unlocked the street gate and left it wide open, the last piece of evidence that the place had been ransacked by thieves.

Then she was out, into the night, slinging the plastic bag containing Thom's possessions onto a nearby mound of garbage. She moved steadily through the streets, across busy intersections, over shafts of light thrown onto the sidewalk from open shops, past the noise of karaoke and shouting televisions, around the corner restaurants whose plastic chairs and tables spilled onto the sidewalk and uniformed beer girls laughed politely at bad jokes. Blue plastic bags wafted in the monsoon breeze, floating no more than an inch above the sidewalk; rats as big as cats scurried among broken bricks.

As she went, she kept to the dark spaces and side streets. Fifteen minutes later, she entered Street 322, keeping a safe distance from the villa in case the guards recognized her. But as she edged closer, she realized these were different men—dressed in the sand-colored shirts of the National Police, with black and gold epaulets and hard, peaked caps. Lights were burning on the villa's top floor—a sign that gave her reason to hope.

Going around the block, she leapt into the dead neighbor's garden. At the foot of the jack tree, she put down the sling full of bottles. Deftly, she undid their caps, dipped the rags in petrol, and stuffed each mouth. Then she climbed the tree, swiftly, silently, and settled herself in the fork of its branches. Once she had tied one end of her second krama to the tree, she sat, ears cocked and eyes peeled for movement.

To the west, the traffic on Monivong sounded like the sighing of a sea. Mosquitoes banked and dived around her ears. She could still leave now. She could climb back down and out of the garden, return to the Naga, pretend she hadn't heard the "thieves." She had come this far, yes, but could she really go further? Someone like her. Someone so weak.

Then Sovanna walked past one of the upper floor windows. The stars were in alignment: they were ordering her onward.

Song inched back down the tree, picked up one of the bottles, climbed back over the wall, and scampered to the edge of the block. When she peered around the corner, she saw the policemen were still there, but talking and making no effort to keep watch. She took a deep breath and pulled out the cigarette lighter. The wick of rag flowered into flame.

She hurled the bottle toward the men, sprinting away, hearing shouts as she scaled the neighbor's wall again.

Now she was a thundercrack, the sun at its midday cruelest, the monsoon rain on the skylight, the pounding music of the Naga. She was her hatred for Thom and her love for Sovanna. She was all the biggest things she could summon in her mind concentrated into the one thing she needed to be in that moment—pure, focused speed—hopping down from the tree and lighting her second rag. Making for the right-hand side of the villa, she punched the claw hammer through one of the liquid black windows of the four-wheel drive, transforming the glass into tinkling shivers of sound. As soon as she threw the bottle onto the front seat, flames rippled up, erect and vertical. The third bottle she hurled in the direction from which the guards would come, creating a barrier of flame that she hoped would hold them back. The fourth exploded on the grill of a downstairs window. The fifth smashed and exploded inside, the dragons painted on the closet coming alive in the firelight. The sixth landed perfectly on the upstairs balcony; she had a feel for them now, their precise weight and flight. Sprinting back to the wall, she threw herself into the foliage, clutching in her hand the very last bottle—her insurance policy should she be cornered by the guards.

Trembling with adrenaline, her toes curling in friable earth, she was captivated by the bright banners of flame, the sharp shadows on the walls and decorative plasterwork, the flickering illumination in the garden, every leaf and flower lit and aquiver. She felt connected to a great power that had started as a vision in her mind and traveled through her hands. She was the Naga come to life, each of her heads spitting fire.

From where she watched, dark silhouettes ran from the house, shadow puppets trapped in hellfire. Which meant she was safe, on the side of the angels, no longer trapped in her own burning world.

13

After the Land Cruiser had roared away, locals appeared from nowhere. One, who was lugging an orange jerrican, attempted to splash gasoline over Amos's cuts.

"Get the fuck away!" he screamed. "My shoulder! Just do it, man."

As Amos lay back in the dirt, Fearless braced one foot under his armpit. Amos didn't even grimace when he pulled the shoulder into place, but leapt to his feet and began searching in his rucksack. From its depths, he produced a khaki-colored plastic box the size of a walkie-talkie, with a short, stubby antenna. Fearless watched as he held the box aloft, the dust swirling in the light of the shacks on the crossroads.

Then Amos heaved his bike up and kick-started it roughly. "F-F-F-F-Follow!" he shouted.

So *that* was it, thought Fearless: it was a stammer that made Amos so reluctant to speak—not rudeness or distrust or instinctive aversion.

The two of them rumbled into the darkness, past warehouses, wastelands, depots, and truck yards, turning off the straight highway onto a road that curved and doglegged. As he stamped through the gears, Fearless shook his head. Alyosha had always had his finger in dozens of pies—jeans, cigarettes, fake Napoleon brandy: small stuff. But what the hell was going on here?

Amos slowed down and Fearless caught up as the open fields were interrupted by an outbreak of shops and houses.

"Where the hell are we?"

"Somewhere to the w-w-est of the city. Between the airport and the center of t-town."

Amos braked, held the box up, and led them down an alley barely wider than a car. The houses were constructed in concrete and red brick, all of them on stilts with tall, pitched roofs. Save for the pink and blue flash of televisions, there was no sign of life and no sound louder than their engines.

"C-c-cut it," Amos said, as he turned off his engine, letting his bike coast freely around a corner. Then he dismounted, pushing it silently along the rutted track. Every fifteen feet, he would stop and consult his box. Struggling to read the machine's display, he kept searching for patches where moonshine broke through the trees.

At the end of the lane, music floated from a house—a garish Cambodian pop tune with a nasal vocal. Moving in slow motion, Amos returned the machine to his backpack, leaned his bike on its kickstand, and motioned for Fearless to do the same. Then he drew out a handgun, a Browning or Sig Sauer: a weapon whose brutalist look made Fearless's blood run cold.

Crouching down, they edged their way toward the house. Inside the open gate sat the Land Cruiser that had sideswiped them. A weak light burned in a second-floor room, the music pouring from its unshuttered window.

In the darkness, Amos's lips were blue against his Black skin. His short, dense dreads, silhouetted by the moon, were the bent legs of a tarantula, still and tense. Then a light clicked on in another room and they heard the sound of trickling water. At the same time, a stifled groan went up from the other room. Alyosha: the timbre of his voice was unmistakable.

Then the DJ announced another song and the music began to blare a fanfare. Under its cover, they scurried to the bottom of the stairs. As their heads reached the level of the second-floor veranda, they could see Alyosha's feet and then his naked body, gagged and bound to a wooden chair. On top of the battering he had taken in the crash, his back was marked by bloody, raw tissue where the skin had been burned, wounds upon wounds. A clothes iron on the floor told the story.

Holding his gun out, Amos scuttered in, Fearless behind, rushing to Alyosha, lifting his slumped head from his chest.

As another stifled mumble escaped Alyosha's lips, the sound of trickling water in the bathroom stopped abruptly. The man who had been torturing Alyosha was there, his feet breaking up the line of light under the door.

Amos reached out to Fearless and handed him the gun, motioning that he should keep it trained on the door. He swiftly pulled the tape from Alyosha's mouth, cut through his ropes, and pulled the sheet from the nearby bed.

They heard the sound of a flush. The pipes began to rattle.

Fearless held the gun out stiffly in front of him, pea-sized beads of sweat breaking out on his scalp. He could feel the texture of the stippled gun grip imprinting itself into the flesh of his palm.

At the moment Amos draped the sheet around Alyosha's shoulders, the bathroom door opened and the gaunt man—bare-chested and heavily tattooed—stepped out. As soon as he saw Fearless's gun, he raised his hands, a little smile creeping into the corner of his lips.

Something came out of Fearless's mouth—enough to indicate that he was willing to shoot, though in truth it was just a dumb expression of terror. The man stared back, his body perfectly still. Fearless tried to focus his gaze on the man's face, but he was transfixed by the eyes tattooed under his collarbones, each of them the size of an open mouth. Below them, across the whole of the man's chest and abdomen, a standing Madonna cradled the Child in her arms, rays of heavenly light fanning out in a semicircle around her head, winged angels gazing down from either side. Above his forearms—covered in lines of Cyrillic script—both of the man's shoulders carried a trompe l'œil epaulet, the braided tassels of their bullion fringes draped perfectly straight over each upper arm. Fearless had learned about these tattoos in Russia. They signified the man was a vor—a Russian "thief in law"—who had consecrated his entire life to criminality.

Amos finished swaddling Alyosha's burned torso. Finding a water bottle beside the bed, he raised Alyosha's head and made him drink. The room quivered with every beat of Fearless's heart. He tried to keep his eyes focused on the man as Amos lifted Alyosha and swung him onto his shoulders. But somehow the man vanished: so instantaneously that if the scene had been captured on film, his body would have appeared motionless in one frame and, in the next, completely absent.

"No!"

The shaking of Fearless's gun hand set off his whole body. Amos, carrying Alyosha as if he were a child, stepped over and skillfully uncocked the weapon, took hold of it, and cocked it again once he had it in his grip. Then he turned and made out of the room, Fearless stumbling after him, face flushed with blood, a howl lodged deep inside his gullet. Halfway down the stairs, Amos fired a warning shot as Fearless lost his step and clattered down on his back.

A minute later, they were roaring northward, heading toward the distant orange glow of the city. Alyosha, half-conscious, his body slumped against Fearless's back, moaned and huffed at random intervals. Under cover of night, a hot tear gathered in Fearless's eye. He resented the endless darkness of this little kingdom and the sense of terrible smallness he felt within it.

He should never, ever, have been trusted with the gun. Amos had probably assumed he was courageous, believing the old story about saving Alyosha's life. More than ever it felt like a hex he would never remove.

When they were in Sarajevo together, Alyosha had taken him to photograph a nursing home that was eager for someone to publicize its plight. The director had welcomed them, introducing them to his daughter, a nine-year-old who no longer had a school to go to. He then left Fearless to document the building and the fate of its frail, uncomprehending inhabitants.

And then a rocket ripped out the first floor.

A colleague, Tim Greenaway, snapped Fearless escaping the wreckage, blackened by smoke, dragging the unconscious Alyosha, with his other arm clutching the director's daughter to his body: an image of a hero irresistible to any editor. When the picture was published, there was a stupid misprint: the cutline "Fearless Joseph Nightingale rescues Sarajevo bombing victims" omitted the *Joseph*, which led to people dubbing him "Fearless."

But Fearless was no hero. His instinct after the rocket strike had in fact not been to save, but to raise his camera. During those first vital moments, he snapped flame and smoke before something heavy had knocked him to his knees. In crawling out, he found Alyosha and the girl by chance.

A good world requires people not just to avoid doing harm, but to strive wherever possible to help one another. Alyosha knew this. And he actively lived it. The nursing home was an opportunity for him to do kindness, which is why what ultimately happened hurt Fearless even more.

"Amos!" shouted Fearless, but Amos didn't hear. He rolled on, the Browning cocked and ready in his hand, glancing over his shoulder for beasts coming behind them, hell-bent on trampling them into the dust.

14

Great curls of smoke gushed from the bottom of the fire, a black cloud stacking up three times the height of the villa.

From her vantage point, Song could see the policemen's peaked caps and frantic arms. Beyond them, shadows scampering behind the curtain of flames; the staff of the house, she guessed—a cook, a cleaner, the driver. And then the silhouette she had been anxiously awaiting: long hair whipping back and forth like the bead strings on a monkey drum.

In an instant, Song was scaling the garden wall again, pulling herself up hand over hand on the krama. Dashing around the corner, she saw Sovanna being shoved, angry, arms flailing, berating a policeman who now turned back to join the struggle against the fire.

The sound of sirens strobed and pulsed into earshot. Neighbors emerged and gathered in clusters, hands clamped firmly to mouths and noses. There was no need for Song to worry about being seen; Sambo, the Wat Phnom elephant, could have lumbered past unnoticed. She hurried up behind Sovanna and slid her hand into hers.

When Sovanna turned, her eyes looked straight through Song.

"It's me, bong. Sovanna—it's me."

Sovanna staggered back, her eyes alarmed, the pupils so round and black one could detect no color in them. The air between them crackled, cinders swirling like tiny gnats.

Song made to embrace her but Sovanna retreated. She bent forward and raised a flat palm to ward her off.

"It's me, Sovanna. I know. I can't believe it either."

Song moved forward again but Sovanna shook her head violently. She raised her hands to grasp two handfuls of her hair. Then she wheeled and started to run, with Song chasing after, saying, "Bong! I know. Come back. It's me." It was like her memory of them running through the rice fields, only now they were on a city street. And they were crying, not laughing.

"Sovanna! Chop!"

And then, as Sovanna reached the crossroads, she staggered and turned and the two of them fell into each other's arms, Sovanna's chest heaving, sobbing, shaking. They pulled back to look at each other, Sovanna's eyes focusing on her, and buried themselves deep in each other's arms again. Song breathed her in. They were finally together.

Brakes screeched beside them.

"Get in now, sisters!"

It was Bun Thim. He leaned over and opened the rear door of the Camry. The whites of his eyes shone in the darkness of the cab.

There was no time to question how he had known they were there. Song pulled Sovanna behind her onto the back seat and they tumbled across the vinyl, the car wobbling on its suspension.

Bun Thim roared onto the busy boulevard, the door slamming shut as he swerved into the traffic. He weaved the car back and forth between lanes before turning right into the backstreets.

The sisters held hands. Apart from her eyes, which seemed blacker than in the memories that Song had guarded, Sovanna seemed the same: just how Song would have been—complete, perfected—if the accident had never happened.

As Bun Thim serpentined through the city, it was impossible not to think of the last time they had ridden in this Camry, in that pitch-black moment, crossing the Japanese bridge.

They had been happy, so happy, the car speeding along in the early hours of a Sunday morning. They were laughing at a little joke or in relief that the night was over; their visit—to a respectful client—had been unremarkable. There was loud music playing, the windows were down, the wind whipping the girls' hair around their faces. It felt as if they could take off as the bridge climbed up, as if they were on a ramp that led to the stars.

As they began the descent into the city, a motorbike appeared beside them and held steady alongside Song's open window. She recognized the rider, a fat kid they called Mao due to the extraordinary resemblance he bore to the Chairman. She saw his fat-fingered hands gripping the motorbike's handlebars—hands that had once paid to knead her flesh.

Bun Thim was the first to register the danger. He shouted at Song to wind the window up. But before she could react, the bike accelerated, revealing a man riding pillion, struggling with something. In the same moment she saw what it was—a black plastic bucket—he pulled open its lid and let the contents fly. A wave of liquid arced in rushing air. Cold water, she thought, when it touched her skin. But where was her blouse? She was naked. Naked! Daggers and fire were savaging her face, the car out of control, flashing back and forth in a fishtail. There was something inside her nose, sharp sticks of pain. Her head burned all over, stabbed by a million toothpicks. Sovanna was cowering in the footwell below her, shrieking.

Assailed by the same images, Sovanna leaned in. There was nothing that needed to be openly said. They had learned to survive, escaping to rooms inside their minds that no one on earth could enter save the other.

As Song buried herself in the sweetness of Sovanna's hair, festoons of lanterns rippled in her vision, hung between the lampposts along a stretch of beer gardens. She imagined they had been taken back in time to the fork at which they had once been separated, and were finally free to take the other path.

15

Fearless held his head in his hands and stared at the vinyl floor. The gentle breeze of an oscillating fan lifted the hairs on the back of his neck. Muffled howls came from behind the partition.

When they had arrived at the clinic—a large, detached house—the doctor had been waiting expectantly at the gate. "This is the last time. Now we're even," he muttered to Amos.

He was a tall, lean Australian, with a head of unkempt curls and the laid-back, battered demeanor of a surfer. But as soon as he saw what had happened to Alyosha, he switched into professional mode, rushing him into his surgery, giving him oxygen and attaching an IV drip. Once Alyosha was stable, the doctor asked Fearless to wait in the waiting room. Now, after stitching the worst of his wounds, he was debriding Alyosha's burns, cleaning and dressing the damage. In the silence between Alyosha's groans and howls, surgical tools clattered in a metal tray.

The moment the vor had fled gnawed at Fearless. The monster was free, circling in the darkness, with the lean flanks of a greyhound, the head of a wolf. The thought of losing Alyosha—the vacuum it would create inside him just when he thought there was nothing left to suck out—was inconceivable. Jimmy, Luke, Lucy, Conrad: without Laure, what did he have, save his handful of friends?

When he closed his eyes, he and Alyosha were back in Kosovo, coming under fire as they walked down a dirt road, bullets fountaining up from the dust on either side. Alyosha sprang to the right and he dived to the left and the two of them lay hidden under the cover of bushes. He could hear the crack of the twigs, feel the springiness of the pressed grass beneath his back. They had spent six hours rooted to those spots, waiting for darkness, when they might creep away under cover, emptying their canteens with a thousand sips. And to while away the time they had told each other everything—Fearless his father's story; Alyosha his experiences in Afghanistan, the fallout of Chernobyl and what it had done to his grandparents' world. He had spoken of the boom years after the fall of Communism, the deals from which he'd now been brutally exiled—deals that the dealmakers would measure in centimeters.

"Centimeters?"

"The thickness of a stack of dollars! Five centimeters. Ten centimeters."

"Like the size of your dick," Fearless joked.

"Yes," Alyosha deadpanned. He bowed his head. "It's true. My penis is small. Only two or maybe three inches when excited." He remained silent, caught Fearless's eye, and burst into laughter.

All the while they talked, Alyosha picked wild blackberries from a bush, lobbing them over to Fearless to stave off his hunger. It was also during this conversation that they discovered they were both only children and that they—what were the odds?—shared the same birthday, four years apart. Fearless told Alyosha about his mother's madness after his father's death—which for a long time everyone had thought was a kind of grieving. In return, Alyosha talked about the treatment he had received at the hands of his drunken and violent stepfather.

It felt like a kind of falling in love, that talk: strange, new, unsought but essential.

"There's something, Alyosha, I'd like to ask you," Fearless had blurted out.

"Yes?"

"Tell me. Where do you think I come from?"

It was the question put to every person in Sarajevo in those days: Who are you? What are you? How do you identify yourself? Which, to an outsider, seemed absurd: for if you could not tell the difference, why on earth should it possibly matter?

"What do you mean?" Alyosha threw him another blackberry.

"I mean: what do I look like to you?"

And like that, though he never called it this, Alyosha became the keeper of his secret, which he never betrayed. In fact, Alyosha always relished the deception, didn't he? "We're the pretenders, you and me," he liked to say. He would even shave Fearless's head for him when he needed it, spurting the foam out, and with deft, delicate movements, drawing the disposable razor across his skull, little whipped meringues gathering at the tips of the plastic, his fingers touching his scalp, gently repositioning his head.

"Anyone who could pass in this world would do it," his mother had always maintained. "Don't follow your father. Whatever God gives you, you use."

It was good for professional reasons—that was Fearless's justification. Passing as white, being purely English, anointed him with authority and aroused less suspicion. It gained him entry to places, usefully set him apart, or won him the right to be ignored on his own terms. In Africa especially—ironically—it was an asset. As much as it irked him, what his mother had dictated therefore became something he consciously chose. But if it had to be hidden—which took effort and attention—his Blackness also had enormous meaning. It had to be as powerful as the privileges of his father's color and class, which Fearless was expected to assume—and which his father longed to be free of.

In those early days then, Fearless and Alyosha's friendship was an infatuation, stacked, day upon day, week upon week, with an intensity of experiences that was new and shared. Bosnia and Chechnya had been exceptional conflicts, where they were free to take risks and go where they wanted. Before that, governments had already started marshaling photographers, managing their images from Grenada and Panama, the Falklands and the Gulf. Now, almost always, they kept photographers under their wing. Instead of making your own way in a combat zone, talking to and documenting people on each side, you had to be embedded and wear their fucking uniforms.

Yes, their time was special. In war, Fearless found himself. If depression was a disproportionate response to real events, there was a logic in seeking out real events in proportion to what he was feeling. It was clever to think of it like that. As sweet as those blackberries. Even when this rationale did not hold, there was always drink and oblivion and the knowledge that Alyosha would scoop him up, dust him down, and somehow put him to bed.

Yes. Alyosha guarded part of his life that no one else knew. If anything happened to Alyosha, that part would die.

A groan of pain came through the waiting room wall again and Fearless got to his feet and began to pace. A noticeboard pinned with thank-you notes caught his attention: children's drawings of Dr. Andrew, messages on postcards with the *i*'s dotted with hearts, photos of smiling, expatriate babies. These images were the polar opposite of the headshots at Tuol Sleng: faces that had so much living to look forward to, faces that looked into the darkness behind the shutter and saw sympathy and kindness and reflected love.

Then suddenly he was staring at a picture of Bun Thim and Song, with Dr. Andrew standing by their side. Song's face was undamaged, no scarring or burning or discoloration—her black hair loose, her smile serene. She was radiant. Bun Thim was clearly Dr. Andrew's patient, both of his hands wrapped in thick bandages like bag gloves. This must have been the time he got the burns on his hands—but why was Song with him? What was their connection?

As his hand reached up to hold the corner of the print, Alyosha screamed and a door slammed in the foyer. Startled, Fearless unpinned the photo, slipping it into his pocket as Wish burst in. Without acknowledging Fearless, Wish made straight for the examination room, where he was immediately greeted by the doctor's angry shouts.

When he reappeared, Wish sat down on one of the plastic chairs and fumed—again refusing to look Fearless in the eye. It was not the time to confront him, Fearless decided, as Alyosha groaned once more behind the wall. But maybe that was an excuse? He always withheld his anger—a magma chamber that bubbled and couldn't find a conduit. When Wish glanced up for the shortest moment, he turned down his lips and spat on the floor.

Wish was living proof, Fearless saw, that his photos *had* had an effect—though not in a way he'd ever intended.

It had been hot up in that tower block, back in Bosnia; they had dripped with sweat from every pore. For some reason, Wish had abandoned his sniper position. When Fearless found him, along the corridor in an office strewn with paper and broken furniture, he was sobbing uncontrollably, head bowed between his knees. Above him, on a shelf, someone had left a sunshade for a car windshield: a pair of laughing cartoon eyes. Fearless took the shot—the weeping sniper and the cartoon eyes—and sat by his side, letting him recover himself.

"I spoke to the girl, like you said, and she laughed!" Wish stammered. "She said I was a kid. She, she . . . laughed in my face!"

Three days later, when Fearless returned to the U.K., the image made it onto the front page of *The Times*, which in turn led to syndication around the globe. And when Fearless went back for his second stint in Sarajevo, which already paled in comparison to the high of his first trip, he found Wish insulted, proud, and defiant—and utterly determined to get his revenge.

Now, Amos opened the door and beckoned Wish in. Fearless darted over to listen after it had closed.

"They got Colonel Vasiliev's house! Petrol bombs, they had," Wish said. "At the same time they broke into the Naga and smashed it."

"Th-th-three attacks. In one n-n-night," said Amos.

"It must be Kraus. But how could he reach us here? And Thom is gone. No one knows where." Wish lowered his voice. "There is one more thing. They take Colonel Vasiliev's girl. What do we say to him?"

Amos didn't reply. Apparently, it required some reflection. Who was Vasiliev's girl? And why—above everything—was *she* the thing that they were worrying about most?

"She alive?" said Amos. "L-Leave it with me. First, take some men and go to this address."

There was the flap and crackle of a map being unfolded and the rattle of someone reaching into a jar of pens.

"And this is the n-n-number plate of the Land Cruiser he was driving.

Take it to the Chief. Do this first before anything else. Ssssssee what you can turn up and report back immediately."

Wish hesitated. "How's he doing?"

"He'll be okay. Less than ten percent burns. C-cuts and bruising. We got there just in time."

There was movement in the room and Fearless stepped away. When Wish came out, he hurried out of the building. Amos nodded to Fearless before he closed the door.

Shortly afterward, the voices of the doctor and Amos came closer.

"He's not going anywhere. He'll have to rest for several days."

Fearless moved away again before the door reopened and the two men came out into the waiting room. The doctor stepped toward Fearless and shook his hand.

"Your friend will be fine, mate. Amos knows what to do. I'll be sending a nurse to look after him as an outpatient. For now, go home and get some rest."

"I have called B-B-Bun Thim," Amos said to Fearless. "He's coming to t-t-take you back to th-th-apartment. There was a robbery there tonight. Check your things are safe."

"I'm sorry about earlier, Amos. I let him get away. Did I put you in danger, going to the Killing Fields?"

"He m-m-makes his own calls," said Amos, nodding ruefully. He had the air of a weary parent apologizing for a willful child.

"Why would someone do this? It's so extreme. What's he mixed up in?"

"He doesn't want you to worry. I mean—there's really n-n-nothing to worry about."

When Bun Thim pulled up, the windows in the Camry were down. Unusual, given his love of air conditioning. But as soon as he got in, Fearless realized why: the back seat absolutely reeked of petrol.

Surreptitiously, he pulled out the photograph he had stolen, the faces of Bun Thim and Song flashing up under the regular stripes of streetlight as they drove. He noticed now that there was a digital number in the corner, dating the picture to three years ago. Twice, Fearless tried to open a conversation with Bun Thim, to create an opportunity to ask him about the image—and twice he ignored him, not even looking in the rearview mirror.

Fearless finally came out with it when he was getting down from the car.

"Bun Thim. Wait. I have this photo of you—see. The girl who cleans here. You know her, don't you?"

Bun Thim looked down and gave an uncomfortable laugh.

"What was it that happened?"

"No no. No unnerstand."

"This is when you hurt your hands, isn't it?" Fearless tried to touch his arm, but Bun Thim scampered back around the car.

"I late. My wife. Sorry sorry!"

And with that, the Camry was driving away and turning onto the riverside.

Entering the building, Fearless went immediately to Song's cell, but her door was wide open when he got to the landing, the room empty, her crate of possessions on its side. Back in his own apartment, things had been scattered around, but nothing was missing save the bottle of antiseptic he always kept in his first aid kit.

He sat down on the bed, a wave of tiredness overwhelming him. The brothel, the blackout, the nightmares, Tuol Sleng. The crossroads, the showdown at the house on stilts. It was all too much.

But when his head hit the pillow, something solid hit him back. Something hollow yet hard, concealed inside the pillowcase. Wrapped in newspaper—a garish image of a Khmer woman with an elaborate bouffant—was a VHS tape with yesterday's date scrawled on its label.

Bemused—and nagged by the suspicion that he had seen the woman somewhere before—Fearless went to the sitting room and turned on the television. The mouth of the video player swallowed the tape and the rickety machine hummed and whirred into life. A white room flashed up in front of him on the screen. There was a massage table in the foreground and a triptych of paintings behind it. Colonel Vasiliev lumbered into the scene and sat down heavily. A heavyset, bullnecked Black man followed him, Vasiliev reaching out to shake his hand.

Then the two men made a space, the Black man patting the table. Vasiliev beckoned to someone just out of shot, then reached up slowly to unbutton his shirt.

16

"You didn't think about what would happen next?" Sovanna walked to the window and gripped the bars of the grill.

"We'll go to Battambang. And we won't get caught this time."

Sovanna turned and pushed her hands into the roots of her hair. "That's it? Battambang! What is there in Battambang?"

Song's nausea floated up to her throat. She had assumed there would be nothing but joy in their reunion. When Bun Thim had driven them to his house on the outskirts of the city, and his wife, Morivan, had let them wash and prepared a meal—which Song had devoured but Sovanna refused—it had seemed like they might coast on a wave of wonder forever.

Sovanna had reached up and unwound Song's krama and kissed her all over her face and head. "It should have been me," she had murmured. "I'm sorry, oun. So sorry."

Song held her and told her no; she was glad Sovanna was her perfect mirror. "When you live in an ugly building you never have to look at it. And whenever I look out now, I will see you."

Sovanna had explained that after the acid attack, when it seemed Song was over the worst, the Chief had taken her on a trip to Bangkok. When she returned he told her that Song's condition had suddenly deteriorated; there was a complication with her breathing; she had died unexpectedly in her sleep. (Did you believe it just like that? Song wanted to ask.) The funeral rites had already been performed, the Chief insisted: a grief on top of a terrible grief. For how could Sovanna not have been there to send her sister on her journey? How could she let her set out alone?

Afterward, the Chief tried to sell Sovanna as soon as he could.

"He still comes to the Naga, Sovanna. He sits in the hall and asks me to sing."

Sovanna curled her lips. "The fucking liar! Does his bitch wife know? Bet she doesn't."

As soon as it was common knowledge that Sovanna was up for sale, Colonel Vasiliev—who had for so long monopolized the twins, who had always been so pleased with himself at being able to tell them apart—purchased her.

"I got a good deal on you—that's what he always tells me."

Sovanna's life with Vasiliev had been relatively simple. Bereft without Song, but better in other ways. There was Vasiliev, but that was only three minutes' work a day; the rest of the time was hers to fritter at the health club, usually under the watch of one of Vasiliev's men—someone she felt was "a sweet guy, funny." She would swim or doze on a lounger or play table tennis with other club members. She laughed about how much she had come to love the game. It was a way for her to talk with all manner of people: the barang on holidays, the wives of the rich and powerful, the Presidential Guard and the boys that worked as pool and gym attendants. And she was a good player; she hustled her opponents, pretending she was hopeless before catching them out with smash and spin.

Song had little to say about her life in return. Why trouble Sovanna with the drudgery and beatings? Even the good things—Bopha, Samnang, Rathana, and Dara—couldn't be alluded to without letting darkness in. But after Sovanna had mentioned the Colonel's kind man, she nonetheless found herself revealing how Fearless had helped her. It seemed important to show she knew a good man too.

As the discussion turned toward what they would do, Sovanna's questions became more urgent and worried. "Where are we meant to go? And how will we survive?" She was crossing her arms tightly, each hand cupping the opposite elbow and scratching the skin red and raw. "They'll be coming for me," she muttered. "They'll be sending their men."

When Song joined her at the window and tried to put an arm around her, Sovanna shrugged her off. "They're coming for me," she repeated.

The sound of an engine outside made her jump. She pressed her palms to her chest and inhaled sharply. But it was only Bun Thim, driving his car into the ground floor room.

"See. It's okay," said Song, as Bun Thim called out to Morivan.

But it wasn't okay.

"You leave now!" Bun Thim said. "They know! The new barang—the one with the shaved head—he had a photo of Sovanna and me. He knows I know something—and he knows I know he knows."

Sovanna gave out a loud cry that made Bun Thim flap his hands at her.

"How could they know?" said Song.

"Because someone must have seen us. How else?"

"But if that were true, they'd be here already. And he's not one of them. He's not the same as the others."

Bun Thim sneered. "They're all the same. I know them better than you."

As soon as Bun Thim said it, he realized its stupidity. The girls had seen these men do things he couldn't imagine.

"I'm sorry. That was stupid. But you cannot stay here, sisters. If they find you, we are done for—me, Morivan, the baby."

"Bong," said Morivan, coming up behind Bun Thim. She jerked on his sleeve and pulled him out of the room. Outside, you could hear the hissing consonants of her whispering.

Sovanna leaned in. "Will we sleep in the street like dogs?"

"It's only till tomorrow. And then we'll leave. We'll start out early. Ma and Pa, our home, we can make it." Song wanted to take all the senses and memories of their childhood and compress them till they were a hard, perfect diamond and give it to Sovanna to hold in her palm.

"But they gave us away, oun!"

"What do you mean, 'gave us away'?"

"Pa and Ma gave us up. They sold us. Why go back?"

"That was Saveth just saying that. It was another big lie. Just like the story they told you about me being dead. We weren't like the others. We were kidnapped. I remember. In the middle of the night. They threw us in their car."

Flashlights in the field where she had gone to pee. Her golden teddy bear tucked in the crook of her arm. Yellow circles of light: she remembered them dancing across her. Still squatting, arms grabbing her, pee trickling down her thigh.

"They *made* it look like a kidnap, Song, so we wouldn't think badly of them. We're like everyone else here: orphans with parents. Who can blame them? Why stay there, eating tamarind, salt, and rice? The village people were right when they said twins were bad karma."

Song shook her head, and Sovanna softened her tone.

"They were told, maybe, that we would have a better life somewhere else. That we would go overseas and have good jobs as servants. They probably thought it would be for the best."

When Bun Thim returned, his shoulders were bowed. "Okay. You can stay tonight—but out in the shed. It's not nice, but you can lie down. In the morning, you go."

"Thank you, pu. Oh, thank you! You're doing so much."

In the other room, the baby coughed and grumbled in its sleep. Morivan went to comfort and feed it, while Bun Thim led them down to the yard. There, he showed them into a small hut they used for storage. They ducked their heads as they entered, squeezing their bodies together on a narrow rattan mat.

"Keep this close," Bun Thim said, pointing to the tools and, in particular, the heavy blade of a machete. "I'll come at dawn. I'm sorry I can't do more."

As soon as she lay down in the dark and the heat, Song's stomach pains started to assail her again.

"Was it the food?"

"No. I've been having this pain awhile."

"How long?"

"A few weeks. My stomach is tight and hard."

Lying beside her, Sovanna stroked her belly in circles. How many years it had been since she'd been touched so tenderly.

"Is that okay?"

"It's good." The nausea passed. Tiredness spread out and radiated through her limbs.

"Will you tell me the story, Sovanna?"

"What story?"

"The story about the bridge."

"The bridge."

"The bridge between the houses that we'll have. The story you used to tell in the old days."

"The bridge. Oh. Yes. I haven't thought about that in a long time."

"Me—I think about it every single day."

Sovanna was silent. Her hand kept making circles. "You sleep now," she said.

"You too. We must rest."

"I can't sleep. I don't sleep. But don't worry. It will be fine."

There was something not right. Part of Sovanna was being kind—but it was wrestling with another part that was hard and unforgiving.

But there is a tomorrow, Song told herself, as her eyelids grew heavy. Tomorrow: a word that now held possibility.

"We'll make a plan, bong. We'll make a plan in the morning."

But at first light, when the door creaked open and Bun Thim peered in, his face etched with more worry than it had been the night before, the mat beside Song was empty.

17

Vasiliev's friend tapped the table several times and a small boy tentatively stepped into the frame. Prodded in the back, his chest jerked forward, his pigeon-toed feet struggling to keep up.

There was no sound on the tape, yet over the next unsettling hour, the room was clearly full of noise—snarling and grunting, screaming, pleading.

Fearless fast-forwarded through the action, unable to stomach the events. First came the Black man and his chest-heaving laugh, and then the hulking flab and flesh of Vasiliev; there were more children—so inured they didn't resist—all of them barred by lines of quivering static.

A small animal flexed in Fearless's throat—he knew one of the faces: the little girl, Bopha. He remembered being lifted by little brown hands. Hands on his arms and legs. Hands cradling his head.

Barbarity, depravity, malevolence, filth. Horror, outrage, shock, disgust. No words he could summon conveyed the content or the feelings the stream of images provoked.

He shut off the machine and ran to the bathroom. Afterward, on the balcony, he dragged hard on a cigarette, affronted by the purring cars and scooters, the canned laughter from TVs, the brightly colored goods in the shop directly opposite with its teddy bears hanging from threaded ropes like garlic and its infant formula stacked in shoulder-high pyramids, and the river, the river flowing endlessly on to the sea. The evil of that inch-thick plastic box radiated within him, as did the thought of his new burden: for it was Song, surely, who had left the tape behind for him. She had wrapped it in the newspaper cutting as a kind of sign. The tape was a barb of responsibility—stuck in his conscience now, impossible to remove.

But what the hell could he do? Vasiliev himself had bragged about the police being in his pocket, that Cambodia was a zone beyond the rule of law. And the room in the Naga was a zone within that zone, where anything was permitted, no desire taboo.

Fearless threw the tape, a street map, and a bottle of water into his shoulder bag. Alyosha would be appalled at what his "boss" was up to, but Fearless would have to wait for morning to see him. In the meantime, he would follow the river to the north, to the last known location his father had visited. Maybe seeing it would be easier under cover of darkness.

No more than five minutes away, looming over a six-foot wall topped by a six-foot metal fence, was a monumentalist block of stone: the former French Governor's Palace. Here, on the final day of his trip, his father would have stepped down from the chauffeur-driven Mercedes and passed through the entrance, the doors held open for him. This was to be the crowning glory of his tour: a personal audience with Pol Pot—Brother Number One.

Fearless lingered on the other side of the road, where he could best see the upper floor of the building. A scene he had dreamed many times blossomed in his mind: translucent white curtains billowing in a breeze, the room empty save for two throne-like chairs on a dais, Pol Pot and his father facing each other—his father animated and enthusiastic, Pol Pot elegant and unruffled, dressed in a pale gray Nehru jacket.

What did they talk about? The physiocrat economic theories they both admired; the progress Cambodia was making, its example to the world? But what else? What turns did their conversation take that could possibly explain his father's murder? He imagined Pol Pot beckoning an advisor as his father leaves. He whispers in his ear. The man nods slowly.

That night, his father had been upbeat and effusive. According to the accounts of others present, he had suggested a nightcap to toast "Brother Number One" before retiring early, then flying home and delivering the gospel to his followers.

But he would never open the suitcase he packed that evening. It would be shipped back to Fearless and his mother a month later; Fearless remembered it sitting bleakly in the hall, the baggage tag in his father's writing dangling from the handle. For in the middle of that night, the residence was woken by shouts. A group of cadres stormed through the building, found his father's room, and shot him twice in the chest. He was the only target of the attack.

Fearless had searched for the faces of those men at Tuol Sleng. They simply had to have been there in the ranks of headshots. They were traitors, the Khmer Rouge had announced in the aftermath, traitors who had killed his father to smear the Party and make Cambodia a pariah. It was bullshit, of course. They too were victims, tortured on the bed frames for doing what they'd been told.

Whoever shot his father, they weren't truly his killers. It was the man who gave the orders, who made all things possible.

Perhaps his father had overstepped the bounds of propriety; while agreeing with Pol Pot's ends, he had objected to his means: enough of a provocation to unleash the devil's temper.

This idea—which gave Fearless some comfort—was also the deepest source of his fear. If his father's death was the consequence of his unbending convictions, why do anything that might imitate or emulate him? Better to make a virtue of not believing in anything, to be an observer who focused on form and shape and color: on how things were arranged and not on how they might be.

A night guard appeared from the booth in front of the Palace now and wagged his finger at Fearless, laying his hand on the butt of his gun.

Just five months ago, in April, on the very day it was agreed he would face a tribunal, Pol Pot had died in his jungle hideout of a "heart attack." His body was cremated before an autopsy could be performed. Now, no one would ever know what had been said during that conversation. For a while, his father's words had existed, if nowhere else, in Pol Pot's head: if there had been honor in them, decency, a final flash of courage, it had lived for twenty years in the dark matter of that mind.

For the remainder of the night, Song flitted through Fearless's mind, her face shrouded by her checkered krama. And where were the children? Sleeping or being subjected to yet more horrors? They were all connected now by what they'd done for each other.

When the night sky began to lighten, a dark blue seeping into the charcoal black, Fearless walked a slow route to the Hotel Le Royal. On the way, his mind played devilish tricks; at one point, as he circled the chalky dome of Wat Phnom, he could have sworn he saw Song hurrying past in the distance. Not the Song he knew but the Song from the photo: her head uncovered and unscarred, her long hair rippling.

As the rose glow of dawn seeped up from the earth, spread between the gaps in the houses, and gilded the leaves of the trees, he came to the broad sweeping driveway of the palatial hotel, its pale facade a block of beige against the cobalt sky. A rooster's crow tore a ragged strip from the silence. Standing in front of the hotel's colonial stylings, you might think you were entering a different era—a time where power and responsibility were in the hands of a supervening power. It didn't escape Fearless as he crunched across the gravel that, in coming here, this was exactly what he sought.

The first thing Alyosha did was ask how *he* was: "This is all I care about. The rest is meaningless." Fearless had to be insistent to make himself heard.

Like him, Alyosha had to fight the urge to puke—even though Fearless had warned him what was on the tape. Perched on the edge of the sofa in his suite, Fearless watched his face work its way through colors: the jaundice yellow of queasiness; the flushing pink of shame. Finally, sheer, scarlet fury.

After a few minutes, Alyosha shut the video player off. The veins in his temples pulsed and fluttered.

"You were right to come. This tape is . . . Tell me, where did you get this, bacha?"

"It was on the floor," said Fearless. "The thieves must have found it when they turned over the apartment."

"Were there other tapes?"

"I didn't see any."

"I need to know how deep this goes." Alyosha winced, his eyes squinting hard—at the situation or the pain of his burns or perhaps both. "Have you shown it to anyone else?"

"Who would I show it to? I know Vasiliev has connections—I could hardly go to the police."

"He has connections, yes. But so do I."

Fearless breathed in relief. "That's what I was hoping."

Alyosha rose and walked to the window, his hand reaching out to touch the pleats of the lace curtains. "If the people on the tape come to know that we have it—well, we're in danger. Do you understand that, Fearless?"

"I can imagine. Look, what's all this about, Lyosha? The rest of it, I mean. Are you out of your depth?"

"Can you trust me to resolve this?"

"Of course. But what will we do?"

"Not 'we.' *Me.* With everything that's going on: the attack, this tape, not to mention the terrible things you have to deal with—it's me and me alone who will make this right."

"Okay. What will *you* do then?"

Alyosha turned to face him. "You have to trust me. Even if it seems like I'm . . . going around. Remember how you didn't believe me when I said I could get a meeting with Khattab?"

The meeting with Samir Saleh Abdullah al-Suwailim in Chechnya had been Alyosha's greatest triumph during his time as Fearless's fixer: somehow, he had made a connection and arranged an escort to Khattab's secret location high in the mountains. "I can track anyone down," Alyosha boasted afterward. "No one escapes me."

Alyosha clasped his hands together and swung an imaginary bat. He was referring to one of his favorite anecdotes—to little Alyosha coming home from elementary school. Cornered by a group of drunken men in the courtyard of his building, he had picked up an iron pipe and screamed like a banshee, making his attackers scatter and run.

"I trust you. Of course I do. But where will you begin?"

"First of all, with Mr. Thom—the little king of the Naga bar. There is no way he's not involved in all of this. Once I get my hands on him, I will know my next step. For the moment, stay here and sleep—you look like you need it. Amos!"

While Amos helped Alyosha to put on his clothes, Fearless splashed water on his face in the bathroom. Wondering if he might scrounge a Valium again, he took a peek inside Alyosha's toiletry bag, carefully removing the Rolex lying across it, its casing engraved with a capitalized name: "Электромаш." But between a can of shaving foam and a bottle of exclusive-looking moisturizer, the only pills Fearless could find were a blister pack of flunitrazepam: white pills, not the blue ones they had taken on the plane.

"Whatever happens," he overheard Alyosha muttering, "leave Wish in Cambodia to clean everything up."

When Alyosha and Amos left, Fearless tried to sleep, but his mind wouldn't let him. Getting up, he idled around the room, a burgundy strip in Alyosha's travel wallet catching his eye: apparently, Alyosha was now a British citizen. Chuckling to himself, Fearless picked it up to investigate, uncovering a further surprise—stuffed inside was another passport, this time with a navy cover and Hebrew lettering. Fearless always took a childish pleasure in passport stamps and Alyosha's collection was—as expected— exceptional. Moldova, Sofia, New Delhi, Singapore, Luxembourg, South Africa, the British Virgin Islands. In the British passport: Kabul, Mehrabad, Baghdad; a stamp of Arabic letters Fearless supposed was Saudi Arabia. Having restored the documents to their rightful place, he opened the French windows that gave onto the hotel's courtyard and smoked for a while, watching the other guests enjoying the swimming pools.

As he reached the end of his cigarette, the Black man from the videotape walked into the courtyard—bare-chested and wearing garish Bermuda shorts, his rubber sandals clacking on the tiles around the pool. Fearless gasped: behind the man trailed two girls aged between eight and ten and a woman in her twenties, her voluminous torso wrapped in African fabric.

Fearless went to Alyosha's closet and found a pair of swimming trunks and sun cream. *Looks like I'll be hanging around the hotel pool after all.*

He draped his robe across a lounger. The little girls were swimming, throwing a beach ball between them, but the Black man had disappeared, leaving them with the nanny. Fearless dived in and swam a couple of widths before floating on his back at the edge of the pool. When a stray throw sent the ball in his direction, he laughed and threw it back, asking the girls if he could join in; one way or another, he would find out who the man was.

"Sweet kids," he said to the nanny, as he toweled his face and chest after the game of catch had ended.

"They really are," she replied, in an Aberdonian brogue.

"So you're from the Granite City and they're from . . . somewhere terribly English like me."

She smiled. Underneath the heavy smear of red lipstick and the dead crown of badly bleached hair on her head, there was a pleasant face hiding if you tried to look for it. Not many people did, he suspected. She might warm to a bit of attention. "Good guess," she said. "But they're from the Ivory Coast originally—though they do go to boarding school in England—you're right."

"The Ivory Coast. You go there often?"

"Oh no. General Traoré—their father—is hardly ever there. I take care of them back in the UK."

"He's a widower."

She laughed. "Oh no. His wife's in Paris." She lowered her voice. "Buying clothes in Chanel that wouldn't suit a woman half her size."

Fearless beckoned the pool boy. "I'm getting a drink. Can I buy you one?"

"Oh, I . . ."

"Come on. You're on holiday—just like me, no?"

By the time the drinks arrived, the nanny had opened up; he had learned about her sister in Edinburgh, her childhood dog, and her love of dressmaking and ethnic fabrics. Bit by bit, Fearless steered the conversation back to the General.

"It's a different culture," she said.

"Macho?"

"Patriarchal. They're not interested in the girls, but the older boy, they obsess about." She adopted a posh voice. "He boards at *Eton*."

"I went to a public school," said Fearless.

She blushed and apologized.

"I'm teasing you," he said. But it was true. After his father's death, with his mother hospitalized, Conrad, already his designated guardian, petitioned his father's family to create a trust to pay for his fees and needs—even if those same family members refused to take him in or even meet him. Conrad told Fearless that it was not Fearless's fault—his father's family had never gotten over their anger at his father for snubbing them. But Conrad and Fearless both knew otherwise; Fearless could pass with other people but *they* knew his color, which was also a marker of class: not upper, middle, or working, but second. "Sod 'em," Conrad said, whenever they used the money. "Take your flying lessons, buy a piano, if that's what you want."

The doors to the hotel foyer swung out. A heavyset man dressed in a white dress shirt and slacks held them open for General Traoré to return.

"Is that the time? Good talking to you," Fearless said as he rose and draped his towel over his shoulders. "Perhaps I'll see you again. Will you be here long?"

"That would be nice. Another two days. We'll be by the pool."

"Good afternoon!" Fearless said brightly as he passed the General. "You must forgive me for distracting your charming employee."

So he had found out a name. A country of origin. Length of stay. The son's school. The wife's shopping trips. Alyosha would be impressed.

When Fearless woke, splayed across a king-size bed, he saw his duffel lying on the floor.

Alyosha was sitting on the suite's other bed. "Amos—call the nurse to redress my burns. Bring the antibiotic cream. And also the painkillers."

"You've brought my stuff," said Fearless.

"Yes. Everything. I'm sorry I put you there. I had no idea what was happening in that place. My God. Mr. Thom has run away, that's for sure."

Fearless wanted to reach out and touch Alyosha reassuringly but didn't want to cause him any further pain.

"Alyosha. Listen. The Black man on the tape is staying right here at Le Royal. His name is Traoré."

Alyosha groaned but did not respond.

"Did you hear me? He's a general from the Ivory Coast. He's lounging by the pool! He'll be here two more days."

Alyosha sighed. "I know who he is, for God's sake! I know all about that bastard. But, like I said, we can't call the police. We need to think. We're in dangerous territory—which is why I need you to leave right now."

Fearless swung his legs off the bed and sat up. The air conditioning sent a shiver across his collarbones. "What do you mean?"

"Tomorrow morning—you go to visit the temples. I have booked you a ticket on the boat to Siem Reap."

Fearless was struck by a sense of déjà vu. It was like the original offer to take him to Cambodia: arrangements already made; no say in the matter; Alyosha reverting to his old fixer ways. But he couldn't go to Siem Reap. He remembered the smile on the girl's face: little Bopha, so pleased with her letter on a string.

"From Siem Reap, Fearless, you fly home via Bangkok. You don't return to Phnom Penh. It was an idiot idea, bringing you here!"

"Don't be silly, Lyo—"

"No. You listen! I take care of everything." Even in his pitiable state, Alyosha's will was implacably strong.

Fearless felt a distance opening up between them, as if their two beds were life rafts on a sea, borne apart by unseen currents.

Alyosha turned and laid face down on the bed again, burying his forehead deep into the bedspread. "Such wickedness," he said, his words muffled by wadded fabric. "Don't you worry about this, bacha. We will have our vengeance, I swear."

18

Song could tell from the way the necklace was laid out: Sovanna intended it as a parting gift.

"So this is the thanks I get," Bun Thim said, when he saw that Sovanna was gone—as if she, who only last night he had wanted away, was causing him yet another inconvenience.

"Where would she go, pu?"

She read the answer in his face. The twitchiness. The restlessness. She had known it, crouching in the dark among the pitcher plants, as she watched the loose-limbed silhouette in the blue light of the television. She had known it but hadn't wanted to bring herself to admit it. She reached for her waistband but knew she wouldn't find anything. The money Fearless had given her and the money she'd stolen from Thom were gone.

"How should I know where she goes?" Bun Thim muttered.

"It's okay, pu. I will leave now too."

"No, no. No one wants you. It's her they are looking for." It was a statement of fact, no reproach or pity in it. "Stay, bong. Keep your head down. Morivan will look after you."

Bun Thim closed the door and went back into the house. A minute later, there were raised voices from a nearby window. There was something about a customer for the Siem Reap ferry. Then Song heard the Camry's engine clearing its throat.

In the shadows inside the hut, hot tears streamed down Song's face. The anger was at herself: she should be running out of the house, calling and shouting Sovanna's name. Yet it was one thing to bind her head and scurry through dark streets and another to draw attention to herself in broad daylight. They would see the burns around her eye and think she was a freak. It was pathetic to admit it, but she was relieved she could stay in hiding.

The door opened again and a chink of light fell across her lap. "Come into the house," said Morivan. "There's no need to stay here."

Inside, Morivan picked up the baby and pressed it directly into Song's arms, pretending not to notice her red eyes and wet cheeks. Then she lit the gas ring and fried the onion for the bobor. Soon, the white-yellow broth was simmering in its pot.

The magnetism of the baby's eyes, its little movements, the tightness of its grip when Song placed her finger in its palm: all of these things banished the worries from her mind. The child seemed to cast an orb of radiance around her, as if her whole body was singing with light.

For the rest of the morning, Song made herself useful cleaning and cooking, though whenever she thought of Sovanna, she would weep, then cough, then sob uncontrollably.

A little after lunch, Bun Thim returned. Agitated and terse, he took Morivan aside. Morivan didn't talk back, but her air was defiant.

Midafternoon, while the baby was napping, Morivan sat beside Song and spoke in a low voice. "He told me not to tell you, but you have the right to know. He is sure that Sovanna has gone to see Sokha. He lives with his friend on Street 211. It is very close to the Olympic Stadium."

Sokha. Anger rose inside her, but its object was far more than the man who'd scarred her. It was the Naga and Thom, it was the Chief and Saveth, it was the whole damn world that had beaten the shape of their lives.

"Why?" She knew the answer already.

"Sokha sells yama."

"Will he tell the Russians?"

"No. But the Russians are looking everywhere. They have many men and the police. They will surely find Sovanna."

19

At first light, Bun Thim arrived to drive Fearless to the Siem Reap ferry. Haggard and drawn, sullen yet jittery, he would not acknowledge Fearless's greeting.

Fearless was also tired and uneasy. He never liked to leave the scene.

"What the hell are we waiting for?" Alyosha had said to him so many times.

"We're waiting for something good to come out of this."

"Nothing good will ever come out of this."

But Fearless would hold out for the possibility of grace.

As Bun Thim shut his door and turned the ignition, Amos descended the hotel steps, opened the opposite door, and got in beside Fearless.

"I don't need babysitting," Fearless said.

Amos didn't respond.

"Shouldn't you be keeping an eye on Alyosha?"

Though Amos stayed silent, Fearless sensed a new softness and thoughtfulness to his diffidence.

At the quay, passengers gathered while men in oil-stained shirts ran back and forth on a long, white boat, clanging wrenches and shouting. Fearless and Amos leaned on the Camry's bonnet. No passengers would be embarking until the boat was fully functional.

"You were army?" said Fearless as he lit a cigarette, sensing for the first time that Amos might talk.

"I was in Bosnia like you. In Srebrenica—three years ago."

"Srebrenica? There were no British soldiers in the safe area."

"Ha."

A crash from the boat's hull resounded across the water.

"I wasn't a ssssoldier there. I was just an observer. Though when the sh-shit happened I didn't observe anything. I heard it. A single gunshot. Silence. Another shot. And so on. We thought that the planes would come. We relayed the coordinates. But that was never the play. One came. One plane only. It p-passed on the other side, as my mum would have said. Afterward, all they wanted was for me to sign my name. Forget you ever saw it, they said. Nondisclosure." He spat on the ground.

"So why this?"

"This life? I don't know any other kind. After I left, I ssssset up a skydiving school. My passion. The way you feel free in the air. But it went t-t-tits up." He turned to Fearless. "Sometimes there's no way out—don't you reckon? You can't wipe the slate c-c-clean and start afresh."

Amos leaned in, his black eyes fixed on Fearless. "I'm curious about something. How'd you know to be in N-Nairobi?"

"What do you mean?"

Someone else had asked about Nairobi in Cambodia. But who? Where?

"On the d-d-day of the bombing. How'd you know to be there?"

"I didn't know. I was just visiting an old school friend who works there. What's your connection to Nairobi?"

"We don't have a connection. I was just wondering about h-h-how you get your leads."

"But let *me* ask *you* something. That night in the Naga. You know that I wasn't drunk. Someone spiked my drink. Who would do that?"

"Spiked? What makes you think that?"

"I've been drunk before."

The wrinkles on Amos's forehead clenched and his nose scrunched up.

One of the men who worked on the boat came onto the stern and whistled. "Come come!" he shouted. "Time is going!"

Under Amos's thoughtful gaze, Fearless walked along the quay and handed his bag to one of the porters clamoring for it. He found a place to settle on the roof of the boat, resting his feet on the railing along its edge.

Two minutes later, the motor began to churn. As the boat drifted away and he raised his arm to gesture goodbye, Amos stepped toward the edge as if he'd just remembered something. He cupped his hands to make his voice heard. "Don't! D-D-Don't go to the guesthouse—the one he told you to."

"What?" shouted Fearless.

"It's a shithole. Find another place! There are better places, seen?"

For the first hours of the trip, the river meandered, past floating villages and shacks of timber and tin, thatched with rattan and sun-bleached reed. Corrugated roofs caught the sun in rhomboids of blinding white light. Fishermen looked up from long, narrow boats, deft hands unpicking fine meshes of net.

Fearless dug the stolen photo out of his duffel to study Song's face again, beaming up at him. As the wind riffled the picture, he noticed something new: in the bottom left-hand corner, Song's hand was resting on another. It was the hand of someone lying down, an IV stent attached to it. So there was someone else involved in the moment that had brought the doctor and Bun Thim and Song together, someone else tied to the illness or accident.

What did it matter? He had left it all in Alyosha's hands. He could go home if he wanted. But go home to what? "Just put yourself first," Alyosha had told him seriously. "Bacha, you're recovering from the most terrible time."

Several hours later, the river opened into an immense sweep and was subsumed by the vastness of the Tonlé Sap lake. When the rains hit Phnom Penh and combined with Himalayan meltwater, the river expanded here, flooding fields and forests. It was a river that didn't respect the definition of rivers: it ran two ways and not always to the sea.

The boat engine stopped. There was a murmur of concern. A curl of oil smoke wafted beneath Fearless's nose.

Silently they bobbed on the still sheet of water the color of smoked glass and as smooth and shiny. A mist spread around them and swallowed them whole, turning everything under its spell to a milky gray.

20

When Song arrived on Street 211, Sokha was standing in his front yard, staring at the ground, in conversation with his fat accomplice. Mao was sweating profusely and supporting his weight on a shovel.

Song positioned herself so she could watch them through the fence. Leaning in, she could even make out what they were saying.

"If it hadn't been us, someone else would have done it. The fucker would have given us away in a second."

"He had it coming," Mao agreed. He spat on the mound of earth and rubbed it in with the sole of his sandal. The mound was about seven feet long and half as wide.

"He'll be rotten soon enough."

"He was rotten already!"

Mao gestured toward the house. "What's she doing in there?"

"She's off her face."

"I don't like it."

"She's insurance. If they come for us, we'll bargain with her. You'll see."

The gall. It didn't matter that Thom's body had to be under that mound—a man she had wished dead a thousand times; it was their attitude, the blithe manner in which they maimed and killed because other people's lives were nothing next to their own.

Sokha squatted down to examine a large sack of white powder. "I don't get these instructions. They're all in English."

"I've never done concrete."

"Fuck it. I'm hungry. Let's do it tomorrow. Besides—there's a way we can enjoy this situation."

Mao raised his fat hand to stroke his chin and Sokha laughed lasciviously, leading the way inside.

Their casual attitude would be their undoing, Song thought to herself: even in the process of burying a dead body, they hadn't bothered to padlock the gate. It was a bitter pill that her life had been changed irrevocably by these idiots. She looked at the shovel Mao had leaned against the wall and knew she would do what her anger bade her.

When loud music began to buzz from the windows, she pulled up the bolt and slipped inside. In less than five seconds she had darted across the dirt, picked a tennis ball–sized rock from the ground, and grabbed Mao's shovel.

Standing outside the door, she stopped for a moment and breathed, thinking through the steps she was about to take. Then she reached up and deliberately unwound her krama. *I'm still here*, she wanted to say. *Laugh at my face if you want. You bastards will never break my spirit.*

She inhaled and hurled the rock in the direction she'd come from, its clang on the gate resounding around the yard. Immediately, footsteps hurried on the other side of the door. As the latch began to turn, she raised the shovel in both hands, the way a protester brandishes a placard.

Music rushed out through the opening door and without looking, she swung hard, smashing the head of the shovel straight into Sokha's face. She smashed him and the Chief and Thom and Vasiliev and every single cowshit bastard she had ever known. Out cold, she smashed him. Flat on his back. And then, without pausing to look at what she'd done, she stepped over the body, on the alert for Mao, hoping she would see Sovanna.

A scream went up in the corner of the room. There she was, recoiling and pressing her back to the wall. She was topless, with only a small thong on her bottom half. Song rushed to her, kicking through the paraphernalia on the floor: a plastic water bottle with a short and long straw, thin strips of metal, disposable lighters. In an instant, she could see how empty Sovanna was—not just because of the yama, but through the accumulation of what they had lived through.

But before Song could scoop Sovanna up, a hand pulled her shoulder. She heard an angry grunt and a solid metal click—something tense, on a spring, yearning to be released.

21

"Bitch," Mao grunted.

Then his body went limp, as if his marionettist had thrown aside the controls. Song heard the slap of his flesh on the tiles and the dull, flat thud of his fat, heavy head. Drops of something splashed on her cheeks and clothes—warm, like the first rain at the beginning of the monsoon.

As she turned in shock, two white men were beside her, one of whose fists flashed gold with a knuckleduster. The other carried a gun, a silencer attached to its barrel.

"Nyet!" the first man said as more men entered, kicking Sokha's body aside as they fanned through the house, barking short, quick words in Russian.

Then Colonel Vasiliev appeared. Standing over Sokha, he prodded him once, then twice with his cane. "Slap haey," he murmured. Already dead.

His eyes fell on Song, lit up in recognition, and then turned their gaze on Sovanna's corner. Two of his men were holding her up by the armpits, her limp legs incapable of supporting her weight.

Vasiliev shook his head. "Here," he said, digging deep into his trouser pocket. He gave Song a handkerchief to wipe Mao's blood from her face.

Sovanna did her best to open her eyes—just long enough to reveal their glazed, hazy state—before the men half-lifted, half-dragged her to the door.

From the other side, one of Vasiliev's men appeared at the window. Song couldn't be sure of the individual words but she could sense the meaning from the context well enough.

Vasiliev hawked up phlegm from his throat. "Mister Thom," he said. "So they got to him first."

Then he lumbered toward her as Song remembered her krama, wishing she could remove it from around her waist and safely cover her head again. Instead she stayed frozen as he lifted her chin, his meaty hand firm but respectfully gentle, tilting her face so he could examine it in the light.

"You still have beauty spot here, I see. That's how I tell which one is which."

Satisfied, he turned to one of the rattan chairs nearby, giving Song the chance to attend to her krama.

"Say goodbye to your sister," he said, the knuckles of the chair's palm stems wincing under his weight. "Pavel—take Sovanna to the truck."

"I go also," said Song in English. "Som toh."

Vasiliev burst out laughing. "Your sister does not belong to me anymore! She did—until yesterday."

He was speaking as much to himself as to Song, it seemed.

"See what she is now." He raised his palm. "My fault. But what can I do? I am in love with my memory. So beautiful. You too. And the two of you together. What a gift God gave! Sit, sit. We will talk. But please—stop this crying."

When he waved, she sat uncomfortably on the edge of the chair opposite him, cupping her hands limply in her lap.

"You're my sister-in-law. Did you know? Isn't that funny? We're family. Though now she is being taken by this . . . fucking prick!"

As a gesture, he tried to remove the wedding ring from his finger, but the finger was too thick and he couldn't make it budge.

"What happened to him?" he said, waving his hand at Sokha's body. "Little shitboy. Making his clever plan with tapes to blackmail and get money. But not so clever now. What happened here? You tell Colonel."

Song kept her head down and didn't say a word. Slap haey, slap haey, slap haey, slap haey.

"Never mind—but it would have been easier to beat it out of them. There must be more tapes. Nikolai! Load the bodies and search."

He grunted as he put his hand into the pocket of his slacks again, extracting yet another handkerchief, this one to mop his brow.

Tapes. So Fearless *had* done something with what she'd left. And that something was making waves; she could sense Vasiliev's anxiety. She looked to the door. Would they let her go? Or would it be easier for them to kill her too? How stupid it had been to imagine a different future. To imagine any future at all.

"Don't you worry yourself," said Vasiliev. "You can go, Song. Do what you want." He reached forward and picked up a bunch of keys on the low table. "Here. These look like the keys to this place. You stay here if you like. Makes no difference to me."

He rose to his feet and watched the men heaving the bodies out to their trucks.

"You were always the clever one. You'll survive well enough. Sovanna's gifts—how to say?—were in other matters."

Four or five men came back and gathered on the threshold.

"We have taken bodies, see? We don't leave a big mess. Isn't that right, Dmitri?"

Dmitri said something to Colonel Vasiliev and he laughed.

Once again, Song knew enough to catch the sense: how hilarious, they were joking, to have a cleaner at the scene, already in position, ready to work!

Slap haey. She could still feel the clang of the spade on Sokha's head, the vibration that ran from the blade down the shaft, which was still reverberating inside her bones.

"Here, take this money." Vasiliev held out a ten-dollar note.

Song reached up and pushed his hand away and he grunted, scrunched the note into a ball, and threw it onto the chair. Then he turned and walked out into the bright noonday sun, his form turning white before disappearing.

While she sat, motionless, the men set to work. First, they gathered around the television in the corner of the room, checking over the VCR and bagging two or three tapes. Then they ripped the place apart, overturning everything but moving delicately around her: the eye of their tornado.

They upended furniture, pulled out drawers, and scattered their contents. A bed grated painfully as it was dragged across the floor. They flipped it over and the slats came clattering onto the tiles—like the sound of a giant roneat being dismantled and shattered.

Dmitri went to the door, wiping the sweat from his forehead. "Nothing!" he shouted out.

"Check the yard—then we go."

The men began to file out. Car doors slammed. Dmitri came in, walked to the kitchen, then returned. As he left, he placed a bottle of bleach on the table. "You're welcome," he said in English, nodding to himself.

After the trucks had pulled out, one of the men shut the gate, leaving Song in her new property, cold and quivering. There was blood spattered here and there, much of it smeared by boot prints. There were fragments of other little things—bone, hair—that she didn't want to think about too much.

Flies were already buzzing, swarming into the room.

She rose to her feet and opened every window. If she wanted to stay here, it was true, she would have to clean. She fashioned her krama around her nose and mouth, tied the knot tightly, and got to work.

22

By midafternoon, Fearless was climbing the vertiginous steps of Angkor Wat's sanctuary. At the top, in the dark stone interior, he caught his breath, a Rorschach of sweat across his back. He gazed out over the crenellated temple-mountains, the pitch-roofed colonnades, the lily-padded moats. It was something out of high fantasy, this ancient place, with its carved friezes of epic myths and legendary battles, its libraries and staircases and rain-stained balustrades, its complex matrix of water channels and reservoirs—a temple of the gods, as Tolkien would have imagined it. It was the ancient past and, at the same time, so alien that one might believe it had arrived here from outer space.

Leaving Angkor, he took a motodop to see the sunset at Ta Prohm—the next temple on the tourist trail, and the one that had loomed largest in his mind for twenty years. It was renowned for the way the jungle trees had grown into its fabric, the serpentine roots of silk-cottons and strangler figs draping themselves over its columns and pediments, worming tendrils deep into their fissures until root and stone were inseparable. There had been a photo of his father taken at Ta Prohm, mailed to them after his death by an American member of the tour party: the only visual record of his father's trip. The Khmer Rouge were happy for them to take pictures of the temples: this was the mystic state of the realm before it had been infected by the West. His mother had ripped up that photo in her hurt and grief.

Resting his hands now on the trees' thigh-thick tentacles and feeling their power moving into the stone, Fearless retrieved the creased photograph from his pocket and looked once more at Song's smiling face. If he left Cambodia he would never know if she was alive or if there was anything he might have done to help her survive. Moreover, he would be turning down the responsibility that Song had given him: the righting of the terrible wrongs on the videotape.

As Fearless left the temple, the sun was sinking, stretching his shadow to the proportions of a stilt walker. The angry heat of the day saw reason. "Take me to a hotel," he said to his motodop. "But not The Paradise. No Paradise—understand?"

He was dropped off in front of a white monstrosity on a strip where an endless line of "wedding cakes" was being constructed.

At reception, he placed a call to Lucy, hoping for an outside perspective. But he didn't have the chance to begin his story. "Thank God you called," she said. "You need to come home. There was a fire at the cottage. They're saying it was arson."

"What?"

"The whole thing's burned down."

In her voice, he could hear the tears welling in her eyes.

"Everything's gone," she mumbled.

The click of the cradle as he put down the receiver felt like a door, closing on a former life.

After speaking to the receptionist, Fearless reserved a taxi to Phnom Penh, set to leave at the crack of dawn. Then he picked at a bowl of rice and fish amok—the sole diner in the deserted restaurant. Later, in bed, insomnia troubled him. Questions circled—a shiver of sharks, silently closing in, with blank, black eyes and dagger-toothed underbites.

PART 3

23

When she had finished wiping up all the blood, guts, and spatters and had scooped the drug paraphernalia into a wastebasket, Song realized, to her surprise, that her body needed food. As she was searching the kitchen, the hairs on her neck bristled. Someone had entered and was standing behind her. She yelped, turning and brandishing the mop.

"Ot ey tee," said the man. "You speak English?" He was Russian, but not part of Vasiliev's crew; there were dark blue tattoos winding around his forearms and a stiffness to his body that spoke of long, unchosen hardships.

The man let the duffel he was carrying fall from his shoulder and pulled a blue plastic bag from its open mouth.

She kept the mop pointed at him, its thick ropes dripping pink.

"Bread. Fruit," he said. "Here. Take." He laid the bag between them, bowing his head slightly.

When he retreated, Song moved forward and snatched the bag. At no time taking her eyes off his face, she tore pieces of the baguette and ate greedy mouthfuls, trying to supplant the taste and smell of blood.

The man sat down in one of the chairs, his eyes clenched as if he was looking into sunshine. His fingers toyed with the fringe of her spare krama, which she had thrown over the arm of the chair before cleaning.

Minutes passed. Then he reached into his bag again and drew out a pocketknife that he placed on the floor and kicked. He was passing it to her so she might cut the fruit; inside the bag was also a ripe mango.

"You speak English. Yes? I'm your friend. I know where is your sister. I know where they take her."

He looked at her face, monitoring her response. What did he want in return for the information?

The man gestured to the wreckage. "What they look for? What they want?"

Song cut a slice of mango and sucked its flesh. The juice of the fruit was sweet and light.

"Where is she—my sister?"

"They take her to villa."

"Where?"

"What can you do?" His sarcasm crossed the language barrier, intact.

Song wiped the juice from her chin with the back of her hand. She was still cautious but sensed he would do her no harm.

"You want your sister. I tell you. But first tell me what is happening here."

She cut another sliver from the fleshiest part of the fruit. "Who are you?" she asked. "You work for Colonel Vasi?"

"No no." He tapped his chest. "I work for only me." His eyes were defiant, but not unkind. "My name is Viktor. What is your name?"

"Song."

"What I want—Song—is Federenko. You know Mister Federenko? He is man who has your sister."

So that was what Vasiliev meant. He had given Sovanna up to *him*. Had leaving the tape with Fearless been a terrible mistake? "Ot tee," she said out loud.

"Yes. Federenko. I see him take her. I know where they are now."

It made no sense; if this man knew where Federenko was, why was he here, asking her questions? He was alone and powerless like her in some way. She remembered one of the proverbs the Chief liked to repeat: *The enemy of my enemy is my friend.*

"The tapes," she said. "The Russians. They are looking for videotapes."

"What tapes?"

"Of the men. What they are doing in the Naga."

He narrowed his eyes. "How do you know?"

"I . . . I gave tape to the Englishman," she said.

For several seconds the man didn't move or blink. Then he rose to his feet and shook his head, walked to the window, hesitated, then turned back.

"The Naga Bar is finished. They take everything out. Chairs. Tables. I saw them on street. And police are everywhere up and down riverside." He swept his hand through the air. "They put children in van . . ."

She felt every organ inside her tighten. "The children . . ."

The man snapped his fingers. "Everything changes. Now Federenko is boss of Vasiliev. The Tsar. The big man."

While he spoke, his eyes were searching the floor in the attitude of a beachcomber. Then he strode straight toward her and she flinched and stepped back. But he walked past and heaved the small fridge from the wall, its metal feet crunching and scraping on the concrete. Behind it only a solitary cockroach sampled the air with its antennae before vanishing into an invisible crack.

Song scanned the room too; maybe Vasiliev's men had missed something. But there were no other appliances. No fixtures to unfix.

The man strode out. She heard him moving things in the bedroom.

As she stood there, listening to him crash and ransack, her eyes alighted on the decorative frieze on the wall: a giant relief of Angkor Wat over six feet wide, three feet tall, and at least three inches deep, the temple raised from its painted background of sky, grass, and slender-stemmed palm tree. There were finger marks in the dust around the relief's edge: not so long ago, someone had rehung it.

When the man came back in, he caught the line of her gaze. He wedged his fingers beneath the frieze's edge and shunted it from the wall. "Help!" he groaned as he struggled with its weight in a vertical position, jerking his nose to the corner closest to her. The two of them tottered, grimacing and staggering as they lowered the massive picture onto the coffee table.

The backing of the relief consisted of a plywood panel, secured with several frayed screws around its edge. The man gestured to her to fetch the knife he had given her and got to work with the blade. Once he'd finished, he lifted up the plywood and slid it away.

There, in the hollow mold of Angkor Wat, with the same labels and handwriting as the one she had left in Fearless's pillowcase, were two dozen VHS videotapes, each one numbered, each one dated.

Viktor put his hands on his hips and chewed the corner of his mouth. "Number 175," he said. "Street 51."

24

Viktor carried the tapes to the player, stacking them on the floor in three teetering towers.

175. Street 51.

The black-lidded eye of the television screen opened up. A girl appeared, tottering backward, a man following afterward, guiding her by the waist. The man put his hands on her shoulders and pushed down. Viktor's face remained impassive.

Song turned away. Children's faces swam up inside the dome of her skull: smiling, fearful, numb, dissolving.

Desolate, she went into the other room, heaved the bed right side up, and wrestled the mattress back into position. Outside, people and motos and cars passed in the street, but the video player's clacking and ratcheting drowned out their sounds; Song could feel hands pushing down on her spirit.

After half an hour, Viktor shut off the machine. She heard him open the door and go into the yard. Through the window she could see him smoking a cigarette, a little muscle in his cheek twitching involuntarily. Then he went back inside and inserted the next tape.

Song drifted off on the bare mattress. When she emerged, she found Viktor asleep in a sitting position, lit by the quivering static on the screen. On the table lay a paper covered in Cyrillic scribbles, with four-figure numbers indicating times on the tapes.

Feeling her nervous hand on his shoulder, he shuddered himself awake. "I go now," he said, jumping to his feet and picking up his backpack. For a moment he looked at the stack of tapes. "I take this one," he said. "But you stay here. Put the other tapes back in picture. I come with food." He walked up to her and gently gripped her upper arm. "We will work together, you and me—okay? You understand?"

Song found herself nodding. "Where do you go?"

He waved the tape. "To use this. I have idea."

As he opened the door, she wondered why on earth he would be so kind.

"When I come back, I do like this on gate," he said. He gave one knock, two short knocks, one knock, three short knocks.

After he left, she ensured the gate was padlocked, hid the tapes, and managed to lean the frieze back against the wall.

25

Fearless walked up to the green gate of Dr. Andrew's house. Midday on a Sunday, the street was deserted. One eye closed, he peered through the metal pickets at the single-story house, an old military jeep, and the lush front garden clustered with flowers.

His share taxi had made good time, arriving in Phnom Penh in the middle of the morning. He had gone straight to Le Royal, eager to see Alyosha, but the receptionist informed him that Mr. Federenko had checked out.

"What about our other friend, General Traoré?" he asked, as he filled out the registration form to take a room.

"General Traoré checked out also, sir."

"I sign here, yes?" Fearless adopted an absent-minded air. "I guess the General's visiting his son in England."

"On this line, sir. Yes, I think he was flying to London."

After showering, Fearless tried to call Alyosha, but the sound on the other end was high-pitched and continuous. Then he took a motodop directly to the Naga—or, rather, to the place where the Naga had been. The steel door to the stairs hung open and the walls were splashed in bright white paint. In place of the bar, he found an empty tiled room, devoid of tables, chairs, shelves, the pool table, and, most noticeably, the carved, wooden Naga booth.

This was a good sign, Fearless felt. Alyosha had taken steps to put things right.

Outside, not even the incentive of a few thousand riel could draw any information about Song from the motodops. She had spent every day no more than fifty feet from them but they didn't even seem to know of her existence. Dr. Andrew was now his only lead.

Fearless rapped hard on the gate and then once again. Finally, a middle-aged Cambodian woman appeared.

"Dr. Andrew," Fearless said through the gap in the fence.

The woman opened the door, put her hands together, and then led him toward a circle of rattan chairs on the veranda. Through the half-open French windows, he could see a tower of cardboard boxes, several of them open, bubble wrap strewn everywhere.

Dr. Andrew came out, fastening his shirt buttons. He made no attempt to hide his irritation.

"Look, mate—it's the weekend. Family time."

Fearless sat up. "I'm sorry," he said. "The last thing I want is to bother you, Doctor."

Before Dr. Andrew could reply, Fearless took out the photo.

"Song's missing. She helped me when I was in trouble and I need to know she's okay. That's all. If there's anything you know . . ."

Dr. Andrew's mouth opened. He took the photo. Fearless watched his face, remembering his reluctance the night he had helped Alyosha.

"Please understand, Doctor, I'm not involved in my friend's business. I'm just a guy on holiday. I want to make sure she's safe."

The doctor sat down, his shirt still half-open. The skin over his collarbones was red and leathery, the curls of hair on his head wet and loose from a shower. He stared at the photo for a very long time.

"This isn't Song, mate. It's her twin sister, Sovanna. Funny you asking me: people are searching for Sovanna, too."

A twin. All this time he'd been looking and staring and reflecting on someone who wasn't who he thought she was.

"So both of them are missing."

"Looks that way, doesn't it. You know what? Song *is* in this picture." His finger pointed to the small brown hand with the IV drip. "She wouldn't have agreed to have her photograph taken. I expect that's still the case today."

At that moment, a little Khmer girl—between two and three years old—ran out of the house, her sandals pattering the polished concrete. She evaded Dr. Andrew's grasp and ran onto the lawn before returning to the veranda to clamber onto Fearless's knee.

"Hello!"

A Khmer woman hurried out of the house. She smiled and nodded in an apologetic way.

"Hello. What's your name?" Fearless said.

"Lee-ak," said the little girl, wriggling on his lap.

"Go back in with Ma, Srey Leak," Andrew said. "How about getting some iced tea for Daddy?"

Dr. Andrew's wife repeated his request in Khmer and the girl got down and ran into the house. The doctor's rough edges softened for a moment.

"So you don't know where Song is?"

The doctor leaned forward. "To be honest, you're the first person who's mentioned her in the last couple of years. I treated her and Bun Thim here after the . . . accident. And then she was taken. I . . . did what I could. I wasn't in a position to be asking any questions."

The doctor's wife reappeared bearing drinks on a tray, the little girl holding the hem of her sampot. She put the iced tea down and led the child onto the lawn.

"Can you tell me what happened?" Fearless asked.

The doctor kept on staring at the picture in his hands. "I'm sorry, mate. It's been a while since I thought about these girls. And now twice in two days. It's not a happy story." He sighed and looked back at the cardboard boxes. Their open lids fluttered in the breeze of a ceiling fan as if they were building up the courage to take flight.

"They were prostitutes—you get that? The stars of the show. At a place called The Sunflower, which was high-end—as high-end as any place you could get in Phnom Penh at that time.

"To have one girl so beautiful would have been pretty extraordinary, but to have identical twins—well, you can just imagine. They were hot property for the owner—a local bigwig. The Chief of Police. Well—you can probably imagine him too.

"The thing was, this Chief wasn't just happy with the business. He fell in love with Sovanna and spent every spare second with her. He'd get Song to sing karaoke in the bar while they . . . canoodled.

"He lived it up. But, soon enough, his missus found out. If it had been just sex, she wouldn't have cared. But the old fool was head over heels. Doolally. And word got out. People she knew were talking. Laughing behind her back. They said the Chief was Srey Ya and Sovanna was Ros Sothea. So the wife hired some guys to take her revenge. Not on the Chief, of course, but on the girl—to make her suffer.

"So . . . one night, when Bun Thim here was driving the girls, as they were crossing over the river on the Japanese Bridge, two guys pull alongside on a moto with a bucket and lob acid into the car, all over Song. A fair amount of it splashed over Bun Thim too, which is why his hands are bandaged like this in this photo.

"It wasn't s'posed to be Song. It was Sovanna they were after.

"When they brought her to me, I thought: no hope in hell. The fumes alone in an acid attack can be enough to kill someone. But Bun Thim's quick thinking had made the difference. He pulled the car off the road and dragged her into the river. He kept her there and locals brought soap to wash her— which must have done a lot to counter the acid. It's not like a thermal burn, you see, where the damage is done in the moment of the trauma. The acid carries on burning silently, slowly, until you can find a way to neutralize it.

"Anyway, I don't know how, but Song pulled through. She bloody well fought. The debriding. The grafts. The washing of the wounds to fight infection.

"And the Chief didn't walk away—I've got to give him that. He paid her medical expenses. Gave her a place to live and a job. He was guilty— for him, for his wife, what she'd sunk to. It's worse than murder, really, being attacked with acid. To destroy someone's face so they don't even recognize themselves.

"As for Sovanna, she was passed on to your friend's boss, Colonel Vasiliev. That's why I'm surprised you don't know about her. He bought her and married her—what could be better? And so they all lived happily ever fucken after."

A cold wave curled up behind Fearless's back.

The doctor rose to his feet, chewing his lower lip. He looked out into the garden at his wife and daughter.

"You can buy the freedom of these girls with money or favors. With the skills you have—if you have skills that they need. I did that for Tina. I'm still doing it, I guess."

He sighed. "Anyway. That's Song's story. And the story of how I ended up with so many plants. Tina loves her plants. Plant pots everywhere!"

Fearless looked at the woman bending over to inspect a flower. She called the little girl: "Come look. Come see." The child did not appear to be of mixed race. He remembered Alyosha saying that the Naga girls' tubes were tied and guessed the even deeper story of the family around him, the wants, the compromises, the sheer force of will. It would be tempting to compare these stories to matryoshka dolls. And yet, when one story opened to reveal another, the new story was never smaller or easier to grasp; it was just as complex and led, in turn, to still more stories, some of which couldn't be opened and some whose interiors unfurled into space.

"Where could Song have gone?"

"I can't help you there. I know their family comes from somewhere up near Battambang." The doctor looked at Fearless and shrugged. "Wherever Song goes, it won't be easy. Acid damage can never be fully repaired—not here. Maybe with the best plastics guys in the West you could mitigate it, but her face and head will be scarred forever. If you do find her, you tell her Dr. Andrew wishes her well."

Fearless rose from the chair and shook his hand. "And Alyosha? His back is going to be okay?"

At the mention of Alyosha, Dr. Andrew withdrew his hand. "He saw me before he left for Bangkok. But I don't make a habit of talking about my patients. Not even to friends of theirs. I've already said too much."

Bangkok. What was there? A hub for flights elsewhere.

The two of them walked down the driveway.

"Bye-bye, Mister," called the little girl from the garden.

"Bye-bye, Leak. Thank you for bringing my drink."

As Dr. Andrew held the gate open and Fearless stepped onto the street, he turned to shake the doctor's hand again and thank him for his time.

"One more thing. Can you tell me what the drug flunitrazepam is?"

The doctor creased his eyebrows and pushed his lips forward slightly. "Roofies. Rohypnol. It's a benzodiazepine for insomniacs. Or rapists, for that matter—I expect you've heard of it. Once you take it, you're gone, you forget what's happened to you."

"Can you die from them? Could you kill someone with them if you really wanted to?"

"You can die from anything, mate. It's just a question of quantity."

As Fearless took a moto back to Le Royal, disconnected images and memories collided and latched onto each other: the blister pack of Rohypnol in Alyosha's toiletry bag; the view from Wish's crow's nest in Sarajevo. He was surer than ever that Wish had spiked his drink. Only he and Amos would have had access to Alyosha's things.

He would never forget the last time he saw Wish in Sarajevo. The young sniper glanced over his shoulder when Fearless came in, then turned, gluing his eye to the scope of his rifle. The spirit Fearless had formerly captured on film—vulnerable, sympathetic, and troubled by conscience—had been effaced. Only bitterness now remained in its stead.

"Come see, it's your girl with blond hair," Wish said to Fearless. "An old grandma, too. They are waiting at crossroads."

There she was: the girl that Wish had fallen for, the girl that Fearless had encouraged him to approach.

"So which one shall I kill today? The choice is yours."

Fearless exhaled, shook his head, and stepped away from the rifle.

"I don't joke, Mister Big Shot. Speak now. You have one chance."

Two, three, five seconds passed. Then Wish fired, adjusted the windage on his scope, and fired again, his eye never leaving the crosshairs.

Both women lay on the ground.

"How does it feel?" said Wish. "You could have saved one of them—but you stood by and watched."

Fearless dashed from the room and clattered down the stairwell, leaping the last six steps of every flight. On the street, he sprinted across the tarmac and threw himself onto his knees. The girl's skin was already bleached of life, the bullet hole on her forehead a perfect red bindi.

He slid his arms beneath her body and lurched down the boulevard to his jeep. Her limbs were lifeless, her mouth open to the sky. *Psst psst*, the bullets whispered over his head, missing him, as he knew full well, on purpose.

Back at his room at Le Royal, Fearless found that the maids had drawn the curtains and lowered the AC to abattoir temperature. He would shower, he decided, and recharge his batteries before he started to plot his next move.

When he turned back from the window, the man who had brutally tortured Alyosha was sitting quietly in one of the armchairs. It was the stark vertical lines on his face that Fearless recognized: a hollowness that resonated an air of menace. A little gym bag rested by his feet—the kind in which a boxer keeps gloves and hand wraps.

The man raised his finger to his lips very slowly. "Sit," he said, gesturing to the armchair opposite. In his left hand he held a simple black prayer rope, ready apparently to speak with his God.

There was nothing more evil, Fearless thought, than someone who tortured, who not only gave pain but stretched it out and made it sing. He wanted to clear his throat and spit in the man's face.

But he did as he was told. He would never have a chance of fighting or fleeing someone like this. To earn his title, the vor would have proved himself many times; he would have given up job and family, renounced money, property, and home; he would have spent years in the toughest prisons, often in solitary confinement; he would have demonstrated that he was a leader and a man of presence and force, guile and grit, rigor and resourcefulness.

Sweat slid over Fearless's temples. He looked at the man's face—the straight mouth, the sharp eyes, the knot of flesh at the top of his nose that suggested he was in perpetual concentration—and tried to guess what he was thinking.

"In the market a few days ago. That's the first time you see me," he said. "I am buying iron. Yes, you are remembering me now."

His body and head didn't move as he spoke; the serene self-possession was eerie and unnerving.

Fearless remembered something he'd once heard about the vory. According to their code, they couldn't deny what they were. "You're a vor," he ventured.

"You say so."

"No—I'm asking. Tell me. Are you a vor?"

"If I am vor I must say yes. Very good! But I am not vor no more. I am . . . nothing. I work alone. Only me. Viktor." He breathed in through his nose. "Enough. You tell *me*: where is Alexei Federenko?"

Fearless could see the muscles in the man's jaw flutter, and a vein of defiance pulsed inside him in response. "I don't know where Alyosha is. And even if I did, why on earth would I tell you? Do you have your iron in that bag? I have a shirt that could do with a pressing."

Viktor remained impassive.

"Well. Do you have your iron or not?"

"No," Viktor said simply, folding his hands in his lap, the black prayer rope still clutched between his fingers. It could have meant *No, I have no intention of hurting you* as equally as *No. I don't need tools. I am perfectly capable of killing you with my hands.*

There was something of the crow about him, Fearless felt. Dressed in black. Sleek and sharp-beaked.

"You won't get any money from torturing me, Mister Vor. I don't have anything to do with my friend's affairs."

"I won't hurt you, don't worry. You and I—we have same . . . friend."

"What friend?"

"The girl. The girl called Song. With the burns, here and here and here."

Fearless held his breath as the man reached into his bag and withdrew a Cambodian gingham scarf. He placed it on the small coffee table between them. There was that scent—the semisweet tang of Song's body. Fearless could see the material was stained with blood.

"Where is she? Is she safe?" He instantly regretted showing desperation.

"First, you tell *me*. Where is Federenko? Only your friend with blond hair remains. All others are gone. They leave Cambodia."

"I told you I don't know. Even if I did, I wouldn't say."

The vor shook his head and then knitted his brows. "I don't understand. Please. What do you do for Federenko? You don't work for him but he gives you money? What he send you to Siem Reap to do?" He had lightened his tone, deciding to play good cop: curious, interested, open to explanation.

"Money? Of course not. Alyosha is my friend. I went to see Siem Reap for the temples, thanks to his kindness."

Viktor burst out laughing. "Federenko does what is good for him! Or his friends in business. His friends in FSB."

"I've spent more time with him than you, believe me. I don't need you to tell me who he is and what he's done. Maybe there's no such thing as friendship in your world."

The smile disappeared from Viktor's face. His unblinking gaze glittered brightly. In it, Fearless could sense a key strand of the Russian character: the elemental belief in something bigger than yourself—a great undertaking of which you are part—and, central to this, the elevation of the soul.

"I don't understand. So explain me please. *You* photograph wars and *he* sells guns. How you are friends? Is it special deal? He makes war so you can take your photographs?"

Guns? Alyosha traded many things, but not arms. And yet there was no obvious way Fearless could disprove it.

"You've got things wrong. He's not selling nuclear missiles."

"Missiles. No, no. Kalashnikovs, grenades . . . These are more dangerous. They kill more people."

It was Alyosha who had taught him to shoot an AK-47 in Grozny. "Don't hold it like that. That's Soviet manual way. Put the stock in the middle of your chest like this. This way you kill men and spare the birds. No one hates guns more than me, after Afghanistan, but it's a skill you must have. Every man."

The vor slipped his prayer rope into the pocket of his shirt. Then he leaned forward in his chair, looking quizzical.

"You really don't know the way Federenko is working. What do you think he is doing with your tape?"

The tape. It was only Song that could have told him. He must have menaced her too, even tortured her.

"He used the tape to get what he wants," said the vor. He sat back again and raised his finger to his lips. "To take the girl from Colonel Vasiliev. The pretty girl—our little friend's sister."

"Sovanna?"

"Yes. Sovanna. With tape, Federenko is boss. He no longer has to play table tennis with her and take her to swimming pool and"—he mimed masturbation—"at night in his hotel. Because Vasiliev is on the tape, yes? What does he do? I know." The vor's lips curled. He breathed through his nose loudly.

Fearless remembered the table tennis bats Alyosha had brought with him, the morning after the night that Song had disappeared. What had then seemed surreal now made sense. What was it that Alyosha had said to him in the Naga? "Lyubov zla, polyubish i kozla." *Love's evil; you'll love even a goat.*

"So Federenko use tape to get his woman. Colonel Vasiliev's house is burned in fire. Silly girl to give you tape—to trust you. Stupid."

Fearless wanted to come back with a killer line, but there were too many facts and details for him to process. First, Vasiliev's house had been attacked *before* he discovered the videotape. The two weren't linked in the way the vor thought. And from what he had overheard of Amos and Wish in the doctor's waiting room, the attack, the Land Cruiser hit-and-run, and the Naga break-in had been synchronized. The vor was holding back much more than he was revealing. There was no way, surely, that he was working alone. Meanwhile, Fearless's anxiety about what had befallen Song was transforming itself into an unpredictable anger. He needed to get control of it, to think before he compromised himself.

He looked up to see the man's gleaming eyes, examining his face keenly for any reaction.

"You say Federenko's your good friend, but really you know nothing. So: let me tell you what *I* know."

Fearless's heart rate rose as the vor reached into the bag again, but it was only to pull out a pack of cigarettes. He lit up and exhaled a curl of purple smoke.

After he had lit a cigarette for Fearless and handed it to him, he reached into the bag again. Now, he laid a revolver on the coffee table between them, less than a yard from Fearless's grasp. "You see. We trust each other. You can relax."

Fearless took a drag on the cigarette, keeping a straight face despite its acrid taste.

"Six years ago. Russia. Early days of Yeltsin. Okay? Capitalism is beginning—the days of big money. Government decide that everyone will be capitalist with vouchers. They give millions of vouchers. One voucher—two Volgas! They have TV ad nonstop. MMM. Golubkov. You make money, you go to World Cup in America."

Fearless knew something about this time. Brown vouchers—a kind of currency that Russians went crazy for. With vouchers, you could buy shares in the recently privatized businesses or just trade them on street corners or station concourses for a quick buck.

"My friend Grigory. He is taking care of our money. You know what is obshchak? It is how the vory share our wealth—the great lake. When you are in shit, when you sleep on the mattresses, you take from obshchak. And when you are outside, you give. These are rules. But in these days, prices going crazy, the vory too do things in new ways. We decide to put obshchak in business and companies. And, like everyone else, in paper vouchers also."

Fearless could guess where the story was going. He already knew that Alyosha's exile from Russia—the exile that had washed him up in Sarajevo and thus into Fearless's life—was tied to a financial innovation of that era: the creation of mutual funds for vouchers in which investors pooled their resources. Alyosha had put himself in the vanguard of the fund creators. By investing his clients' vouchers in companies and sitting on their boards, Russian industry would flourish, and they would rake in the dividends. It was a win–win situation—and for the good of the fatherland. But in a climate of hyperinflation, no one gave a damn about things like hard graft or long-term growth. Currency speculation, leverage, arbitrage, asset-stripping—these were the keys to short-term jackpots. In markets that were completely unregulated, it was a free-for-all. Honest intentions like Alyosha's were trampled on blithely. Like 100-meter sprinters or Tour de France cyclists, you either participated in the illicit behavior or trailed in your rivals' wake. It simply wasn't possible to do the right thing.

"Federenko makes big, big promises to Grigory. He said he invests our money and gives back three times, five times. But he invested in nothing. He sell all the vouchers and then give some money back, saying 'Look. Here's your first profit!' A trick. A fucking dirty trick!

"And when people get this first money they celebrate and put more! More. More. The bosses are happy!"

"I know how this ends," said Fearless. "It got out of control. People lost their money and Alyosha was sorry for it."

"No. You know nothing. Federenko didn't care. He let his own wife go to jail. His own personal wife! And he disappeared and money disappeared, like this. And after that, my friend Grigory is beaten badly. They burn him with iron. They kill Grischa dead."

Viktor's hand quivered.

"At the time I am in prison. I hear what happened but I cannot be there. I think about Grischa. Every day. Inside prison, thinking, waiting. Then at last I get out, two months ago, and I look for Federenko. I find, I follow, watching, waiting. That fucking Black bodyguard always there. But I never forget Grischa and what is happening to him. Do you understand? I never give up. This is why I am here."

"To put Alyosha out of his misery."

"What does this mean?"

"It means you want to kill him."

No reply. Perhaps to reduce it in this way was insulting. Fearless could see the man's logic, his deeply felt hurt, whose rawness couldn't help but stir a mote of sympathy.

Shaking his head, the vor stood up. He walked toward the net curtains, leaving the gun on the table.

The harshness of the afternoon sun was softening now. The light through the curtains was mother-of-pearl gray.

"I see your photos of children. In war. Suffering and—what is word?—innocence. You care about children."

"Of course."

The man turned back to face him. "Then why you are not angry? Your friend Federenko: he *kills* children."

Fearless sighed. He had lost his patience. He was sorry to have let himself soften for a moment. Yes, the grievance about the voucher fund he could believe and sympathize with—but murdering children?

"It's true. I see it." The vor pointed to his own eyes. "The blond man and driver take children in van."

"You saw them killed."

"No."

"So they could have been driving them home."

The vor sighed and shook his head. "They are dead," he spat. "Dead! Always they clear evidence. And what is greatest evidence? You tell me. The things in these children's minds."

"They could have been driving them anywhere. And how is Alyosha involved? You mentioned Wish. The blond one. It's him, the bastard. He's the one who's been trying to kill me, for Christ's sake!"

The vor jerked back his chin and head. Then he blinked slowly, before regaining his composure. "Of course," he said. He lit another cigarette and looked out the window into the hazy light. "I understand that you believe your friend. I am a stranger. Unless you see with your own personal eyes." He stared at Fearless, looking down his nose. "There are more tapes I can show you."

"More tapes?"

"Yes. I have one here. I see more last night." The vor reached down and withdrew a tape from his bag—a tape with the same familiar label and markings.

"I've already seen enough. You're telling me that *Alyosha* is hurting the children?"

"No."

"Exactly. There is no way he would be involved."

"It is he, the one who makes it happen. I show you this. Oh, can you not see? You, me, girl: we are against the same man. I am not your enemy. *He* is your enemy."

Fearless decided to play along. "Okay. So you'll take me to the girl and show me your tapes as long as I tell you where Federenko has gone?"

"So you know where he is."

"She's alive and okay?"

"She is safe. Yes. I can tell you this."

"I don't know where Federenko is—but I can find him for sure. One way or another, we're always in contact."

The vor's attention was drawn by something at the window. He walked back to the chairs and gathered his things. Before he put the revolver away, he opened its barrel and spun it. It had been loaded, every round slotted into its chamber. "Police outside," he said. "Running everywhere, looking for something."

Fearless got up and went to the window: a blur of pale blue shirts and black peaked caps hurried down the path that bisected the pool. A pot-bellied captain brought up the rear, barking orders.

"I let you think," said the vor as he strode to the door. "Because what you think is true . . ." He left the end of his phrase hanging. "When you have something for me, I tell you where Song is. I find you again, don't worry."

As the vor lay his hand on the door handle, Fearless threw him a bone. "I know something about the blond man—Wish is his name. He sleeps with a prostitute who works at the Cambodiana. She's a white girl with blond hair and her name is Larissa. If you find her, you'll find him—that much I can tell you."

The vor didn't look back but paused and nodded before he opened the door and walked into the corridor.

A minute later, dull thudding crescendoed up the stairs. Five policemen hurried in and surrounded Fearless in a semicircle.

Then the captain arrived, his heavy paunch leading the way. "You come with us, Mister."

"Am I under arrest?"

The captain muttered an order and two officers flanked Fearless.

"What are you charging me with?"

As the men applied a pair of handcuffs and shunted him from the room, others began emptying his duffel. In the corridor, Fearless counseled himself to keep his cool. It was a case of mistaken identity; they had taken him for the vor.

"I'm not Russian," he said, as they jerked him past the floral centerpiece in the lobby, the heels of their shoes clacking on the marble floor. "I'm British. *Anglais*. Do you understand?"

As they pushed him outside, onto the broad steps to the gravel drive, Fearless saw the vor standing by the police vehicles, bold as a bull in the middle of his paddock. As the policemen took him to the middle car and opened the rear door, the vor lit a cigarette and blew out a smoke ring.

"What's this about?" Fearless shouted.

"We have videotape," said the captain. "You. At Naga Bar."

"What? I'm not on any tape."

But Christ—the night he'd been drugged by Wish, he was surrounded by girls, sequins dazzling his eyes. Skin the color of honey, everywhere.

He felt himself falling into a soporific trance—as if a hypnotist had uttered a trigger word that sent him spinning. Arms dealing. More tapes. A twin sister traded out of love and shifting power. The bloody krama on the coffee table. But Song: alive and safe. That was something he had to hold onto.

A hand pushed his head down and he fell onto the back seat, the handcuffs pressing their metal gums into his wrists. The engine revved. The sky began to whirl in the window. For a second, before the little motorcade swept onto the boulevard, he caught a final glimpse of the vor, in the shadow of a shade tree, his hand raised to his temple in a perfect salute.

26

One knock, two short knocks, one knock, three short knocks.

Song shifted the edges of her krama to hide her face and hurried out into the dark yard.

Viktor walked past her, head down and shoulders hunched, and she fumbled to reattach the padlock to its hasp. Back in the house, he told her about the meeting with Fearless.

"I don't know where they go. I don't know why police take him. They say for the tape. Is he on the tape you give him?"

"I did not see the tape." But yes, there was every chance he was on the tape if Fearless had gone into the VIP Room on the night she saved him.

"Why give it if he is on it? I don't understand this man."

Viktor threw his bag onto a wicker seat and slumped down. He reached up and held the top of his head in his hands. Then he got up and paced around the room, the streetlights making a shadow-cage of the window bars on the wall.

"So he is like all the others. He is one of them?"

"No. He did nothing. I heard the girls laughing."

"You are sure?" Viktor frowned. "He is stupid, this man. In front of his face, he can't see . . . But he cares about you. He is worrying you are not safe."

"Why?"

"You tell me." He got to his feet again and paced.

Song thought for a moment, remembering Fearless as a zombie, the whites of his eyes, the animal drooling.

"There are many things I don't understand," said Viktor. "But the tapes are safe, yes? If only we can show him."

He closed his right fist and hit the side of his head.

"I am almost out of dollars. At this time I am hoping my job is finished. Now, even if I know where they go, I cannot follow them. And we have these tapes but no way to use them!" He muttered to himself as he dug into his bag. Hard metal objects knocked against each other.

"Where are you going?"

"There is one man of Federenko left in Cambodia." Turning, he held out a revolver, spinning the barrel to check it was loaded. "I am too good. Too weak," he said to himself.

Song thought of Fearless sitting in a bare room, waiting for his interrogators, or his face behind bars. She remembered the moment she had slipped the videotape into his pillowcase. It had been a long time since she had felt such guilt.

After Viktor had gone and she'd locked herself in, it occurred to her that there *was* a way in which she could help Fearless. Or rather, there was someone who could help him on her behalf: someone who owed her more than he could repay.

27

Blood and bright white light pulsed across Fearless's skull. His field of vision fractured into transparent polygons that slid and overlapped then divided like cells. He needed to stop resisting and making requests for the British embassy. When they realized this was a case of mistaken identity, they would put down their batons and offer him an apology.

CORRECTIONAL CENTER, read the English capitals beneath the squashed circles of Khmer script. He had expected to be taken to a police station for interrogation but instead the convoy delivered him straight to jail. After they had pushed him into a hut and forced him to strip to his underwear, they frogmarched him along a path between low sheds, from which shouts and hysterical laughter echoed. Bony fingers wrapped themselves around dirty metal bars.

Inside Block A, the guards shoved him into a cell like a veal crate packed with fifty eyes, twenty-five pink torsos, and ninety or so nut-brown limbs. The ceiling space was crammed with bundles of fabric and crumpled plastic water bottles dangling on lines.

When the door clanged shut, a duvet of humidity fell. He could see no window or means of ventilation—just black walls and flesh and the steam from the inmates' skin.

Fearless looked around and nodded at his neighbors. "Sua s'day," he mumbled apologetically as they parted to afford him a six-inch path.

"You come here," a voice called out. "Yes you! That's right."

A small man with pale skin was beckoning and nodding. "I foreigner like you. From Tokyo. Name is Toshi," he said. The man reached out a limp and delicate hand. He had an asymmetrical face, one eye lower than the other.

As Toshi helped him down onto a mat, a last defiant outburst rose out of Fearless's mouth: "I bloody well demand to speak to my embassy!" he shouted. His voice was ridiculous: a colonial bureaucrat, determined to impose an order that was obsolete.

The Japanese man raised his finger and shook it. "Here, no embassy or NGO allowed."

As Fearless tried to find a comfortable sitting position, his forearms clasped around his shins, Toshi ran through the prison's protocols. The exercise period had been and gone: an item that made Fearless's heart sink further. He had been held by police before, but never more than a few hours, and always confined to offices while his credentials were checked. This was different. Here, he was bombarded by devilish little horrors: the overpowering smell of unwashed bodies; the outbreaks of scabies on arms and chests; fresh welts delivered from gun butts or belts.

"But you know Block A is The Ritz!" said Toshi. "You pay, you have water, soap, more food."

After a while, Toshi shut up and a stupor fell over the men. Fearless bowed his head and silently mounted a defense of Alyosha that trumped anything the vor had said or thought. Yes, he could understand why Alyosha was a bête noire to the vor; some of his business dealings, including the voucher fund, were dubious—*To live with wolves, Fearless, you must howl like a wolf!*—but at his worst Alyosha was just a tolkach—a middleman, who could skillfully navigate the world of blat. Maybe the scale of his operations was different today, but his principles and standards would always remain the same.

In the early evening—or so Fearless reckoned—the cell door opened and the guards brought food: a mush of watery rice and "vegetable" soup, green and spotted with slick bubbles of grease.

"They eat rest," Toshi explained, when they left with half the pan still full. "They live here like us but sleep outside."

After dinner came toilet time—the tenth circle of Inferno. Here, the men lined up at a row of holes, the tiles all around slick with a brown, buttery slime. As Fearless peed into this paradise for flies, he promised himself he would hold his shit as long as possible.

Settling down to sleep on the hard stone floor was nauseating, sweaty elbows and knees and backs rubbing against him. Being six foot two was a distinct disadvantage: no prospect of stretching out or relaxing his limbs.

How long had these men been living like this? Day after day, month upon month: they were tougher and hardier than he would ever be. Already, after a few hours, his spirit was fractured. How the vor would laugh if he knew.

For a long time, Fearless sat awake in the dark, listening to the troubled dreams of Toshi and a medley of prodigious snoring. From time to time, a wave of sweat washed over his forehead—not from heat but from clear, cold terror. Mosquitoes buzzed everywhere—impossible to swipe away— feasting on every last inch of his body. For a short period he attained a kind of half-sleep, punctuated by strange images. A child's plastic doll on a mound of damp ash. A row of flip-flops stamping up and down in thick mud. The glowing teardrop of a flare, high in the sky, descending.

After first light changed the darkness from black to merely charcoal, the cell emptied out at an appointed hour: it was work time for the long-termers, according to Toshi, who would be bussed out to fields or local factories. Then, before the sun started to climb to its peak, the rest of them were finally allowed outside, their eyes squinting in the morning light. Fearless gulped the air and basked in the sun, relishing the heat on his chest and face. Shoved by the guards, he fell in line with the rest of the inmates, who had begun to circle their arms and stretch their legs ostentatiously.

"It is obligatory to exercise!" panted Toshi, squatting down.

Twenty minutes in, the sky changed color. Just as on Fearless's first morning in Phnom Penh, the rains thundered down. In an instant they were battered by curtains of water.

The men began to bellow and whoop, many of them stripping, rubbing and jigging their bodies to get clean. Another group gathered on the far side of the yard as the storm drain overflowed, gushing out sewage and frantic rats. A crack team of them cornered and caught one of the critters—a source of horrible, angry joy.

Even after the men themselves had been cornered and funneled inside, their excitement and ebullience remained contagious.

Toshi loaned Fearless an old T-shirt so he could dry himself and he wiped the water away, feeling almost fresh. The slogan emblazoned across the chest read FRANKIE SAY: RELAX DON'T DO IT!

If a new arrival were entering the compound now, they might have heard his laughter rising up from the windows: the hysterical cackle of a demented loon.

28

When the security guard flapped his hand at Bun Thim, he edged the Camry forward through gold-tipped iron gates. Song shrank back into the shadows of the back seat as he maneuvered under a carport draped with wisteria.

The villa adjoining the carport lay dark and quiet. A bolus of dread lodged in Song's throat. Bun Thim cut the engine and they waited, saying nothing, while the insects buzzed and chirruped their night songs. Her old friend had aged a decade in the last three days. His head drooped and his back had rounded, as if weighed down by an invisible hod of bricks.

A light came on and the hinges of a door whined. The old man, dressed in his habitual white shirt and gray slacks, doddered across the carport toward them, supporting himself on his cane. He gestured to Bun Thim, who ran around the car at once and opened the door to the back seat with a deferential bow. When he climbed in beside Song, his left side facing her, paralyzed and bisected by its dark vertical scar, she made no attempt to join her hands in respect.

"Oun. I wondered about you after they closed the Naga," he said, refusing to turn or make eye contact with her.

They—as if it had nothing to do with him.

"Pu," she said. "There is a barang whose name is Fearless. He was staying in the Naga apartment—I saw him several times. He is connected to Federenko but he is not . . . one of them."

The Chief nodded twice but still refused to look at her.

"Yesterday, they arrested him at the Hotel Le Royal."

The Chief lowered his head and pursed his lips. "Well," he said after a time, "I will do what I can."

It was the response she had expected; nevertheless, she was surprised by the surge of feeling inside her chest. Did he think that installing her in her cell in the Naga and making her toil under Thom day and night had absolved him? She looked at the grand house and the light behind the door and the flowers winding delicately around the posts of the carport. She had paid for it; her, Sovanna, the other girls: their nightly labors had made it all possible.

Deftly, she reached up and unwound her krama, sending the folds of it tumbling into her lap. She shifted her body and lifted the hair from the side of her head: movements that compelled him to turn and look at her.

Paralyzed or not, his expression couldn't help but betray the shock and dismay he felt at seeing her scars uncovered. They had power—these rivulets of welted flesh and tissue—and now she would wield it and no longer be its subject.

"You will do more than what you think you can," she said in her coldest voice.

He breathed out through his nose. "I give you my word."

He was exceptional, she realized. She respected him for that. In this country where so many were experts in forgetting, in burying their deeds and covering them with ashes, the past in him could not be denied. Was that weakness or strength? She didn't know or truly care.

For a minute, they sat side by side in the dark. She kept on staring at him, willing him to look again, but his eyes remained focused on the floor and his hands. How funny, the two of them, each with their facial scars! But his made him a warrior; hers made her a victim.

He opened his mouth as if he were about to say something. She wondered whether he might even dare ask her to sing. But then a silhouette appeared in the doorway. It stood there, a black shadow, its hand on the jamb.

She had never seen the woman herself. The shadow waited long enough to be sure it had been noticed, then slowly turned and walked back into the house.

"It is finished, p'oun," the Chief said in a whisper that almost sighed.

"No. There's something I still need to know. Why was Sovanna told that I had died after the acid? Tell me the truth. Why did you do that?"

"I . . . I couldn't keep Sovanna. I had to let her go." He looked back to the door at which the woman had appeared. "And the Russian offered to take care of her for me."

"But why say I was dead?"

"Because he wanted to be sure that she had no reason to run away. He didn't want her to think there was another life possible. She went on a trip, and when she came back we told her you had passed from unexpected complications."

"You made her world a lie."

"I didn't have a choice."

"Ha!"

The moment the Chief got out of the car, Bun Thim started the engine. The old man steadied himself on his cane and leaned into the window. "Never come here again," he said, before turning away.

That's fine, she said to herself. Let him have the last word.

29

Fearless lay in a fetal position, every sinew and tissue indurated by a second night on concrete. Hrrraaaak, spit-splat. Hrrraaaak, spit-splat. He could hear his fellow inmates traipsing to the washroom, sloshing water in buckets, and hawking phlegm onto the floor.

A guard entered and prodded Fearless's thigh with his foot. He mumbled something in Khmer and indicated Fearless should follow. Riddled with mosquito bites, and dressed only in rigid boxer shorts, Fearless rose and dragged his feet.

Outside, under unforgiving morning sun, they crossed a courtyard to another building, where Fearless was ushered into a box room office. An old Khmer man, a benign-looking grandfather, sat at a desk awaiting his arrival.

When he saw Fearless, the man exclaimed in shock. He reprimanded the guard, who hurried away.

"Ne vous inquiétez pas, Monsieur Nig-tan-galle," the man said. He indicated that Fearless should take the seat in front of him. "Thanks to me, the worst is over."

When he spoke, only one side of his face seemed to move. The other side was divided by a deep, livid scar.

The guard reentered with Fearless's clothes and duffel bag. He tossed Fearless's passport, press card, and driver's license on the desk. The old man nodded, and Fearless began to dress himself while the man reviewed a piece of paper through half-moon glasses. Several small items were missing from the duffel bag, but Laure's engagement ring was still there: too extravagant perhaps to pinch.

"A problem?"

"No. Nothing."

Satisfied, the old man signed and pushed the paper across the desk. It was one of those magic formulae, Fearless realized, that bureaucrats dash off to afford special freedoms.

"If you face any obstacles when leaving Cambodia, this will smooth things over."

He called the guard in again and pointed to a crate of beer, which was sitting in shrink-wrap in a corner of the office. The guard bowed, thanked him, and lugged it away.

"As for the video. Let it go. Is that clear?"

"But what was on the tape that got me arrested and locked up?"

"Let's say this is human error. No harm done. Though I'm afraid that news spreads fast these days."

From his briefcase, the old man produced a copy of yesterday's *Le Monde*, already folded to a quarter-page article. There, beside the famous image of Fearless saving the girl, was a report of his arrest for "agressions sexuelles sur trois enfants," followed by a potted biography that emphasized his reputation for taking photos of children in war. It must have gone to print only hours after the arrest. The coverage in the U.K. would probably be worse, he knew; nowhere else were downfalls greeted by the press with such malevolent relish.

"Before you leave Cambodia, Monsieur, don't ask any more questions. Don't contact your embassy. Mind the hair on your head."

Fearless nodded and picked up his duffel. "To whom am I speaking? Why are you helping me?"

"For that, you must thank your friend—the girl Song."

He was the Police Chief, then, from Dr. Andrew's story: not the self-satisfied potentate that Fearless had imagined but a meek, diffident, weak old man.

The metal hinges whined behind him as Fearless crossed the threshold of the jail. He held up his hand to shade his eyes from the glare. A minivan waited in the street, Bun Thim at the wheel. As he started toward it, the rear window slid down and the vor leaned out, beckoning him closer. Fearless stopped dead. Inside, beside the vor, leaning forward awkwardly, sat Wish. A dark swatch of clotted blood stained the white of his bleached hair.

"Hurry and get in," said the vor. "He does not know where Federenko is. But there is something he will show us. Something important."

And then he saw Song, sitting in the last row. She was free, not bound and bloodied like Wish. He didn't know what to say or do. She had saved and watched over him, disappeared into thin air, and given him—for whatever reason—a heavy responsibility. He had trusted her with a secret he had never told anyone else. What could he say now? Where should he begin?

But it was she who spoke first: "You come with us, please, Mister Fearless. Come."

As Fearless climbed into the passenger seat beside Bun Thim, Wish leaned forward and spat on the floor. "Mister fucking Big Shot Camera." The shirt on his back was also soaked with blood: he had clearly received the same treatment as Alyosha.

As Bun Thim drove them out of the city, Fearless turned to Viktor. Was he enemy or ally?

"Where are we going?" Fearless asked.

"You will see. It's good that you have strong shoes, but take this also." Viktor passed him a red and white checked krama.

"Did you find him at the Cambodiana?" Fearless asked.

"I found him in bed," Viktor sneered, cuffing the back of Wish's head.

The road grew bumpy and rutted and, save for Wish, they reached for the grab handles to steady themselves.

"Close windows," said Bun Thim. "I switch on AC."

Soon they were rattling through flat, arid country, a cumulus of dust billowing out behind them. When they came upon two dump trucks in convoy, Bun Thim slowed the van down to a crawl. The trucks turned and he followed onto a track that cut through a swamp of fetid water, leading to an expanse of scorched earth that was overhung by brown-black smoke.

"What is this place?"

"Stung Meanchey. They bring all garbage from Phnom Penh—dump here."

At a fork, the trucks veered off to reveal a landfill that appeared to be larger than a hundred football fields, where yet more trucks jettisoned their loads and bulldozers with caterpillar tracks tacked back and forth, shunting, jerking, and scrummaging against trash mounds. In the distance, a broad swathe of land smoldered away: a bituminous expanse fronded by fire. Gray plumes rippled three or four yards into the air, the odorless methane searing their nostrils. Lost in the mists and scrabbling everywhere, hundreds of people—garbage pickers armed with sharp, right-angled gaffs and improvised tridents—dug for whatever they could salvage, depositing it in the polypropylene sacks they dragged behind them. They were black with grime—from the soles of their feet to their broad-brimmed cricket hats. Every square inch of their bodies was caked with dirt.

At the edge of the site lay a makeshift village—a huddle of temporary-looking shacks and huts. Bun Thim pulled up in front of it, scuttling a group of children.

As soon as he cut the engine, Bun Thim wrapped his krama around his head and helped Fearless with his, tucking the ends into his shirt.

"What about me?" said Wish.

"Fuck you!" said Viktor.

When Viktor slid the door open, a miasma overwhelmed them while a loose crowd of locals gathered and inched closer.

Viktor jumped down and hauled Wish out behind him, booting him hard in the flat of the back before he had a chance to steady himself.

The trucks they had followed now reappeared from another direction. As each deposited its load, people crowded around, ignoring the warning of its bleating horn, pressing themselves as close to its opening maw as they dared. When the book-sized metal teeth came apart to release the rain of waste, the bravest jumped directly underneath, hoping to happen upon the choicest treasures before they were fair game for anyone. The moment a hill of garbage had formed on the ground, picks and spades were leveling it out, the people a hive mind, efficient and focused as ants.

"Let's go," shouted Viktor. "You show us the place!"

Wish snarled back, but Viktor kicked him twice as hard, propelling him into the sludgy waste.

"I show," said Bun Thim, taking the lead. He stretched out a Khmer machete he was carrying, its blade curved like the beak of a toucan, pointing in the direction of an escarpment at the edge of the site. They set out, Fearless and Song bringing up the rear, Song clamping her hand to her nose, Fearless trying not to gag or fall. After both of them had stumbled several times, their ankles sinking into the viscous waste, they reached out and clasped each other's hands, their forearms pressed together for balance as they climbed and descended a whaleback ridge. Ahead, Wish groaned and fell to his knees, only to be kicked again by Viktor—who never lost his balance nor betrayed the slightest distress at the mephitic fumes and suffocating heat.

Finally, Bun Thim stopped walking and put his fist on his hip. "Here," he said, indicating the bottom of the escarpment. He lowered his head and eyes as little avalanches of waste sifted from the face of the slope.

Viktor reached out and lifted Wish's chin. He pointed to Bun Thim. "He is lying—is it?"

Wish jerked Viktor's hand away. He cleared his throat and hawked a bullet of phlegm in his direction. "Even if they are here, you cannot find them! Everything is burned. Everything is moved."

Viktor withdrew a revolver, unbound Wish's hands, and shoved him. "Start digging," he said.

"What?"

"Start digging!" He brought the butt of the gun down on Wish's shoulder blades and Wish collapsed onto his hands and knees.

"What do I use?"

Viktor opened his mouth and bellowed: *"Use your fucking hands!"*

Feebly, Wish began to dabble in the garbage, his fingers picking out larger bits of trash. When Viktor kicked him again, he clawed out handfuls, his knuckles sinking deep into the black, oozing waste. When he had made an impression in one place, he changed position, muddling around, stopping occasionally to retch and hurl before returning to his diabolical task.

The rest of them stood, holding their breath. This is what Burke meant, Fearless thought, when he said terror is the ruling principle of the sublime. The mind is so saturated by one horrible thing it cannot begin to countenance anything else in the world. The soul is suspended in multiple senses: hanging in space, prevented from carrying on.

Soon, Wish was steeped in rancid slime. The semiliquid sludge of hair and brown waste—the kind you might find in a U-bend or trap, reeking of rot and snot and shit—was up to his elbows, smeared on his face and forehead. A scrap of foil-backed food packaging glittered on his cheek. His lips began to quiver and a sob escaped from his chest.

Fearless had had enough. "What the fuck is this for?"

Viktor kicked Wish. "Tell him what you are looking for."

Wish muttered something.

"Say it louder, bastard!"

Wish was crying now; he was crying like he'd cried that day in the tower block when Fearless had photographed him.

"The children. We . . . the children."

"Children?"

"Tell him which children."

"The children . . . from the Naga Bar."

By now, the sun had risen to its greatest height. Big, brutish flies crept all over their bodies.

"What? Why?"

"It was quick. They didn't suffer."

"Why, I asked you!"

"To make it all go away. Enemies love kompromat. And they love when bigmouths like you do their work. No Naga. No children. No tapes. It never happened."

"Who told you to do it? Was it Vasiliev? The African? The fat Black man Traoré."

Wish met his gaze. "It's Federenko," he said, incredulous. "It is always Federenko who gives the orders." His mouth curled into a scowl. "He told me to do it here because this is where they live. There are people who die every day under the trucks. The bodies get covered with garbage and are forgotten. Everything is Federenko's idea. Let me go!"

Viktor raised his arm and stabbed his finger at Fearless. "D'you see? *This* is what your friend is. I tell you."

But what good was a confession extracted in these circumstances? What wouldn't Wish have admitted in this moment? What wouldn't he have claimed Alyosha had done?

Viktor clapped his hand on Wish's shoulder. "Tell me where is Federenko. Tell me now and you live."

Looking just past Wish, where the escarpment began its vertical climb, Fearless's eyes fell on something astonishing—just there, its red brightness undulled by the sludge: a plastic letter *s*—red and lowercase. He bent down and pulled it out, its leather string wriggling like an earthworm.

The roar of a machine thundered above: a bulldozer working on the plateau of garbage shifted a fresh mound of waste right up to its edge. There was that moment of silence when a giant wave draws back to reveal the seabed before it crashes down. Song screamed and Viktor shouted "Get back!" and they were scrabbling, the mountain now shifting and beginning to avalanche.

They made it to safety, but the relief Fearless should have felt was irrelevant next to the letter, the burning letter in the palm of his hand. *No. No. Please God. No*, every molecule in his body cried out.

Then Wish was rolling on the ground, blood splashing all over his face. His head went one way and then the other as a right then a left then a right fist rained down on him, again and again and again and again. It was him—Fearless—who had thrown himself onto Wish and was grunting and huffing and pummeling wildly. He felt Wish's body crumple before he was lifted and heaved away. As he tried to shake Viktor off his back, Fearless fell backward, thrashing madly at smoke-laced air.

"Go on!" shouted Wish. "Just kill me! Just do it."

Fearless struggled to his feet and stood there, wheezing.

"You don't have the guts!" spat Wish. "You watch and take your photos and that is all you do." He tried to rise but fell backward again before bringing himself up and resting on his knees, his head bloodied and beaten, his clothes smeared with molasses. "Come on!" he shouted, as the others stood around him. "I killed the kids. So what! Nobody gives a damn."

Bun Thim stepped forward and, in one clean movement, with no sound or cry, slashed Wish's throat with his machete. Wish fell face-first onto the mound of trash. Above them, the bulldozer roared closer again, causing the escarpment to shed another layer of waste, and they all staggered back as cubic yards of garbage crashed down, leaving no trace of Wish's body.

Fearless seized Song's hand. Finally, they made it to the edge of the site, the ground sprung like a gym floor by the compacted bottles beneath the dirt. The locals remained gathered at a respectful distance. He wondered if they could guess what had happened on the site. Five had gone in, four had returned.

They got back into the van and returned to the city in silence.

30

Fearless sat on the stoop and smoked a cigarette. Above him, something flitted through the overhanging branches. He caught a glimpse of string; a flash of red; a little brown foot. Then, on the other side of the yard, one of the boys raced across the wall—too fast for the naked eye, made of air and out of reach. Fearless sighed, knowing he was hallucinating, and pressed his fingertips firmly to his eyelids.

After they had driven back to the house from Stung Meanchey, Song, Fearless, and Viktor sat down together and puzzled over the jigsaw of their individual experiences, the adrenaline of snapping the pieces together acting as both amphetamine and antivenom, overriding their exhaustion and neutralizing the garbage dump.

Fearless took in Song's life story, stretching back to her scattered memories of childhood, fragments of images and feelings she shared: a house full of starlight; the old bear she slept with that she longed for even now; a memory of eating buffalo meat and morning glory. Then she led them through the most recent weeks: the priest's whisper over the rice bowl; how she'd saved Fearless when he was strung out on Rohypnol; the night of her disappearance after he had accompanied her in the taxi; the explanation of the gunshots Fearless had heard; the cut on her arm that had bloodied the krama, which Viktor would later place on a coffee table in Le Royal; how she had left the tape inside Fearless's pillow, more in hope than expectation; her reunion with Sovanna; Sovanna's addiction to yama; the killing of Sokha. It was Song, he now grasped, who had set fire to Vasiliev's villa. And the Naga break-in too had been her work alone; this, when taken with Viktor's hit-and-run, was the series of "coordinated" attacks that had spooked Wish and Amos. Crucially, Fearless also learned from her that he himself hadn't laid a finger on the Naga girls.

Viktor told of his journey across the world, of how Amos and Fearless had foiled his revenge in the house on stilts. Fearless listened with vigilant skepticism as Viktor then shared what he knew of Federenko—how his nickname, The Chechen, was an exercise in branding that exploited the time he and Fearless had spent in Grozny, the Chechen Mafia being a byword for single-minded viciousness. Fearless found himself overwhelmed by old memories that were now recast in a stark new light. He remembered Khattab, Samir Saleh Abdullah al-Suwailim, the raven-haired Islamist whom he had photographed in Chechnya. Had Fearless been a tool—a man who provided Alyosha with an armored car, who took photos of his associates that they would use for propaganda—while secretly Alyosha brokered deals for arms? After Bosnia, those photographs of Khattab seemed to be proof that his partnership with Alyosha was blessed: they could go wherever they wanted, secure exclusives beyond others' wildest dreams. Fearless's mind reached back to the first time they had met. When his fixer had been wounded on his arrival in Sarajevo, Fearless had known that finding a replacement would be tricky. But he was desperate to get started—and Alyosha miraculously appeared, at the Holiday Inn noticeboard, boasting exceptional language skills and a line to black market diesel. Fate had brought them together.

Nevertheless, Fearless *had* been sure to do his due diligence. He knew the local legends about being conned by fixers—Fish, at *The Telegraph*, had woken naked in his hotel room, with every last item—passport, wallet, underpants—missing.

"Oh, I insist that you call my last employer," Alyosha had said, producing a *Washington Post* business card from his pocket. "Though you won't know if you can trust me until I prove it. And this is something I will do."

So much of Viktor's case against Alyosha seemed to hinge on Wish's testimony at the garbage dump. In Fearless's mind, Wish's confession merged with the confession of his father's killers, whose accounts had been wrung from them on the racks at Tuol Sleng. What good were such stories? What credibility did they have? But then the image of Pol Pot came to him again. "It is always Federenko who gives the orders," Wish had spat.

Fearless's mind flickered, refusing to settle.

"Look—I tell you. After paying my ticket, the house, the car, I have money only for food for a few more weeks. Understand? It is important that we help each other."

"I have ten dollar that Vasiliev give me," Song offered.

"I need to think," Fearless said, still hoping that some memory might revive the embers of faith in his friend. Like that time in the early days of Bosnia when Alyosha had shown him that the safest place to be was the hole created by the last shell shot. He had led him scurrying, from one to another.

"You must see this," said Viktor. He stood up and headed toward the Angkor Wat frieze that was hanging on the wall.

Song got up too and walked away, shutting herself into the other room.

Viktor had identified three specific scenes for Fearless: not sexual material, but moments in between, when the men had used the VIP room to negotiate and make payments. If they had any chance of finding Alyosha, it would depend on them unpicking the deal he was working on and pinning him down to a time and a place.

In the first scene, the two army men—Traoré and Vasiliev—entered the frame and sat down side by side. There was small talk and then a lengthy shaking of hands. After Traoré prized his fingers away, he handed over a sheaf of papers and then—it was hard to see—a small, dark pouch. Vasiliev, clearly pleased with the contents, walked out of the picture before Traoré received a "sweetener" that neither Fearless nor Viktor could watch. As soon as little Bopha entered in her summer dress, Viktor hit stop and ejected the tape.

In the second scene, Vasiliev was wearing a different set of clothes, sitting beside a man of Mediterranean appearance whose head of curls reminded Fearless of Mercury in Botticelli's *Primavera*. This time it was Vasiliev who produced the little black pouch, full of obvious wariness as he handed it over. When the man peered inside, a blinding flash filled the frame, as if it contained a sun reduced to the size of a walnut.

Finally, Viktor cued up one last tape.

"Wish told you this. The thing I am showing you now."

For a moment, Viktor knelt in front of the television, holding his palm up to block the center of the screen. Then he paused it and jerked his nose to the right-hand side of the picture.

"There. Watch. At the curtain. You see it shine?"

Fearless just caught it: a glint of gold.

Now, a man moved from left to right, blocking the view of the curtain entirely, before something else came in from the other direction, up close, which blacked out the screen completely. And then a hand swung down, a hand Fearless knew, perfectly front and center in the frame. The intimacy of that hand—the exact form of its fingers, the pattern of its veins, the texture of its skin—was repulsive. And yes, it was the exact watch. There: the special subdials with the little squares on sticks. The day Fearless had appeared with the tape at Le Royal, he now realized, Alyosha's surprise had been only that the tape existed. He already knew the depravity it would contain. All along, he had feigned his outrage and disgust. All along, he had lied about serving justice.

"Do people go to Phnom Penh for entertainment?" Fearless had asked. The answer was yes, for the darkest of reasons.

"So you will help," said Viktor. "Help me and help Song."

Fearless didn't know whether he was asking or telling.

"You think you can find him?" Viktor asked.

"I have some leads." The phone number he had was probably useless. But there were the stamps he had seen in Alyosha's passports. Sofia, New Delhi, Singapore, Luxembourg. Kabul, Mehrabad, Baghdad, Saudi Arabia. One of those had to have some significance.

Where to begin? His first thought was to ask Laure. He had to bite his tongue to stop a sob from rising up. What he had to do now was precisely her domain: investigate, dig, nose around, disrupt. She would lift the heavy stones on any path she took, exposing webbed dirt and writhing worms to the sun. He would call Jimmy, at least, when he was in transit in Bangkok, to see what he might turn up on Traoré. It was about time he made use of Jimmy's special access. "I'm Ministry of Defence," he would euphemistically declare whenever a stranger inquired about his career.

Viktor called Song out of her room and they arranged a motodop who would call on Bun Thim to drive Fearless to the airport. Meanwhile, Viktor set to work using Mao and Sokha's tape machines—the little "factory" they had set up with Thom—piecing together a compilation of the scenes he had identified, of which he then made multiple copies. Fearless took two—one to keep, the other to post to a safe address—and left another for Viktor to keep in Phnom Penh. This time the evidence would not disappear.

Song, for her part, cooked and served a simple dinner of rice and fried vegetables.

As she lowered the plate in front of Fearless, a necklace swung from the folds of her blouse, a dazzling pendant that danced on its chain.

Fearless recognized the blue-violet stone at once. "Where did this come from?"

"Sovanna."

"Do you mind—can I see?"

A strange feeling came over him as she placed it in his hand. Yes, it was exactly like the stone he'd bought Laure in Nairobi—now with the power to refract not just light but understanding.

The necklace had to be loose change from a bigger transaction, he grasped. But how stupid to involve tanzanite. The point of using precious stones for payments was the impossibility of tracing their origins: stones were money that laundered itself. But tanzanite—"found only on the foothills of Kilimanjaro," the jeweler had proudly told Fearless in his showroom—gave Fearless a pin to stick into the map.

"It's a beautiful stone," Fearless said, helping Song reattach the clasp. He had the urge to rest his hand on her shoulder.

After they had finished their meal with slices of fruit, and he had elbowed her aside to wash the dishes, the three of them waited outside for Bun Thim. Fearless took a last drag on his cigarette and stubbed it out with his foot in the dust. For a moment, the children were back in the air, racing down the street, past the gate, around the corner. He could hear their chatter and the rain of their flip-flops.

Then an engine ticked and rattled behind the gate.

As he grasped Viktor's hand, they held each other's gaze.

"You have the number I gave you?"

"I'll call. You have my word."

"Look after her," Fearless whispered. "She's alone and has no one."

He caught Song's eye as he walked toward the gate, but it was only when he hesitated that she ran up behind him, took his hand, and whispered, "Good luck."

PART 4

31

Fearless swept the old newspapers and road atlases aside and clambered into the back seat of Conrad's Peugeot.

Up front, Lucy and Conrad looked at each other.

"You ought to see these," said Conrad, passing him two folded newspapers: the English equivalents of the article in *Le Monde* about his arrest. Making that happen had been way above Wish's pay grade.

Lucy's gaze met his in the rearview mirror. She had always looked up to him as an older brother and example. *Why on earth?* he wanted to ask. He dropped the papers into the footwell. "Anything else?" he murmured. "Do I have anything left?"

It was silent in the car as Lucy pulled onto the motorway. There was too much to explain and no way to begin.

For a while, Fearless closed his eyes and pretended to sleep, but he knew what was coming. He clenched his jaw. Of course, there would be no trace of what had happened on the other side, but better to turn his head away and focus on the landscape's shades of green—seaweed, emerald, lime, aquamarine; to imagine time reversing, the road rolled back and trees sprouting from the plowed fields until the country was virgin forest.

By the time Lucy had driven them to the site of the fire, the afternoon light had begun to fade, the road rising, bordered by hedgerows, and then dipping onto the vista of the Seven Sisters: a white slice of chalk-cliff cake crumbling into the sea. There, to the right, should have been the old coast-guard cottage. Now, though the pale white walls and Georgian windows remained, the roof was nothing but a latticework of charred beams, only a shallow wave of tiles still clinging along the gutter.

Conrad and Lucy hung back as Fearless got out of the car. A silent numbness struck him as he lifted the police tape and walked up to the empty wreck. Circling the building, he lingered where the back door had once stood. Near the place where the cupboard had been, two large cast-iron pots sat in their usual position, containing a dry soup of sifted rubble.

Everything else—the records, the books, the diaries, the answering machine through which he might have heard Laure's voice one last time— was gone. Everything that had flowed into Laure and filled her life, of which this cottage had still been the mold, retaining the shape she had made in the world, had been incinerated.

Her folders! More than anything, he wished those had escaped: her thoughts, her efforts, the object of her attention. The investigation on which she'd been working off and on for two years—he knew bits and pieces but wanted to know more. He would have liked for her to guide him along the paths she had cleared; to know why she had explored one fork instead of another; the blind alleys tried and abandoned; what lay at the heart of the labyrinth.

He picked his way across the debris, moving through all the spaces in which they had lived and cooked and talked and loved and slept. Here was a board from the bathroom's tongue-and-groove wall which he recognized from flecks of its yellow paint, there the space their bed had once occupied. He closed his eyes and willed it all to come back to him, and for the merest instant he was back with her. Yes. There. She is standing in the doorway near the full-length mirror, smoothing down the sides of a dress. He is looking into her eyes. He had never looked into a lover's eyes so deeply and long before. It was terrifying. After they'd made love, he would always lie awake, eyes open, looking out into the darkness, listening to the contraction of the beams and the tapping of the pipes, worrying about mice when he heard a little scratching sound, only to realize it was just his own eyelashes on the pillow. But then, at the moment he felt most alone, her hand would reach out and make sure she was touching him.

But then a thought intruded: had the girl he carried from the fire in Sarajevo, across a threshold as charred as the one he was crossing right now, *really* been the daughter of the nursing home's director? Why had her tracksuit been unzipped and hanging open? Even back then, was Alyosha some kind of pimp?

Shaking his head and scowling, he walked into the garden, which looked almost untouched save for the cairn Laure had built. Now all the rocks lay scattered, no doubt lassoed by the firefighters' hoses. Passing through the gap in the back hedge, he wandered down the grassy slope toward the edge of the bluff, the dirty dishwater of the Atlantic lapping at its base in a swirling froth a hundred feet below.

Already, he could not remember her face. How difficult it is to fix it before she turns away, pushes the hair from her eyes, changes her expression in response to something.

As he neared the cliff's edge, he heard Lucy's footsteps hurrying and then slowing down just as he came within reach.

"Don't worry," he said, as she slipped her small hand into his. "I wouldn't have the guts to jump. What about you?"

She sniffed and punched him on the upper arm.

For a while, they remained still as the sun descended pink and low in the sky, ready to slip beneath the purple waters.

"Were your negatives inside?" she asked.

"No. Some things I was careful about saving."

"You think they were the wrong things?"

"Why, don't you?"

Lucy took her arm out of his and walked off to one side.

"I think . . . I think no one has to get beaten up, you know. I think . . . no one's beating you up anymore and you don't have to keep beating yourself up either. And I think that's what Laure always wanted you to feel."

Turning away from him, she bent down, picked a dandelion head, and blew at it.

"Let me ask you something, big brother. Why do you do what you do? Put yourself in danger. Take photos of all those things."

"Do you want my usual answer or do you want the truth?"

She smiled gently.

"I do it—I did it—because I wanted to face death, on my own terms. When you're riding on an animal's back there's no way it can bite you. And because, when I saw other people losing their sons and daughters and fathers, I could see my experience wasn't particular but general—everywhere—and I wasn't alone anymore. All the other pompous stuff about helping people was bullshit. Though I did want that too. I did hope it was worth something."

She turned back to him, the sun a great disc in the sky behind her. "So you took your grief and loss and you made something out of it. You said: I choose this. Which is special. That's the thing, isn't it? To know what you've been given and own it and make it good."

"Like your numbers?"

Lucy had been a math whiz kid, a prodigy who was accepted at Cambridge at the age of fourteen—though she had abandoned her degree before its final year, the first time her mental health had overwhelmed her.

"Like my numbers," she said. "And now you'll do it again."

She was right, he thought—though she had no idea what he was planning.

Beyond them, the sun now sank out of sight, transforming the horizon into a line of fire. A vivid rose light lit up their faces. When the moment was gone, the sea took on an immense gray calm, as still as water that has been left in a clear glass beaker, on a wooden table, in an empty room.

Fearless couldn't bring himself to tell them about Cambodia. Safely ensconced in the kitchen of Conrad and Lucy's house, he kept opening his mouth before pursing it again.

Lucy made a pot of tea. "I'm glad you're home," she said.

Was it home? He'd always convinced himself that he was a boarder, that his time here was temporary because his mother would recover. But since the age of twelve, on and off, he'd lived here for over seventeen years.

"You'll stay here until you're properly back on your feet," said Conrad. "Put things in order, then get back to work."

Fearless took his mug from the tray. "I can't stay. I may not even be here tomorrow."

Finally, he began the story, from taking his first step out of the plane in Bangkok to his last moments with Song and Viktor at Sokha's house. He felt like a toddler: *And then . . . and then . . .* desperately looking for his audience's approval, following the weather of reactions on Lucy and Conrad's faces.

He was most interested in how they responded to Viktor's story: how much did they believe the word of a torturer? "Because it could all be lies, couldn't it? Just look at the things they're saying about me in the papers."

They said nothing.

"I didn't do anything," he added. "Song knows this from the girls. She heard them."

It was all so improbable, so hard to explain. But that was precisely what Alyosha had said, wasn't it? "You make it so complex they must take you on trust." Alyosha: Conrad and Lucy would surely doubt him more readily. They couldn't understand what Alyosha had been for him. Their friendship had been a special island in his life that only Laure had stepped foot on—and only for a moment.

"And then I gave my word to Song," Fearless explained. "I said I'd track down Alyosha. That's why I came back—to start investigating."

"You're going to do what?" said Conrad. "Embark on a manhunt? I understand why you feel a debt to the girl. But she's safe. The children . . . that's beyond horrible. But what can you do? Report it to the authorities— even if the bastards are corrupt. And then what? The police chief asked you to leave the country. The only thing you can do now is what you do best. Find a way to write up the story. Let people know what's going on. Did you take any photos?"

Conrad hated anything to do with Cambodia; it had destroyed Fearless's father, his oldest friend. Even hearing the name Cambodia on the news, he once admitted, left a horrible, acrid taste in his mouth.

"You don't understand."

"Well tell me, then—what am I missing? These men are clearly dangerous."

Fearless felt a hard knot of anger in his solar plexus. He didn't say anything as Conrad pressed on.

"Even if you managed to find Alyosha, what exactly would you achieve?"

"Oh." Fearless scowled and clenched his teeth. "What the fuck do you know anyway?"

Conrad looked down, and reached up to smooth his comb-over.

"And what's the point of that stupid thing you do with your hair? Everyone knows you're bald!"

Lucy opened her mouth, then said nothing. She gathered the mugs and put them back on the tray.

"You need to stay, Joseph. Lucy, just tell him."

Fearless's chair grated on the wooden floor. He heard the door slam behind him. He walked up and sat on the staircase to the first floor, hearing something clattering in the sink, followed by muffled voices.

Beside him hung a gallery of his photos that Conrad had framed. A triptych from his series on arms dealing—factory production line, arms fair, fighter pilot. Just above that, a shot from his piece on the grave robbers of Port-au-Prince. Farther along: Wish, aiming his sniper rifle onto his crossroads and an old Serb weeping, cradling a dead dog in his arms. A vast sky stretching over the sprawling refugee camp at Goma. A grandmother in Grozny holding a dripping paintbrush, the daubed letters on a wall reading PEOPLE LIVE HERE.

How beautiful. How beautiful he had made so much suffering in so many places. In his angriest moments, he had wanted his photos to be accusations. To place viewers at the scene, to deny them an alibi. But instead their beauty just made it easy for them to say, *Ah yes, there are terrible things happening in the world*, before turning to the stocks and shares or showbiz pages. He was a pond skater, darting here and there but always on the surface. Even if he were to break through to the dark depths below, he would only succeed in drowning himself.

The last picture caught Fearless's attention: a line of men in camouflage kneeling on a mountainside, shrouded in mist, bowed in prayer. Here and there, above them, emerging from the fog, were the heads of pale horses and the distant peak of a mountain. This was the meeting Alyosha had referenced when they'd first spoken of Nairobi, the one with Emir Khattab, the Saudi Arabian jihadi who had led his band of fighters in the vivid green hills of the Chechen Caucasus. Of course, it was the Islamists who had been the perpetrators of the bombing in Nairobi: Fearless had seen their toughness for himself, their unyielding hearts and faith.

Khattab came down to him from the landing above. Fearless didn't turn to look, but he knew the sound of his footsteps. He was a big bear of a man, made more imposing by his tall papakha and layers of khaki clothing and his long hair tumbling onto his shoulders in ringlets. There was nothing strange about his presence in Conrad's house.

Long before they'd met, Fearless had seen the propaganda video of Khattab, bellowing in triumph in front of a line of Russian corpses. But the Khattab he knew was placid and soft-spoken. Beneath the hat, hair, and beard, his face was young, its brown skin entirely free of blemishes. He was at ease when Fearless photographed him, happy to oblige every request; his image was his brand, through which he could terrify enemies and seduce new donors.

Khattab came closer and sat down on the stairs just above Fearless. Fearless felt his breath caress his neck, heard the whisper and crease of his waterproof parka. He could smell the leather of the weightlifting glove that Khattab wore on his damaged hand, its fingers blown off in a bomb-making mishap. Khattab reached out and laid that glove now on his shoulder. "We fight to the end," he said, in his soothing voice. "Whether we win or not. Whether we are defenseless or armed." It was Alyosha's voice that Fearless heard when Khattab spoke, for it was always Alyosha who had translated between them.

Fearless didn't turn to face Khattab. But he reached his arm across his chest and laid his hand upon the glove.

"Even if they kill us, Fearless, it does not matter. Because you and I, we know one thing, don't we?"

Then Fearless turned to look. He was about to call Khattab by his real name—Samir Saleh Abdullah al-Suwailim—the musical repetition whose susurration Alyosha so loved, which he used to chant under his breath like a mantra—but there was no one there, just the last light of evening glowing red and green through the stained-glass window.

Down below, Conrad insisted something was true and Lucy groaned back. Then the French windows rattled. Lucy's little dog barked. Conrad muttered something and another chair scraped across the floor.

For the rest of the evening, Fearless shut himself in his room, like a teenager who feels he's owed an apology. He could smell the burned ashes of the cottage in his nose; phrases from the newspapers whispered in and out of earshot.

Later, long after darkness had fallen, a light through the window, at the end of the lawn, caught his eye. A silhouette moved in the trees, ballooned, then disappeared. Downstairs, he let himself out of the back door, his footprints charcoal on the dew of the moonlit lawn. A hedgehog, surprised, curled in a defensive ball. The coppice leaves shivered. An owl hooted above.

The tree house in the broad fork of the sweet chestnut was a marvel, part Dr. Seuss, part Thoreau, built when Lucy was a child. On the porch outside the door, her walking boots sat side by side. Fearless removed his boots too, stubbing out his cigarette and lobbing it into the bushes.

As he pushed open the door, he saw that one of the night-lights was blown out, but another survived to cast a flickering glow over the den, its walls covered with paper tablecloths teeming with scribbled equations and algorithms.

Entering, Fearless remembered to duck his head, dodging strings of origami swans and Mardi Gras beads and the giant paper koinobori in sea green and flame colors which swam in the invisible currents of air. On the floor he stepped carefully between small piles of books, some Lucy's, some Conrad's: Popper, Wallace Stevens, Carl Jung's *Memories, Dreams, Reflections*; texts on number theory; a biography of Turing; his own battered copy of *On a marché sur la lune*. Seeing the slim spine of Zweig's *The Royal Game*, he was twelve again, entering this very same space.

"I taught myself chess," Lucy had said to him.

"I can play. But I'll be too good for you," he had replied; he had already mastered the rudiments of the Sicilian.

But after ten moves, he knew: he could spend his life on variations—Sveshnikov, Dragon, Scheveningen, Najdorf—but he would never see what she could see. She had grasped who he was, how he would play and how far he could reach. She was six.

Even today, he was still her chess king. Of little power and much bigger than her, but always in need of protection.

Now, as the boards creaked beneath his weight, Lucy stirred and turned under her duvet. Her mousy hair—which had not seen a brush in several days—had fallen in a clump across her boyish face and Fearless reached down to tuck it behind her ear.

With Laure gone, she was the last arbiter he had. He wanted her to tell him what to do and how to make something from this mess.

As he drew back the duvet, Large the dachshund raised his head, registering Fearless's familiar presence before going back to sleep. Fearless moved him aside and lowered himself onto the mattress. The last nightlight died, leaving a bitter scent in the air, and he felt a darkness beyond darkness descend upon him, as if the atmosphere of the earth had been ripped away and they were exposed to a vast and starless emptiness. But then Lucy mumbled something and spooned his body instinctively, her arm reaching around and pulling him close.

For a moment, he was taken back to Itum-Kali, to the foolish trip Laure and he had made to the dead city. Never mind that he was falling ill; he had been determined to accompany her. Alyosha had been livid afterward: "You would insult me by going alone!" The weather had turned angry—crazy to brave the mountain passes—and they had been forced to spend the night in an abandoned stone hut, its battered roof punctured with an Iceland-shaped hole. He remembered gazing up at thunderclouds and shivering under a blanket, and then—what grace—Laure putting her body behind him. "I'm here," she whispered.

And then, in the night, he'd stirred and they were facing each other, the little hairs on her wrist touching the hairs on his: just barely, right at the very edge of feeling.

When they got back to Grozny, she went missing for a few hours.

"I went to call Richard and tell him it's over."

"Who's Richard?" Fearless said, even though he already knew the name of her boyfriend.

"I told him I'm in love. Said I would give him back his ring. He didn't take it well."

"Who are you in l—"

"Don't you bloody dare!"

As he listened to the gentle shhh of Lucy's breathing, tears now brimmed in Fearless's eyes. If Laure lived on anywhere, it was in the quest that had driven her: the search for truth; the fight for justice. It was a blessing, really, that Lucy wouldn't wake up. He didn't want to hear anybody's objections.

The next morning, Fearless woke alone in the tree house. He found Conrad at the kitchen table, perusing the paper in his dressing gown.

"There's a plate in the oven for you."

"Good old Lucy. Where's she gone?"

Conrad didn't look up. "Walking the dog," he said quietly.

Fearless sat down opposite him and started eating his bacon and eggs. His eyes took in the old, familiar tableware: chipped willow pattern plates, the big yellow teapot.

"How is she?" he asked Conrad.

Conrad paused.

"Is she stable?" Fearless asked.

"Well. She can go a week without speaking to me. I guess that renders her sound of mind in your opinion."

Fearless laid his knife and fork together in the French way: on the right-hand side, just as his mother had taught him. The knife tip pointed to a pair of yolk-smeared swallows: star-crossed lovers that were taking to the skies.

"She sees someone," said Conrad, "to talk things over. You could do that."

"Does it sound so crazy, everything I said about Cambodia?"

"I didn't mean it like that. I just want you to be at peace. I was wrong to react how I did. I'm an old man—you're right."

"It was important for me to go there. It's funny, but I realized that some part of me had never really grasped that he was dead. And I felt close to him in a way I'd never felt before."

Conrad rested his hand on Fearless's forearm, and then did something that surprised them both. He reached up and lightly stroked the curls on Fearless's head, which were now growing out for the first time in years.

"I saw the moment he died. I could picture it clearly. The shock and the struggle and the quickness of them bursting in. I could feel his surprise and his fear and his pain. I hope it was short. It must have been just a moment." He paused. "As for the rest of what's happened, I know it sounds preposterous."

"Not at all. Only fools think they decide what reality can be."

"So the powerful are fools, then."

Conrad nodded and laughed through his nose. "Touché," he said. "But please tell me, Joe—you track down Alyosha and then what happens? What will you do when you come face to face with him?"

"I'll think of something." Fearless was aware how childish it sounded.

"What matters most to him? *That's* what you need to work out if you're going to find him."

"It's this deal that will allow him to go back to Russia. But then, he's also in love with Song's sister Sovanna."

"Two loves."

"Which are mixed up. He only has her because he has power over Vasiliev."

"Okay. So tell me, then. What help can I give you?"

"He has a private plane. I remembered him drunkenly talking about it. A sports team once owned it. The Cardinals, I think."

"So you might be able to find its registration."

"And track where it's been. Even where it might be going."

"I'll see what I can do. Make some calls this morning."

They went to Conrad's study—a den crammed with papers and hardback volumes, decorated with oppressive Laura Ashley wallpaper. Fearless called Luke to arrange a meeting at his chambers, not stopping a second longer than he needed to give his old friend an explanation, and also made contact with Yelena and Levin to find out whether Federenko had surfaced in Moscow.

"Any joy?" Conrad asked.

"It was always a long shot. It's only after the deal that he can return to Russia. That's what he told me, for what it's worth."

"Okay. Off you go, then. Let me get to work," said Conrad, opening the door and guiding him toward the threshold. "Just one thing," he said, before he closed the door. "Will you see your mother before you do anything?"

Fearless had known that this was coming.

"I'm glad you still visit her, Con. But why? What's the point? Is it guilt? Because I was the one who hid what was happening to her—you remember that."

"You were twelve years old!"

"I knew what I was doing. And when you discovered the truth, you did everything you could. I remember that day on Harley Street. Waiting for the diagnosis. In that big squidgy chesterfield. Funny the things that stay with you."

"You shouldn't visit for her sake. But for you. You know that."

"Do you remember? Going back to the house after they'd committed her. All the orchids dead. She was obsessed with those fucking orchids."

"Let me make these calls. But visit her because I ask you, Joe." His voice was quiet and low and calm.

32

Fearless gulped down a cup of tea and drove up to Euston in Lucy's old car for the meeting with Luke. First he would confirm his plans for the meager money he had left, transferring all of it to a numbered Swiss account. Then he would check over the instructions for his will; Lucy would be named as his sole beneficiary—the future inheritor of the payout from Laure's insurance. She was the closest person to him and also the most vulnerable.

"You've joined the beard club!" Luke chuckled when he entered. He instinctively stroked his thick ginger wedge as if to denigrate Fearless's efforts. "And look at your hair. I like it, I must say."

Luke's office was in its habitual state of chaos: files arranged in haphazard towers; a rusted bicycle leaning against the wall; a leather holdall spewing muddy rugby kit, a handful of aluminum studs tumbling onto the floor. But the visible chaos was in inverse proportion to the clarity of Luke's mind and command of his domain. Before he handed over various papers for signing, he skimmed every page to double-check the contents, wheezing as he peered through his glasses at the text.

"Don't forget to breathe."

"Fuck you, tosspot. If you weighed twenty-five stone and played tighthead every weekend, you'd be snorting too."

While Luke bound and filed the completed documents, Fearless took pen and paper to write a letter for Lucy. He crumpled up a first draft and threw it into the bin before he managed to strike the tone he wanted.

When he had finished, he sealed the letter and attached it to the will, which he signed in all the requisite places.

"I don't suppose you're going to tell me exactly what you're planning," Luke said.

"It's best that I don't."

"I can guess."

"It may not come to it. This is just . . . a backup."

"All the same . . ." Luke sighed.

When they rose from their chairs, he walked round the desk and pulled Fearless into a breathtaking bear hug, releasing his grip only to take Fearless's arms from his sides and position them around him before pulling him even closer. Fearless was happy to be held in Luke's cloud of too much coffee and day-old sweat. In fact, he made sure to breathe it in. If things played out the way he hoped, its memory might be all he had left of his friend, whose love, intertwined with Jimmy's since their schooldays, had been a seam in his life, a message in Brighton rock.

Luke let go of Fearless and guided him out of the office.

"Stop drinking so much, will you—and eating so much pizza," Fearless said.

"Okay."

"And lay off the coffee and cigarettes."

"Fuck off." The best way to say goodbye, it seemed to both of them.

Outside, Fearless strolled around the area for a while, smoking a cigarette under flat, bright sunshine as blackbirds darted through the foliage above, casting lines of song from tree to tree. When a flock of them burst out into the sky, Conrad's request hit him—"Because I know you care"—and he made his way back to the car.

"You're Mrs. Nightingale's . . . *son?*" the receptionist asked.

"I've been living abroad," he mumbled as he signed the visitors' book. But what would it really matter, he wanted to say, if he visited every week, when she didn't even recognize him?

Opening the door to her room, he saw her in profile, her features hidden by frizzy hair. They'd let it grow and pinned it up ham-handedly; her old self would have been utterly mortified. He wondered if she would feel the same when she saw *his* hair.

Unheard, he watched her for a moment, sitting in her wing-backed chair and staring into the dense, green shade of the garden. It had always irritated him: her endless concern for plants and flowers; her obsession with her orchids' flourishing and well-being.

"Is that you, docteur?" she said when she spotted him, in the thick French accent she refused to discard.

"It's Joseph, Maman."

"Jo-zeff. Jo-*zeff*?"

She started to turn and pursed her lips, but then turned back again to watch something happening in the large oak tree, deep inside the dappled light on its broad, lush leaves.

"Zat squirrel is *naughty*. Look at what ee's doing."

Fearless sat down in the plastic chair opposite her. Her face had changed in some ways—the liver spots were more numerous—and her spirit was very different from what he had guarded in his mind. There was an unwavering stillness to it: a hard, inner core.

He had reduced her, he realized, to the thwack of the cane across his cheek, to the year he had lived under cover in his own house. During his first days in Bosnia, he had told himself that that time had been good training: it had taught him how to scurry from one place of safety to another, to skulk in shadows and corners, to live on his own resources; it had taught him that an attack could come at any moment. Most of all, he had learned to make loneliness his calling: the photographer, always apart, even in a stampede.

For a while, his mother told him about the soap opera of garden life: the birds that came every day to the feeder, the vagaries of the weather, the bounty of the fruit trees. It was always a point of principle with him to listen to her attentively—his defiant response to how little he felt she had listened to him. Yet he was struck by the urge to hold her, to kneel down by her chair, to reach out and take her body in his arms.

When she had run through the thoughts that floated on the surface of her mind, Fearless tried to say a few words of his own. He mentioned places and people that he hoped might trigger some kind of recognition: his father; the name of a road on which they had once lived; her favorite actor, Charles Dance; Oxford; Beachy Head. Soon, he had run out of ideas. He contemplated asking about Haiti. Surely *that* would push her buttons. Maroons. Voodoo. The Tonton Macoutes who had disappeared her cousin. But mentioning Conrad was the thing that lit a spark.

"You know Conrad? Don't talk to me about that man. What did he do? I don't remember . . . but it was bad."

He tried to shift her focus onto the garden again, pointing out the giant wafting heads of the hydrangeas.

Then, without warning, she said, "Will Laure come back?"

"What do you mean, come back?"

"She came here only yesterday."

"No—that's not possible."

"She showed me the photo of her baby. I saw it. Black-and-white. Funny-looking thing. Are they okay?"

However he chose to respond, she would forget soon enough.

"They're doing brilliantly."

"That's good. Is the child a boy?"

"A little girl called Rose. Laure is . . . a brilliant mother."

"You're a friend of theirs? You have seen the baby yourself?"

"Yes . . . She looks just like you, they say."

He was going too far—but what harm would it do? He could turn back time. There was, he realized, some comfort for him, a grace, that this was all real to her.

"It's funny, you know. Your eyes are like my son's. But you're older. And . . . from a different place."

Something caught in her throat and she began to splutter.

Quickly, he got up to pour her a glass of water, but she choked on it and angrily waved him away. Each cough grew louder, seizing her body; spittle began to gather in the corner of her lips.

A care assistant entered. "I think we're tired now, aren't we, Agnes?" The plump, rosy-faced woman rested a hand on her back.

"I am *Madame Nightingale*. Not Agnes. Tu vas me tutoyer?"

"Yes, dear. What say we have a nice lie-down. It's about that time. I'll draw those curtains."

Fearless stood to the side as the woman helped his mother onto the bed, plumping her pillows and straightening her body. How difficult it was for her to move just a few inches; hard to square with the vision he always carried in his mind, of her thundering down the hallway, cornering him, and grabbing the cane from the orchid—the first thing to hand she might use as a weapon.

"In one way, it's a relief," Conrad had told him after her diagnosis. "She never meant to hurt you. The person who hurt you wasn't her."

But Fearless had found that her grief and love were both things he could now doubt.

"You have to watch them," his mother whispered after the carer left. "They steal things. But I keep my things safe—in a secret place."

It struck him what a journey she'd had to end up here, inert, on this mechanical bed with its hard metal edges and its black, rubber-tipped levers. And how misunderstood she'd been. She had been a young hotel waitress, pregnant to a strange but charming traveler. Were they in love? Fearless had never been sure but, in any case, he had come back for her to "do the honorable thing" and bring her into his alien English world, in which she had never truly found her ease before he died on an adventure in a yet more alien place. And simultaneously, as if life had been determined to swallow her whole, she'd been struck unexpectedly by mental illness.

And her orchids—he'd never articulated it before—had been her way of keeping home—her Haiti—alive in their house.

My mother.

As he squeezed her upper arm to say goodbye, he made one last attempt to reach her, this time in French. "Maman. Do you recognize me?"

But she shook her head.

"Because I want you to understand that I'm going and I might not see you again. There's something I have to do and if I do it right, I'll have to hide. For a while. A long while. I want you to understand."

She kept on staring into the garden.

But when he put his hand on the door handle to take his leave, she called out:

"Jojo. It looks like rain. Don't forget your raincoat when you go outside."

He stepped into the flowered corridor that smelled of boiled vegetables and synthetic fabrics that no one made any more. "It was never your fault," he murmured, before he closed her door.

At reception, there was no staff member at the desk. As he signed out in the visitor's log, he went back through the pages for the satisfaction of proving that his demented mother had been wrong.

But she had told the truth: Laure had indeed visited. How fresh the pain when he saw her handwriting, its neat regularity, the bold flourish on the tail of her G—written the very afternoon before she had died. So the picture—black-and-white—must have been the ultrasound she had pinned to the fridge and never had the chance to show him in person.

As he drove back to Conrad's house down the winding Sussex A-roads, he wondered why Laure had decided to pay that visit. Fearless had told her it was pointless to tell his mother she was pregnant, and yet she had gone, and somehow got through to her.

"Chişinău, old boy," Conrad shouted as soon as he opened the front door. "That's where the plane is. Landed two days ago. Damned if I can pronounce it. And I have those stills from the videotape you asked for."

"Kee. Shee. Now!" shouted Lucy from the kitchen.

"And I've already found a contact there—though you'll never guess who."

Conrad emerged from his study, still in his dressing gown, waving a pink Post-it note above his head.

"Chişinău. Moldova. Transnistria," Fearless said, remembering his pool-playing buddy Vadim and his stories of life in the 14th Army in Pridnestrovie. Federenko had taken his jet to the nearest international airport and then, in all likelihood, driven to Tiraspol. Fearless remembered hearing him shouting on the phone, angry that the terms of his deal had been changed. What if the goods he needed were being shipped from Transnistria? Maybe he'd gone there to oversee arrangements in person.

Fearless took the Post-it from Conrad's hand.

"You're kidding me. Christ. Does he know what happened to Laure?"

He felt a pang of jealousy even now, after all these years, in his chest at the name and number of someone who had been close to her.

"He must do," said Conrad.

"At least I can tell him in person."

"What do you mean?"

"Alyosha will move on if I wait. I know what he's like."

"But do you? Really? Isn't that the crux of everything that's happened? And we still have so many other leads to explore. Stop a moment and think. Give it one more day."

But Fearless was already heading up the stairs. When Conrad came to find him, his duffel was almost packed.

"I made a call, Joe, and put some money in your account. You can pay it all back when the estate's sorted out."

"I can't take it. I can use my credit cards, Con."

"It was money for a rainy day. And it's cats and bloody dogs."

33

As soon as the plane touched down, the senses and muscle memory of his old self began to stir. Hire car. Road map. Chewing gum. Coke.

The black plastic of the dash bounced the summer heat onto his chest as he rolled down the broad boulevards of Chişinău, wary of the wired routes of the ringing trolleybuses. Mid-century Soviet architecture loomed on either side, but here and there anomalies had survived the century of upheaval: public buildings with French stylings and classical proportions; Greek, Byzantine, and Ottoman-influenced Orthodox churches. Since independence, new offices and shopping centers had sprung up: space-ships from the future, with blue steel columns and mirrored glass facades.

At the appointed meeting place—the tree-covered island of Ştefan cel Mare Park, where towering mulberries and acacias provided shade—Fearless found a bench by the central fountain. Flecks of spray were carried to him by the breeze as he watched young mothers congregate nearby, the fat hands of their babies reaching up from Victorian prams, and teenagers splashing each other on the other side of the water, their forms broken by glistening curtains of spray.

A tall, dark shadow slanted across him. "Small world," a voice said before its owner came into the light.

"One degree of separation," said Fearless, reaching out to take the bony fingers that had been offered. Fearless had seen photos of Richard before, but he was struck by how handsome he was in person.

"Do you know?"

"Yes. Yes, of course. I thought about coming to the funeral, but . . ."

"No need to explain."

"She was an important part of my life."

"And you to her."

"You're being generous."

"You're the generous one—helping the man who stole your fiancée."

"Stole? I think you're overdoing it a bit."

"Wrong word, then."

"She chose you. And she was never sure of me anyway. Still, for a while, I had an unhealthy interest in you. At first, seeing your work would drive me mad. But then I realized losing out to an idiot would have been worse. She chose someone who has something to say. There was comfort in that."

"I had something to say?"

Richard appeared conventional and slightly studious, but Fearless could appreciate the frankness Laure would have valued.

"Anyway, it's a point of honor that I help you now. Otherwise, I'll hate myself for being petty. So—what can I do?"

"I need to know everything—everything I can about Transnistria. It's the place I need to get to. At least, I think it is."

Richard sat down on the bench beside him.

"Transnistria. Okay, then. A thin caterpillar of land—125 miles long, twenty wide, sandwiched between the Dniester River and Ukraine. Most people in the West have never even heard of it. They think you're making the whole thing up when you tell them. And in a sense they're right because, officially, Pridnestrovskaya Moldavskaya Respublika does not exist. Even though it has state institutions and its own flag and money and stamps and even passports for its citizens, it's still not recognized—save by the men who run it."

"It's a breakaway state."

"Yes, with its own micro–Cold War against the country of which it's officially part. And that means you can't do business legitimately there—there are only unofficial or criminal markets—which has made it the western edge of a new Silk Road that stretches all the way to the east of Russia, taking in Siberia, Afghanistan . . ."

"A new *criminal* Silk Road."

"Indeed. A massive zone where Russian is the lingua franca. And that's a key thing: Transnistria is inextricably tied to the motherland. It's common knowledge that it shares profits with Russia from the sale of 'unnecessary' arms and ammunition stockpiled in the old army depositories. Thousands of tons of matériel flow out over the border with Ukraine, which is easy to cross with its farmland and forests of fir trees. It couldn't be simpler— you drive the weapons down the road. From there, they go to Odesa, the Black Sea, and . . ."

"Anywhere."

"The Middle East, Africa, the Caucasus."

"Drugs too?"

Richard frowned. He pulled his mouth to one side. "Money-laundering. Sex trafficking . . . but drugs? Not so big."

"Not necessarily illegal drugs. Pharmaceuticals I mean. You see—the person making this deal also demanded a quantity of needles."

"Needles?"

"I overheard it—it was definitely needles that he said." The phone conversation coupled with the Rohypnol in Alyosha's toiletry bag had convinced Fearless that drugs were a crucial part of the deal.

"Odd question—but was it a *Russian* speaker you overheard?"

"Yes."

"Then maybe the deal involves Iglas. Do you speak any Russian? *Igla* means needle, but it's also the name of the surface-to-air missile system."

"Antiaircraft guns . . . I didn't even think."

"Each of them would be worth maybe fifty thousand bucks. For a deal in this part of the world, that's much more likely."

A big-money arms deal—just as Viktor had alleged. Fearless's mind raced through all the times Alyosha had agreed with him when he railed against the spread of weapons around the globe. "Bullshit!" he muttered.

But then, he could see a logic in Alyosha's view. For years, the USSR had had the best tanks and missiles—a space program—while its citizens had made do with next to nothing. Now, they could cash them in to pay for the things they'd lacked.

"I'm sorry. It's really not bullshit, I assure you."

"I wasn't referring to you, Richard—no offense."

"None taken."

The air felt thicker now, saturated with traffic fumes and biting insects. An Igla, Fearless remembered, sparked the Rwandan genocide, when one of them shot down Habyarimana's jet. He had often dwelt on it—that a rocket from one man's shoulder could be enough to light the touchpaper for a million deaths.

"There are definitely Iglas in the Transnistrian stockpiles," said Richard. "And for all I know, they're still in active production. The massive steelworks in Rybnitsa, the Tochlitmash or Elektromash factories—they're fronts for the manufacture of all sorts of things. On one conveyor belt they turn out goods for the civilian market—transformers, electronics, cables, pipes—and on the other, all manner of weapons. Pistols, assault rifles. Mortar tubes, grenade launchers."

Elektromash. Электромаш. The engraving on the back of Federenko's Rolex.

"How do I get in? If I wanted to."

"To Transnistria? Not difficult. Anyone can see the sites: statues of Lenin, the Heroes' Cemetery—all the Soviet monuments in pristine nick. They might even give you a tour of the cognac factory. But where you're thinking of . . . well . . ."

"I can try."

"Of course. But . . ." Richard sighed. "Look—just ask yourself. Out of all the illegal weapons deals around the world, the billions of dollars in arms—$60, $70 billion every year—how many of these dealers are ever brought to justice? I mean *anywhere*. How many can you name? Soghanalian for selling to Saddam Hussein? What did he get? A couple of years before his deal with Clinton. Who else?

"The problem is this, Joseph. How the hell do you trace these deals? What evidence can you get out of the chaos of a war zone? And what connects the dealers to the arms on the ground? It's not as if they're present when the weapons change hands! And even if you do catch someone, what jurisdiction do you prosecute them under when the deals cross borders and go through secret channels? Under international laws in international courts? As if! And remember, that's not even taking into account the fact that these men are nearly always connected to—or sponsored by—intelligence agencies, military officials, senior politicians, et cetera et cetera.

"No. Arms dealing is the perfect crime. The crime that sums up our age better than any other. Who we are. What we value. Our inability to work together.

"There can be a war on drugs. There can be a war on poverty. But there is no war on war. Not now. Not ever."

"I know that," said Fearless. "I agree completely. But I think Conrad must have told you this. This thing—it's personal. It doesn't matter how foolhardy it seems. I have no choice."

Richard helped Fearless mark up his map: the route into Transnistria through the buffer zone town of Bendery; the capital, Tiraspol, and its principal street, along which he would pass the Parliament Building and City Hall; the approximate location of the military depository near Cobasna, where Vadim and his crew of "peacekeepers" would have yawned away their tours of duty.

"I guarantee that the roads around it will be blocked."

"But I could go cross-country. Just here, perhaps. Park somewhere and go on foot."

"If you want to be thrown into a police cell, sure. Whatever happens, take my address and phone number."

As Fearless drove east, the economic deprivation of Moldova revealed itself. Rutted roads of compacted dirt branched off the highway at regular intervals. Young children ran around in bare feet and old people called after them from porches, a generation of working-age adults gone abroad in search of employment.

Under the circumspect glare of a peaked-capped guard, he passed through the border checkpoint and crossed a bridge that spanned the black expanse of the Dniester. This was the entry into a Soviet dreamland: here, a statue of Lenin on a thirty-foot-high pillar, an asymmetrical concrete wing soaring from his back; there, a Soviet tank squatting heavily on a brick plinth.

Soon, he was rattling across open country again until, as expected, he encountered the first roadblock: a candy-striped gate manned by two sullen guards. He wound down his window and greeted the one who bothered to rouse himself.

"Bună ziua. Good day! Hello."

He'd tucked a wad of dollars inside his passport. He extended it slowly, catching the guard's eye.

The man removed the notes and slid them into his breast pocket, then proceeded to peruse the pages and stamps at leisure. He muttered something to his colleague, who sniggered ostentatiously, before handing the passport back and tapping on the car roof. "You go," he announced, waving his hand in the direction Fearless had come, as if dismissing yet another of his fawning concubines.

Fearless's stomach tensed in anger, but he turned the car and drove off without saying a word. There would be no point trying the other checkpoint. They would surely radio their counterparts there.

And so Fearless attempted his original, ridiculous plan, pulling the car off the road once he'd reached a safe distance. Leaving it under a dogwood tree, he set out across a grassy plain. By his reckoning, the base's perimeter would be half a mile to the north. But he had waded through the knee-high grass no more than four hundred yards when a vehicle roared up a track alongside the field. Two men got out and walked toward him. He stopped and waited.

"We have orders. You go back to border with us."

They searched him thoroughly, patting him down, then took him back to his car and searched that too. No point in claiming it was just a misunderstanding.

Sandwiched between the "police" car and an impeccably preserved lime green Zaporozhets, Fearless drove in a convoy of three. For a moment, he had the urge to drive right off the road. He had a vision of Belmondo in *Pierrot Le Fou*, plunging his stolen Galaxie straight into the sea. But no ocean abutted the side of the road, just scrub and meadow, so on he followed, heading west in a country where all things leaned East, back to the border, through yet more checkpoints. "You're pathetic," he muttered to himself as they rumbled along.

He looked at his watch and added on four hours. He'd missed the agreed-upon time to phone Phnom Penh. He needed to think, be clearer and sharper. Viktor would be waiting in the lobby of the Intercontinental, pacing back and forth, brooding and cursing. If he thought Fearless had abandoned them, then he might abandon Song, and all Fearless would have achieved was to cast Song out and ensure that the only person she loved was inaccessible.

As he drove on, he wondered if everything that had happened to him since Laure's death had been nothing but an excrescence of selfish grieving: an allegory he had cultivated to give himself the hit he needed, to sate the junkie woefully addicted to extremes. He had given up photography but invented a situation that allowed him to carry on avoiding the routine and rules that he'd feared a wife and baby would bring. Now he was distracting himself from facing up to his loss.

And then, there was something that both disgusted and comforted him: on some deep level, Fearless still believed that Alyosha might explain all of this away, or that, even if Alyosha had lost his moral compass, Fearless could somehow set him straight again.

On the outskirts of Chișinău, they pulled over onto a quiet road. The Zaporozhets performed a U-turn and puttered away, while the police car flashed its headlights to indicate he could move on.

"Were you followed?" Richard asked when Fearless turned up at his apartment.

"No. Can I telephone?"

"Not from here you can't."

He went into another room and reappeared with a hooded sweatshirt. "Put this on. We'll take my car to a place I know."

"Is this necessary?"

Richard stared at him with narrowed eyes before he pushed him into the corridor outside. On the street, he walked fast, nudging Fearless along.

"When I open the boot, climb in quick."

"Correct me if I'm wrong. But you're enjoying this, aren't you?"

"Just a little bit. Maybe," Richard chuckled.

At least it's clean, Fearless thought, as he braced himself against the rough, black carpet, the car turning left, then right, then left again.

When Richard opened the boot, dusk was beginning to fall. Fearless had a glimpse of decorative wrought iron balustrades on a first-floor balcony, a curved mansard roof, a line of stuccoed cornice, before Richard guided him up three or four steps and a wooden door opened, an apprehensive woman standing behind it.

She whispered to Richard, who squeezed her shoulder in return, and nodded hello to Fearless as he pushed the hood back from his head. Impeccable silk suit. Matching lilac heels. From the luxurious surroundings, a diplomat or politician.

Richard led Fearless into a library bathed in the glow of heavy table lamps, two leather sofas facing each other in its center. "It's safe to call from here," he said, pointing to a phone on a console table. "But you have no more than fifteen minutes. I'll leave you in peace."

Conrad's bright "Hello" let a chink of light in on his twilit mood. He was clearly delighted to be freed from his usual humdrummery.

"The plane belongs to a fleet under the name Air Irina . . ."

"Irina is the name of Alyosha's grandmother."

"It's a company that's extraordinarily difficult to trace. First, it's registered here, then it's registered there. Moldova, Equatorial Guinea, the Central African Republic, Kazakhstan."

"Not places renowned as aviation hubs."

"At the moment it's incorporated in Monrovia, Liberia. A bloody convenient jurisdiction if you're up to no good. A business registered there can operate anywhere, have its offices wherever, and get the paperwork in a matter of minutes. Liberian law doesn't even demand that the names of executives or shareholders be filed."

"Monrovia," murmured Fearless. He thought of Traoré and the precious stones—two facts that indicated links with West Africa. Liberia shared a border with the Ivory Coast and was a center for the trade in Sierra Leonean blood diamonds.

"And, as for company ownership before the Liberian registration: well, there are different directors named on each document, none of them traceable to anyone concrete. There are headquarters with nothing but a P.O. box for an address. Business offices located in residential blocks of flats."

"And no Alexei Federenko."

"What do you think?"

"So what now?"

"The only way we could get a better picture is to look at the records on the planes themselves. The logbooks, insurance documents, all the paperwork pertaining to airworthiness."

"Oh, why didn't you say? I'll call up my international police force and we'll dispatch men with search warrants."

Conrad ignored his sarcasm and rustled some papers. "There's one more thing that Roger found out. Not long after you arrived in Phnom Penh, the jet went in and out of Dubai."

"It can't have been Federenko—he was definitely in Cambodia."

"So the plane went without him. In fact, it goes to Dubai regularly. Several times over the last few months."

The Mediterranean-looking man on the videotape. The man who Alyosha must have picked up from the airport on the night Fearless had been drugged and left for dead. Of course, it had to be him—Traoré had already arrived in Phnom Penh.

No time to reflect; more calls to make. After several attempts with crossed lines and blank silences, Jimmy's voice emerged across a field of static.

"So Traoré's known to your lot in intelligence?"

Jimmy glossed over Fearless's lack of discretion. "General Wilfried's a model citizen. One of the good guys. A shining light for modern Africa."

"But—*our friends*—they say otherwise?"

"What friends? The first step is to exploit the open sources. You can thank a junior colleague of mine who spent a day in a corridor in Abidjan, waiting for some pompous mandarin to see him."

If Fearless hadn't been so wrapped up in the present moment, he might have been touched by all these kindnesses.

"And so?"

"My colleague got access to a number of documents—the most interesting of which he copied at some expense. I now have in my possession the most expensive photocopies of end-user certificates in the world."

"End-user certificates?"

"The standard document for weapons sales. They certify the buyer who will be the recipient of the goods, ensuring that weapons remain at the approved destination and don't end up in embargoed or enemy states."

"How does a piece of paper stop anyone taking them somewhere else?"

"It doesn't—unless you have law enforcement agents who track and investigate and ensure that borders are secure. And that's what's interesting about the certificates Traoré has signed. Over the last year, you see, these have been rather . . . idiosyncratic, including some purchases that landed in Abidjan, which are unusual requests for an African army. The one I have in front of me includes handgun silencers. And on two occasions there are references to 'farming equipment' that include massive quantities of TNT."

"So these items, you're implying, are destined for other places?"

"The majority of goods in any one shipment may stay. But I'd bet some leave the Ivory Coast and go elsewhere."

"What was the air company that brought them?"

"Let me see."

He could hear Jimmy shuffling and riffling through pages.

"Irina. Air Irina. Flying from Kyiv. Though the company appears to be under Kazakhstani registration. Ha ha!"

"What's so funny?"

"The registration prefix for Kazakhstani planes is UN. As in flight UN-8475, UN-2394."

"As if the planes are making runs for the United Nations. Deliveries of tons of weapons in the name of world peace."

"Clever buggers."

"So Traoré supplies the end-user certificates. And he gets a handsome cut, which pays his kids' school fees. And then the weapons go to . . . ?"

"From Côte d'Ivoire? Liberia, maybe. And from there, it's a stone's throw to Sierra Leone."

"Traoré to Charles Taylor to the RUF."

"It's possible."

"Liberia again. It keeps coming back."

"And Liberia makes sense," said Jimmy, "for another solid reason. Over the last six months, our friend Traoré has been back and forth to Monrovia."

"So I guess I'm going to Monrovia, then."

"Okay," said Jimmy. "When?"

"Straight away. If there's a lead, then I take it—that's my plan. And this is the best lead on the table at the moment."

He paused. The line whispered and cut out for a moment.

"Are you still there?"

"Yeah, I'm here, Joe. Can you hear me? Look—I'll meet you there."

"Where?"

"In Monrovia."

"You'd do that?"

"I would. But I have my own motives in this. You may have stumbled on something big. And with me along, you'll do better. I have contacts. Networks. Where are you now?"

"In Moldova."

"Moldova?"

"I'll explain when I see you."

"Okay. Moldova. You'll still reach Monrovia before me . . . When you get there, check in to the Mamba Point Hotel. Have you got that? The Mamba Point. I'll see you by the pool."

Fifteen minutes later, Richard drove Fearless back to his car. This time, Fearless sat in the passenger seat. "Thank you," he said when they'd arrived. "You've gone out of your way. I know you did it for Laure."

"I did it for you, too," Richard said. "There's a photo you took—I don't know if you remember. The imprint of a body."

"In the grass in Kosovo."

"Yes. I have an old photocopy of it. Pinned above my desk—I look at it when I'm struggling. Driving you around and helping you make a call? Well, let's just say it doesn't repay it."

He reached across, grasped Fearless's hand, and held it.

"I don't know what you're looking for, but I hope you find it."

34

Song had come to develop a genuine affection for Viktor. It wasn't just because he always did what he said he would do. It was something else, something she had noticed in a quiet corner of her feelings: even if she had been desirable, he would not have desired her. It wasn't in his nature. His intentions were pure.

They had come to a tacit understanding: Viktor would go outside to get food and supplies and do anything necessary to ensure their safety, while she would take care of everything indoors.

"But you can go out if you want, Song. You tell us this yourself. No one is looking when you go outside."

Viktor didn't push her when she pretended not to hear. Besides, cooking and cleaning and washing the clothes here was a very different thing from her toil in the Naga—it was her choice to do them; he had not asked, let alone compelled her.

But the question of Fearless and what he was and wasn't doing hung over them—an ominous cloud of unknowing that mingled with the bitter smoke of Stung Meanchey, which in turn was infused with her grief and shame at what these barang must think of her country. *There are decent people everywhere!* she wanted to tell them.

Now Viktor came in from the yard, rubbing his concrete-covered hands on a rag. She plunged the shirt she was washing into a bucket of suds, swirling it back and forth in a figure of eight. "Finish," he said, gesturing outside, where fresh concrete lay over the earth where Thom was buried.

He cleaned his hands in the kitchen sink, picking out the crescents of grout inside his fingernails. Then he showered and changed into a set of fresh clothes.

It was time: he nodded and set off for the Intercontinental.

An hour passed of pacing back and forth. In the bedroom, she discovered a plastic bag on the bed containing bras in different sizes and several pairs of underwear. She laughed out loud, and then wept at Viktor's thoughtfulness, then went to the bathroom to try them on. Her breasts were heavier these days, the areolae more round and brown than they'd ever been. Just there, she could see the pattern of veins beneath the skin. It must be her age, she thought; even in her heyday in the Naga, her breasts had been too small to merit a bra. But then, she had seen Sovanna naked before the Russians took her. Age hadn't seemed to change *her* body. It spoke of a more profound separation between them than the fact that they had been confined in different places.

Two and a half hours. She cleaned the bathroom and kitchen meticulously. Three. She washed the windows inside and out. Four. Scraped the corners of the ceiling of cobwebs. Finally, Viktor returned, anger flushing his cheeks. He had hung around in the hotel lobby for three hours, he grumbled. But no: nothing. How gullible they had been!

Half an hour later, thinking she was asleep, he crept out the door and into the yard. She listened as the street gate creaked open and shut. A little later, she tiptoed into the other room and checked his clothes.

Yes. He had worn the silky short-sleeved shirt she had washed yesterday. It was comfort he was seeking. He wouldn't abandon her yet.

35

In the end, Jimmy reached Monrovia well before Fearless, whose circuitous journey took him to Paris, then Abidjan, before the Weasua Airlines flight to Roberts International. Even the most seasoned traveler would have balked at the Russian Antonov, with its tires as bald as Formula One slicks and its sunburned, soused-looking Ukrainian pilots—but the service was reliable and packed to the gills, mainly with ECOMOG soldiers and a group of East Asian men, dressed in impeccably pressed shirts and slacks.

"You're Chinese?" he ventured to the man sitting beside him.

"No no. Taiwan!" he shouted back.

China had broken off diplomatic relations with Liberia, he explained, when Monrovia agreed to recognize Taiwan's sovereignty in return for a cool $200 million in aid. It was a game that Transnistria no doubt dreamed of playing, Fearless thought: sprinkling cash over the impoverished states of the world to make the quantum leap from "real" to real.

The bright yellow taxi he hailed when he landed at Roberts was a dented saloon with its indicator lights smashed. It was riddled all over with black daubs of body filler. "My friend, wel-calm to Monroviahhhh!" cried the lively driver over the blaring sound of Warren G's "Regulate." "My name is Quincy—like da famous TV show. Gentleman—you are about to entah the fascinating sphere of forensic medicine! Hahaha."

"Or Quincy Jones," said Fearless, meeting his eyes in the mirror from which heavy strands of beads swayed back and forth.

"Exactly!" Quincy roared again, handing Fearless a business card, the heavy gold bracelets on his wrists tapping together like the ball bearings of a 1980s executive desk toy.

After they had passed the bombed-out former airport and the abandoned vats of the Firestone rubber factory, the city began to emerge from its rubble-strewn periphery. People dodged through traffic with little regard for safety while motorbikes puttered past on the band of asphalt between the side of the taxi and the aggregate on the roadside. While the bright colors of walls, doors, awnings, and signs—turquoise, lemon yellow, peppermint, tiger orange—blared life, everywhere were the hallmarks of trauma and violence: no wall without pockmarks, no painted surface unchipped. The English language had the perfect adjective to describe the city and, no doubt, the human spirits within: distressed. Even in the heart of the town they were crawling into were ruins or buildings whose construction had begun during hiatuses of peace—future ministries, schools, hospitals, health centers—only to be abandoned in yet another wave of war.

The Mamba Point, its car park crowded with Pajeros and Hiluxes, their doors painted with big black U.N. capitals, was an oasis of air-conditioned, satellite-TV luxury. Fearless found Jimmy at a table by the pool, poring over the contents of a large box file, his hair longer and more unkempt than usual. Barbed wire ran along the perimeter wall behind him—a circular scribble across the horizon of sea and sky. The two men embraced and sat down opposite each other, saying nothing for a while, smiles of bemusement on their faces, in a way that only the oldest of friends might manage. Then, taking a deep breath, Fearless plunged into his story, trying to gauge if Jimmy would reckon him as mad as he himself partly suspected he had become.

But Jimmy was excited by what Fearless had discovered. Riffling the edges of a thick wedge of paper, he rattled off information, hypotheses, strategies.

"So Irina Air and Federenko's private jet. Over the last six months, they've both visited Monrovia. Look, I've arranged dinner with someone who might help us. A reliable source—he'll arrive in a few hours. Take a nap if you want first."

"Who's this?"

"You can call him J. D.—like we do."

By now, the sun had sunk and snagged itself in the barbed wire. The sky was salmon and seashell pink and brushed with crimson.

"You're excited about unraveling this. I get that, Jim. I do. But it's not the ins and outs of the deal that concern me. I want to help Song get her sister back and confront Alyosha. I want to see him clearly in all of this."

"That's ironic," Jimmy muttered, shaking his head.

"What?"

"*You* seeing clearly. Go and get some rest." Jimmy thudded one ream of paper onto another and shoved the whole wedge into a Tesco carrier bag. "Just don't be late for dinner. Eight o'clock sharp."

J. D. moved in an elegant, light-footed way. As he crossed the hotel veranda, his shirt was a block of white against the dark. Behind him, there was little suggestion of a city—only isolated islands of generator-powered light. On the beach, Fearless could make out two or three charcoal fires above which golden faces tended to evening meals, the midnight blue sky flecked with a spray of innumerable stars, as if someone had sieved icing sugar onto a jeweler's display.

J. D. offered Fearless a warm, limp hand. "Pleased to meet you," he mumbled, refusing to make eye contact.

But Jimmy soon put J. D. at ease. Fearless could see how his sober manner and perceptiveness made him ideally suited to managing informants. After five minutes, J. D. was in full flow, explaining his work as a jack-of-all-trades for a coterie of the Liberian elite that included the President.

J. D. revealed that he had met Traoré—a man he was told to treat with the utmost solicitousness—a dozen times over the last four years. As the waiters brought beer and pizza to their table, he related Traoré's penchant for gold and diamonds, his ballooning weight, his quirky obsession with model airplanes.

At a propitious moment, Fearless pulled out an old photo of Alyosha. "Do you know this man?"

"No."

"He's a little fatter now."

"I've never met him."

Fearless watched closely for any glint of recognition, but there was nothing to suggest he wasn't telling the truth.

Shortly, J. D. excused himself to visit the bathroom.

"What he's telling us is uncovering what this deal's about," Jimmy said.

"I told you—I only care if it takes me to Federenko. It's all well and good that J. D. knows Traoré. It's all well and good that Federenko's planes have visited here. But if he just brokers everything over the phone, he could be absolutely anywhere. And I need to tie him to a place, here and now."

Jimmy remained silent, pushing the breath through his nose. Behind him, the night sea surged on the shore, leaving a glittering fringe of surf in the shape of a snake. On its edge there could be conflict or peace, grief or ease, but beyond, in the dark waters, all this was irrelevant. The depths were indifferent to the machinations of people, their squabbles and desires and selfish hopes.

J. D. came back, tracing a line of right angles through the restaurant tables. He gestured to the waiter to bring more beer.

"Can I show you more pictures?" Fearless asked. He offered him one of Wish from Bosnia. Then a still of Vasiliev taken from the videotape—one of the ones that Conrad had made.

"No. No. But this one: this is Mr. Hossein," said J. D., holding up the still Fearless had least expected him to identify, of the unknown Mediterranean-looking man.

"Who?"

"Mr. Hossein. I meet him at Roberts many times. Several times I take him to the Hotel Africa. They send me because I speak Arabic after my training in Libya."

"He's Libyan?"

"He's Arab—which country, I don't know. And he's quiet. Like the Sphinx. Believe me, he says nothing."

"Why did Mr. Hossein come here to Liberia?"

J. D. laughed. "It is not my job to ask questions! No, no. I took him to the Boulevard Hotel to meet with some big army men. And they don't let me in—they can talk without an interpreter. Then the next day they tell me to take him to buy boots. Strong boots before we take the helicopter to Foya."

"That's a town on the northern border," said Jimmy.

"I will handle the needles myself," Fearless remembered Alyosha saying. "The certificates signed, the meeting with our *foyer* friend."

"It's a stone's throw from Guinea and Sierra Leone," Jimmy continued, "a dust bowl through which goods pass back and forth freely. Weapons, ammunition, drugs, diamonds. Is that what Mr. Hossein was interested in?"

For a moment J. D. hesitated, looking from Jimmy to Fearless and back. "He was meeting with the general who runs things in Foya. A general called Doe—no relation to Samuel. And yes—it was for diamonds in exchange for weapons. This I know. A lot of carats."

"When was this meeting?"

"A few weeks ago."

"When exactly?"

J. D. pressed his hand to his forehead and held it there. "It was the day they played the first match of the World Cup. Brazil and . . ."

"Scotland," said Jimmy. "Early June, that makes it." Not long after Hossein had received his little pouch in the brothel.

J. D. excused himself once more and got up.

"Extraordinary," Jimmy said, leaning in and shaking his head. Then he sat back and knocked twice sharply on the tabletop, making the unused set of cutlery jump up and down. Fearless could see two sides of him vying with each other: the enthusiast, excited by what they were uncovering, and the professional who had been conditioned to exercise skepticism.

"You're thinking: terrorist groups. The Middle East," Fearless said.

"The Lebanese have had a stake in the Sierra Leonean diamond markets for decades—way back before the Second World War. They're everywhere around here—the Ivory Coast, Senegal—and always with strong working ties to *les grands*."

"Hezbollah then?"

"It's possible. A tried and tested revenue stream. Maybe the handover on the tape was a gesture of goodwill—a sample that proved Federenko could reliably broker the sale, making use of Traoré's end-user certificates."

"And then Hossein, the buyer, flew here on his private jet and headed straight to Foya in his brand-new desert boots."

"Direct to the source. To seal the deal in the flesh."

Fearless drained his beer and wiped the sheen of sweat from his forehead. He remembered the celebration that night in the Naga Bar; was this what he and Vasiliev's men had been toasting, a supply line for diamonds and arms being secured? This was their gusher roaring out of the earth. This was their river of precious black gold.

Still, there was nothing that declared *Federenko is here*.

"This could be worth taking to the Americans," Jimmy said. "Because to investigate this deal—to gather all the evidence, to track all the names and places—requires more resources than you and I can muster. After the Cold War ended, most countries slashed intelligence budgets across Africa. No more maneuvering to sway countries' sympathies. No need to invest in labor-intensive networks. Right now, the CIA's the only player that counts. The Foreign Office has been on a death march since Suez."

J. D. was walking back toward their table, weaving slightly unsteadily after all the beers he'd downed.

"We are wondering where Hossein is now, J. D.," said Jimmy. "Do you know where he flew to or where we might find him?"

J. D. smiled and leaned back in his chair. Then he chuckled and let his chuckle grow into a stuttering laugh. "That's easy," he said. "This time I have an answer."

"Where? In Africa? Is he somewhere on the continent?"

"No!" J. D. gave another little laugh. "But he'll be right here in Liberia the day after tomorrow. I am going to Roberts to pick him up myself."

Early the next morning, after half a dozen attempts, Fearless got through to the Intercontinental payphone.

"Is that you, Viktor? Viktor—can you hear me?"

As soon as he heard a grunt of acknowledgment, Fearless ran through everything in a flurry, hoping it would make up for missing their last call.

"And how's Song? Is she safe? Is everything okay?"

"So—after everything—you don't know where is Federenko. Yes?"

Fearless had decided not to mention his greatest hope—that J. D. would agree to a meeting with the Americans and that, CIA on their side, they would have Federenko—for if he did, Viktor would surely be appalled, his chances of getting to Federenko severely compromised.

"Not yet. But with each clue our odds get better, Viktor. We're close. Believe me. Viktor? Christ, this damn line!"

When his voice came back, Viktor was cold and unambiguous.

"You think you can do this your way and what I want is not important. But Federenko killed my friend and you *will* find him."

"Viktor . . ."

"You listen. If you care about the girl, remember who keeps her safe. This is my job and I do it because you do your job. But if your job you do not do—what do I do with her? She cannot survive alone. She cannot go out of the building.

"What is phrase you taught me? Put her out of her misery. Is that what I do? Yes? The next call—bastard—be sure you don't miss."

36

Viktor left the street gate open and strode across the yard.

"What did he say?" Song asked as soon as she opened the door.

"Out!" he shouted, taking hold of her arm and yanking her. "He said nothing at all. He goes to England, Europe. Africa. Nothing else!"

"Please stop."

He turned her to face him and placed a finger on her breastbone. "Teach me how you say in Khmer: 'shut up.'"

"What?"

"Shut up."

"Bith mort. Can we go back inside?"

"And now, you tell me how you say, 'Don't stare.'"

"Kom meul."

"Okay . . . And how do you say, 'Mind your business.'"

"Kith pika rorksi khluon eng."

"Good."

"I go inside?"

"No. You come with me. And you take this stupid thing off you right now." He put his fingers in the knot of the krama and unpicked it, letting the first wrap of fabric fall away.

"No!"

"Yes. You did not wear it with Sokha and this police chief. So why not with me? Are they better than me, these assholes?"

He tossed the krama on the ground and, before she could scream, hustled her across the yard and onto the sidewalk, keeping a firm grip on her upper arm. Motos dashing. The rainbow colors of beer-branded parasols blinding her. The thunder of a dump truck punctuated by the hammering of a pneumatic drill. She tried to jerk her head to fan her hair over her face and shrink down and back and away from this world.

"You come now. You walk . . ." *People everywhere.* "You are not afraid!" His arm was already steering her along the sidewalk.

"Where do we go?"

"To buy food. From now on, it is your job."

"The market?"

He didn't respond and she wasn't able to look at him. She kept her head low, her eyes fixed on the sidewalk tiles and their pattern of squares and circles forming the shape of hundreds of eyes.

Were people looking? She couldn't tell—though she sensed dark forms hovering at the edge of her vision. Walking with a barang would have drawn enough attention, even if she hadn't been so scarred or scared.

Now her feet stepped into a corridor of shade. The noise around her contracted, then boomed and echoed: they must be under the roof of one of the market's alleyways. The sounds came into focus: clattering and chattering. Her leg brushed against a vat of rust-red chilies and plastic packs of turmeric stacked waist-high. There was a puddle of crimson: rancid blood from a butcher's stall. The thudding must be his cleaver coming down on the chopping board.

She wanted to scream. She wanted the Naga. To be back there, where she was safe and unseen.

Viktor's hand now appeared beneath her chin, waving a square of folded riel. "Stop your crying. Take this. We need fish. Rice. Some fruit. Mango or rambutan—whatever you prefer. But nothing expensive—we have to be careful."

Another sob started to balloon in her chest. She realized now what he was trying to do: throw her in at the deep end, teach her how to survive. Was he leaving her? Was that what he had decided after the phone call?

There were deep baskets of layered fresh fish at her feet now. The light danced on their sides. Their ammoniac smell burned her nostrils.

She looked up to meet a pair of squinting eyes. The woman's chapped lips grimaced a little in shock.

Viktor stepped forward. "Kom meul!" he said.

Then he pointed a finger at her and added a sentence in Russian.

Song didn't understand and nor did the woman, but the message was obvious: he wouldn't tolerate any nonsense.

He pointed to the fish and nudged Song's elbow. Somehow, the words she needed spilled from her mouth.

The fishmonger weighed and bagged the fish at once. When she tried to hand it to Viktor, he waved toward Song and then turned to let Song handle the rest of the transaction.

After that, they did the same at the fruit and vegetable stall and then again with the seller of rice and pulses. The vendors noticed her face, but didn't make anything of it.

Still, she was overwhelmed. The words *whatever you prefer* echoed in her head; the idea that you might prefer one thing over another. And then there was the money: she was the one in charge of using it.

When they emerged out of the alley into the bright light of day, Song had a feeling inside that she couldn't recognize.

As they walked back into the yard of the house, she grasped it fully: Viktor was being a father to her—the feeling of which she had forgotten. He had shown her patience and listened and understood what she needed after her years of being enslaved and dependent. Accept the weather of other people's thoughts and minds, he was telling her. Be proud under the monsoon rain and the heat of the sun, equally. And he was doing the hardest thing a parent could do: taking her into the world and letting her go.

37

"You understand that what you're suggesting is criminal, Joe." Jimmy shook his head and rose from the table. He rested his hands on the parapet and sighed. "If you're caught, I'll be powerless to help. Why would you risk it? Just stick to the plan and we'll have something for the Americans."

Fearless walked to Jimmy and placed a hand on his shoulder. "I'm doing it. We only have a couple of hours. All I need is the extra camera. Can you help me or not?"

Jimmy went back to his bag at the table and returned with something matte and silver in his hand. "Here. With the chain attached. Exactly as requested."

"Jimmy, I love you." He had a talent for unscrambling. Like an expert Rubik's cuber, he could survey a problem and restore order with an elegant twist of his wrists.

Fearless had only seen a Minox once before. But the solid yet featherlight ingot felt familiar: his kind of weapon.

The day before, after thirty-six hours of waiting, they had finally received J. D.'s call and hurried to the lobby of the Boulevard Hotel, where they posed as two Westerners in Monrovia on business. When Hossein entered the building, it was the stiff gait Fearless recognized, then the hair, oiled and parted in the middle, framing his head with its crown of shining curls. Fearless and Jimmy watched from wing-backed armchairs, pretending to talk, as he retrieved his key card from reception. At that moment, the plan came to Fearless. All he needed was Hossein's room number and a Liberian he could trust who would take on the role of hotel maintenance man.

"Fully functional?" said Jimmy.

"Looks like it. It's loaded."

One of the Mamba Point waiters waved from across the pool. "Mr. Nightingale, sir! Your taxi has arrived."

Quincy was beaming when Fearless climbed in.

"Look at you," said Fearless.

"My friend! New polo shirt. New trousers. Look at dees pockets. Pockets on my thighs. Pockets on my ass!"

"You have the card? And the toolbox."

"Chay. Don't worry."

"Once you're carrying it, no one will question you, believe me. You remember what to do?"

"Ehhh. I'm a natural showman—even in dees dreads."

"No showman stuff, Quincy. You need to blend in. That's what I'm paying you for."

"Chaaa. Look at me! I take off my links. I don't take my links off for no one but you." He lifted up his arms and turned his bare wrists. "I'm ninja. A car-mee-li-ahhhn. Ha-ha-ha-haaaa."

Quincy stopped his taxi a hundred yards from The Boulevard and Fearless got down and approached on foot. Inside the lobby, he headed to the reception desk and bothered the receptionist with a string of questions: room availability, facilities, the dos and don'ts of navigating the city. While the receptionist was distracted, Quincy walked in, lugging his heavy toolbox with a lopsided lope. He did, as hoped, blend in perfectly: the maintenance man carrying out his daily rounds. After crossing the lobby unnoticed, he passed through a door to the stairwell.

Fearless thanked the receptionist and sat down in the waiting area, making himself comfortable beside a small side table on which there was an internal phone and a preposterously large table lamp. He counted sixty elephants and then sixty Mississippis before an elegant-looking African couple came out of the elevator. Sixty alligators later, a cleaning lady passed by, waving a feather duster at the furniture desultorily.

Finally, another guest approached the front desk.

While the receptionist was occupied, he picked up the internal phone and dialed Hossein's room.

"Good morning, Mr. Ho-ssein?"

"Yes."

"Dis is hotel recepshan."

"Yes. What is it?"

Hossein had an impeccable English accent, no doubt from the kind of public-school education Traoré had been buying his children with gun money—though clearly he had been pretending he couldn't speak English with the Liberians. To gain some advantage in negotiations, Fearless supposed.

"I'm sorry to disturb you, suh, but da guest on da floor above you has repartted a wata leak and I must send an electrishan to check dat dere's no damage to your room."

"Damage? There's no damage. I can check for you myself."

Hossein put the receiver down, sending a loud tock into the earpiece. Fearless could hear him walking away and then opening and shutting the door of his en suite.

"I can see there's absolutely no damage at all."

"I understand, suh. But it is hotel policy dat we must check da lectric lights and sockets at once." Fearless pretended to be reading his lines from a staff handbook: "Your safety, sah, is our prime-ry carncern."

"Okay. If you must. When will you come?"

"Right away, suh."

Hossein sighed and puffed out air. "Okay. Come immediately. I'm leaving in ten minutes."

Fearless put the phone down and walked casually to the stairwell door. He stepped inside and whistled up into the light. Quincy, up above, whistled in reply. Everything would depend on his acting talents now.

Tiny beads of sweat broke out at the roots of his hair as Fearless allotted a number of seconds to each step Quincy would be taking. Walking down the corridor. Fifteen seconds. Knocking on the door. Ten seconds. Hossein letting Quincy in and telling him to make it quick: twenty seconds.

Quincy would open his toolbox and get to work, walking around the room and checking sockets with his multimeter. Then, he would mention casually that he needed to cut the electricity and remove Hossein's key card from its plastic slot on the wall. He would busy himself with a socket before declaring everything was okay. Now, the critical moment Fearless had worried over: he would return Hossein's key card to the slot—except it would be a replacement card—before leaving the room with the real card in his pocket.

When the time was right, Fearless went back to the stairwell. After a few seconds more, he whistled—but there was no reply. A sense of panic quivered just above his pelvis.

Then a door slammed and heavy boots clocked on the stairs. A beaming smile appeared at the top of the half-flight. Quincy put his finger to his lips and slowly descended, before producing the key card from one of his pockets with a flourish. "I wait for you in the taxi, Mr. Fearless," he whispered. "Original gangstaaaah," he added, as he walked out into the lobby.

After thirty seconds Fearless went back to the lobby and settled down, this time in an armchair with a view of the entrance.

Five minutes later, J. D. walked in and sat down on a sofa nearby. Fearless took out a newspaper from the briefcase he had brought with him and hid behind its pages while J. D. ignored him.

Then the hotel elevator pinged and Hossein emerged. Neatly pressed shirt and slacks. Rigid gait. Finical facial hair. J. D. rose and took Hossein's right hand in both of his; then they exchanged a few words in Arabic before walking onto the forecourt.

Ninety seconds later, Fearless stepped into Hossein's room. He shut the door behind him, put the key card in its holder, opened his briefcase, and pulled out a pair of latex gloves. Then he took a deep breath and cleared his mind.

He started with the closet, but his heart sank when he opened the door: the safe had been used and locked with a code. He tried 1111 and 1234—to no avail. After checking the pockets of a jacket, he withdrew a small, wheeled suitcase and inspected the neatly folded items inside. There were a series of pastel-colored shirts—one pink, one pale blue, one bright white—all Turnbull & Asser, all perfectly starched: the kind of shirts that Alyosha would covet. He imagined Hossein, sitting on a bottle-green Chesterfield in the deep shadows at the rear of a Jermyn Street shop, a brisk attendant in his early sixties presenting him with an array of styles.

But there was nothing hidden beneath or between the shirts.

Closing the closet, he went to the bed and carefully lifted up the edge of the mattress. Nothing. Except a specialist pornographic magazine dedicated to women with supersized breasts.

Fearless sighed as he riffled through the soccer ball–sized mammaries. *So Hossein couldn't get what he wanted in Cambodia*, he said to himself.

Then, nestled in the magazine's centerfold, sandwiched by a close-up of swollen labia, he found a slim A6 notebook of eighty pages, every one annotated in a precise, regular hand, in Arabic, in English block capitals, and with numbers: row upon row of accounting and calculations.

There was no time to examine it—he needed to get photos. This was where the Minox's metal chain came into its own. Two feet long, it had small nodes at various points: eight, nine and a half, twelve, and sixteen inches. For text this size, the sixteen-inch distance would be ideal, allowing Fearless to keep the handwriting in focus.

There were flight numbers, to-do lists, amounts of dollars and pounds, all of which were linked to dates in both the past and future—all of them leads that would keep Jimmy and Conrad busy. This was more than Fearless had hoped for—more than pouches of diamonds or briefcases of cash. On the middle page—the centerfold of the notebook within the centerfold of the magazine—he spied a PP with the address of Le Royal.

After he had taken twenty shots, the whole room blared with noise, the ceiling and floor quivering and humming.

"Christ. Fuck."

It was the fire alarm, its vibrating bell pounding his chest and back. Was it a drill? When he dashed to the window he saw hotel staff and guests spilling out of the building and congregating on the lawn. Beyond them, where the hotel drive met the road, he could see Quincy walking backward, waving frantically.

Fearless rushed back to the bed and took several more shots of the names and phone numbers before he returned the book to its place under the mattress. Picking up his briefcase, he walked straight out of the room, shutting the door behind him and hurrying down the corridor.

At that moment, the doors of the elevator slid open to reveal Hossein standing in front of him with an irritated expression, his key card—the false key card—in his hand.

Blood flushed Fearless's cheeks. He had left the real key card in the room slot: when Hossein finally gained access to his room, he would immediately know something had happened.

Fearless held up the flat of his palm and shouted, "Monsieur, not the lift! We must go down tout de suite. The fire alarm rings. We cannot stay 'ere."

Before Hossein could respond, Fearless had reached him and grabbed his upper arm to steer him politely toward the stairs.

"Quickly quickly!" said Fearless, as he half-pushed Hossein along. "I saw smoke at my window. This is not a drill!"

Thank God for Quincy, Fearless said to himself. Waiting behind the wheel of his cab on the street, he must have seen J. D.'s Hilux returning. He had run in and set off the fire alarm to warn him.

Hossein shrugged Fearless's hand away and submitted to going down, though he was clearly perplexed when he noted Fearless's latex gloves.

"I am docteur," Fearless said as they took the first flight, half-smiling and half-grimacing when he noticed Hossein's hand slip the key card back into his jacket's side pocket.

It was at the door into the lobby, Fearless calculated, that he would make his move to retrieve the card. The door should open into the direction of escape; that was the principle—they would have to push through it.

As they turned onto the last flight, Fearless came up behind Hossein's shoulder and then, at the bottom, made to overtake him, jostling into his side, slipping his left hand into Hossein's pocket and extracting the fake key card Quincy had left in the power socket.

"Fool!" said Hossein. "There's no need to push and panic!"

"So sorry! Pardonnez-moi, Monsieur. Please go ahead."

Hossein dusted himself off, tutted, and strode out of the lobby, Fearless slowing down and sighing in relief. Now, when Hossein finally returned to his room, he would think at first that he had lost his key. When reception opened the door for him, he would find it in its slot. He would doubt himself—*But I'm sure I had the card in my hand*—and put it all down to a moment of forgetfulness.

"Think about shape . . . and color and . . . size," said Jimmy, translating Hossein's hard-to-read Arabic script. "The really . . . bright white color is the one . . . dealers like.

"It's like a beginner's guide. Dealing Diamonds for Dummies. Names, addresses, numbers of various contacts. Antwerp, London . . . here's one in the U.S. Right next to it: 'Will buy uncut up to one hundred dollars per gram.'"

"Would that be legal for a U.S. dealer?" asked Fearless. "To buy diamonds that come from this part of the world?"

"Who would know? You can't prove where diamonds come from or under what circumstances they've been mined or through whose hands they've passed. It's not in dealers' interests to ask questions. In their line of business, it's a breach of etiquette."

Jimmy looked out over the glimmering surf and squinted.

"Diamonds. It amazes me. What are they really worth—save when they're used on a saw blade or grinding wheel? They're not even scarce. They mine hundreds of millions a year. It's De Beers that hoards them to keep prices artificially high."

Jimmy widened his eyes and turned back to the desk, once again poring over the minuscule text.

"This page of dates with numbers beside them—not phone numbers but more like some kind of code. And look—the end of this month underlined in red. It looks like it's going to be a critical time."

Fearless's gut told him that the thirteen-digit codes were key. Bank account numbers, maybe. Computer passwords or access codes. Combinations for safety deposit boxes or vaults.

"Seventy-five percent up front," mumbled Jimmy. "And look here, a list of weapons."

"Worth checking against Traoré's end-user certificates?"

"There's matériel you definitely don't find in this region. Not if the destination is Sierra Leone. SA-8 missiles—never used in West Africa. BM-21 launchers—incredibly rare. Night vision goggles. Mine detection equipment. Radars. Laser range finders. Dragunov sniper rifles! Not much use in wooded hills and mangroves with coked-up kids who shoot and strafe from the hip. Much better for somewhere with long, flat plains, where you can pick the enemy off from a mile away."

"Afghanistan," Fearless suggested, thinking of Federenko's passport stamps.

"Not likely. Hezbollah isn't involved over there." Jimmy's finger swept right to left across the page. "Cigarettes. Baby formula. Designer T-shirts. Jeans. This is really small-time stuff."

"But what happens when you add thousands of small deals together?"

"It's a way of evading attention. Maybe. It's possible."

Fearless thought of market traders with stalls of knock-off jeans. The Jack the Lad with his bag of cigarette cartons in the pub. Ants: little ants all over the world, contributing their little shares to a much greater fund. Not so different from how Viktor had described the obshchak. Or the builders of Angkor Wat—or any of the great constructions to which individuals contributed a tiny part—York Minster, Santiago de Compostela, Petra, the Great Wall—with no hope of seeing or even understanding the finished whole.

Jeans. Cigarettes. Hints of Alyosha—but no concrete reference to him in Hossein's notes.

"Just the mention of Le Royal," said Jimmy, reading his mind. "There must be a broker who connects all the dots."

Jimmy called for beers and began to think out loud. There was a triangle, as he saw it, with three parties at the vertices: Federenko, Hossein, and whoever he represents—"let's call them group X—" and, lastly, a circle of corrupt West Africans who were most likely connected to the RUF in Sierra Leone. Federenko was delivering arms—sourced from Transnistria—to West Africa, most of which went to the West Africans themselves. The West Africans paid for these arms in diamonds, but not to Federenko—it was Hossein who received those. Hossein, for his part, also got a portion of the arms: the weapons that were clearly better suited to other conflict zones. And in return, Jimmy presumed, Hossein completed the triangle, by paying Federenko in the dollars he needed.

"In cash," said Fearless. "Because Federenko needs liquidity to make things square for him back in Russia. 'Once this big deal is done,' he kept saying, 'I'll be back where I belong.' So Federenko sells arms and receives dollars in return. And the West Africans receive arms and pay in the unique, untraceable resource they have access to: diamonds. And Hossein . . ."

"Hezbollah doesn't make sense at all—no. They already have networks—why go to all this trouble?"

Fearless didn't need to be told. He felt the warm breath of Khattab lingering on his neck, the gloved hand on his shoulder.

"Al-Qaeda then."

"But diamonds is not how those guys do business. Unless . . ."

"What?"

"It's far-fetched. But think. These groups have powerful backers. A lot of big money. And where do they keep it?"

"I don't follow."

"In banks. They keep it in banks like you and me."

"So what?"

"Until now, their targets have been in *their* world. A hotel bomb in Yemen that killed a couple of hotel workers. But now they've struck American embassies, the stakes have completely changed. Before they were a blip on the CIA's radar, but now they're a pulsing, pinging, alarm."

"So they're worried their millions in the banks will be frozen. Somehow, some way, they need to get that money out."

"To turn it into a commodity. Something small you can transport."

"Which can't be traced. Which you can turn back into cash when you need to."

"The diamonds are not a way of *making* money, Joe. The diamonds are a way of *hiding* money. Hossein receives arms and achieves something even better: he changes all his dollars into diamonds via the deal. And whichever African parties are involved, they get a new line of credit after the Italian military ruined things with their Operation—what was it called?—Cheque to Cheque."

"So the whole thing's an elaborate bureau de change. I get it. But Federenko—where's he? How does it lead us to him?"

"It doesn't. But it's enough to get the Americans interested. If we can convince J. D. to talk, with them on board, we might get to him."

Jimmy clenched his fists and rose to his feet. "I need to make a call. Get me another beer."

A grim smile formed on Fearless's lips. Something he'd done had reaped results. In his mind, the coded numbers spun in a slot machine. With the CIA's help, the reels might align.

"I'm telling you all: this is the end of days!"

That's what Alyosha had claimed years ago in Sarajevo, blind drunk with the other correspondents and stringers holed up under siege in the Holiday Inn. Yes, Fearless had conceded, day and night the Serbs were bombarding them, while an hour away people were sauntering through the Uffizi, downing steins at Oktoberfest, applauding prancing Lipizzaner, oblivious to the hell their neighbors were living through—but why give in to such disillusionment? Cynicism doesn't speak truth to power. It cannot prick the consciences of ideologues or bend pragmatists from their course.

Fearless was proving it right now. He was walking the talk.

His mind took off on an improbable flight of fancy. He would face Federenko again and compel him to answer his questions, admit what he was and was not guilty of, make amends where necessary, and seek forgiveness. Traoré would be unmasked; Sovanna released and reunited with Song. And whatever misunderstanding had resulted in Fearless being jailed would be brought to light and confronted head on.

Fifteen minutes later, Jimmy returned. "J. D.'s on board—and I've spoken to the Americans. But we may have to wait."

"How long?"

"A couple of days. Look—it's a bureaucracy. It has to pass across people's desks."

Before Fearless could lament, they were interrupted by a waiter. There was an urgent call for Jimmy, who left the table once again.

"I take it all back," Jimmy said, shaking his head when he returned once more. "Not only will they sit down and question J. D. tomorrow, they're going to fly in analysts from Langley to do it. From Langley—direct. You've really made waves.

"I'm gobsmacked. Direct—from Langley," Jimmy repeated.

Waking early after a restless night, Fearless braced himself to phone Phnom Penh, a flow chart of different conversations branching in his mind, some with outcomes that led to Viktor pacified, others to Song wandering destitute and alone. But he had barely said hello before Viktor interrupted him.

"He's back."

"Who's back?"

"He arrived in Phnom Penh last night. Very late, with Sovanna. And the giant Black bodyguard."

"Listen. Viktor. Don't do anything. Do you hear me? I'm coming at once. There'll be others that follow. Can you—"

The line went dead.

"Viktor . . . ? Viktor? Are you there?"

He tried to call again but the phone rang and rang. On the fifth attempt, a stranger answered, cursed him in Khmer, and slammed down the receiver.

38

Viktor had spotted the shaven-headed one first—the one whose skull protruded like the melon of a beluga—lounging at a riverside café table. A whole group of goons were slurping tins of Angkor and wiping sticky strings of pizza cheese from their chins, basking in the sun and in the sense of their own impunity.

When Viktor followed their car, he came to the doctor's place, where he glimpsed a Land Cruiser behind the gate. At once, he knew that Federenko had returned—but why? To get more treatment for his burns? Surely he could buy expert care anywhere. But there was no chance of lingering: two guards manned the gate. If it came to it, later, he would get information from the doctor personally.

"Sovanna's back?" Song said when he told her the news.

"I don't know."

"Maybe they will hear from Vasiliev that I am here. And Sovanna will come for me. And they will find you."

"Let them come—though I don't think Vasiliev will talk to Federenko. They are enemies now. Your sister is part of that." Viktor took a gun and laid it on the table. "I go to make phone call at Intercontinental, okay."

On his return, Viktor told Song that Fearless was on his way.

"He wants that we wait for him before we do something."

"Why?"

"I don't know. But I am doing right now—no waiting. If I wait, Federenko leaves Cambodia again for sure."

"I am coming with you."

"I go alone," he said. "You must stay here for now." He turned to look for his bag.

"Viktor, I'm not afraid. I can go."

"I know. But—"

"I am coming!"

He put the bag down, walked toward her, and took her by the shoulders.

"I know. You are strong like me, Song. This, I know. But I go first because I have only myself—do you understand? You—you have Sovanna."

Before Viktor departed, she served him rice and curry that he sat down and devoured: fortifying himself for the fight. When she reached down to take the empty bowl, he gently took her hand and held it in his.

He waited for the tapping of her foot to stop, for stillness to fall over her body like a sheet. "They try to take it," he said, making a circle around his face. "They try to take—how do you say? Your beauty. Yes?" He reached out and placed the tip of his finger on her stomach. "But it is here. Not there. Inside. Inside you."

She placed her hand on top of his. And he placed his other hand on top of that.

After he had gone, she paced back and forth for ten minutes, her heart leaping every time an engine rumbled by. Then—she didn't know why—she found herself in the bathroom, examining her face in the mirror, following each contour of her marbled scar. With her fingers she gently traced its undulations, its colors like a hurricane swirling over a weather map.

"Me," she said, looking herself in the eye. It could have been worse. Her eyelids hadn't been burned off. She had all her senses. Her hands were untouched.

When Viktor returned to the house, his frustration was obvious: he had tried the doctor's, the Hotel Le Royal, and even the building where the Naga had once been. He made a fist and thumped his solar plexus. "Even the other big hotels, no one has seen."

The next day brought yet more disquiet. Song waited as Viktor visited any site he could think of, extending his search to the other big hotels, monitoring the riverside bars and restaurants.

When he told Song the doctor's house was locked and shuttered, the plant pots and outdoor chairs taken away, she felt a ball of anxiety inside her stomach.

Cords of rain hammered the roof.

"He will be here today?"

"Maybe. It's possible."

If earlier Viktor had dismissed the idea of waiting for Fearless, now his arrival was a weak ray of hope.

Then, not long after the rain had stopped and the trees and buildings glistened in the newly revealed sun, the steel gates exploded, taking to the air like metal wings.

The door spun across the room. Shadow men darted past. Viktor was on the floor. Animals were hunkering over him.

They spoke Russian. They had pistols. Things came into focus. She managed to take her hands from her face. Viktor was now on his stomach, yelping, as one of the men kneaded a gun in the back of his neck. She tried to cry out, but her voice had disappeared.

Seconds later, another four-wheel drive swerved into the compound and Federenko stepped down from the passenger seat. Vomit rose up inside her gullet; she gritted her teeth and swallowed it back. Amos strode around the vehicle and opened a rear door for a whirl of rushing black hair that rippled across the courtyard.

And then she was lifting her hands to cup the back of Sovanna's head, her breath hot and anxious, her heart beating thunderously, the warmth of Sovanna's body enveloping her entirely.

But Viktor?

"I begged and I begged!" Sovanna moaned into her good ear. "He kept saying no. But when I said what was happening to you, he changed. He did change." She leaned back a moment to kiss Song's forehead, before pulling her even tighter. "He's not so bad. He does what I want and what I want is to be with you, Song. For you to come and live with us, okay? It's going to be okay."

Sovanna came out of the embrace again and looked Song in the eye. He let her be high—that was why she ran to him.

"Just follow what I do, oun," Sovanna said. "I know this one. We're friends. He thinks I'm smart. Me—the smart one!"

There was no time to say more: Federenko came up and gently parted them. At the same time, someone else approached from the other side. Song's mouth opened when she saw Dr. Andrew, his face grim but full of the warmth he'd always shown her. "There's barely a chance this is possible," he said to Federenko.

"Take care of it and your obligation to me is over."

"You said that the last time."

"I give you my word."

"Hello, stranger," Dr. Andrew gently murmured to Song, reaching out to lay a hand on her upper arm.

At the same moment, Federenko issued an order to his men and they hauled Viktor to his feet, his arms braced behind him, all the blood suddenly drained from his cheeks and lips. As they wrestled him to the bedroom, she could see his shoulder blades flexing. He glanced back at Song with the doleful look of a dog abandoned as Dr. Andrew guided her in the opposite direction.

"Come with me, sister," the doctor whispered in Khmer. "There's nothing to worry about. Just do what I say."

As he led her to the bathroom, the doctor spoke again. "Give us a moment. We'll be three minutes, maybe. Four minutes max."

As they walked into the tiled room, Song's ears were pricked for a crash or shot or terrible scream of agony. But there was silence—not even furniture scraping on the floor. Even the sounds of the nearby building site—the relentless hammering that had punctuated their days—had miraculously stopped. It was as if the Russians were standing quietly in a circle, surrounding Viktor and saying their prayers.

Dr. Andrew closed the bathroom door. His bleak look melted into an expression of pity as he reached into his pocket to withdraw a thin cardboard box.

"You need to pee on this," he said, removing a short, plastic stick, half blue, half white, with a kind of empty window on one end. "Do you know what this is?"

"A test?"

"That's right. It's something he's doing to please Sovanna, I think. It's really not possible, the thing that he's asking."

As she lifted her sampot and lowered herself onto the toilet seat, the doctor turned his back to give her privacy. She watched his shoulders droop and his back begin to hunch—as if he was a schoolboy who had been put in the corner.

The dribble of pee fell over the end of the stick, echoing loudly in the water in the bowl. There was no sound from the bedroom, nothing from the main room. Time slowed down, as if measured in the drops between her legs, as if the workings of her body controlled who did what and when.

Finally, she stood up and let her sampot cover her legs again, holding the dry end of the stick in front of her. She looked at Dr. Andrew and wanted him to look back but, when he took the stick from her, his head remained bowed.

39

The gods were on his side, Fearless told himself, as he made it safely through passport control at Pochentong. J. D. would be meeting with the analysts from Langley; they would assess his story and the evidence from the notebook and decide how to act on Jimmy's hypothesis. But then, when the taxi pulled up at Sokha's house, he saw the violent buckle in the panel of the street gate.

Fearless edged on tiptoe through the gap in the gate. The front door was ajar but no noise came from within. His hand trembled when he pushed it open and saw a wicker chair overturned and balls of cushion stuffing. Fragments of china crunched underfoot.

He checked the kitchen: empty. No one in the bathroom. His teeth were clenched so hard his jaw began to smart. A bead of sweat slid across the tragus of his ear and gathered somewhere in his beard near his jawline.

At the door to the bedroom, a firework of blood burst across his vision.

Oh, Viktor, he wanted to cry. Face down. Unconscious. A crimson pool around his head—or, rather, the space where half his head had once been. His right hand clenched a handgun loosely. Outside, drilling from the building site started up.

Pointlessly, Fearless reached for a pulse.

Смерть не месть. Мертвые не страдают, read the tattoo on Viktor's forearm: *Death is not vengeance. The dead don't suffer.*

His body had been a book in which you could read his history—and now his present.

Fearless released the wrist and let it lie. For a brief moment, he put his hand on the soft white skin of Viktor's back. It was warm to the touch. If he'd come an hour earlier, he might have been able to prevent it—or maybe his body would be lying here too with a gun in its hand to mimic a shoot-out.

Quickly, he searched the room for any clues or leads. In Viktor's bag he found a photograph of Viktor himself, bare-chested and smiling, his arm around another man's shoulders: Grigory. Apart from that, Fearless found only clothes, a roll of riels, a couple of well-thumbed books with Cyrillic script. Here, a scrap of paper marked a page in the *Works of Shakespeare*: the last scene of *Macbeth*—a play Fearless despised.

He slipped out of the house and approached the motodops on the corner, taking a roll of dollars out of his pocket.

The white men had arrived in 4x4s, he learned.

A Cambodian girl came with them and another one left.

The second girl had something wrong with her face. But she stared at them angrily—she had no shame.

There was another barang also, on his own, in a military jeep.

"What time?" Fearless asked, pointing to his wrist.

"One hour," said one of the men.

"Baa baa. At four o'clock."

"Where did they go?"

Fearless reached into his pocket for more dollars, but was met with nothing but straight-mouthed smiles.

"You. Take me to Rue Pasteur, som toh."

At the moment Fearless swung his leg over the Daelim, another motodop rumbled up alongside his own. A conversation ensued between this man and his driver and before he knew it, riels were exchanging hands again.

"You come with me," the new man said to him. "I know place where your people go."

40

As the Land Cruiser rolled through Phnom Penh at a stately pace, motos gliding past its tinted glass, Song tried to hold back a surge of memories.

The bead of sweat hanging from the tip of his nose.

"Keep still, I told you. I said: don't move."

Afterward, Federenko standing in the corner. His back turned, his shoulders hunched, as he struggled with his belt.

"Orkun charan." *Thank you very much.* He had actually had the nerve to say that.

She had tried to put all these moments in a space outside the story: wash them away; clean herself up. They should have gone into the river and been borne by the current till they dissolved and were lost in the waters of the sea. But the river flows two ways. It brings everything back. She remembered Bun Thim's grimace as he raised his machete over his head. That was everyone's story; everyone she had ever known in her world. The past came back—it needed a moment, a spark—and you were there in your horrors again, in a time you'd thought was over.

Was that Sovanna squeezing her hand?

"I was right, oun. See? I was right."

"Open your eyes. Empty your mind," she had chanted to herself when he had been on top of her. "What's happening in the present will pass." She had believed it.

And what were they doing to Viktor right now? "Viktor!" she cried out.

"Don't worry, oun! Forget him." Sovanna stroked her face; her pupils were saucers.

When the Land Cruiser pulled into the drive of an imposing villa, Song was relieved to see Dr. Andrew's jeep. With him, she had someone trustworthy to guide her—a polestar in a dark and clouded sky.

Federenko himself opened the car door for her. She could sense that something had changed. As she got down, he reached out a hand to steady her and guided her gently in the direction of the house.

"Take a seat, Doctor," Federenko said, as they all walked into the villa's high-ceilinged atrium—a palatial space with a sunken seating area, Western-style fabric sofas, and tall plants in terracotta pots. Then he shouted in Russian at one of his men, who ran to an adjoining room to attend to something. When the man returned, Federenko pointed in his direction. "Go wash," he said in Khmer to Song. "There is a bedroom and bathroom. We will find you clothes."

When Song looked to Sovanna, she nodded in encouragement, taking her hand and leading her into the wet room.

As she stood under the water, she could see the garden through the concrete grill: fronds of swaying leaves, harsh sunlight, and no escape: a guard paced back and forth across the grass.

When she had finished, Sovanna was waiting for her in the bedroom.

"Bong—where are my clothes?"

"Those rags? Don't be silly."

On the bed, Sovanna had laid a pair of her hot pants and a floaty shirt—the kind of clothes Song used to wear during their working days. Beside them, a length of heavy silver silk was clearly intended to take the place of her old krama.

"This blouse is Guess," Sovanna said. "He bought it from a famous shop in London called Harrods."

"But I want my old shirt, and . . ." She wanted to explain, but Sovanna was already lifting the top over her head.

"He says he's going to take me to Paris and Moscow."

She was crouching down now to put Song's feet into the shorts. Song felt naked, her thighs and collarbone unclothed. And she was conscious of being exposed in another painful sense: during their separation, Sovanna's plans and wants had diverged from hers.

"Sa'aht!" cried Sovanna, stepping back to admire what she'd done. "And now we put makeup—like this. And this—"

"No no!"

Sovanna had a small zippable pencil case packed with plastic tubes and brushes. It was as if she meant to pretend that none of it had ever happened—or was it just the heedlessness of the drugs? She waved a blusher brush in circles around Song's face, the soft filaments whispering against her cheeks and eyelids. Song gave in to the feel of her finger and thumb, the way they tenderly, kindly, steadied her chin. She wanted there to be nothing between them anymore—that was the most important thing—no distance or hurt or lie or sense of guilt.

"Now this," said Sovanna, reaching for the fabric.

"No. I don't want it, Sovanna. It's okay. Leave it there."

"Good. You don't need it. Not at all." Sovanna nudged her back into the main room, whispering. "He's really not so bad. I think when he smiles he's even handsome. Last night he took me to a restaurant on our own. He is going to give us freedom—not like with Vasiliev. We can decide where we want to go. And then, you know the best thing . . ." She leaned in and lowered her voice even further. "Afterward, he tried, but he can't get it up!"

He can when he's forcing himself on someone, Song wanted to tell her. There were plenty like that; Sovanna knew better than anyone.

Federenko and Dr. Andrew were waiting for them in the lounge.

"Leave us now, Sovanna. Yes yes. You heard me."

After Sovanna had gone up the stairs, Federenko stepped forward. "Did they not leave you something to cover your head?" he said to her.

She stared back at him silently, thinking of Viktor.

"You come with us," he said to her, adding an awkward "please," leading them into another room, a small study whose walls were lined with empty bookshelves.

"I need to take some blood," Dr. Andrew said. "It will help us do tests to make sure everything is okay. You can give us some privacy," he added, nodding to Federenko.

"I will stay."

"No, you won't. As you yourself know, I extend the same courtesies to all my patients. You leave or I leave."

When Federenko had shut the door, Dr. Andrew opened his doctor's bag.

"Have you been feeling ill at all, Song? Tell me. Tell me everything."

"I've been sick sometimes. Vomiting. And tired all the time."

"And your periods?"

"My . . ."

"Your bleeding. Is it regular?"

"It comes. But never at the same time. Always different."

"Same same but different," he muttered with a grim smile. "But when was the last one? The last time you bled."

"Not for a long time," she said. "A long, long time."

She could hear him exhale. "You are going to have a baby," he said. "Do you understand?"

She nodded, but she knew that it couldn't be possible. "But . . ."

"I know it's hard to believe. The blood test will confirm it."

His attitude—of kind, caring concern—and the fact that she trusted him made everything worse. Worse because sympathy opened up floodgates to feelings that she didn't need to overwhelm her now.

"I don't want to ask, Song, but I have to—understand." He leaned in and reached out to lay his hand upon hers. "Have you had sex with anyone other than . . . *him?*"

To say yes, to confirm beyond all doubt that the baby was Federenko's would ensure that she—and the child—were cared for, and that she could stay by Sovanna's side. But equally, it would mean she would be tied to a monster who had given the orders to kill Bopha—sweet Bopha—and Dara and Rathana and Samnang too.

What if she lied? She could say it was Thom's child—that, all along, in their rooms, he had been using her for sex. No one could deny it and she might be allowed to go, but Sovanna would be lost and so might the child, without the right treatment to make sure it was healthy.

Because this is my *child*, she thought for the first time. *It is mine as much as his. It's part of me.* It was inconceivable—as inconceivable as making her scars disappear—and yet it was true, this wonder she had always discounted. For a moment, she sensed the baby—a kind of warmth in her arms; an energy spreading through her and hovering around her skin.

"No. Only him. The child is his. I'm sure."

Dr. Andrew nodded. "That helps me to know how far along you are." He turned to the door to the atrium and took a deep breath. "Come in!" he called out. He spoke in English now.

Federenko entered, his face drained of color. "So?"

"It's yours."

"One hundred percent?"

"She's sure."

"I just take her word?"

Dr. Andrew's face flushed red—not in embarrassment but in warning. "There's no way of being one hundred percent sure. Not before the child is born."

"But we can take DNA—from me, from the fetus."

"That would require an amniocentesis: inserting a sharp needle into the uterus. With the past procedures Song's had, the risks could be catastrophic. As it is, you'll need the best obstetric advice and tests to rule out an ectopic pregnancy. After all that, if she carries the baby to term—and I must stress the odds in this case are compromised—DNA testing could easily be done."

Sovanna now hurried into the room, pushing past Federenko. Her pupils were even more dilated, the smile on her face a mask; her limbs and fingers trembled perceptibly.

"Leave us, Sovanna! Can't you see we're still talking?"

"It's okay. I stay." She put her hands on Song's shoulders. "And Song is staying also, isn't that right?"

"Go, Sovanna!"

"No. She lives with us, yes? Yes? You answer."

Federenko's repressed anger had a concrete target now. "She will stay. But get out! Come on. Get out!"

Sovanna didn't move. She jutted out her chin.

"I need help! Someone now. Get in here, I say!"

Two men hurried in.

"Take the girl upstairs."

Song reached out for Sovanna but the men dragged her away. Behind the slammed door, her cries faded, then disappeared.

Federenko moved closer, lowering his voice.

"You tell her this. I don't want anything lost in translation. She lives with us and has the baby. But we keep this . . ."—he gestured to himself and then to Song—"secret."

Song nodded her assent when Dr. Andrew finished his unnecessary translation. She herself no longer knew how Sovanna would handle the truth.

Now, an angry scream rose up outside the house. Sovanna had broken away and the men had cornered her on the grass. Song moved to the window and saw her trying to sidestep them, her hair flashing this way and that around her shoulders. There was spirit still inside her—her old, fiery intelligence. In the midst of everything that had happened, it had been Sovanna who had seen what Song had been unable to: that the story she had been telling herself could not hold. Behind the deadness of the junkie's eyes, the embers of the real Sovanna were burning, alive to possibility in a way Song had never been.

She put her hand on her stomach and felt its warmth. For the first time since her face had been stolen, she had something precious that someone else wanted.

That was what Federenko was really scared of. That she could use what she had inside her to mess with his little plans. She could demand that Sovanna be taken off the drugs. She could make Federenko help her wean Sovanna off them. She had found Sovanna in body—and now she would nurse her spirit back to life.

41

Just as Fearless arrived, brimming with rage, the goon at the villa's entrance turned and lumbered away. Fearless saw him heading down the side of the house where his colleagues were struggling with a writhing animal— a spinning ball of black hair and limb. Then Amos appeared, moving the other men aside to take control.

Fearless made straight for the villa's front door, his fists white-knuckled, his forearms jar-tight.

Entering, he stood in a vast, high-ceilinged square. Ceiling fans wobbling over a rectangular, sunken lounge. Two low-backed sofas facing each other. Not a soul. But then he heard a familiar voice.

". . . lost in translation . . ."

". . . she will live with us and have the baby . . ."

". . . but we keep this . . . secret."

When he tiptoed toward a half-open door, he caught a glimpse of a nut-brown arm.

Now he heard Andrew's voice, talking in Khmer.

What baby? Had Federenko returned to arrange some kind of adoption? But then he remembered Song complaining of a bad stomach, scurrying to the toilet after the day at Stung Meanchey. But the girls' tubes were tied; Federenko had said that himself.

He pushed firmly on the door. Song was in front of him. She wasn't wearing her krama; he could see the glabrous swirl of her acid burn. Her arm was wrapped with a Velcro cuff; Dr Andrew stood beside her, pumping its rubber bulb in his fist. Federenko, slightly apart, turned around to see him.

"What the hell!"

Then Fearless was flying straight at Federenko's throat, his right foot sweeping his legs from beneath him. They were both on the floor, Fearless straddling his torso; he was throttling him, Federenko's fat hands flapping around.

A few more seconds and he would finish Viktor's mission. He had never really known how strong he was. Federenko's eyes widened and began to bulge; his feet started to twitch and tap on the floor.

But then Fearless's body took to the air and the back of his head hit the concrete-tiled floor. His vision capsized before flipping and righting itself. He saw two Amoses, both ready to strike.

When he pushed up, he felt something warm on his neck. The side of his head hummed; a high tone rang in his ears.

More men gathered in the doorway. Had they killed Sovanna? Beaten her senseless?

Federenko staggered to his feet, retching and clutching his throat.

"You sent me to die in Siem Reap," Fearless spat.

"Where have you come from? Are you out of your *fucking* mind?!"

Fearless pressed his hand to the well of his collarbone, looked at the blood, and wiped it on his jeans.

"I see it now. The shock on your face! You sent me to die in Angkor. You put me in that jail."

He knew the truth of it in his body.

"And . . . you already tried to kill me . . . at the Naga . . . Of course. It was *you* . . . It was *you* who spiked my drink."

He remembered the morning after the night Song saved him. The two Khmer boys had come into his room first. They had been sent ahead to carry his body out.

Alyosha scowled silently and reached both his hands to his throat again.

"Why? Tell me why!"

"What's happened to you, Fearless? Really. What the—"

"I saw the Rohypnol. I saw it in your toiletry bag."

"So what. I have sleeping pills. Why would I spike your drink? I don't even know when it is that you are talking about! Most probably it is Wish. He's the one who hates your guts. What the hell. Why are we having this conversation? You just appear out of the blue, ranting and raving."

Fearless stayed down. It could have been Wish.

"Why did you kill the children? Tell me—what purpose did it serve?"

"Kill who?"

"The children. You gave Wish his orders."

"What? Tell him, Amos. We have nothing to do with children."

Amos's eyes remained fixed on the floor. "We have nothing to do with children," he repeated.

What did Amos know? Fearless wondered. Wasn't he just a faithful servant who Federenko used and micromanaged, who knew no more than Federenko needed him to? Each person was a pawn in Federenko's reality: sacrificed or exchanged, but always a vehicle for his works.

"Did you watch the tape? Because I saw you there. Your hand was resting on the curtain. That shiny Rolex watch. You were there. Watching. You knew everything that was going on."

He was taking a risk—he ought to keep the existence of the other tapes a secret. But Federenko couldn't be sure he wasn't referring to the original.

"You saw a Rolex. What? A Rolex on the tape." He flapped the placket of his shirt back and forth. "But of course you did! The Colonel—Vasiliev—has the same." He raised his hand and tapped on the golden dial. "One of our partners gave him the exact same gift. Did you see me on the tape? I mean *me*! Of course not—"

"I saw your hand," Fearless said, under his breath and unheard.

"Why? Because I wasn't there. You know it. In your heart. You listened to that madman, didn't you? That crazy faggot with his revenge and his orders from the FSB. Please. What the fuck has happened to you, Fearless?" Alyosha lifted up his head and tutted.

FSB—the same accusation Viktor leveled against Federenko.

"He saw Vasiliev's watch and thinks it's me!" Alyosha said to Amos. "Are you hearing this? He is saying now that I'm watching those bastards."

Was it true? Had Fearless got everything wrong? He remembered a watch face looming up in the Naga Bar. A golden circle, with three smaller black circles within it: it was Vasiliev, pointing to the time before he left him in the booth. But he pushed on. "You did nothing with the tape. You just used it to get Sovanna from Vasiliev, didn't you? And then to get me thrown into that shithole of a jail."

Now Federenko's voice had a note of weariness. "What the hell," he sighed. "First you claim I try to kill you. Then you say I got you arrested." He waved his hand. "Get him out of here."

Fearless looked up at Song, whose eyes were turned away. In the avalanche of rages and realizations tumbling around him, he had forgotten what had brought him to the villa in the first place. The scratch of tearing Velcro split the silence as Dr. Andrew removed the blood pressure cuff. She was pregnant—and the baby . . . He looked at her, willing her to meet his gaze.

Federenko's men hauled Fearless to his feet and dragged him to the lounge before he could say another word. They hustled him across the tiles, through a door into a box room, which lay empty save for a solitary wooden chair, and hurled him to the dusty floor, locking the door behind them. On his feet, he tried the handle and kicked the bottom rail, only to provoke angry thumps in return on the other side. Then he took his anger out on the wooden chair, smacking it across the room, leaving it upended in the corner.

What now?

He couldn't shape his scattered thoughts into sentences. There was only the splatter of blood around Viktor's head, Song's stomach distended with Federenko's baby, the thrum of the blow he'd received to his temple. He circled the four walls, kicking up dust from the bare concrete. He slapped the cold plaster with the fat of his hand. Twice he tried to jump to test the barred window, but it was set high in the wall, well beyond his reach.

After he had sunk down to the floor in despair, he heard something outside—Russian voices: two men patrolling the garden.

"Dima heard him say. Where I go, they go. He won't let them out of his sight for a second now."

"As if she isn't enough trouble—"

"Beautiful trouble, mind."

"But now this sister—this one with the face."

Five minutes later, the same pair returned. He could hear the scratch of a match and the first drag on a cigarette. But then the men moved, just out of earshot.

He pressed himself as close to the wall as he could.

"The nineteenth." He was sure that he heard "The nineteenth." There was something about "dust" and something about a "border."

After that, there were no more patrols in the garden. Fearless sat on the floor, his arms crossed around his knees. Outside, he could hear the noise of traffic on a distant boulevard. A man with a hoarse voice walked past in the street, shouting words that sounded like *Edge-eye! Edge-eye!*, metal wheels trundling and squeaking along. After an hour or so, the daylight began to dim, slipping through the colors of dusk in minutes, one moment flat white, the next Prussian blue.

Then a key rasped in the lock and Federenko entered, his hand flicking the switch of the bare bulb above. He nodded upward to signal to the men who came behind him. "Leave us," he said, waving his hand past his ear. "It's okay. He can't kill me. Tell Amos to bring us a drink."

"Fuck your drink," said Fearless.

"And bring food. He must be hungry."

When the men had gone, Federenko closed the door behind him. He walked toward the wall with the high, barred window and stood, his hands joined together behind his back. Then he turned, set the wooden chair upright in the middle of the room, and jiggled it to ensure it would bear his weight. When he sat down, he let out a long, loud sigh.

"Mon frère, this has all been a big misunderstanding. How could you even think I'd hurt you for a minute. And kill innocent children. Come, come. Please. If you care so much for the children, find Vasiliev. That's what I'd do. Why look for me?"

"Because you are Pol Pot."

"What?"

"You're Pol Pot." Fearless said it like an automaton, speaking it in a dream, saying it before he even thought it. "Wish told us everything."

"Wish! He has lost his mind. You saw it in the Naga. He's mentally and spiritually weak. Wasn't that why you took your photos in Sarajevo? His fragility. His vulnerability. Anyway, he's gone. A fact that tells you everything. He sinned and ran away."

"He killed on your orders."

"No, Fearless. Please." Federenko rose to his feet and walked back to the barred window. "You don't know what it is to be a leader of men. There are times you give instructions. When you want something done.

"*Fas*! you say. And you do not specify the means and ways. But I cannot do everything. I cannot be everywhere. I cannot hold Wish's hand or Amos's or yours. And I tell them! Every time, before they go, I tell them. Control yourselves. Don't let things get out of hand. But men don't listen. They take things too far. I see this many times in Afghanistan. They explode. Sometimes it's only way for them to stay sane. Some made necklaces of ears, I tell you. Dried, human ears. Necklaces of them.

"Please. What happened, Fearless? How do you believe this shit? If ever I see Wish again, I'll give him what he deserves."

Could it be true? Wish had implicated Alyosha only after Viktor had tormented and beaten him.

"You're emotional, bacha. My God—the things you've been through. When we grieve, when we're under stress, we fall prey to ideas." He pressed his fingers to his cheeks and sighed.

Was he right?

And yet Fearless recalled Richard's words—how he'd maintained it would be impossible to pin Federenko down, that even when he walked around with bloodstained hands, none of his crimes would ever be substantiated. Fearless felt like a teenager in an Introduction to Philosophy class, faced with the contention that the falling tree in the forest makes no sound when no one is there to hear it—or that nothing exists save the contents of one's own mind: things obviously untrue but impossible to disprove.

"Why do nothing with the tape? What about the children? What about the shit those bastards were doing to them?"

"I told you to be patient, to wait. To leave it to me."

"You took a videotape of little children being abused and used it. Used it to trade a girl, a slave for your own pleasure."

Fearless could see the muscles in Federenko's jaw tighten. Federenko turned his back to him and put his hands on his hips.

"Do you ever get tired of being . . . so . . . fucking . . . naive? All those years I was jealous of you, in awe of everything you are. The tape was worth nothing! Can't you see? Not here! No justice would have come from it. So yes—yes, I use it—not to buy a girl but to free her! I'll be damned if I apologize. Not now. Not ever. I *love* Sovanna and have suffered to see her in pain."

"You suffered so much you slept with her sister!" Fearless remembered the Rohypnol in the silver blister pack. "Of course. You drugged Song and forced yourself on her. You sick fuck. Why? So you could pretend she was Sovanna?"

Federenko turned and scowled at him like a cat. "I was drunk! Nothing more. And she was grateful for the attention. What business is it of yours? You want the freak for yourself?"

"And the gobstoppers," Fearless muttered. "You bought those little kids sweets. Special sweets—all the way from little England. Jesus. When were you there?"

Federenko was sweating now; little beads glistened along his hairline. "The tape," he said, "was an opportunity. You cannot blame the bird of prey for carrying off the lamb. An opportunity, Fearless—do you even know what this means? You people don't get it because you have already everything. A cream for every pimple. No kasha for every fucking meal. And jars of birch juice and sauerkraut again and again. The idea of rejecting things! Your father was the extreme—turning his back on a lordship! To become a Communist professor! That is just . . . fucking ridiculous. And all of you—you have the luxury of being observers. Observers of history and never its victims. No, no. For us, when opportunity comes, we must take it."

Opposite views of the same set of facts: had it always been this way between them?

"In life, Fearless, there are people who read the writing on the wall. And there are people—like me—who do the writing. When we act, we create our own reality. And while you're studying that reality, we act again, creating new ones. When will you understand?"

Federenko shook his head, faster and faster and faster, as if the action was powering some dark dynamo inside him.

"Life's a fight! You bite and scratch! That's what you do, Fearless. How many times I tell this very thing to Amos!

"And just tell me—what is love? Or kindness? Only the desire to make yourself feel good. And what is compassion if not a way of flattering yourself, of trying to take your little worries away? All the bastards staring at your pictures in their newspapers! So sympathetic—and yet they will never admit that their big houses and fast cars are built on other people's misery. And fairness? Something only the weak believe. When you understand, you see you must satisfy only yourself. That, in the end, is everything."

His tone grew lighter, as if he had cut the anchor rope to Fearless's accusations.

"This is the story of Russian history. For Communism to triumph, we wipe out everyone who stands in our way. The purges, the terror: the end justifies the means. For capitalism to defeat Communism, we put the law in the hands of criminals: once again, the end justifies the means."

Fearless thought of his father in the French Governor's Palace, sitting on the dais, face-to-face with Pol Pot. Was this the logic he had dared to question? He might have quoted Gandhi—that the means are, in the end, absolutely everything. Fearless spoke the words out loud, faltering:

"If I want to take your watch, I shall surely have to fight for it. If I want to buy it, I shall have to pay for it. If I want it as a gift, I shall have to beg and plead for it. According to the means I employ, the watch is either stolen property, my own property, or a donation. Different means produce different results. That's what Gandhi said. As the means, so the end."

Federenko tapped his fingernail on the crystal of his Rolex. "All that is important is that this watch is mine. And you will never have it. God damn it: *this* is system. Communism, capitalism, all the ideologies people like to invent: they are costumes on the body of our deeper human nature—over what we are and cannot change."

Fearless's head spun. "So we're all selfish, then. All of us? Corrupt."

"Corruption. Selfishness. Use those words if it makes you feel better. In the end, it is the only breach against chaos."

A kind of drowsiness fell upon Fearless's shoulders—as if someone were pushing down with heavy hands. Federenko's certitude was an intoxicating drug. Why weren't selfishness and sybaritism legitimate ways to live? After all, Fearless had tried everything else and failed.

And yet there was still part of him that wanted to fight back.

"What you forget is all the people struggling against what you're talking about. People who value kindness. Altruism. Equality. Maybe your side is winning: God knows you and I have seen the evidence. Maybe it has always won—but that doesn't mean it's over. Me. Laure. Conrad. So many. Devoted to realizing the justice you love to belittle. Who *are* free and *do* question this human nature you speak of."

Federenko chuckled, then threw his head back and laughed. "You people more than anyone are part of the system! Perhaps the most crucial, vital part there is. You aren't free. No! You've never been free."

"Fuck you."

"You are a product of the system, Fearless. You have been groomed by it, nurtured by it. You have been educated in a certain way. You have succeeded because who you are and what you believe and do is acceptable. You went to the right school. You dropped out of the right university. You know the right people who themselves know all the other right people."

Fearless remembered the network he had drawn on: Conrad, Jimmy, Luke, Richard.

"You forget how much time I have spent with you, Fearless. In your little club, with your standard responses to the world. At least in the USSR we knew we weren't free. We knew we were being policed every second of our lives. You people aren't even aware of how much you are controlled. You go along like lemmings, without even knowing. You have been selected because you have a talent for being the people you are. Because it pays to play nice, and costs dearly not to. You can think and act freely—but within limits that are already set.

"And then you flatter yourself that because there is a Watergate or—what's this British minister's name—Aitken?—that you are free to—what's your phrase?—*speak truth to power*. Bullshit! Even now you refuse to see it. You're like a fly buzzing against a window. I open it and try to wave you out but still you throw yourself again against the glass.

"And your photography! Don't get me started on your stupid photography. I have watched you—with Wish—now there's a good example!—taking dozens of pictures, shot after shot. And then you choose the one with the expression that fits, that conveys the message you already decided upon. It is always the situation as *you* want to see it."

Now Federenko adopted a wheedling voice: "Alyosha, we go to the barracks today. Alyosha, this afternoon you take me to the morgue. Take me to the places where there is evidence of the evil I've already imagined."

"How clever you are," said Fearless under his breath. "How brilliant, standing there, mocking me all this time."

It was in Grozny, Fearless saw, that he should have put two and two together. In addition to his work as Fearless's fixer, Alyosha was obviously dabbling in other things. Fearless made nothing of it, for it never got in his way—Alyosha was always available, ready to take him where he wanted. And even though Fearless knew that serious money was being made as unscrupulous officials seized control of oil wells and metal exports, he had always told himself that Alyosha's business was just small-time.

He'd been too caught up in his work, he realized now. He had prided himself on being nonjudgmental. And then, love had drawn him across its event horizon, swallowing him whole and leaving him blank.

That was an excuse, though! Christ, he had been blank already. What had he ever really known about people? How to frame them? What angle of light worked best on their faces? The forms around them that would set them off perfectly in a square? Did he truly know anything about what other human beings thought or wanted, what the masks of their faces did or did not conceal?

"Were we ever friends?" Fearless's voice was barely a whisper. "No. It was all . . . What was it? Tell me."

Federenko grew terse: the frustrated parent of a toddler. "I've done what I can. How much I have done, tried to spare you from everything. Ask yourself this: if I was really the bastard you say—a child killer—why would I bring you here to Cambodia? What purpose would it serve? I brought you here to help. And not only do you have no gratitude—you decide to make trouble! I leave on urgent business and you get yourself thrown in jail."

Alyosha walked back and forth, his shadow tracking him. It was clear he felt he was the victor of the debate. He'd worked his way through the thickets of Fearless's objections and broken out into clear, open meadow.

"And how do you think you even got out of jail? By magic? It was me that made calls. It was me that used my influence."

It was a stone-cold lie. Finally, an icy wave broke across the fantasy that Fearless might somehow be mistaken, that this whole thing might be a gigantic misunderstanding. It was Song who had freed him: a story so improbable that Federenko could never have imagined it was true. How he lied, spouting the first thing that entered his head, so confident that he not only knew the limits of other people's knowledge but could set and adjust them according to his will. This, Fearless realized, wasn't the opposite of Alyosha's love for him. It *was* his love. He had always remembered what Fearless had confided, making him feel that he was known and complete. In the long wake after his mother's forgetting, that had been a life raft for him to cling onto.

Federenko sat down again on the chair, hitching up the knees of his slacks as he did so.

"How I've loved you, bacha. But we're living through the end. I want you to see. Can't you see? The beginning of the end was your Industrial Revolution. From that, everything follows. Like thread from a ball of wool. No! Like toilet paper from the roll. Yes! That's better."

For so long at Vasiliev's beck and call, surrounded by thugs with no interest in the life of the mind, Federenko needed someone to appreciate his Weltanschauung—someone whom he considered his intellectual equal.

"Once this thing is set free, it goes to the end. To destruction. And that means life is so simple. He gets it. This new prime minister. What's his name?"

"Tony Blair."

"Yes. Toe-nibbler. You see it with his big American grin. How he has accepted the truth, that there is only this choice."

He put his thumb and forefinger together and used them to punctuate the beginning of each question, as if he was throwing a series of darts.

"Do I live wholly, completely, for myself? Do I live focused on what I want? Yes! Your people made this choice a long time ago. Whether you want to accept it. Whether you like it or not. Never pursue a phantom, Pushkin said. Or waste your efforts on the air. Love yourself, your only care! And now my people can make that choice too. This is the freedom I talk about. Freedom. At last."

Federenko's thumb and forefinger closed into a tight, quivering fist and he rose and slowly walked to the window bars. One could feel his will to power following behind, a dark puma, biceps flexing beneath velvet legs.

How grim, Fearless thought, that he had spent so much time with this bastard—more time with him than all the honest people in his life combined.

Satisfied the conversation had come to an end, Federenko turned sharply on his heels and faced him. His voice was managerial, devoid of emotion.

"You know, Fearless, I'm sorry our friendship is over. But I will not forgive the accusations you have made. Tonight, we leave Cambodia and you won't see me again. Not after everything you have said. No, no. Anyone else in my position—being attacked, being insulted—wouldn't think twice. Not in this world. They would show no mercy. But I don't forget you saved my life. I am a man of honor."

Inside, Fearless laughed bitterly. But why answer back? Let him enjoy his little story about debts and obligations.

Federenko walked to the door and reached for the handle.

But there was a flaw in his philosophy—a gap through which Fearless might reach:

"One thing, Alyosha. If it's true there's no future. If it's true there's no point in living for anything but yourself—why care about this baby that

Song is having? Why not let Song leave? I'll make sure she's looked after. You'll never hear from us again."

"What is this girl to you? Why do you care about her so much?"

"I was in a state. She cleaned me up. God knows what would have happened if she hadn't been there."

"Well, I'll tell her you said thank you. How's that? Are you satisfied?"

"Let me see her, at least. All I ask is one minute."

Federenko opened the door. "Okay—whatever." He crossed the threshold and reached back for the handle. "You're right. I shouldn't care. But it's hard to resist the old thinking. Sometimes, I guess, we can't help ourselves." He shut the door and Fearless heard his receding footsteps.

"Sometimes we can't help ourselves," Fearless echoed under his breath.

A few minutes later, the door swung open and Amos appeared, with Song following behind. "Two minutes," said Amos. "Then we take you to Pochentong."

Amos shut them in the room, but positioned himself behind the door, his feet breaking the line of light under its sill.

Song kept her head down. She did not look at him. He wanted to rush to her, but something—a strange kind of etiquette—froze his limbs.

"Viktor is dead," she whispered.

His mute response was enough.

She looked up at him fiercely. "You go now too. Far away! Back to England."

"There's no way I will leave you here."

"You must go. You have to go."

There was something in her eyes—a glittering hardness, a determination—that he had never seen in the short time he'd known her. She had discarded her krama out of pride, he realized—while he was still wearing his same old long-sleeved shirt.

"This is the best place for me," she told him. "For the baby I am having." She reached up reflexively to cradle her stomach. "And I will be with Sovanna again. We will all be together."

Before he could think how he might respond, she raised her voice and began to shout at him in Khmer. The words came thick and fast—a twang and thrum, like guitar strings wound too tight, ringing through the air.

"What are you doing, Song?"

She was yelling, the pitch of her voice rising. She was accusing him, disabusing him—or just plain abusing him. The dark shapes under the doorsill shifted and grew. The handle of the door began to turn.

"Go now!" she whispered harshly before the door came away from the jamb. "Forget this. Please. And never come back."

Amos burst in. "Right—out!" he shouted. "Whatever this is, it ain't carrying on."

Before Fearless could remonstrate, he was being pulled out of the room. Reflexively, he reached for the photo in his pocket, of Viktor and Grigory smiling, their arms around each other; he dropped it on the ground for Song to pick up. Then he was tripping across the steps in the villa's atrium, into the sunken lounge, across it and back up, into the foyer, out of the front door, into the night air thick with heat and dust and the relentless, infernal buzzing of the cicadas.

PART 5

42

Back in the air, en route from Pochentong to Bangkok, as he knocked back first one gin and tonic and then another, Fearless did his best to make the facts do his bidding.

"Go now. Never come back!" she had said. The words reverberated inside his cranium. It was a different Song from the one he had left in Phnom Penh—as if the time she had spent in Viktor's company had forged her glowing metal into tough, unbending form. The airplane goblet cracked in his grip. After wedging it into the seat pocket, he lurched to the toilet.

"Am I just like *him*?" he muttered: the Great White Bastard who does what he pleases—abusing people, saving them from abuse, believing that they want and need him.

Safely inside the toilet, he had a vision of himself from a higher point of view, floating in the darkness at twenty thousand feet, the mists running off the fuselage as it roared through moonlit cloud. He could see himself through the plane's carbon fiber skin, sitting in his locked box, head in his hands: an impossible X-ray photograph that he could only take inside his mind.

"I will not feel. I will not feel until I have to," he chanted to himself—but the mantra had long lost its power. Feeling was no different than the sound of the pressurized cabin, the constant drone of gas rushing through the plane's vents, seeping through the hinges and the gaps in the plastic fascia. But with it there was also the clear, hard knowledge he had gained over the past four weeks: that he could no longer remain a bystander, riding on death's back as a way of making sure he never came face-to-face with it; and that there was a difference between the thwack of the bamboo cane on his face and his father's death (two things long merged in his mind), which was also the same difference between Laure's death and the children's horrible fate: the latter were man-made things that could be reconciled by man.

And that man would be him.

"Where the hell are you?" said Jimmy.

"In a hotel in Bangkok. Tell me what's happened before we lose the line."

There was silence—not the silence of satellite gaps or crossed wires.

"Did J. D. meet with the men from Langley?"

"Yes, but . . . I don't know what to say. It was a failure. A . . . fiasco."

"What do you mean?"

"He called me afterward. He was in absolute hysterics."

"I thought you said that this guy could be trusted."

"He can. The Americans met him as arranged—at a hotel in town. But then they drove him to an apartment, to a room with other men that they didn't introduce. They sat him down, hooked him up to a polygraph, and grilled him—not with one or two questions but on and on. Five hours. They didn't let up. Why was he lying? they said. How much was he being paid? They questioned everything I'd told them. They said he had a drug problem. They didn't give him breaks. No food, no water. Just the same bloody questions. He lost it—who wouldn't? He cracked, started screaming. He told them that everything he had said was true while the polygraph needle went crazy on the charts.

"Then they showed the paper to him and said it proved he was a liar. Said they should take him to the police—but they'd show mercy and let him go."

"What the fuck?" Fearless said. "Why do that?"

"I don't know."

"You have no idea?"

"It's Traoré. That's all I can think. That Traoré for them is somehow untouchable. That for some reason they'll protect him—whatever he's implicated in. In return for services rendered. A line of information. I don't know. But that's what my instincts and the little digging I've done are telling me. Traoré got his degree at Bentley College in the U.S. And his military training courtesy of Gaddafi in Libya. He moves between worlds, making himself useful. You know how this works. Who pays Mobutu?"

"But even if Traoré's untouchable, can't they do something about this deal? There are other parties involved. And I have a specific date and place. They'll all be in Foya a little after the nineteenth of this month."

Awkward silence again, like a banker before a Select Committee: obligated to speak but loath to answer.

"They're leaving this alone, Joe. And so must I."

Frustration caught in Fearless's mouth, stuck on the hooks of old loyalties and discretion, before his anger ripped it free in little shreds.

"Fuck your orders! And fuck whoever orders you around."

"What the hell! I'm trying to help. People can't always be vessels for you to accomplish the things you want. When will you learn that? You're a fucking grown man. What do you think this means for me? I made J. D. promises. I lost my professional compass. And now my ability's being questioned."

"There *has* to be something we can do, Jimmy, please."

"There's no plan B."

"What about the codes? The flight numbers? The registrations."

"There's nothing more on those."

"You mean you've checked and turned up nothing? Maybe someone at GCHQ might know something."

That silence again.

"You haven't checked and you won't. At least have the guts to say it."

"You think intelligence is about discovering the truth. Is that it? You moron. It's like any other work in this world. People don't like doing any more than they have to. That means being suspicious of information you didn't generate—let alone information that overturns everything you believe. These guys have their reality. They don't want an alternative!

If they discredit J. D., then a threat to their narrative is gone. All the buds and branches of an intricate bough are pruned right back, nice and neat. They wave their polygraph paper and say, 'Here. We proved it was bullshit.'"

"If that's true, Jimmy, then all the terrorists and troublemakers in the world have to do is . . . be original! The more imaginative, the more unconventional they are, the more likely it is that no one will suspect a thing. They just do what no one expects—like drive a ten-ton truck bomb into the U.S. embassy in an East African city."

"Put yourself in their shoes," Jimmy said. "Everyone's scared of the unknown. And this is so unconventional it beggars belief: Islamic terrorists, the RUF, arms from Trans-Dniester, blood diamonds. No one would ever—"

Feeling that he was about to fall from a great height, Fearless lowered the receiver back into its cradle. The ground raced toward him. He could see his reflection: plummeting through mirrored glass, clothes flying up behind him.

He realized now how much he had wanted the legitimacy of the official world. It was seductive: the confirmation that what he was living through was not chimera and shadow. He remembered Jimmy's enthusiasm when they had first met with J. D.: the Americans will "run with it"—he'd said it a dozen times. *They'll run with it*—a newspaper expression Fearless should have recognized: the enthusiasm of the assistant editor before the chief says no.

That night, in an unremarkable bar in Bangkok, Fearless hunched over a string of double whiskeys, only vaguely aware of the dark forms of other customers passing back and forth under the dim light of paper lanterns. On a mute television above the bartender's head, CNN's ticker scrolled news about falling markets.

"Et tu, Jimmy?" he whispered under his breath.

How do you live without the continuity other people bring to your life? Without Laure, without his mother, and now, it seemed, without Jimmy. Who would be left to bear witness to who he was, to all the things he had done, to all the places and times he spanned? That was another thing that Federenko managed effortlessly, jettisoning the ballast of his past as he rose relentlessly into a stratosphere of wealth and power.

He picked up his heavy tumbler and brought it down, its bottom making a hard, resounding tock. The bartender paused in his toweling of the bar, raised his eyebrows, and carried on.

"He let his own wife go to jail. His own wife! Can you believe!" Viktor spat in a corner of his mind.

"Vera. Yes," Fearless said out loud.

There *was* ballast that Federenko could not shed. He remembered how Federenko had called her a *wet hen* when he had first arrived at the apartment in Phnom Penh—which one might translate as *old bag* in this context; a hundred and thirty pounds' worth of sand lodged in his balloon's wicker basket.

He slid some dollars and a handful of silver baht across the bar and headed back to his room to pack his bags. There was a direct flight from Don Mueang to Istanbul, wasn't there? From there to Kyiv: how hard could it be? And from Kyiv it would be no more than an hour to Odesa. His mind was a giant airport ticker board, split flaps flipping and rattling destinations. He had nowhere else to go; this was the final call.

43

After Fearless had been removed, Song was allowed to go upstairs to the room Sovanna shared with Federenko. When she entered, she found Sovanna curled up on the double bed, her eyelids ever so slightly open. Song sat on the floor beside her, watching a wisp of hair ribboning in Sovanna's breath. Over Sovanna's shoulder, she could see Federenko's toiletry bag by the bedside—a repulsive and intimate reminder of his dominion.

When Sovanna stirred, the two of them stared at each other for a moment, a slight smile touching the corner of Sovanna's lips. "You're here. I knew it," she murmured, reaching out a finger to run across Song's cheek. "I had a dream, you know. That we had a little girl. And we were her mothers together, the two of us alone. And we were always there, even when she was old. That's what we'll do. I feel it in my bones."

"I hope so, bong. I really do."

"You mustn't mind him. Though we won't let him know that!" She chuckled silently and let her legs slide from the bed. "We play our cards right," she whispered, looking to the door to suggest they might be overheard. "We can have a good life here, you and me."

For a moment, Song saw a Sovanna that almost seemed lucid. But when she went to the bathroom and came back a few minutes later, her eyes were glazed again and her words heavily slurred. She slumped on the middle of the bed in a starfish shape, apparently transfixed by the ceiling's blank screen.

By the time darkness had fallen, Song had decided: she would have to take control of the situation. Later, when they put a meal in front of her, she played the willful toddler, pushing it away from her and across the table.

Amos drew his lips together, holding himself rigid like a palace guard. Above them, the ceiling fan rotated lazily. Cicadas buzzed in the foliage outside. After thirty seconds, he stepped forward and edged the plate back. But once he had retreated Song pushed it away again.

Knitting his brows, Amos left the room.

"Eat!" said Federenko as he strode in a minute later. "You must—for the sake of the baby. Come on. Eat."

He tapped on his belly and she had a vivid memory of its flab, covered in curly hairs, hanging over her body. She kept her eyes on a point in the middle distance and did not blink or open her mouth.

"What is this?" Federenko asked. His eyes had widened. He looked to Amos, who remained impassive.

Half a minute passed with no one moving or speaking.

"Sovanna must stop the yama. And you will make her stop," Song said finally.

Speaking in Khmer with him made her seem bolder. She had to speak without euphemism; there could be no question of diplomacy. Moreover, he found it difficult to set the tone. She relished the irony of this; she could have spoken to him in English, but he assumed her English was as broken as Sovanna's and that his rudimentary Khmer was superior to it.

She could see Federenko was now calculating something. Would he deny Sovanna was a junkie? In the end, he thought better of it:

"I cannot stop how Sovanna is."

Song summoned Viktor's stillness, the way it radiated inner strength. "You take the yama away. You shut her in her room. And you make sure someone watches her all the time."

"No, no." Federenko put his hands on his hips. His left foot tapped quickly on the floor several times. What could irk a man who relished controlling everything more than his inability to meet a straightforward demand?

"It's simple," she said, knowing why he couldn't admit otherwise. To do so would be to declare outright that Sovanna was being paid—no longer in money but in the yama she couldn't survive without. He would have to profess he was no more or less than Vasiliev, that Sovanna and he were not, as he averred, real lovers. She saw Sovanna rising in the light of the television, her arms reaching up to the ceiling and entwining, her body lowering down, her head disappearing.

Federenko stroked his chin and put his fingers to his lips. "If you do this, it will hurt Sovanna very, very much. It might destroy her. Do you understand what you're asking?"

Of course she understood: many a Naga girl had been lost in the fog of yama. She had seen the rage, heard the muffled pleading through the walls, the talk of fits and tremors, of dark nightmares, of slashed wrists. "I will be there," she said in the harshest monotone she could muster.

Federenko started nodding. "Fine, fine!" he said brightly. "It will take a few weeks to get her better. So first we go to Bangkok. Then, somewhere else for a few days. When all these trips are over, we will start. Okay."

Song reached out, put her fingers under the edge of the plate, and flipped it off the table, sending it smashing to the floor. Fragments of china scattered across the concrete, strands of curry sauce and sticky rice clumps splattering. "If it takes a week, we stay a week. Right here. We don't move."

Federenko glared at her, neck flushed and cheeks reddening. But what could he do? Start slapping her around? What Song carried inside her rendered her untouchable.

Bodies tense, the two of them faced each other, like the cockfights in the village she remembered from childhood: that moment before the birds fluttered and flurried and ripped with their sharpened spurs, when they were completely still, sizing each other up, their slick black feathers shining, their necks pink and stippled like white men's balls.

Federenko shouted for the housekeeper to clean up the mess. When the woman came in with her dustpan and brush, Song resisted the impulse to get to her feet and help. Instead, as she listened to the tinkle of shards being swept across the tiles, she reached out and picked up the table knife that had been left for her. Holding it out no more than an inch above the table, she turned her gaze to its gleaming blade, not moving a muscle, just watching it catch the light.

Federenko didn't know she cared about having the baby—and she would make sure he thought she hated carrying it. She would be unpredictable. Capable of anything. What was growing inside her was not only a child, but power—a force she had never felt and didn't care for but would wield if she had to.

Federenko said nothing for twenty seconds, then turned away. He walked out of the room, shutting the door behind him.

Early the next morning, the shouting began. She heard a fist beating on a door, then a bolt rattling in its strike plate. When Song rose from her bed and looked out into the corridor, Federenko was there, striding toward her. "You come here," he said, beckoning her, as she rubbed sleep from her eyes.

In the small bathroom, he held up a transparent plastic bag, packed with lime-green and strawberry-red pills. After emptying them into the toilet, he pressed on the flush. As they watched the pills sink and struggle against the whirlpool, they heard thuds and cries coming through the wall.

"Okay?" Federenko said, holding up his finger. "But this week we go to Bangkok. The hospitals and doctors have things they don't have here, understand? Downstairs the cook makes whatever you want. Go eat."

Though she knew Amos had seen her devouring the breakfast, when Federenko looked in, Song picked at it sullenly.

From time to time, she glanced at Amos, trying to detect what Fearless had seen in him: someone who was more capable of sympathy and human decency than the others. After breakfast—following orders or unilaterally, she couldn't tell which—he beckoned her gently and led her to Sovanna's room. Inside, a guard loomed over the bed—though they had already handcuffed Sovanna's hand to the supporting post of the headboard. "Give them a m-m-minute," said Amos, waving him away.

Song pulled back the hair that hung over Sovanna's face, leaned over, and brushed her lips on her cheek. Then, as Amos went to the window and looked out, she climbed onto the bed and spooned her as best she could. She wanted to get closer, to hold her tight, to somehow find a way through Sovanna's unresponsiveness. She didn't know if Sovanna was asleep or not, but she whispered in her ear, summoning up the happiest things she could think of—like the memory she'd had of the time they were all together, eating buffalo meat, all four of the family.

But then, the next day, Sovanna was wretched and bitter again.

"That buffalo story of yours is nonsense. Don't you remember? You and Ma had gone to visit Uncle and there were soldiers fighting around the fields. Pa and me lay down on our stomachs in the furrows. Bang bang bang. Shooting the walls of the house. The buffalo was caught in the crossfire and killed."

"That can't be right."

"*I* was the one who worked the fields."

And so it went on for those first three days: Sovanna was confused and exhausted. She couldn't think straight. There were bouts of screaming and ardent pleading. Catatonia. Sweat. The rancid smell of vomit. Only very occasionally tenderness.

"Remember—you chose this," Federenko reminded Song.

The atmosphere in the house grew fractious and tense. The men, with nothing to do, were starting to get crotchety. They were below decks on a ship being tossed on Sovanna's emotions, waiting for the cycles of storm and doldrums to pass.

While they scowled and grumbled, Song thought on her strength, and plotted, and worried about how amenable Sovanna was to Federenko. She found that her singing could calm Sovanna at her worst and tip the balance of the scales in her favor. When she had sung all the old songs, she would make up her own, little hums and vowels and sweet words with choruses that she would repeat and refine with each repetition.

When Sovanna was less fretful, she would rock her in her arms and whisper in her ears that all her suffering was Federenko's doing.

"*He's* the one who's torturing you, Sovanna. I begged him not to, but he won't give in."

She had never lied to Sovanna before—the thought of it disgusted her—but this was not the real Sovanna, Song told herself—not yet. In time, she would uncover the true one, just as she had uncovered her scars. And she would make that happen by any means necessary.

44

Larissa, Wish's favorite, was dead, found in a Hong Kong hotel room, face down beside the corpse of an Austrian investment banker. In the *International Herald Tribune* that Fearless bought in Istanbul Airport, he happened across the syndicated report: multiple stab wounds; a crime of passion; unattributed sources. There was no mention of prostitution or links to Phnom Penh, no more information on Larissa except that she was a Russian national under thirty.

By the time he touched down in Odesa, darkness had fallen; in the taxi from the airport, he couldn't tell if the city had changed since Laure and he had visited here three years ago. "I must show you," Alyosha had said to him back then, "what we are building with your money—don't you think?"

While most of the people they knew lived in dour Soviet blocks, Vera and Federenko were building a detached property, directly opposite one of Odesa's cemeteries, sandwiched in the shadow between two concrete towers. They lavished Laure and Fearless with hospitality that evening, insisting that they take their double bed while they camped out in one of the unfinished rooms: "Once we have a baby, this will be our nursery," Federenko had said. Laure and Fearless slept only fitfully, thinking of them huddling on the dusty floor among drip-smeared paint pots and sheets of *Uryadovy Kuryer*. Fearless remembered thinking how much he admired Vera and Alyosha's stoicism: cast out from Moscow, where they had wanted to settle, they were making the best of the opportunities they had. Laure had thought to bring a small gift—a set of delicate china bowls—that drew a bright smile from Vera.

After checking in to his room at the Londonskaya on Primorsky Boulevard—an imposing, Petersburgian building with thick carpets and marble columns—Fearless went out on his own into the city. In the dark, he wandered among the crumbling grandeur of baroque buildings, their dirty pastel colors powder gray in the moonlight. A few blocks from the sea, he found a basement bar called Gambrinus where he relished the heavy food, a big stein of beer, and the booming klezmer skank of an accordion and violin.

Ten hours later, in morning light so bright it needled his eyes, a taxi took him from the hotel to a quiet, deserted street. Maintained immaculately, the single-story house and its garden were now finished, its flower beds bursting with red carnations, its dwarf fruit trees full of the small talk of birds. Still unsure of what he would say, Fearless lingered in the street in the shadow of a lime tree. Federenko had maintained that he would always do right by Vera; what could make her take Fearless's word over his?

A door opened at the side of the house and Vera appeared, carrying a basket of washing. Over the hedge he could make out her shoulder-length red hair, the outline of her trim body through the loose clusters of privet, her simple V-neck sweater and stonewashed jeans as she bent and stretched and pinned clothes to the line. There were no men's shirts, he noted. No children's vests. Her fingers were nimble, clipping pegs to legs and shoulders. Something about her brisk, easy manner gave him hope.

When he knocked on the front door a minute later, she cracked it open and stared out with narrowed eyes.

"It's me, Vera. Fearless," he said in English, waving his hands across his growing curls. "Do you remember? We visited—Laure and I—three years ago."

She opened the door wider, and he moved a half step forward, smiling broadly.

"Fearless?"

Her obvious surprise was a relief: no one had warned her.

"Why are you here?"

"I've had a long journey. Can I wash my hands? It's through there, yes?"

He walked confidently into the house, taking off his jacket. Inside the bathroom, he ran the taps, in case she had decided to listen outside.

Swiftly, he opened the bathroom cabinet. The glass shelves confirmed what the clothes on the washing line had already told him. No razor. No aftershave. Only one lonely toothbrush. No sign of Western beauty products or designer perfumes: if Federenko kept her, it was within a limited budget.

As soon as he emerged, Vera appeared at another door. She had quickly brushed her hair and applied lipstick—not that she needed to: the delicate beauty that had once captivated Federenko had not been dimmed by time but burnished by it. "Why are you here?" she asked again, with a mix of hesitancy and guarded suspicion.

He gambled that she didn't know he had seen Federenko recently and also that he had told her nothing about Laure.

"I'm trying to find Lyosha. I haven't seen him since Laure died. Did you know that? Laure—she was killed in a car accident."

Her mouth opened. "What?"

"A terrible crash. Over a month ago."

"Bozhe moy," she said, making the sign of the cross on her chest. "What are you saying?" She approached and walked past him down the corridor.

Following her, he passed an open door, through which he glimpsed a small room with a bunk bed and toy cars queuing in a line at a tiny service station. Then they entered the kitchen, where she pulled out a chair. He saw her shoulders rise up, pause, then fall. He remembered now, sitting in the garden outside after dinner. Alyosha had taken him there to smoke cigars—how ridiculous, he had thought—on cheap plastic chairs. Fearless had looked back at Vera and Laure talking at this very table, sharing some kind of confidence in the golden light inside. "Women," Alyosha had said to him. "What's the phrase you have in English? As thick as thieves, yes? I *love* this expression!" Laure cast an easy intimacy. He was so used to that gift he had forgotten its magic.

"I was scared to meet her," Vera said now, looking up at him, as Fearless took a seat at the table opposite her. "I thought she would be here"—she raised her hand up above her head—"and she will think I was nobody. But she wasn't like that at all."

"She was humble."

"She knew people. She understood their character. Let me make some tea for you. I will take one too."

Everything in the kitchen, he noticed, was simple and spare—a far cry from the fussy interiors he had usually experienced in this part of the world. This was not a bold, stylistic choice, he sensed, but something that derived from Vera's personality—an asceticism, a simplicity, a lack of interest in excess—perhaps the result of her stint in prison. As she spooned tea leaves from a metal tin, he noted colorful drawings stuck to the fridge beside a handwritten shopping list and a calendar.

Vera brought the tea and they talked more of Laure. Despite his determination to steer the conversation, he couldn't resist the urge to unburden himself. It was something about the way Vera allowed him enough silence and the sense of her own sadness merging with his. By the end, tears had started to well in his eyes.

"I should have been there," he said.

"Ah—but she loves you."

"I see now that the being-there is everything. It's what counts. It doesn't matter what excuses you have or how good your intentions are."

He looked over to the open door, as though expecting Laure to walk in, as if it had all been a test. Then Vera asked: "Why come here? Why come all this way? Tell me the truth."

A look of fear passed over her face as he reached into his shoulder bag and pulled out the videotape. He hoped his air of sleeplessness and vulnerability would make him somehow more believable.

"I didn't want to show you this. But it's serious, I'm afraid. I am worried about Alyosha. He's involved with bad people." He laid the tape on the table and pushed it toward her.

Vera's cheek twitched. But behind the face that had melted when they were talking about Laure a defiance and obduracy now reemerged.

"This is not my business. I never see Alexei now. From time to time he phones. But I leave him to his work."

She pushed the videotape back, the black plastic box almost sliding into Fearless's lap.

"Shall we eat something, yes? There are plums from the garden."

She got up from the table and went back to the counter.

Shortly, Fearless himself rose and took his tea to the window. He had one more card to play. "You have children?" he said, raising his teacup to the garden, where a small plastic slide sat on the concrete patio.

"My nephew and niece come one time a week." A chink of light broke through the cloud of unease he'd cast. She rinsed the plums in an old enamel colander.

Casually, he moved toward the papers stuck to the fridge. "So these are their drawings, then."

"Last year we ski in France."

Fearless pretended to admire the felt-tip chairlifts as his eyes scanned the other papers on the fridge. There was a number written in red pen that caught his attention—a string of thirteen characters that matched the ones in Hossein's notebook.

"It's a shame you and Alyosha never had kids yourself," he remarked, his heart beating faster as he scrambled to memorize the numbers. "A shame for the world—two lovely people."

As she lifted the dripping colander, she didn't look up, but he could tell she wasn't uncomfortable or offended. He bet no one dared ever mention her childlessness. He grimaced, thinking of the blow he could strike.

"Alyosha told me that you came close one time," he added.

She reached for some bowls. "Yes. We tried for many years."

"That must have been hard."

"It changed things, maybe."

"He told me it was tough for you. That you thought it was your fault."

She turned off the tap. "Did he say that it is *me*?"

Fearless said nothing.

She shook her head, opened the tap, and rewashed the plums. "It is never something with me," she murmured.

Fearless felt as if he'd been walking in the shallows on a beach, only to find the seabed fall away. They lingered on the edge of icy waters that swirled with the yearning for things that had seemed impossible.

He had set everything up, but the situation was worse—or better—than he had imagined: what would he do with it? If he revealed right now that Federenko was having a child with a prostitute, then that would surely challenge her loyalty. But who would he be if he manipulated her like that?

Fearless looked at the plums in the bowl she handed him. It was one of the bowls Laure had given Vera on their visit. Laure had been wary of Alyosha, right from the beginning, while both he and Vera had loved and trusted him.

"I guess Alyosha lies about a lot of things," he said. If he couldn't get what he wanted without cruelty, it wasn't worth it.

Vera laughed gently and shook her head. "Tell me. Did he ever speak of the time he and I meet?"

"You mean when he chased the men away with the pipe?"

She laughed ironically. "He chased the men away," she said. "What happens next? Go on. Tell me."

"Well . . . the men ran away. They were scared of him, thought he was crazy."

"No, no. They never run. They chase him and catch him and pull off his clothes. I helped him when he was alone and naked in the street. I put my coat on him, borrow him my brother's clothes. From that moment he said he loved me but he doesn't even know me. I think often if he even wants to know the . . ." Her words seemed to catch in her throat.

"The real you," Fearless said.

Federenko got infatuated. He was infatuated with Sovanna. Back in Grozny, he'd even been infatuated with Laure. No, it was more than infatuation with him. His desire would glue itself fast on an object as . . . what? A form of salvation? Perhaps. Or, better, a means to access another dimension, far from his shame, way beyond his wickedness.

Sovanna's appeal was not her radiance but her *emptiness*, Fearless realized. It was ridiculous, unbelievable, but also entirely logical: a troubled addict could be the vessel for what he had exiled himself from: virtue; the idea that he was really a good man.

"Alyosha is weak," Vera said. "He needs people to do his dirty work. In the old days, I slaughtered the chickens he bought from market."

Vera picked up their bowls, plum juice dotting the ceramic like blood, and took them to the sink. Her back turned, she placed her hands on the counter and braced herself. He could see her chest rising and falling again.

"Everything to him, Fearless, is about being . . . inside."

"Inside what?"

"That circle. He doesn't hate the men. Yes? They mocked him and called him a Jew and he thought it was secret. They *mess* with him. Do you understand what I am telling you?

"For him, being inside is the most important thing. More important than love. More important than family. More important than his grandmother in her shed in Pripyat. I know him better than everyone and I know what he cares about. There is a saying in Russian: *the appetite comes with the eating.*"

He saw Federenko now—the small, naked boy. Alone in the street and clutching himself in modesty. He saw where the determination to get back "inside" came from. He knew that feeling himself. But he didn't need to be like him.

Vera turned and walked out of the kitchen without a word. He heard her in another room, opening and closing a drawer. When she came back, she pushed a slip of paper across the table.

"You know what this is? This is what teaches him another lesson."

"It's a voucher." Fearless remembered what Viktor had told him.

"He didn't get the right people. He didn't have the connections. It wasn't like Frank Sinatra in 'New York, New York'. When there are no laws, you need the most powerful people to like you."

"So you took the blame."

"What happens with the vouchers taught him he is being naive. He believed—I was believing too—that we can do things honest. We were going to own a factory. Work hard and save. Make something you can hold. Timber. Metals. This was our dream. To be a Stoltz in a world of Oblomovs. To keep socialism but have it gentle, gentle. But you can't be honest." She held up her finger. "Only one honest man spoils the game for everyone else. And we were desperate! In the markets they were starting to sell press cakes. Like in war time. You don't even know what press cake is!"

Fearless took in the room: the matching teacups on hooks; the artificial flowers in their green glass bottle.

"And I have this house—so what!" Vera said coldly. "I see you look."

"I . . ."

There was no point in denying that he had judged the life she had chosen, that he had calculated how expensive a skiing holiday in France for three might be. And there was no point in admitting what they both well knew: that her anger and bravado concealed a bitter truth. She could have had as many flowers as an opera diva on opening night—real ones: roses, gladioli, peonies—but they wouldn't have masked the lingering, subtle scent of her loneliness. No one had been there for her for a long time.

"You keep it," she said, tapping her finger on the voucher. "A souvenir. You can say now that Vera gives you something. You're a bad actor, you know. You and he are no longer friends. You are wanting to get him—and you are wanting me to help you."

Vera turned and took a lettuce out of the fridge. She rinsed it in the sink and started noisily ripping off leaves.

"But I can't help you because I don't know anything at all. I was telling you the truth. I mind my own business."

Fearless rose from his chair and moved toward the fridge. "There *is* something you can tell me."

She stopped ripping the lettuce. "What?"

"This number. What's this number you've written down here?"

She turned her head back to the sink, chewing her lower lip. "The number on the calendar? It's a code for money he sends me."

"Codes for money? Like a bank account."

"No. I give code to a man at an office near the port."

"At a bank?"

She took a tea towel and dried her hands. "It's a place for sending money. A little office behind a laundry shop. The Muslims that are here—they use this office all the time."

"So you give the code and then they give you Alyosha's money."

"What good is this to you?"

She folded the towel and hung it. Fearless held her gaze but chose to say nothing.

"I give the code to a man—Mr. Roy, they call him—and he telephones to Dubai. He speaks to a man in English—an Indian called Mirza. I know this because they always talk about this cricket. Mr. Roy explained me: it's sport you English and Indians play. Then Roy reads the code and Mirza gives permission. Mr. Roy takes the money out of a safe and gives to me. Okay? Big deal. What good is this to you?"

She turned away, looking for something to do. But everything was neat and tidy and in its place.

Dubai: the flights that Amos made for Federenko. Amos, Fearless saw, ferried money back and forth.

Vera saw Fearless's narrowed eyes. "I know nothing else—believe me. I'm sorry. Nothing."

"I do believe you. Don't worry."

Fearless rose to his feet and thanked her. He apologized for coming here with bad intentions. As he walked to the door, he tried one last thing.

"Maybe there's something you could do for me, Vera—in case you happen to speak to Alexei."

"Yes?"

"Tell him I was here. You were scared that I was crazy and you slammed the door in my face, told me to go away."

"You are crazy. I was scared," she repeated. "Okay. I can do that." She turned the latch and opened the door for him. He smiled as the sun poured upon them, transfiguring her red hair into a sheet of white gold.

He stepped forward for a moment and cupped her head in his hands and kissed her gently on the top of the head. She didn't shrink away. And then he turned into the light and didn't look back.

45

Sitting behind him in the taxi, Song could see a nervous spasm in Federenko's cheek. As they crawled along the clotted arteries of Bangkok, he shook his head and muttered to himself occasionally, turning around to steal glances at her and Amos.

Over the last few days, in the buildup to the hospital trip, his agitation had increased with every waking hour. He was tormented, Song hoped, by losing his hold over Sovanna; without her addiction, she was no longer dependent on him, while she leaned ever harder on Song's support and care. "That's why I'm getting better now, oun. When you were gone, the yama made everything easier. It filled up the emptiness. But now I have you back."

In one of these increasingly frequent moments of clarity, Song had told Sovanna about the children, what she felt for them, and what had happened at Stung Meanchey. "But don't say anything to him, bong—just keep your feelings inside for now." Sovanna had nodded, her forehead bowed and furrowed. She turned the loose strap of a gold watch Federenko had given her around and around her stick-thin wrist. But the next moment, she was holding the watch up above her head, catching and refracting the light with its diamond-studded dial, suddenly distracted: a child with a short attention span.

Still, Song felt the tide beginning to turn. Maybe this was why Federenko had insisted Sovanna stay in Phnom Penh. It would suit him if she lost her bearings and began to fret again. That would explain why Amos also had to accompany them; he was the only one as invested as Song in Sovanna's recovery. Last night, when Song had tried to sit up with Sovanna, it was Amos who had kept watch and insisted she rest. The night before, when Sovanna woke screaming from a night sweat, it was Amos who had been there to take her to the bathroom. Amos possessed the impulse to care and the inability to repress it. This morning, when Song had felt nauseous, he had laid a hand on her stomach, innocently, simply: the kind of guileless touch she wasn't used to.

Now, in the taxi, he leaned in and whispered to her. "Stop worrying—ot ey tee. Sovanna is getting better."

He was right: Sovanna had got through the worst of the withdrawal, she told herself. It really seemed that she was on the path to the old house of her self, ready to cross the threshold, open the shutters, and let light in. Even the world gliding by through the taxi window—of high-rises and overpasses and the giant pillars planted for a train in the sky—reflected this sense of a new hope and beginning. This is the future, they said. This is what Cambodia would have been if its history had been different. There was so much wonder in the world, Song thought. Only an hour ago she had been flying. She couldn't get over it. He hadn't let her see it or touch it, but he had got her a passport. The little rust-colored book that could take her to places she had only dreamed of. Inside the hospital, they were now rising in a glass elevator through the marble and air of a cavernous entrance hall. Shards of light sparkled off the polished terrazzo; foliage waved gently in the atrium garden. It was a palace of the gods and she was floating inside it like an angel.

Song and Amos took seats on easy chairs in an open lounge while Federenko filled in paperwork at a reception desk. Amos got a nurse to bring toast with butter and jam. Then Federenko beckoned Song and they began a circuit of examination rooms, blood tests for both of them, a health check and ultrasound.

"No problems," said the sonographer as he wiped her bump with his scratchy blue paper, "but you see the specialists now. They will call you shortly."

"But is it—?" said Federenko.

"Yes, it's a boy. Congratulations."

The dream of a girl: she had known it wouldn't be given to them. But she controlled her face. *Don't move it*, she told herself. *Make it serene, like the head of Jayarvarman.*

Then there was more waiting, and Federenko was called again. When he came back, there were sweat patches on his pastel blue shirt, as if he'd wedged two fountain pens under his armpits. He went to the water cooler and drank several cups in succession and then gestured to Song that they were ready to see her too.

"So, to say again," the doctor said in an American accent, when they had settled themselves in front of him in an examination room, "the earlier blood test and the new results confirm that your wife is HIV positive. I'm so sorry to be the bearer of this news."

The girls that had "retired" over the years raced through Song's mind immediately. The ones who suddenly went back to their villages. There was Vannary—so skinny—with the purple sore on her face.

The younger doctor turned to Song and inclined his head. "You are HIV positive," he said to her, nodding.

Song pretended that she didn't understand, but the floor beneath her chair had opened up and she was plummeting, spiraling down a dank, dark tunnel shaft. It was death and disappearance, not hers but the baby's, cursed even before it had come into the world.

Federenko squatted on the edge of his chair, his hands on his knees, elbows out to the sides. "The doctors are saying you have a kind of malaria," he said to her in Khmer. Perhaps he didn't know the word for HIV, she wondered, and was using malaria as the closest equivalent. "This malaria," he continued, "is something the baby might catch. But the doctors will give us special tablets to stop that."

The second doctor leaned forward and offered a printed sheet of paper and a clear, plastic box with little compartments. Federenko took hold of them before Song could react.

The doctor pointed at the colorful grid on the paper. "This is your regimen with three kinds of tablets, each tablet to be taken two times a day. I think you have heard—yes?—of the AZT."

The doctors then talked about *viral loads* and *transmission*. Even the younger one gave up the pretense of addressing her. It wasn't a language issue: even if they had believed she could speak English—even if she had told them that the customers who'd taught her were in all likelihood the men who had given her the disease—they would have addressed themselves to Federenko and Federenko alone.

Now the first doctor turned to her and carried on his translating: "These are the tablets you take until the baby is born. We do this and everything's fine. Understand?"

"She just takes the tablets," Federenko repeated in English. "Tell me again."

"Don't worry, Mr. Federenko. Stick to the regime and the baby will be virus-free. There is little or no chance—I assure you."

"Not too late?"

"We wouldn't start treatment in the first trimester anyway."

Federenko had gone from fretfulness to meek subservience. He nodded and mmm-ed and looked cloyingly at the doctors. Since they'd entered the room, color had come back into his face. It was relief, Song realized: he had been worried *he* had caught HIV! From her. That was why he'd had a blood test also.

"After the baby is born, you must avoid breastfeeding," the doctor said. "On the second sheet you can find details of what to expect. And it's important for your wife that she gets specialist advice on how she will manage her condition in the future."

Federenko lifted the first page to glance at the one below. He made no effort to translate what the doctor had just mentioned. She was an incubator; he didn't care what happened to her after the birth. In fact, if she was going to die, that would suit him just fine.

So be it, Song said to herself—but he would never have the child. She would start planning for that now. She'd find another shovel if she had to.

Outside, someone switched on the fountains in the hospital gardens and water sprayed up in a giant sweeping rake. The mist appeared in the picture window behind the doctors, arcing back and forth through space and sunlight. Ignoring the men, Song walked over to the glass, captivated by the sparkling, rainbow-striped jets. Water—not to drink or cook or wash or nourish—but just to catch the eye and distract the mind.

The rest of that day would pass in waves of excess as another taxi swept them around the boutiques of Bangkok, Federenko getting out, hurrying in, dashing back, carrying big rectangular bags made from glossy colored cardboard with little handles made of the finest white rope, while they waited, silently, in the dark, cold car interior and the world spooled on behind tinted glass.

46

"Just the flights that went to Dubai, Conrad. And only the private jet. The one that was owned by the sports team. The Cavaliers."

"The Cardinals."

Bits of paper seemed to crackle and scrape on the end of the line as if Conrad was holding the mouthpiece to a pan of frying bacon. Sitting at a desk in his room at the Londonskaya, Fearless pictured him in his dressing gown and briefs, reading glasses balanced on the tip of his nose.

"I wouldn't mind the magic word from time to time," Conrad grumbled. "Okay. Here it is. Twenty-fifth of June. Then one in July and . . . one more in August." A picture was emerging, but of what exactly Fearless didn't know.

After he had spoken to Conrad, Lucy came onto the line and gave him a London number to call.

"Look," said Jimmy when he picked up the phone. "This J. D. business . . ."

Fearless said nothing for a moment. He knew he owed Jimmy a sincere apology.

"The thirteen-digit codes, Jim. I found out something."

"What?"

"They're a way of moving money."

"How do you know?"

"I saw Vera, Federenko's wife, here, in Odesa. Every month she gets a code that she takes to an office where a man—Mr. Roy—releases her allowance. Mr. Roy makes a call to a Mr. Mirza in Dubai. A cricket-loving Indian who verifies the code."

"An Indian man in Dubai."

"Yeah. An Indian in Dubai."

Fearless knew the pause that followed; he'd felt it a hundred times at school: Jimmy was taking a step toward solving something, the first x or y in a simultaneous equation.

"An office in Odesa," said Jimmy. "So—you were right. That's how they win."

"Win what?"

"They imagine things that to us are unimaginable. Do you remember at school when Northcote-Green read us that Lawrence poem: 'Touching the unknown, the real unknown, the unknown unknown.'"

"What?"

"Hawala," said Jimmy. "Our friend is using the hawala system."

"Hawala?"

"You must have heard about the Indian bribery scandal. The Jain brothers case from earlier this year. I've encountered hawala a few times in my work—though it's outside my remit—more North and Horn of Africa."

"Hawala."

"It's a form of transferring money—or value, to be precise—outside the traditional banking system. Goes back to medieval times—maybe as far back as the days of the old Silk Road when traders traveling thousands of miles didn't want to carry money and leave themselves at the mercy of bandits. Today, migrant workers use it to send money home—builders on construction sites, domestic servants in the Middle East. It's an elegant thing. Moving money without moving it."

"It sounds like magic."

"Well, it is magic—if trust and faith are magical to you. Say I want to send you a hundred pounds from London. I could go to a bank, sign forms to make a transfer, pay commission, factor in exchange rates, and wait a few days. But if I go to my hawala office run by friendly Mr. A, I give the money to him and specify a password—a thirteen-digit code, say—and the destination city."

"Like Odesa."

"Like Odesa. Mr. A calls his contact at the hawala office in Odesa—Mr. B—and gives him details of the sum and the code. Meanwhile, I call you and tell you where Mr. B's office is and the thirteen-digit code you need to withdraw your money. Get it? And so, you make your way to the office in Odesa, meet Mr. B, and tell him the code, for which he releases the sum in your local currency—what is it there . . . ?"

"Hryvnia."

". . . taking a small commission for his trouble. Et voilà! Fast. Convenient. Cheap."

"But that makes no sense at all. Mr. B's given a hundred pounds' worth of hryvnia away for nothing. What difference does his little commission make?"

"No difference. Well, not immediately. But Mr. B has the knowledge, the promise, that Mr. A will one day settle the debt. In due course, someone will come into Mr. B's office in Odesa, wanting to send money in the other direction; then he will call up Mr. A, and they'll adjust the tally between them. That's the beauty of it—everything happens by trust—which is also the thing we in the West wouldn't tolerate. The hawaladers depend on being as good as their word. The system doesn't rely on laws or policing."

"But that still doesn't work. A hundred pounds might be all right. But what about the kind of sums we're probably talking about. Ten thousand pounds, a hundred thousand, millions, or more? How long will Mr. B put up with being owed a massive sum? In the end, they'll have to resort to the real banking system, surely."

"If the books need to be balanced when there's a huge payment on one side, then they employ different tactics. Under- or overinvoicing, maybe. Because most of the time these transactions take place in the context of import/export businesses. Think of a piece of merchandise—"

"I dunno. A table tennis bat."

"What? Okay. Fine. Sports equipment. Let's say you owe me 66,000 rupees and I'm going to be buying 100,000 rupees' worth of sporting goods for my business. You buy me the 100,000 rupees' worth of sporting goods and ship them with an invoice for 34,000—which I pay. The debt is settled.

No money-laundering investigators or taxmen are alerted. Alternatively, forget all the invoicing and goods—just send a man with an amount of gold equivalent to the money you owe."

"Or a little pouch of diamonds."

"QED."

"And of course—there's no paper trail."

"Nothing apart from the hawalader's ledger, which might just be a list of names and numbers and dates. Incomings and outgoings—not much more sophisticated than something a market trader might have. And even if you had one of those ledgers, it would be useless. Remember, this is a vast network. If you owe me that ten million rupees, maybe I owe three million to another hawalader, five to another, and two to a third, and to even things up, I get you to settle my debts with each of them—which would mean there would be a web of transactions, not all of which are recorded, stretching here, there, everywhere . . ."

"But . . . I don't need a ledger," Fearless muttered.

"For what?"

"Just tell me. Do you think you can find that office?"

"What office?"

"The Indian's office. This Mr. Mirza. His opening hours. I'll call you as soon as I land, okay? I'm catching the next available flight to Dubai."

There were no scheduled flights till early the next morning and Fearless was far too agitated to sleep. He tried to burn off his nervous energy with push-ups and sit-ups, but the exercise only made him more wired.

Putting on his jacket, he headed into the night again, this time wandering in the direction of Odesa's harbor.

Surely nothing was enough to compel a man to part with his child. Even the most die-hard capitalist knows some things are priceless. He remembered looking in on their future nursery, seeing Vera and Federenko huddled under a blanket on the floor.

From the top of Eisenstein's stairs, he gazed at the burning lights glittering along the fringe of the bay. Nearer by, on the dock, cargo cranes were illuminated by floodlights—giant metal heron heads, bent to the water. For decades, wheat had been loaded at this port, from the rich black soil of Ukraine to Europe's kitchens. But now, he knew from Laure's reporting on the post-Soviet economies, the trade in oil and liquefied gas was even more coveted, most of it in the hands of the Neftemafija, who had acquired the contracts to operate the refineries.

The fall of Communism was a heavy stone dropped on these still waters; while he had been focused on avoiding its shock waves, photographing the way the spray split the spectrum, Laure had seen the bigger picture, concentric ripples beyond his view. She had tracked what couldn't be photographed. The flows and flight of capital. Money laundering and high-stakes property deals. Policies of deregulation and liberalization.

Somewhere out on the water, a distant foghorn sounded. He imagined a stack of bills of lading on the desk of a captain's bridge, the top sheet branded with the stamp of Federenko's shell company.

"For negotiating, you must know the red lines, yes? The lines the other person will not cross. Once you know what is impossible—everything follows."

What would Alyosha do and not do? What was impossible for him? He had lied and dissembled, but there were still things Fearless knew about him that no one else did. Habits. Assumptions. Prejudices. Reflexes.

He thought of himself, of everything he'd put into his photography. "Our desires are always weaknesses," he muttered. Fearless had thought he could escape his own tragedy by immersing himself in other people's. But what you most wanted could hurt you, be used against you.

He remembered what Richard had said about arms dealers never being present when the weapons change hands. But Richard didn't know how Alyosha hated to delegate or how this deal was more important than any other. "I guarantee it personally," he had said.

"The appetite comes with the eating," Vera had told him. Mirza had the money, which was everything to Federenko, and if Fearless could take it from Mirza, then anything might be possible. There were some things Federenko had hungered for even longer than a child.

But even if Fearless managed to get the money and used it to bargain for Song, Federenko would surely hunt her down for the child. Fearless would have to protect her. They would have to hide away. And even then, they would go on living their lives in fear, knowing that he could come for them at any moment. "I have a gift for it," Federenko had said. "No one can escape me, Fearless."

Now a line of light broke across the horizon, the soft yellow of a table lamp on a dark winter's night. As it widened, Fearless could make out the colors of the funnels of the cargo ships, the blue and scarlet stripes of the Black Sea Shipping Line that once would have been crested with a golden hammer and sickle. He pictured himself brandishing the hammer in his left hand, the sickle flashing high above his head in the right.

By the time the light spread across the underside of the clouds, racing across the water over the bay toward the steps, Fearless knew precisely what Alyosha would do—and how he would outfox him.

47

The ping-pong ball looped high in the air before Sovanna, gritting her teeth, smashed it home. Her growl of determination crescendoed into a squeal.

"Twenty-twenty," Amos said, shaking his head.

"Your serve," said Sovanna, hunching down to receive.

Song, sitting level with the net, her legs dangling against the side of a mahogany credenza, looked from one player to the other, their eyes and grins locked. Like them, she was entranced by the rhythm of the game, whirled higher and higher by each successive rally. Intent on the pocking of bat against ball, the angles, the variations in spin and speed, Sovanna couldn't hear the call of her addiction.

When she looked at Sovanna now, Song was filled with a growing wonder. She could feel an energy surging into her and, with it, a true respect. For Sovanna had been right about the story they had told each other. It was an invention, a kind of comfort. They weren't meant to believe it. The holes in the walls of the house that let the light in and scattered "stars" on the floor weren't a wonderful memory; they were the scars of war. With the buffalo slaughtered in the crossfire of fighting, the family's fate had been sealed, though they struggled on for two seasons, scrabbling and scraping for any food they could come by. Yes, her parents had sold them into slavery. From their perspective, to receive an offer for the girls was good fortune.

"Twenty to twenty-one!"

"Aaargh. Your match point," said Amos.

He too, Song noticed, was now graced by a kind of magic; so long as they played, his stammer lost its hold on him; he could joke, tease, and shout without fear that his voice would snag on the brambles of his brain. Now he served with backspin, Sovanna lunged forward, and with each shot of the rally—five, then ten, then fifteen in a row—the string of thrill between them grew more and more taut. Amos hit hard and Sovanna stepped back to defend, then he feinted and played short, drawing her back in. Their eyes were wide open, laughter danced in their breaths. Amos lobbed. Sovanna smashed. Amos defended. Sovanna stretched to save.

But Song's sharp shout of delight was cut short by Federenko. As he walked into the room, Sovanna caught the ball.

"Amos. Let's go. I have made the arrangements. It's Dubai tonight to collect the advance."

Amos moved closer to Federenko and lowered his voice. "Dubai, tonight? Isn't it too s-sssoon? We still have l-l-l-l-leeway."

"What do you mean? You think you're the one who decides now, is it?"

Amos didn't answer.

"No. You're not, Amos. That's not your job." Federenko tapped his golden Rolex. "Go straight to Mirza. The same as always—except for this." He took a slip of paper from the pocket of his trousers. "Memorize the name and then forget you ever saw it. Clear?"

Amos faltered. "No. B-but yes. With d-due respect, she isn't over the y-y-ya—"

"She's fine. She was fine when we went to Bangkok. And she's even better now. Just look at her running around and enjoying herself."

Amos stepped even closer to Federenko. "It's still a crucial moment. The time she's most v-v-vulnerable. She needs professional help, not just Song and me. What I'm saying is t-t-two more days of what we've been doing. That advance is not going to go anywhere, is it?"

Federenko shook his head, but he hesitated for an instant. Amos had built up a reserve of respect that even he couldn't dismiss out of hand.

"You go too far, Amos. I don't like last-minute . . . But fine. Two more days. And then Dubai before Moscow." Federenko stepped back, turned around, and spread his arms. "Ladies. We take our plane trip in a few days. Start to think about packing—the normal clothes you wear. It's going to be hot. Ah, let me show you how this is done. First to five!"

He took Amos's bat and motioned to Sovanna for the ball.

When he served with a downward motion, no trace of spin, Sovanna hit it back, flat and fast, the ball hitting his stomach before he could react. "Ha ha!" he cried, before serving again and receiving the same treatment.

After Sovanna had won the first three points, Song started to worry. Tensions were being played out on the table. She had told Sovanna to keep things inside—the special skill they shared.

Not yet, she warned Sovanna silently, *not yet.*

On the fourth point, Federenko decided to give it his all. He bent at the knees and narrowed his eyes. There was something childish and desperate about his need to prove himself. She must have refused him; Song recognized the whiff of rejection. The night before, he must have asked to be alone with her.

She guessed that to accept a refusal must have been love in his mind. To delay his plans. To defer what he wanted.

Federenko's shot was too high; a smash came back, bouncing up at his chin. He had to take evasive action, ducking to one side.

Zero to five.

That was that.

Sovanna shrugged, tossed her bat onto the table, its wooden handle clattering hard on the surface, and without comment walked casually from the room with Amos following. Song had noticed something about them just recently: the blossoming of an idea, the feeling that fates could be changed.

Song looked down at the floor, away from Federenko. With women, he knew only how to worship or enslave—both of which made you smaller, both a kind of hatred.

"Lucky streak!" Federenko said brightly, chuckling to himself, picking the ball up and knocking it on his bat, up and down, as if all of it—everything—was just a game.

For the rest of that afternoon, Song waited for an opportunity to deliver her own killer blow, but when she was finally allowed to see Sovanna, the moment had passed. Darkness had fallen and the bed was littered with the shopping bags Federenko had brought from Bangkok, little balls of red tissue paper tumbling onto the floor. Sovanna was trying on a pair of heels, cardboard labels dangling from her hem and sleeve. She was captivated by her dark reflection in the window; all that mattered to her was the shape of things now—and not the shape of things to come.

And then, later that night, Song heard music playing and furniture being dragged across the floor. Someone shrieked—in laughter, not in pain. It was Sovanna, and then a low murmur in answer that could have been him, the voices moving away, then slowly returning. And then there were heels that, even when Song placed the pillow over her head, could be heard clacking back and forth relentlessly in circles.

48

Fearless had a feeling Jimmy would be waiting in Dubai—out of guilt or curiosity or the desire to see this through. He had become to Jimmy what he supposed his father had been to Conrad, unable to read and respond to the other's good sense due to emotion, dogmatism, and sheer bloody-mindedness.

"You're humoring me," Fearless said as they embraced over the arrivals barrier.

"I'm saving your arse. That's what I'm doing. Because how will you get Federenko's money *out* of the country? Did you even begin to think through that little part of it?"

"How would *you* get it out?"

"I've arranged reinforcements."

"Who?"

"A mutual friend. Or, rather, a family member." Jimmy produced a slip of paper. "Here's the address of Mirza's office. I'm presuming at least you have a plan for that part."

Fearless led him through the fluorescent unreality of the brand-new concourses of Terminal 2 until they found a small concession that, along with photocopying, fax, and internet services, offered the printing of business cards while you wait.

"Do I look like a Michael?"

"More aristocratic."

"Miles?"

"Too jazz."

"Cosmo."

"Bit flighty."

"Digby."

"You a dog?"

"Alasdair."

"That might work. Posh enough. Boring enough. And we'll add a double-barreled surname. Baden-Powell is one I use. You can bring up your illustrious ancestor as a diversion."

Fearless added an address in the City of London and, while the cards whirred through the machine, went shopping for a suit. It was relatively easy to find an overpriced navy pinstripe. Remembering Hossein's range of Turnbull & Asser shirts, he picked out a pale blue that he had seen in his hotel closet.

When he returned, Jimmy dusted off the shoulders of his jacket. "You pulled off Liberia, you can pull this off too," he said.

Fearless nodded. "Let's do it." His eyes searched for a taxi sign. "But after we arrive, keep the engine running."

Through the Nissan's tinted windows, a gleaming city sprouted along Sheikh Zayed Road, as if money itself was erupting from the earth's crust, conglomerating into gunmetal and glass stalagmites. Between the buildings, lush grass and artificial lakes repudiated the power of sun and wind and sand.

"One day this place will be like the Fortress of Solitude," Fearless said as they cruised under the double shadow of the Emirates Towers' columns.

"There's no oil here. Though people always assume there is. Sheikh Mo's master plan relies on financial services: that's the thing they've really made their own."

"No questions asked."

"It'd be rude to even think it."

After navigating a grid of streets where new construction alternated with plots of laterite wasteland, they pulled up to a long, three-story, white cuboid punctuated by building-height strips of tinted glass. A sign for a travel agency was planted in the lawn.

"As-salaam-alaikum," Fearless said to the man seated behind the desk as he stepped into its freezing, air-conditioned semidarkness. The man was brown-skinned, South Asian, with a preposterous horseshoe mustache. A large image of a Norwegian fjord formed a crescent around his head.

The man rose from his chair and proffered his hand. "Wa-alaikum-salaam."

"Do you speak English?"

"Yes, of course."

"I am here to see Mr. Mirza."

"Yes, certainly. Follow me please, sir."

The man did not ask Fearless his name. He led him through a side door into a short, narrow corridor, which in turn led to a long, luxurious, wood-paneled office. At the end, silhouetted by the bright sun shining through a shift of net curtains, an elderly man sat behind a mahogany desk, his fingers steepled and eyes half-closed. He was dressed in a plain white salwar kameez. Half-moon reading glasses hung around his neck.

As they approached, Mr. Mirza lifted his head from his posture of meditation, rose to his feet, and stretched out a bony yet elegant hand. "Good afternoon," he said in a perfect English accent, gesturing to the chair for Fearless to be seated.

Fearless made himself comfortable, adjusting the cuffs of his shirt. There would be no need for Alasdair Baden-Powell, he realized; no questions asked. He contemplated saying *You must have been expecting my colleague, Mr. Amos,* but then thought better of it.

"May I go ahead with the code?"

Mr. Mirza withdrew a ledger and opened it to its current page using a marker ribbon. Then he put on his reading glasses and looked at Fearless with an unblinking, walleyed stare. "Yes. I'm ready."

As Fearless recited the thirteen digits he had identified from Hossein's little notebook, Mr. Mirza placed his finger on the grid in front of him. Then he nodded and turned down the corners of his lips.

"We have been expecting you. Everything is ready as agreed. There is just, this time, the matter of the additional password," he said, his index finger resting within the grid lines of the ledger.

The bottom dropped out of Fearless's stomach. "Pardon me, Mr. Mirza. Could you repeat that?"

"The password."

"Ah—my thoughts were a million miles away."

Fearless shifted his weight to the tip of his toes. Mirza removed the glasses and leaned back in his chair. "It's a name. Our mutual friend suggested the extra measure."

Electric pinpricks of sweat broke out over Fearless's body.

Federenko. Vasiliev. Traoré. Igla. Elektromash. Foya. Sovanna made sense. It was the obvious choice.

He was about to say it, the hiss of the *s* already sounding behind his teeth, when a different name came to him like distant music across a valley. "Samir Saleh Abdullah al-Suwailim," he said. He felt Khattab's breath on his neck once again, the tangy leather aroma of his weight-lifting glove. *We fight to the end, Fearless. Whether we win or not. Whether we are defenseless or armed.*

Mr. Mirza reached forward and pressed a buzzer on his phone. A red light flashed and he spoke curtly into its microphone.

A door swung open. Fearless shifted to the edge of his seat and slowly began to raise his hands in surrender.

But instead a teenage boy walked backward into the room, struggling with a heavy, wheeled Samsonite suitcase. "Leave it there, baba," Mirza said to the boy, shutting the ledger firmly and rising to his feet.

"Samir Saleh Abdullah al-Suwailim," Fearless whispered. He rose and grasped the suitcase's retractable handle.

When they shook hands, Mirza held on for a moment longer than normal. "It is always a pleasure to work with our Chechen friends," he said. "It is global what we have now. They cannot imagine how it grows."

Back at the airport, Uncle Archie—the reinforcements Jimmy had mentioned—sat at one end of a bank of steel and leather chairs. Behind the glass, jumbo jets glided silently across asphalt. A pushback tug shunted a plane toward a departure gate. A ramp agent signaled with orange lollipop wands.

Archie hadn't changed a bit in the two years since Fearless had first met him. He was as upright and stoic and clear-eyed as ever, his silver hair brushed back, no thinner or less lustrous. He was still dressed in the same manner—a tweed suit, the very picture of an English gentleman farmer. But his tie—dark navy and embroidered with silver greyhounds—gave him away to the initiated observer: a Queen's Messenger, one of a now decreasing band of special couriers who hand-carried British diplomatic bags.

Jimmy and Fearless sat down on the opposite side of the aisle, leaving the Samsonite suitcase positioned between them. None of the men looked at each other.

Archie's gaze flickered down to the suitcase for a moment and then returned to the oppressively bright sky. When he spoke, he barely moved his thin, red lips.

"When young James here called me, I had assumed we were talking about films. Because last time I helped you it was rolls of camera film, yes? Not . . . *this*. Something this size is rather . . . Well. Problematic."

"It can't be done?" said Jimmy.

"I didn't say that, dear fellow. But my personal luggage doesn't receive any special treatment, you understand. And this bag is not sealed. It has none of the necessary documentation. So what you chaps are asking requires not just taking something through but adjusting the documents of Her Majesty's Government. These things need stamping and addressing. What you're asking is something very different indeed."

"You would have said no."

"I bloody well would." Archie let out a heavy breath. For a moment, his cheeks flushed: white blotting paper pressing on a drop of red ink.

"Just tell me it's a good cause. Make me feel better about it at least."

"It's more than a good cause."

"I'd rather hear it from James."

"Uncle Archie. You have our word. We wouldn't ask for nothing."

He harrumphed. "I dare say I'll find some way to do it."

"We'll be on the same flight. At Heathrow, we'll hand it over."

Fearless glanced up at the departures board overhead. Had news already reached Federenko of what he'd done? If so, he'd unleash every force he could. There'd be people on their way, right now, this minute—a pack of rabid hunting dogs.

On the flight, as if determined to compound his anxiety, Jimmy unpicked each element of his plan, the two of them leaning into each other, whispering under their breath.

"So let me get this straight. You'll meet Federenko in Liberia."

"Yes."

"In Foya. Where he's personally supervising the handover of a shipment of arms."

"Yes."

"He'll bring the women there. Sovanna and Song. You'll make him?"

"And then I'll give the go-ahead for the return of his money by satphone."

Jimmy's eyes narrowed. "So he hands them over. And then you get into a jeep and drive off into the sunset."

"We leave by plane. On the plane that's delivering the arms. The jeep is what I'll tell him to provide for us beforehand. It's what he'll expect and what he'll plan for."

"He'll track it."

"Exactly."

"And then I come in."

"I will land the plane at the place we've discussed."

"Where you want me to be, with transport for you all."

"So he won't know where we're starting from or where we'll disappear to."

Jimmy leaned back in his seat and stared at the tray table. "But why make the exchange in the middle of nowhere in Africa? You could do it anywhere. You could disappear anywhere! Why drag everyone out to Liberia?"

"You think we could disappear in London? If I did that, he would go after everyone in the U.K. who knows me, Jim. He would expect them to hide me or know where I am. Everyone would be dragged in. Hassled and hounded. He'd be on Conrad's doorstep. Making threats. Barging in. If we disappear in Africa, we buy ourselves—and everyone else—time and space. As far as he knows, we vanish in Western Sahara. So far off the radar he could search for a thousand years.

"Besides, Jim. Think of the advantages of Liberia. Where else could we escape, untracked, by air? Where else would I have you, my very own regional expert? And he needs to think it's crazy—that's the whole point."

"But you yourself would be in the most vulnerable position imaginable. Why make him take Song and her sister all that way?"

Fearless reached over and patted Jimmy's thigh.

"It doesn't make sense," Jimmy said.

"Let's get another drink. I'll call the hostess."

Most of Jimmy's objections would be nullified by the endgame Fearless had carefully devised in Odesa—but that was a puzzle piece he could not reveal. If Jimmy knew the complete plan, *he* would think Fearless crazy. Or, at least, no longer the Fearless he knew and loved.

"Just trust me," Fearless said.

"I suppose you won't even tell me how the hell you're getting to Foya."

"Oh, I'll tell you that. And you'll like it too. It involves our dear old friend—Wilfried Traoré."

"Our untouchable friend."

"I'll be touching him all right."

49

"I know you can s-ssspeak English. Or at least understand it," said Amos. Song froze.

"Don't worry," Amos added, "I can keep a secret."

She wanted to trust Amos. Each moment they had shared in their struggle against Sovanna's addiction had distilled, drop by drop, a spirit of faith between them. He knew why her pillbox had so many windows; he knew how she had ended up carrying Federenko's child. At times when she and he were both in Federenko's presence, Song sensed that Amos was disgusted with everything. There was honor in him, she felt, like a hard rod of chrome that held him straight and would not bend.

But then again, he was just doing the job his master had given him. She ought to resist the hope it might be more.

And so she closed her mouth and didn't reply. In the bedroom adjacent to the balcony where they were sitting, they could hear Sovanna stirring and sighing. When she had woken from her last sleep, she had been itchy and crotchety: "Just get out!" she had screamed. "Just leave me alone!"

When Song stole a glance at Amos, he inclined his head. She was fascinated by him, the way he was different from everyone else. On the street, with his Black skin and his dreads and his height—a head taller than any of the Russians, let alone the average Khmer—he was as much a magnet for stares as she was with her scars.

"If you don't want to talk, I respect that," Amos said. "B-b-but . . ." He shook his head. "I want you to know something about all this.

"A long time ago, you see, I . . . I drank. Much too much. I, I was like Sovanna. I couldn't see that there could be another way to l-live. I fought anyone who said I should stop what I was doing."

"So how—?" Song started to ask.

"How did I change? I joined the army. I made f-fighting my drug and my job and, for a while, that worked. But then . . . well, fighting. You end up getting hurt. Or you get hurt by the hurting you've done. Or both at the same time.

"But that's not the thing, Song. What I want to say is this . . . I never had any f-family to help me. But Sovanna has you. That's the difference."

He had never spoken like this. She should use this, she realized. Viktor would do that. Survival was everything, he would have told her. With Amos's help, escaping would be less of a pipe dream.

"You give Fearless warning in Siem Reap," she said. "He told me you help him. Why do you do this?"

Amos's brows knitted. His mouth opened slightly. He shifted forward on the concrete bench. The thumb of his right hand kneaded the palm of his left. "He changed," he said. Then he shook his head and pursed his lips. "Did he change?" He shut his eyes and put his fingers on his eyelids. "I had an *idea* of him. That's a b-better way of saying it. When I joined him, I thought there were lines he wouldn't cross."

Before he could carry on, a strangulated roar pierced the air, coming from both outside and inside the house.

"But how could they know the fucking name? How? No one knows the fucking name except me!"

It was Federenko—not Sovanna—screaming into a phone at the top of his lungs. There was the clatter of smashing plastic as he threw it to the floor. Then the crash of something heavy—a large piece of furniture—before they heard his loafers slapping across the terrazzo.

As the door to the balcony opened, Amos rose to his feet. Federenko ran at him, his face beetroot and puce, and started hitting him, taking little jumps to get to him.

"Why the hell did I listen to you—you stupid Black bastard! If we'd gone like I wanted, the money would be safe."

He rained wild punches on Amos's raised forearms.

"Someone stole the money. From Mirza, from his office! Just yesterday. Do you hear? Someone stole my fucking money! Did you give the name?"

"Of course not! I've been h-here with you all the time."

Then Federenko stopped and lifted his fists, shook them in the air and roared through his teeth. Like a windup automaton, he pounded the side of his own head—right, left, right, left, right.

"They stole the fucking money."

Federenko's thugs were spilling out of the house now, gathering in the driveway and on the lawn below, looking up at the balcony with open mouths and raised eyebrows.

"Fucking AIDS and a fucking drug addict! I should have done it myself. There's not *anyone* you can trust. Just as everything was in place. I was close. This fucking close I was!"

Then he continued his rant in garbled Russian, his words running together and over themselves until they were one long stream of consonants which ended in "pah!" and "paaaah!" as if he was trying to spit out something that couldn't be dislodged—a tangled mass of foul, rancid bile.

50

Just after eleven a.m., Traoré came out of London's Dorchester hotel, closely followed by his teenage son. Fearless observed them through the spray of a fountain in the small, landscaped garden as they climbed into a cab. Hailing his own taxi, he tailed them down Hill Street until they got out at Selfridges on Oxford Street, where he shadowed them browsing designer leather handbags before taking the escalator up to menswear.

When Traoré took a pair of trousers into the fitting room, Fearless slipped into the adjacent cubicle, removed the A4 stills he had in his rucksack, and slid them under the partition. Both of the images showed Traoré naked. Bopha was with him. Not a sound came from the cubicle, no creak, no breath, no crack of plastic hanger.

Bending down, Fearless could see that the stills remained on the floor, next to Traoré's loafers, their laces still undone. Fearless stepped out and pushed back the edge of Traoré's curtain. When he spoke he kept his voice quiet but clear.

"In two minutes, General Traoré, you will walk out of this fitting room. You'll tell your son to take care of himself for half an hour. Then you'll make your way along Bond Street till you get to the Tube station. At the McDonald's inside, order yourself a Big Mac and start eating. I'll sit down beside you and tell you what you're going to do. Do exactly as I say. Don't call anyone. Don't try to run. I have the videotapes these pictures come from. And I have a team working with me. If anything should happen to me, they'll make your life very unpleasant.

"Two minutes exactly. Starting now."

"Who do you think you are?" Traoré said fifteen minutes later, when Fearless sat down opposite him. Fearless checked the Big Mac. Traoré had done as he was asked: there were small, nibbled crescents on the sesame seed bun.

"Lost your appetite, I see. Who I *think* I am is irrelevant."

"You were in Phnom Penh. By the swimming pool at Le Royal."

"The elephant never forgets. Look—let's not waste time. Around the nineteenth, Mr. Traoré, I will be arriving in Foya. We both know what is happening there and we both know who will be there. On the exact day in question—which, right now, you will specify—I will wait in the central market at midday. From there you will provide me with an armed escort to the handover point."

Fearless took the small bag of French fries and upended it, scattering fries over the table and onto Traoré's lap. He took out a pen and scribbled on the greaseproof packaging.

"I'm writing everything down. Just so we're clear. After I've met with Federenko and let your deal happen, I will leave under my own steam—don't worry about me."

Traoré shook his head. He began to laugh in a slow, exaggerated hiccup.

Fearless stared back unblinkingly, counting each sound. Four. Five . . . Seven. Eight. Then he leapt forward, grabbing the back of Traoré's head, his fingers latching onto a cigar-sized roll of neck fat. With his other hand, he scooped up the Big Mac from the table, shoving it into Traoré's mouth, and hissed into his ear, "I'll fucking rip this fat off your fucking head, you fuck!"

The group of teenagers nearby stopped talking, Quarter Pounders poised between table and mouth. When Fearless looked across, they turned their gaze away.

"Eat," Fearless said, tightening his grip on Traoré's spongy flesh.

Lettuce ends tumbled from Traoré's lips before Fearless released him, pushing him back into his plastic seat.

Traoré gasped and wiped his mouth with the back of his hand, smearing mayo and pickle across his gleaming cheeks.

"What you're asking is not possible! I don't know how I can do it."

Fearless chuckled. "Eat your burger," he said in a cold, hard voice. "Everything is possible! That's one thing I've learned. It's just a question of thinking bigger. Of letting your imagination have free rein.

"You know, I've spent a lot of time thinking about you, General. I've been thinking about your son, Charles-Henri, at Eton. How you give him a life beyond most Westerners' dreams. A far cry from where you come from. Séguéla, isn't it?

"Me—I don't have children. But if I did, I'd do the same. I'd move heaven and earth to give them the best so they would know how much they were loved, so they would love and respect me. Because to not have that respect would be a terrible tragedy, wouldn't it?"

Fearless reached into his rucksack and took out a large padded envelope. On the front of it, he had written in bold, black marker:

Charles-Henri Traoré
Holland House
Eton College
Windsor
SL4 6DZ

He positioned it on the table so that Traoré could read the address, then slid out the videotape nestled inside. Traoré put the Big Mac down into its waxy box. A yellow-white twist of melted cheese and mayonnaise dangled from the hairs of his wiry mustache.

Fearless slid the tape back into the envelope and patted it. "Tell me everything is possible and this will never be sent." Then he rose from the table and pulled a scrap of paper from his pocket. "There's one more thing you will do for me, Wilfried. Tell Federenko to call me. On this number here. At one p.m. tomorrow, U.K. time. But under no circumstances reveal that you and I have met or what you have agreed to do for me in Foya."

"But how do I explain how I got this number and the time?"

"Like I said, General. Use your imagination."

51

"Don't shit your pants. It's just the pizza delivery guy."

Fearless and Jimmy sat back down as Luke hurried over to the door of his office.

But it would be the perfect cover, Fearless wanted to say. A guy in a helmet; a quick, sharp headbutt. He'd be through the door and have them incapacitated in seconds.

Sitting astride the suitcase stuffed with dollars, Fearless shifted his weight uncomfortably. Within reach, on Luke's desk, lay an antique Beretta shotgun, its sideplate engraved with mallards rising from bulrushes.

"Glad to see you've taken my dietary advice to heart," Fearless remarked when Luke returned with the pizza boxes. Luke lifted a slice high above his head until he snapped a stubborn string of mozzarella. He pushed the box in Fearless's direction and waved at Jimmy, but both declined.

Fearless's eyes returned to the phone on the desk. The wall clock ticked. He could hear Luke crunching on crust. After a flurry of chatter and planning, the three men had run out of words. Once, Fearless asked for reassurance again—"The railway arches have a separate rear vehicle entrance, right?"—and once, Jimmy returned to the bright idea they had belittled—"I still say we steal his money and give it to charity"—but their attempts to fill the silence ultimately shriveled up.

When the phone finally rang, Fearless jumped like a startled dog. He slid to the edge of the Samsonite case and picked up the receiver as if it might explode.

For the first few seconds, not a word was uttered.

"Tell me what you want," Federenko said.

"Simple," said Fearless, trying to slur his words. "Girls' freedom in exchange for the suitcase I have." He wanted Federenko to think he was drinking and out of control. He was unpredictable. He shouldn't be provoked. Had Vera told Federenko she thought he was crazy?

Luke channeled his nervousness into his next slice of capriccioso.

"How?" said Federenko.

"You will hand the girls over to me in Foya."

"What's Foya?"

"Let's give up the pretense. I know exactly where, when, and what you're doing. I'm making things simple. You give me the girls there. We hand over the money in London. It's a kind of dead drop. Didn't you people invent it?"

"*You people*," Federenko scoffed. "Spare me your insults."

"Listen. Are you listening? I won't say this again." Fearless switched from slurred to staccato to create the impression of instability. "On the day of the deal, at 13:00 British Summer Time, my man enters the square outside the British Library. He'll leave a copy of the Koran on the stone bench there. The stone bench that surrounds the statue of Newton.

"Your man—who will be alone and have a mobile phone with him—will pick up this Koran. Are you writing this down? Inside the Koran's pages he'll find a piece of paper: a map of the surrounding area, with a walking route and address."

As Fearless spoke, Jimmy scribbled something and held it up. Fearless put his hand over the receiver and nodded.

"At all times on this route, your man will be watched. At all times people will be checking he's on his own. If there's any sign he has someone with him or that he's carrying a weapon or bag or there's a vehicle in tow, the deal's off. And your money will be gone forever."

"What will happen at this address that my man will go to?"

"He'll hand the Koran to the security men and they'll search him and let him in. Once inside, the door will be locked and he'll be shown your precious suitcase. Then he'll call you to confirm that everything's in order. This means you'll need to have a satellite phone in Foya.

"When you've had your confirmation, you'll hand the women to me and we leave. In a four-wheel drive that you will provide. Full tank of petrol. Extra fuel tank. As soon as we're safe, I contact my people in London to release your man and the suitcase of money."

There were several seconds of silence.

"Are you out of your goddamn mind? You want me to take a pregnant girl halfway across the world and hand her to you in the middle of the African bush! You're crazy. To think I would give the girls to you *anywhere*! The woman carrying my child. The woman who I love."

"If you don't like the deal, I'll happily keep your money. After all, I've only myself to live for, Lyosha. These days, I'm living wholly, completely for myself."

"You don't need the money. You have Laure's insurance."

"It's not a question of how much *I* need the money. How much *you* need it is all that matters."

Thirty seconds is a long time to stay silent on a phone. Even Luke stopped eating to listen for Federenko's response.

Federenko was cogitating, Spassky to his Fischer, conscious that the more audacious his opponent's strategy, the greater number of weak points he would have to exploit. "I wonder where you'll go once I've given you the girls," he said.

"Have you got a pen and paper handy? I'll give you the forwarding address. That way you can send us cards and presents on our birthdays."

Federenko exhaled audibly—a long, breathy sigh. "Fine," he said in little more than a whisper. "Thirteen hundred hours. On the twenty-first. In Foya."

"That's 13:00 hours British Summer Time—midday Liberian time."

"Okay. Understood."

Fearless put the receiver down and pushed the phone toward Luke. "Call your whole rugby team. Props, locks, and number 8."

Luke reached for a napkin to wipe grease from his ginger beard. "I'll call the full fifteen if that's what it takes."

52

How do people pray? No one had ever taught her. She wanted to pray to the spirits whose house she had toppled, to Lord Buddha, to Jayarvarman, to Vishnu, to every god. She had an image in her mind—of a tall transparent cylinder, with two jugs pouring into it—one of water and one of oil. And if there was enough water, by the grace of all those gods it might rise and fill the cylinder right to the brim, pushing all the oil right up and over the edge. And the baby would be hers then. Nothing of Federenko would be in it.

The last twenty-four hours had passed in a blur. At the airport in Bangkok, they had boarded a passenger jet to Dubai. A screen showed an icon of the plane blinking farther and farther west over blue and green masses. Had they left Cambodia forever? She couldn't ask, and no one would tell her. It was freezing in the cabin and her lips felt dry and chapped. Sovanna, in the aisle in front, had huddled under a blanket, knees pressed beneath her chin. Only once did she move during the flight's first hour, stretching and complaining that her arms felt numb.

Song stood up and leaned over to touch her. "No," she said. "It's fine. Sit back down, oun."

What had Federenko said to her? Through the gap between the seats, she had watched him leaning over and whispering in Sovanna's ear for a long time. During the years they had been apart, whenever she had dreamed of their reunion, Song had never thought they wouldn't tumble back into closeness. But there seemed to be some distance she couldn't breach, a distance that wasn't only the result of the yama—or the conflicting perspectives they had on their childhood. It was as if she had lost her twice: the first time when they were taken from each other, the second when the years between had rendered them strangers.

Amos, at least, could still reach Sovanna. When he spoke to her, she listened and agreed to sip a little tea. In Amos's face, Song could read a brooding like her own, even with the cabin lights dimmed and shutters drawn down. She willed him to stop being Federenko's whipping boy. He could be one of the carved Naga heads, she wanted to say to him—coming to life, the beng wood transforming into coiled scale and muscle, darting out and striking at the rats beneath its fronds. *Rise up*, she wanted to whisper into his ear. *Rise up and hit back and help us escape all this.*

Federenko became more anxious as the flight went on. He walked back and forth along the passage or leaned against the toilets, squeezing himself against the door as the hostess trolley passed. At all times, he held his arms straight by his sides, pressing his fingertips deep into the meat of his palms and dragging them up to the base of his fingers over and over and over again. She could smell his vulpine yearning for the money that had been stolen; it emanated from every pore, no different from Sovanna's desperation for yama.

"But just listen," he heard Amos say to him at one point. "You have a woman you l-l-love. Isn't that something?"

Federenko scowled and turned his back on him.

When they reached Dubai, cars took them straight to a luxury hotel, where Song was given a room of her own. Pushing back the curtains, she found a skyline of lights: the red eyes of a hundred cranes glowing in the dark. As on every night since their visit to Bangkok, Federenko entered and doled out her tablets.

She recoiled at the thought of the tablets touching his hand and then touching her tongue and entering her body. In her working days, the ones who liked to force themselves never returned; they didn't want to risk seeing themselves in your eyes. But now he was here, in her face, handing her water.

Was he still giving Sovanna drugs too? It would explain her pinballing moods: one moment rising and, for an instant, hanging serenely; the next, plummeting flat into the darkness of oblivion. If he was, she would rip his tongue out, tear out his eyes.

Song swallowed the pills and showed him her tongue, remembering his knees pinned on either side of her head. Satisfied, he went to the door and turned out the light. In his mind, he was already looking after his child, she realized, tucking it safe and sound into its cradle.

Late the next morning, they continued their journey—this time by a gleaming private jet, its interior beige leather and gleaming walnut. In this plane, there was no electronic map to follow, though she had heard someone say they were heading for a place called Liberia.

By the time the plane touched down, night had fallen again. From the windows of the taxi she saw crumbling buildings and African faces, fires on street corners and makeshift houses. When they arrived at their hotel, they led her directly to a room with the black rectangle of a TV and a mirror she didn't need and little paper packages of tea and sugar and creamer.

This time, when Federenko dispensed her pills, he had something to say: "You should know that tomorrow we see our old friend Fearless."

He *was* the thief, then. Part of her had longed for it. Now she had to tell Sovanna the truth about the baby. Then she wouldn't stomach Federenko either.

Federenko put his finger to his head and twisted it. Did he mean Fearless was crazy or that Fearless would also be shot?

"We will both get a chance to say goodbye to him. And in the end, you will stay with Sovanna and me."

53

Tk-clk. Tk-clk. The second hand of Fearless's watch echoed inside his ear.

"Fresh plantaaaiiiin! Sweet plantain! Fresh plantain! Sweet plantain!"

He stood alone on a dirt road, bombarded by heat and dust, a stone's throw from the point where three countries meet: Liberia, Guinea, and Sierra Leone. The hubbub of Foya's central market—a locus for farmers and traders from hundreds of miles around—reverberated around him in its mix of languages and dialects. People were bartering at dozens of four-postered platforms covered by rusty corrugated roofs or picking their way through bright blue tarps spread with dried fish, peppers, cocoa beans, and palm kernels.

From the moment he had left Monrovia at four a.m., as the taxi juddered over the undulating washboard, Fearless had gnawed unremittingly on his worries. What had he forgotten or failed to consider? What missed stitch in his plan would reveal itself when he held it up to the light? Maybe Federenko had already tracked down the money and, right now, his men were storming Luke's lockup. They would be seizing the suitcase, laying waste to the whole rugby team, to Lucy, to everyone foolish enough to have been co-opted into Fearless's scheme. And now, having received the news that his goons had accomplished their mission, Federenko would slay him too and keep the girls.

No, he told himself. The suitcase was safe. And it made him impregnable to threat or violence, just as Song was protected by her pregnancy. No one would touch them. The aces were all theirs.

"Two dollar only. Yes—for true-o!"

They could torture him, though, couldn't they? But then he would show them that he had nothing left to lose, that he was already broken.

Tk-clk, tk-clk. One of the traders was waving to him now, beckoning him over to view his display of goods. Fearless stepped back, turned aside, and hunched over a cigarette. It had been stupid to choose such a crowded place. He needed somewhere public, but this was too much. "Poomwee, poomwee, poomwee," he kept hearing—clearly the local dialect for *white man*. A group of children approached him from the direction in which he'd turned, whispering it behind their hands and giggling at the very idea of him. He moved to the other side of the street, crossing one of the planks laid over a deep concrete gutter whose dark, dank interior had the smell of piss. Any minute now, he reminded himself, Lucy would arrive from the east, wearing a flowery headscarf and her Jackie O sunglasses. She would head down the Euston Road, choked with double-deckers, turn right, and pass under the monolithic redbrick portico, emerging shortly afterward onto the British Library's broad piazza.

Yes. She is sitting down on the stone bench beneath the giant bronze of Newton. From the pocket of her raincoat, she produces the Koran.

"Who is he that intercedeth with Him save by His leave?" Khattab's voice again whispered in his ear. "He knoweth that which is in front of them and that which is behind them, while they encompass nothing of His knowledge save what He will."

And somewhere, out on those streets, a man—Federenko's envoy—is converging on the same place. Now, he is sitting on the stone bench too, reaching for the book as if it had always been his to take. Lucy has long gone—she is hailing a taxi on a side street. She leaves her wig and headscarf in a public bin. Federenko's man looks up to get his bearings, his finger on the route marked in fluorescent ink on the map.

Sudden engine noise scattered these images in Fearless's head and sent the gaggle of children running toward the market. It was an open-top army jeep, arriving on the dot: the transport he had stipulated on Traoré's French fry packet.

Traoré, he realized, had spat in the soup: Fearless had demanded a vehicle to take him to the rendezvous but specified nothing about who should be driving it. Of the four, at least three of them were soldiers in their teens. The driver's head was covered with a blue translucent shower cap with a kind of ladies' cross-body fanny pack strapped at nipple height across his chest. Behind him, two younger kids sported bright neon wigs—one of them pink, the other platinum blond—both of them balancing AK-47s on their thighs. The pink-wigged one rose to his feet as they drew near, revealing the fuchsia flash of a high school prom gown bodice.

The jeep screeched to a halt directly in front of him, the words ONLY GOD CAN JUDGE graffitied across its doors. The shower-capped driver sprung down beside him, his Wellington boots making a satisfying crunch. He opened the rear door to usher Fearless in. There was no need for them to verify his identity; who else in this market could possibly be their customer?

"Come," boomed the eldest soldier, who was riding shotgun. He wore a military beret and puffed smoke from a blunt. "We come for you, Misser Fearless. Get in with my men." Fearless nodded, swung his backpack down from his shoulder, and climbed up, squeezing in between the wig-wearers on the back seat. A petal of polyester flower brushed against his cheek, giving off a bouquet of petrol and stale sweat.

The leader turned and chuckled sheepishly. "He worried," he said, pointing his blunt in Fearless's direction.

The one with the pink wig pulled the feather boa off his neck and draped it ceremoniously around Fearless's shoulders.

"Don' worry, be happy," he half sang, as its feathers tickled his ears. "N'mind ya, Misser Fearless, our hearts is white."

Then the jeep roared off, heading straight out of town, the people on the roadsides stepping back or darting away.

"What's your name? What do I call you?" Fearless shouted above the engine's racket.

"Still Waters," cried the leader.

Were they RUF from Sierra Leone? Remnants of Charles Taylor's NPFL? One of any number of ethnic militias? It made no concrete difference to know; questions of allegiance made little sense to fighters who did the bidding of whomever fortune favored.

Soon, the red dirt road plunged down into jungle. Every shade of green rippled at the edges of his vision. The wind rushed his lungs. The engine noise deafened him.

"Traoré said give this," Still Waters shouted. Over the seat, he passed Fearless an AK-47 and the army knife Fearless had also specified. Once he had wedged the rifle between his knees, Fearless withdrew the eight-inch blade from its vinyl sheath, its serrated teeth catching the light in tiny crescents. As the jeep picked up speed, he tucked it into the side of his backpack, checking off the rest of his bag's contents in his mind, items he had hurriedly sourced before rushing to Heathrow: a hydration pack; purification tablets; a small stainless steel pot; a lighter and a flint and steel and matches; a large sheet of plastic folded as small as possible; one ball of cord and one of wire; a Leatherman multitool; his old scouting compass; his headlight; the first aid kit that never left his bag. A last essential: three packs of Camel Filters.

Now the road climbed to a crest and opened out. A small convoy waited: a canvas-roofed army truck and two similar open-top jeeps, all three packed with teenage boys. Without slowing, Still Waters' driver stabbed the air and the vehicles revved and fell in behind them, the boys either standing or hanging off the sides.

It dawned on Fearless then that the "chauffeurs" Traoré had sent him were also the team who were collecting the arms.

They lurched to the left, veering off onto a narrow track, arrowing deep into a dense thicket of ten-foot scrub, brittle branch ends clattering and scraping the bodywork as colorful birds rose from nests and flashed through boughs. The noise of the convoy grew yet more brutal; each jolt from the rocky track jarred Fearless's joints. But no sooner had the grinding of gears become intolerable than they burst onto a grassy veldt stretching out for a mile, bathed in scintillating, eye-piercing sunshine. On the other side of this strip, a group of vehicles awaited: another open-top army jeep and a four-wheel drive crammed under the meager shade of a small stand of palm trees.

The passenger door of the four-wheel drive swung open and *he* got down, dressed in a short-sleeved shirt and chinos. Reflexively, Fearless's hands reached for the gun, tightening around its burning grip and barrel.

No plane. Fearless had hoped that some stroke of luck might have brought it early. Just as the driver began to slow to a stop, he took the blunt from Still Waters' hand. He sucked on it and then, as ostentatiously as possible, puffed out a cloud of smoke in Federenko's direction.

He thought he saw Federenko's mouth open a little. Perhaps he was registering the hair on Fearless's head, the dense little curls he had never seen before.

As the vehicles pulled up, Federenko walked forward, flanked by two of his men carrying Kalashnikovs. At the same time, the fighting boys leapt out of their jeeps and truck, forming an irregular phalanx in the space between. Beyond Federenko, Fearless now spotted another jeep, its heavily tinted windows concealing its occupants.

The girls had to be there. Or maybe this was the joker; the trick Federenko had been keeping up his sleeve.

As the two parties faced off, Still Waters raised his arm with a flat hand; once he seemed confident that his men would hold their position, he walked forward nonchalantly to take Federenko's hand. After a cursory exchange, he then ceded the ground, seeking out the shade, his boys following obediently to join Federenko's crew and their vehicles under the palms.

Fearless was now alone. He could sense everyone's eyes on him. The gun radiated its hard heat into his body, its black metal branding his skin through his shirt. A bead of sweat dripped and burst on his eyelashes, creating a coruscating ring of light around his vision. "Where are the girls?" he called, unable to stop his voice quavering.

"In the four-wheel drives. One here, one there."

"Show them to me."

Federenko didn't turn but waved his hand. From the shade of one of the trees, the big, beluga-headed henchman emerged, his white face pork-chop-pink in the heat. He opened the rear door of the nearest four-wheel drive and moved aside.

A black silhouette stepped out, shielding her eyes. When the hand dropped to her side, it was Song's face that appeared: Song's face as it would have been had it never been burned; Song's face in a parallel world where this moment could not have existed. Her beauty was undeniable.

Then Federenko waved his hand in the direction of the more distant vehicle and Amos stepped down. He looked even taller and more solid than Fearless had remembered, and all eyes shifted their gaze onto him at once. Still Waters' boys observed him with curiosity. He was Black and older and on the other side: as outrageous to them as they had been to Fearless. When Amos opened his rear door, it was Song—the real Song— who stepped down. At first she moved hesitantly, cradling her pregnant bump, but, upon seeing Sovanna, she headed toward her at once. When they met, about forty yards away from Fearless, there was some kind of ill-tempered exchange of words. The beluga tried to separate them with his ham of an arm, but Song pushed him aside and pulled Sovanna close. For a moment, she held her face in her hands. Then she cried out; there were cross words in Khmer; Sovanna scowling; Song shaking her. Amos was now beside them, prompting Federenko to shout out, in the tone one would use for a disobedient dog:

"Amos—get back! I said, get back right now!"

He shouted again in Russian and the beluga separated them all, marshaling Amos and Song back to the vehicle they had come from. Song was still shouting, but Amos's back was in Fearless's line of vision and all he could see of her were gesticulating arms.

"Okay, you've had a look at them," Federenko said. Fearless watched Song and Amos getting back into their vehicle as Sovanna refused to climb back into hers. She shook off the fat hand that had been laid on her forearm and the beluga allowed her to remain under the shade of a nearby tree.

"The vehicle you requested is that one," said Federenko as Fearless lost sight of Sovanna among the teenage soldiers. He pointed out the four-wheel drive in which Song and Amos were sitting. Then he reached into his pocket and lobbed a set of keys to Fearless. "I have the satellite phone too. But look—it's not too late." He kept his palms open and lowered to his sides. "It's been a difficult time. Who would blame you for trying to escape from reality? Not me. Not after everything. We both loved Laure. But it's not too late. Just think. We call this off. I make sure you get home. And the two of us forget it ever happened. How about that?"

Fearless ignored him. He threw the car keys back. "I don't need the extra vehicle. I'm changing the deal. The girls and I will fly out on the plane—after my friend Still Waters and his crew have their weapons. I will give the pilot instructions and he will leave us where I request. Then, he'll be free to take your plane home."

Federenko growled. "That's impossible!" he spat.

"It's me who calls the shots. *I* say what's possible."

"But the vehicle's just here!" Federenko raised his arms in the air. "I give you a driver, an armed guard. Whatever you want!"

Fearless was surprised at Federenko's surprise. Surely he would have guessed that he knew the vehicle was compromised. Had he really thought he wouldn't have another plan?

"The plane—we leave on the plane and that's that. When it lands, you tell your pilot to keep the engines running. Tell him that he answers to me and me alone.

"After that, Song and Sovanna will come with me. Once I'm sure we're safe I will contact my associates in London, who will let your man leave with the money as promised."

It was a reverse ransom—kidnapped money released upon payment of humans.

"But what's to stop you from never giving those instructions?" Alyosha shouted. "How can I know you won't keep my money as well?"

Fearless shook his head and gave an almost imperceptible shrug. Federenko would have to trust him—there was no point in saying it. Once again, Federenko looked closely at Fearless's face. Fearless hoped what he saw was a man at the end of his tether—deranged, unpredictable, a loon who couldn't be bargained with.

Now Federenko changed tack. "One pilot isn't possible. Not in this kind of plane. It's normally a crew of five."

"Well, it's lucky you've got a spare vehicle for them, then. I said one pilot only. I'm starting to lose my patience."

Now Federenko turned and took two paces to the right, before turning on his heels and pacing back again, his hands coming up to clutch the sides of his head. "Look. Understand. The plane won't finish its run when it lands. Foya is just a drop-off before a second destination."

"That's not my problem. We fly out on this plane. With one pilot only. This is my only offer."

But while Fearless managed to be clear and terse, the idea of extra cargo in the plane set his mind spinning.

"Take your precious cargo off right here if it's so important," he said. "You have friends with trucks and jeeps."

Federenko glanced over at the palm trees and shook his head. Then a smile broke out on his face and he began to snigger: a laugh that slowly grew more bitter and maniacal. He turned and headed back toward the vehicles. For a moment he seemed to disappear in the shade under the trees before reappearing next to the tinted glass of the jeep.

When Amos wound his window down, there was a bitter set to his face. Federenko talked at him, low, clear, and stern, and Amos spoke back, but not loudly enough to hear.

Federenko reached across Amos and snatched something from the passenger seat: a cheap blue plastic bag, which he clutched in his hand as he turned. "I'm telling you," he shouted to Fearless, "when the plane lands, the crew will get off like you asked. Then Amos will take over. He's the only pilot who can handle things alone."

Ice-cold water flooded Fearless's veins. This was it: the unforeseen turn of events; the joker he had fretted about. In his plan, the pilot was meant to be completely anonymous. Not Amos, not a person to whom he had some kind of connection. His eyes lost focus again in the glare of the sun. Federenko was holding out the blue plastic bag and speaking.

What was he saying?

IV. Something about an IV. He was peering at him as if anticipating some kind of reaction.

"The sheet of paper inside has the schedule of drugs."

"Okay."

"You understand what you're dealing with?"

"I understand—don't worry."

But Amos. It would have to be Amos, Fearless was saying to himself.

"The plane comes soon. Until then, I wait for the phone call from my man. The girls and I stay by the cars. You stay here."

"What? No tea and chitchat with an old friend like me?"

Federenko raised his finger and shook it at Fearless's face. "For the record, I never did anything to harm you—old friend. I never dreamed of harming you. Not until now."

Alone, in the blistering sun, Fearless looked inside the blue bag at rectangular cardboard packets and a paper with a printed grid. *HIV* was what Federenko had said. Beads of sweat broke out at the roots of his hair. Squinting hard, he kept his eyes fixed firmly on the sky. But there was nothing, just flat white—more absence than color.

Under the trees, the only sound was the chatter of the boy soldiers. In contrast to Federenko's tense, uneasy crew, they were relaxed, confident that this job presented no worries. They passed weed around and joked in the dense shade under the branches, silhouettes reaching out, moving apart, coming together. Some of them, he noticed, tried to talk to Sovanna. For their part, Amos and Federenko were absorbed in conversation again. Now Amos was no longer angry, it seemed—though he would not face Federenko, his jaw clenched tight and shoulders slightly turned. Fearless could see his hands gripping the steering wheel at ten to two—the bones in his knuckles pronounced, the bands of muscles in his forearms tensed.

On and on, the skies stayed white and empty. Fearless picked a lone leaf from a struggling shrub and pulled its flesh from the central vein. He put it between his teeth. It tasted of nothing.

Across the grass, which was long and flattened, Federenko reappeared from his black spot of shadow. He raised his hand and shook a thick black phone in the air. Then he stepped back. It was signal enough. His man had made the call: he had the suitcase in London.

Fearless lit up and smoked a cigarette, his eyes moving from the line of the horizon to the glowing filament connected to his lips.

The sun glared down like a furious patriarch. Then, finally, it appeared: a pinprick of blood on the endless white-blue, growing and growing—a fruit fly, a mosquito, a sparrow, then an Airfix, its wings and body looming into focus. Now he could see its turboprops, four of them rippling, plumes of black smoke streaming out behind and disappearing. A humming spread through the earth and seeped into the silence. The men who had sat or squatted on their haunches stood and walked a few steps forward, faces raised to the sky.

Everything closed in now, as if the petals of a leaf shutter were slowly drawing in, each across the other, focusing the world's light onto this one spot. There were only the engines and the silent clanging of the sun.

Now the plane tilted, banking slowly into position, floating around till it reached alignment with the veldt.

It was here now—he couldn't believe it—their chance at freedom. It descended surprisingly gently, snowflake-slow. Heavy but graceful, it touched down on the seared grass with barely a trace of bump and rumble, just little puffs of dust rising up from the landing gear.

The men sprang into activity. Still Waters' crew jumped into their vehicles and roared to its rear, forming a vulturous circle around its opening metal mouth, the hydraulics of its cargo hold hissing out hot air.

Federenko, flanked by gun-toting thugs, was the first to enter its belly, closely followed by Still Waters. Amos went too, still not looking at Fearless, disappearing into the deep darkness at the back of the hold.

After a minute, Still Waters reappeared to give a signal to his boys. As they went up in groups, lugging metal crates of mortars, rifles, and rounds between them, two white men also emerged from the plane—presumably the pilots. In little more than ten minutes, the boys had loaded their truck. Still Waters swung himself up into his jeep. "We coming to go!" he shouted to his men.

For a moment, his head turned in Fearless's direction. Was that the trace of a nod? The black lenses of his Ray-Bans gave nothing away. Then his gold-ringed fingers tapped on the jeep door and his driver roared off, the convoy falling in behind.

Fearless stood alone, a dozen men lined up against him. On Federenko's signal, the beluga opened the rear door of the farthest four-wheel drive and

Song descended onto the grass. Hesitantly, she walked out with small steps toward him, while Sovanna emerged from the shade of the tree nearby.

As each step brought her closer, Fearless tried to read Song's expression, but she gave nothing away, neither joy nor twist of regret. Sovanna was lurching forward and swaying as if slightly sunstruck, the beluga, carrying the cases, butting her shoulder with his head.

Federenko's voice began to crack when he spoke. "Here they are," he said as they reached his side. "You have them. And Amos is in the pilot's seat."

Federenko's men then parted and the girls walked forward, Song leading the way and Sovanna listlessly following. The beluga accompanied them for half of the distance and then left the bags, retreating backward like a cautious courtier.

Fearless bent down to search the suitcases. How ridiculous he must look, on a secret airstrip in the West African bush, down on his knees, rifling through girls' underwear. Satisfied, he shut the bags and got to his feet. "There's one more thing," he shouted. "I want your watch too."

Federenko said nothing.

"You heard me. Your Rolex. I'll have that Rolex off your wrist."

Federenko unclipped it and chucked it in his direction, its golden circle spinning like a gyroscope through the air. Fearless caught it smoothly and attached it to his hand. It was loose on him but he admired its cold, solid feel. "As the means, so the end," he murmured to himself.

Then Fearless lifted the cases and nodded to Song, who tugged on the arm of the ashen-faced Sovanna. Sovanna resisted, turning back to look at Federenko.

"Sovanna wants to stay," Federenko said, raising his finger. "You're taking her against her will. Is that how you work these days?"

"Something's wrong with Sovanna," Song said to Fearless in a low voice as they walked to the plane. "Where are we going? Will the journey be long?"

"I can't say. I don't even know if we're safe yet."

Only when they clambered up the ramp did Fearless grasp the sheer scale of the plane, its hold cavernous enough for a dozen military jeeps or more. Between the cargo area and the cockpit was a small passenger compartment, where he motioned to Sovanna and Song to sit down. Sovanna slumped heavily, her hand covering her eyes.

"Is she sick?"

"She's on drugs. She's high on something."

"She must have taken whatever those kids had on them."

"No. It's him. He gives her the yama in secret."

When he bent down close to Sovanna, Fearless could see she was breathing heavily, her forehead and cheeks gleaming with sweat.

Sovanna's eyes opened. "So this is our new master. Ha." Her chest almost rose in a scornful laugh.

"Fearless is our friend," Song said. "We have no masters anymore, bong."

"There's nothing we can do right now," said Fearless. "I must first speak to Amos to get us away from here."

"No masters," Sovanna muttered as Fearless headed for the cockpit. "Who cares?" Her head rolled and she laughed silently again.

"You have charts?" Fearless barked as soon as he entered the cockpit, letting his pack fall from his back onto the copilot's seat. Hundreds of black dials and switches with white Cyrillic lettering covered every side of the cabin and arched over their heads.

"Here," Amos said, handing him a thick, folded sheet.

"You need to do as I say if you want your boss to get his money."

Amos was too distracted by Sovanna to focus on Fearless, looking over his shoulder as Song continued to fuss.

"Hey. Listen to what I'm telling you."

"Sovanna's in trouble. Let me see her. We can delay the flight for a moment. Nothing will happen."

It was a trick.

"She'll be fine. Get us airborne right away. Do you understand? We go here," Fearless said, planting his finger on the chart. "You have a ruler and a protractor?"

"I know what I'm doing. But that has to be no less than five hundred yards long."

"It is. And make sure the transponder's switched off."

"Do you think it's ever on, on a plane like this?"

"Close the ramp. Get this heap in the air. And we stay low. Below five thousand feet."

Fearless turned and headed back into the compartment. "Belts on," he shouted as he made his way back into the hold.

Quickly, he edged sideways through the stacks of crates, remembering the way he'd beaten Wish and leapt at Federenko's throat, praying that his anger would come to him again. Through the open ramp of the cargo hold he could see Federenko, a semicircle of his crew still gathered around him.

This is what he hadn't been able to reveal to Jimmy, his extra motivation for making the handover here. In Liberia, or wherever the hell this technically was, he might have an opportunity to kill Federenko, get away with it, and free them all forever. Nowhere else would this have been possible.

Fearless swung the rifle straight up to his chest, his left hand grabbing the barrel, his right the pistol grip, just as the lower half of the rear entrance started to close, the ramp lifting back into flight position. "Put the stock in the middle of your chest," Alyosha had taught him. "This way you kill men and spare the birds."

Now the overhead door swung down to meet the lower ramp, its hydraulic closers starting to retract. The men outside wouldn't see him in the dark, raising the rifle, placing his eye against the sight.

For an instant, Federenko's men scrolled across his vision till the crosshairs settled on Federenko's face. He couldn't possibly know that Fearless was looking at him, but he stared directly back, his lips moving silently.

I'll find you, Fearless imagined him saying. *I will always track you down. You know this.*

It had to be now; in less than five seconds the opportunity would be gone. A reel of images rippled through Fearless's mind. The carnage in Nairobi. The letter *s* in the trash. The hair falling away from Song's face to reveal her burns. He tensed his forearms against a shiver of terror and concentrated all his will onto one shining focal point.

"Mon frère," he muttered under his breath.

The fire ran down his shoulder, through the tendons and muscles—a fuse wire burning its way to the trigger.

54

The voice took a breath and then started to scream again: a diamond-tipped bit drilling into his ear canal. Struck by the vertigo of being lost in the dark and jostled by the plane rattling over the potholed strip, Fearless let his gun drop and reached out with his hands. He felt the sharp, hard angle of a supporting strut, then a crate as cold as a mortuary drawer.

"Ot tee! Ot tee!" The scream resolved itself into words. It was Song.

Amos bellowed back over the noise of the engines, which keened higher and higher as the Antonov accelerated.

Fearless's stomach turned in on itself. He hadn't taken the shot.

As soon as he opened the compartment door, Fearless saw Song slumped over her sister, holding her body in her arms and rocking it. The two of them were on the floor, a mess of hair and limb.

"Ot tee!"

"What's happening?" shouted Amos again, the plane rumbling on, the frequency of the engine noise at such an earsplitting pitch that it felt like they were trapped in a swarm of locusts.

As the plane lurched and rose, Song pitched back, revealing Sovanna's unconscious body. The whites of her eyes beneath her half-closed lids were little crescents like fingernails. An ivory dust, like fine-sifted sugar, powdered the inside of her lips.

Song's face looked to Fearless, wrenched in horror. All language deserting her, she let out a strange yelp.

Sovanna was unresponsive and clammy when Fearless examined her. He pulled on each of her eyelids in turn. He thought he saw a spark of life still flickering. Each second would be critical. He shook her. He tapped her cheek.

"Can you hear me, Sovanna?"

Lightness floated inside their bodies as the plane bumped down and then left the ground.

"Sovanna. Sovanna! Can you hear me, Sovanna?"

Without pausing, he ran his fingers down her chest, located the sternum, and placed the heel of his right hand above it, the left hand following, fingers interlacing. He leaned over, arms straight and shoulders over his hands, and quickly began to push: two inches down, release. When he felt a hard lump, he moved his hand and pulled out a plastic bag from her blouse, tucked into her bra, full of pills. He threw these to the side and compressed her chest again. Two inches down, release. Two inches down, release. He crouched down to feel her breath on his cheek: nothing. He pinched her nostrils, pressed his mouth to hers, and breathed, watching her chest rise, then gave her a second breath.

As he began another cycle of compressions, Song whimpered and rocked back and forth. "Bong srey," she kept saying. "I did this. I did."

She had told Sovanna about the rape and that Federenko was the father, but the response was not at all what she had expected.

"Why say this to me now?" Sovanna had said. "Why not tell me right at the beginning?"

"Why would I lie, bong? I was worried you were out of your mind!"

"You do lie. He wasn't trying to hurt me like you said. He didn't want to make me suffer, I know."

"I did this," Song mumbled. She had tried to play Federenko's game.

Two breaths. Thirty compressions. Two breaths. Thirty compressions.

Soon Fearless's own breathing started to grow frantic.

The plane leveled out but still rattled and whined.

Two breaths. Thirty compressions. Two breaths. Thirty compressions. His triceps were on fire, his shoulders hunched and knotted.

"I will not feel. I will not feel." He was muttering it out loud in sync with the compressions.

He lost all sense of time and space. The sky was flat and white. How many minutes had passed? He was probably underestimating; his feverishness and Song's sobbing dragged every second into an eternity. At least ten, maybe twelve. He had to keep going.

Then Amos was kneeling with him, his face a wretched grimace. "It's on autopilot. You're flagging. Let me take over."

"One more. . . . Twenty-eight. Twenty-nine. Thirty."

"She's been in detox," Amos said. "Her tolerance . . . next to nothing." He put his hand to his forehead, held it there, and didn't move.

Fearless began the count from one to thirty again.

"How long has it been?"

Fearless didn't answer. They both knew too much time had elapsed. If there'd been any hope, she would have revived within five cycles. But now fifteen, twenty minutes had passed. He pushed even harder. There was a crack: a breaking rib.

Amos moved him aside and took over the compressions. He was doing it for Song. That was the only reason. To show her they had done everything they could.

Song had stopped wailing and entered a state of shock, with Sovanna's dead hand draped in her palm.

After a minute, Amos stopped, placing his hands on his thighs. Fearless became conscious of the plane once again, the rumbling of it like the sound of a kettle's rolling boil. With the back of his hand, Amos wiped his forehead. Fearless looked away; he could see that Amos was weeping.

What had Amos planned with Federenko before take-off? Certainly not this. No one would want this.

Amos rose and went to Song. He put his arm around her shoulders with enormous tenderness. Then he touched his lips to her hair for a moment before rising to his feet and lurching to the cockpit. Fearless heard the rusty springs of the pilot's chair creak and metal switches being flicked on and off.

Fearless remained kneeling at Sovanna's side. Twice he reached out to stroke her cheek with the back of his fingers. Her skin was as soft as a child's, it seemed to him. It was a stupid thing to think, because that's what she was. She would never grow up. She would never grow old. Even now, there was a radiance to her that could only be felt in her presence.

His eyes searched for a blanket or some piece of cloth. He couldn't bear to leave her lying there exposed. But there was only a curtain in that rough, dusty fabric used in old trains—and it was hardly enough to cover her. "Song," he said. He leaned over Sovanna to touch her. "Song. Please listen." But Song wouldn't raise her head.

There was no time to waste; he rose and headed for the cockpit. This was the moment he had been dreading.

Seeing the emotion Amos had shown for the girls had spooked him. He paused on the threshold, watching the back of his head. Slowly, his gaze fell on Amos's neck. He stretched out and flattened his hand, keeping it by his side.

He had seen the strike done once after a karate class, when a group were messing around in the changing rooms: a strike to the carotid with the side of the hand, and then, if necessary, another on the other side—an instant knockout if performed correctly.

His left hand reached for the knife hilt in his pocket. Afterwards, he knew he would have to use it too.

Amos turned. "Just do it," he said, immediately turning back to the controls. He pointed to one of the switches in front of him. "The landing gear's here. But be warned, she's a beast. You'll have to wrestle hard when you take her down."

When had he worked it out? Probably before they boarded. Fearless could have done it, he could have, if it had been one of those bulky Ukrainians, with their ruddy faces and beer bellies and sunburned forearms.

"Amos, what are you talking about?"

Just the oddness of Fearless saying his name was enough to reveal that Amos had guessed correctly.

"No need to do me harm. There's another way," Amos said.

"What do you mean?"

"What have you got in that bag?"

"The rucksack? What I'd need to survive if the girls and I get stranded. If worse comes to worst."

"Well, that's already happened."

Amos looked at the dials and made a minor adjustment to the throttle. He was weighing something up that wouldn't keep still on the scales.

"You don't have to kill me. I'm not going to fight you. And you won't have to kill yourself either trying to land this thing—I mean: how will you determine the wind? There might be game on the strip and you'll be forced to do a go-around. Are you used to getting the approach speed as low as you'll need to? Listen, let me take it down. I'll leave you at your rendezvous. Then I'll fly off again, in the direction of the drop. But I'll never make it there. The plane will crash and b-b-burn." He reached out for the chart and flapped it out with one hand. "Here. Here. Or here. Or here. They're all n-national parks. Pretty much uninhabited. Miles from any towns or villages or roads."

Fearless took the map and stared at the green spaces. "Why would you do that? What about you?"

Amos gestured to the well beneath the seats that led to a small space inside the plane's nose. "I'll bail out. There's a parachute in the navigator's booth. And I'll have your survival bag to see me through."

"But . . ."

"I'll be fine. I told you about my skydiving, didn't I?" He pointed to the shape in Fearless's thigh pocket. "The alternative is having no odds at all, no?"

Fearless sat down listlessly in the copilot's seat. "For God's sake. Just land the plane and do your job."

"Just listen. I've had enough of all this. I've some money stashed away— I'll be fine if I make it. Don't you see? With the amount of explosives in this hold, everything will be vaporized and we'll all be reckoned dead. Not a skeleton to trace. Nobody will search. For you, for Song, and not for m-m-me either."

Fearless pictured the explosion. The wreckage of ash and soot and metal. It was too good to be true: he wouldn't have to kill anyone.

"Not bad for a pacifist," Fearless murmured to himself.

It was better than he could have hoped. Iglas, TNT—the entire waybill in Hossein's notebook: a giant firework display that no one would ever see. The tree falling in the forest. The dark side of the moon. And the

Islamists' bombing campaign would have to wait; maybe, now, they would rethink their ambitions. And Federenko? If Fearless and Song were dead, he wouldn't get his money. No phone call would be made. His man would leave empty-handed. He would be waiting right now, under the railway arches at King's Cross, surrounded by a rugby team in black balaclavas. They would tell him no deal and turf him onto the street.

"Hold on," Fearless said, turning back to the compartment.

In his absence, Song had pulled Sovanna around and lifted her head into her lap. She was holding it tenderly and intoning a Khmer song. Fearless knelt down and waited for her to finish, the words falling to a whisper, then little more than a breath.

Then, much to his relief, Song looked up and recognized him. She came back to the present, to the buffeting of the aircraft, to the rippling vibration of its propellers in their bones.

Her lips parted slightly. She saw Sovanna in the rice fields, running the straight path that ran beyond the horizon. And this time she didn't shout "chop!" but run. Run on, run fast, and don't ever look back. For a moment—crossing the space between Federenko and Fearless—she was unbound.

"She is free," Song said.

Fearless reached out and laid a hand on her shoulder. They could be free too; Amos's plan was the only way. By not existing at all, they would never be found.

"Song—once Amos has landed the plane, you and I will leave. I have a friend who will help us escape."

"Together? You and me."

"Of course."

"But he will find us! For the baby."

"No he won't. We have a way."

"I know what you're thinking," Amos said when Fearless returned to the cockpit. "You're thinking: he's just saying what he has to—to get out of this. And why should you believe me? I understand why you wouldn't."

Fearless placed the survival bag beside Amos's seat. He remembered the warning that Amos had given him as the ferry pulled away from the dock in Phnom Penh.

"I trust you." Fearless drew the commando knife out of his pocket. "I'll put this in the bag. I hope you won't need it. And this too." He removed the Rolex from his wrist.

"Get her strapped in. We don't have much time left."

"But what would have happened in Siem Reap, Amos? Tell me. If I'd stayed at that hotel. The Paradise."

"You need to be strapped in. I'm bringing her down."

"Did he mean me harm? I just don't understand."

"For fuck's sake. He wanted to know how much you knew. And the truth was . . ."

"What?"

"It's better not to know."

Fearless relented and went back into the compartment.

"Hold tight!" shouted Amos. "It's gonna get bumpy. Keep those seat belts on!"

They were already level with the green canopy of the jungle. The plane began to shudder, buffeted by unseen forces. Fearless could sense Amos grappling with the controls, trying to slow the giant before it touched the ground. A little whine came from Song; her grip tightened in his as the plane smacked down once, rose, then smacked down again. As the wheels beat thunder, their bodies were hurled forward, Sovanna's corpse sliding away like a loose piece of luggage.

Now they were pressed back violently into their seats, Song's feet and lower legs swinging up involuntarily. The whole fuselage groaned, straining against its momentum. And then—just as terror began to stuff their throats closed—Amos had it under control and they were rumbling to a coast.

"I see them!" shouted Amos. "I see your people. They're waiting for you."

"We go now," said Fearless as soon as the plane juddered to a stop.

With Song still in shock, he unbuckled her seat belt. He took her by the arm and guided her out past the weapons crates as the hold's metal doors parted to reveal Jimmy and his driver, the two of them scurrying toward the plane.

"Those your people?" shouted Amos.

"Yeah, yeah. That's them!"

"I have the phone!" shouted Jimmy as they made their way through the hold. "Give your bags to my driver—he'll take them."

"We won't need the phone, Jim—I'll explain to you in a moment."

"But Sovanna!" said Song, pushing Fearless away. She turned and went back. She needed to tell Sovanna. She needed to tell her that she'd been right all along.

"Where is she?" said Jimmy.

"She's dead. She just died," Fearless said, his face creasing in a bitter grin of pain. "Song! Come back!"

But in seconds, Song was in the plane beside Sovanna, on her knees, cradling her face in her hands.

"Leave Sovanna with me," Amos said to Song, kneeling beside her, his hand on her back.

"Ot tee! Ot tee!"

"Song. Listen to me. You have to go. She'll be burned in the sky. She'll be the closest, I promise you, she can ever get to heaven."

"Ot tee! Ot tee. Ot tee. Ot tee." Song lifted her head and looked at him for a moment. Then she turned back to Sovanna, smoothing her hair.

"Jaa," she said, "Jaa."

"She's gone!"

"I know."

Her voice was now just the tiniest of whispers.

Song reached for Sovanna's hand and held it against her cheek. How she loved that hand, which only now she could see was not like hers at all, with its subtle differences wrought by a lifetime of different gestures—as the drop of water shapes the rock face, as experience shapes the soul. She had loved holding that hand in the dark and whispering. She had loved its fingertips, pressing little circles in the earth so they could play Bay Khom when the rains had finally passed. She had loved being her shadow. She could have been her shadow forever.

She placed a tender kiss in the middle of Sovanna's forehead, rose, and hurried out of the plane.

As the Land Rover picked up speed to drive them away, Fearless looked back to see the Antonov turning around. For some reason, the side door to the hold had been left open, but it was too late to warn Amos—and irrelevant at low altitude.

As they rumbled down a track and plunged into the bush, Fearless kept glancing, waiting to see the plane emerge. Song leaned away and pushed her head into the vehicle's canvas; occasionally a sob rose and fell in her chest. And then there it was, soaring magically into the air: extraterrestrial, unnatural, climbing higher and higher. Soon, it was nothing but a drop of ink dissolving in the endless, unknowing, implacable blue.

55

Amos had known that Fearless would misinterpret him. He said he'd had enough of this life, implying he wanted to make a fresh start. But not everyone can change. Not everyone can start over. Life isn't a TV episode where a good deed or aphorism can change the shape of your spirit and turn of your mind.

Maybe he had learned something from Alyosha after all: the art of managing what—and how much—people knew. He was like a novelist, Alyosha, creating characters and deciding where they would go.

But it's the gaps in stories that always tell you the most, isn't it? The things unsaid. Unspoken. Unmentioned. The things that lie beyond what you intended.

For instance, Amos knew this: it had not been Wish who spiked Fearless's drink. Wish liked people to know the harm he did. It was a point of principle—the polar opposite of his sniping days.

Once Amos had got the plane into the air, he pored over the charts, calculating distance, altitude, and speed. Soon enough, he had rejoined the original flight path. Safely above 5,000 feet, he switched on the transponder. This way there was the possibility the plane would appear on radar before it began its descent and disappeared forever.

Satisfied that he had everything set, he put the plane on autopilot and ducked into the nose turret, where he pulled out a battered parachute pack. Swiftly, he moved to the compartment where Sovanna lay cold and ripped the pilot chute and bridle away. Once he reached the main canopy, he unfurled the fabric. Its color was fitting: wasn't white the Cambodian tradition? And it was also right that her body would end in fire: they cremated their dead to release the soul from its cage before it could alight on some other being.

Then, not stopping to consider why he was doing so, he removed his T-shirt and took the water from Fearless's survival pack. He shivered a little to be bare-chested at this altitude. It would get worse when he went into the hold, he thought.

Wetting the fabric, he wiped Sovanna's face, the white froth from her lips, her right hand, her left hand. Gently he worked, smoothing the little hairs on her forearms.

Then he took the canopy and spread it out on the floor, lifting her lifeless corpse into the middle of the fabric.

He had the urge to lean down and kiss her on the forehead. But he didn't have the right. She belonged to no one now.

Deliberately, slowly, he wrapped the canopy around her, lifting and moving her body as tenderly as possible, struggling to keep the frictionless nylon from slipping away. When he was finished, he tucked the folds of fabric beneath her, so she was as close to a perfectly swaddled mummy as she could be. He thought about saying some kind of prayer or, at least, trying to say what made her special. But he couldn't think of any words and was scared of opening his mouth, for a sob was waiting there, ready to overwhelm him.

Then he got up and went to the radio operator's panel, located just behind the copilot's seat.

"Mayday, Mayday, Mayday," he croaked. "This is Uniform-November-One-One-Zero-Zero-Seven."

He paused, counted to five, and then spoke once again—this time making more effort to inject panic into the transmission.

"Mayday. Uniform-November-One-One-Zero-Zero-Seven. Mechanical failure. Ditching aircraft. Position: close to Benin–Togo border. Altitude fourteen thousand feet. Airspeed: three hundred knots. Heading: eighty-five degrees. Four persons on board. *Four persons on board.* Uniform-November-One-One-Zero. . . ."

He flicked off the switch and checked the altimeter. He would have around a minute of free fall, he reckoned. Then he disengaged the autopilot, set the plane into a shallow descent, and turned back to the passenger compartment.

He hadn't answered Fearless's question about The Paradise, but he hadn't lied. It was better not to know and better not to have killed. It would make Fearless more able to deal with the things that haunt you, he thought, the voices and noises that come when you're alone. Which was always. A single gunshot. Silence. Another shot. And again. Forget you ever saw it, they told him.

Sometimes he had been arrogant enough to think that he could outrun it, that he could just go on living and die before it got to him. But the vulture was lean and hungry and could see more and further. Looking down from its vantage point, it always knew where he would arrive. And when he got to his destination, it would swoop down blithely, perching in the corner, preening its feathers, waiting.

Goose pimples appeared on his arms in the cargo bay. The noise of the wind and the turboprops roared and throbbed. The open side door swung back and forth on its hinges, expanding and closing the sector of light on the floor. He thought about his mum, holding her hand on the walk to Sunday school. What were the words? *Greater love hath no man than this—that he lay down his life for his friends.* She would have known the rest and been able to quote it. But he hadn't listened. He never bloody listened.

As Amos reached out to grip the cold metal of the doorframe, the thought of his first mother—his real mother—also came to him. The feeling he had always had of being in her arms. It wasn't possible, he knew: he had been given up after birth. He hadn't been with her for more than a few minutes. But the picture gave him comfort; it was as meaningful and beloved as any real memory he had.

He leaned out then back in, before hurling himself into the sky—head up, arms out, arching his back, flying free. After the first rush of air took the breath from his lungs, he settled, his body taking over from his mind. There were no more decisions to make. No plans or possibilities. No seconds to count. No cord to reach for. Nothing but this light falling every-where around him and the world stretching out from his wide-open arms.

From box position, he rolled to his left, then onto his back, before bring-ing himself around, belly-to-earth. Hands retracted and legs straight, he shot forward through the air; then, his legs bent and arms out, he slowed, then reversed. He turned in circles, relishing the 360-degree view. How beautiful it was—no tessellated fields or crisscrossing roads, just forest and plain, all of it virgin. He could see nothing that man had done, no evidence of his existence.

This is where we began, he thought. *This is where I end.*

Flowing between positions and changing speeds at will, he conducted the movement of the air around him, his body a foil to louver and tilt. All anxiety had left him. He didn't have to think. Only the winds that rippled his cheeks and flapped the fabric of his shorts made the flight feel any dif-ferent from floating weightlessly.

For the sheer hell of it, he threw himself into a somersault, surfed forward for a moment, before inverting his body. He was headfirst now, pointing straight down toward the earth. With his surface area next to nothing, his speed increased dramatically: 135, 150, 160 miles an hour. He held himself still and straight and true—a dart, a black arrow, a hard spear of steel. From the ground, if you had seen him, you might have noticed a flickering speck—glimpsed for a split second but too fast for the naked eye. If you were near enough you would have heard it: a dull thud on solid ground.

But no one was there to see it, and no one would ever know.

PART 6

Those who sharpen the tooth of the dog, meaning
Death
Those who glitter with the glory of the hummingbird, meaning
Death
Those who sit in the sty of contentment, meaning
Death
Those who suffer the ecstasy of the animals, meaning
Death

Are become unsubstantial, reduced by a wind,
A breath of pine, and the woodsong fog
By this grace dissolved in place

T. S. ELIOT
from "Marina"

EPILOGUE

"Craa!" calls the boy, "Craaaa! Crrrrrraaaaa!"

Fearless leans his head around the sitting room door. The child is bashing two wooden blocks together.

"Doucement, Joseph, s'il te plaît! Dou-ce-ment."

The Barbapapas on the television transform themselves into parachutes and float an elephant down to the earth.

Apart from a single wrinkle under each eye, the boy looks nothing like Federenko—thank God. Not a day goes by without Fearless being grateful for it. With his features, his complexion, his demeanor, his spirit, he's the spitting image of Song and Song alone.

"He's more like his auntie," Song maintains—for, of course, Joseph's face is free of scars.

Fearless marvels at that: the way Song speaks of Sovanna. He still can't manage the same with Laure. The fog of his grief has now dispersed, but he does not see more clearly than before. She is fading. Her face, her voice, her touch. That habit she had when she was deep in thought of touching her upper lip with the back of her ring finger. He can't let it go. And yet it disappears. All roads to her will be gone, as will those to the people and places and experiences to which she'd led him.

"Are you ready yet?" he shouts, removing one of the orchids from the kitchen sink where it's been soaking.

"Un instant," Song replies from down the hall. "Deux minutes—max."

After two years of living on the outer edge of Paris, Song's French is almost perfect, both spoken and written, the latter all the more remarkable given she started from zero. From the first day they had moved into their apartment in the nineteenth arrondissement, in the shadow of Les Orgues de Flandre, one of the monolithic seventies housing experiments, it had been their rule that they would principally speak French. Another was that they would stick—no exceptions—to their new identities. Thomas was his new name, Sothea hers: her name in childhood.

Their life in Paris had been part of the original plan Fearless had conceived on that night in Odesa: what better place was there to hide than a working-class neighborhood in a European capital, a world not just overlooked but actively ignored? He'd learned French through his mother but had never had any connection to the city. Only Jimmy, Lucy, and Conrad knew they had survived. Even Luke was led to believe they had perished in the plane crash: Fearless needed him to execute his instructions without raising suspicion. This was hardest on Jimmy, who, in addition to handling the bureaucracy—from securing the Consular Death Registration via the nearest high commission in Ghana to drawing on a web of connections to create their new identities—had to stand by as Luke's grief unfolded in front of him, while faking a heartbreak he didn't feel.

The doorbell rings. "Craaaa!" calls the boy again.

"The babysitter's here, Sothea! Let's get on the road."

When Song sticks her head out of her bedroom door—her hair, wet from the shower, leaving damp patches on her shoulders—she sees Fearless leading the sitter into the kitchen. He will be telling her the times for Joseph's bottles of formula and the special trick he has for getting him down. Fearless can never do enough for the two of them; it's his way of making amends for his past. There is nothing he will miss. He will always be present. To Song, he spins it differently: "I just want you to be able to make the most of this new life."

And it's true: there's so much to take in. Sometimes, she feels as if she has been dropped from the skies. There is new food—"You can ask for more if you want more," he had actually said to her!—there are new clothes, new kinds of stares in the street, new kinds of shops and money to spend in them (if Viktor had astonished her by putting cash in her hand, Fearless had arranged her own bank account and card). There are demonstrations, with *casseurs* smashing windows in the street. She begs Fearless to go with her—people taking power into their own hands! There are the intensive French courses, every minute of which she devours: she is a schoolgirl, just as she has always longed to be. And that isn't the end: you can use your learning for action; she has signed up as a volunteer on the Croix-Rouge *maraudes*, on which she pays special attention to the most vulnerable addicts. Then there are books and all the worlds and times they open to her, from the classics she reads such as *Le Petit Prince* and *Le Petit Nicolas* to the English albums Fearless likes to perform for Joseph ("Unscramble yourselves!" he shouts when he does *What Do People Do All Day?*—a phrase that, for some reason, sends the boy into hysterics). At the public library, on a shelf labeled INDOCHINE, she discovers several histories that help her grasp the truth of her parents' lives. They were children themselves, she learns, robbed of their own parents and childhoods, uprooted and then returned to a home forever changed. Then there is her body and all its wants. Your body can feel pleasure; it can need pleasure; it can seek pleasure out. For so long she had separated herself from it, but now it was hers again. The body that held Joseph in its arms and let him fall asleep on it: this body full of inexhaustible warmth and light.

Sometimes, when Fearless watches Song taking all this in—new feelings and moods and ways of responding to the world—the person he thinks of most is Federenko. Freedom without limits was a dangerous thing. No one, after all, had taught Federenko how to be free. No one had taught him how to use his power when he finally had it. One day, he knows he will have to convey this to Joseph and ensure he learns the lessons his father had not. This magnanimity comes to him from Song, for she never speaks of Federenko except to mention all that she has to be grateful for. Without him, she says, she wouldn't know she was HIV positive. She would be living under a death sentence she wouldn't have been able to escape.

The drive to the Normandy coast takes almost three hours. For most of it, they stay silent. Song gazes out over the dark seams of the brown fields, at the lines of the new wind turbines marking the horizon, at the white hulks of the Charolais on the lush green hills. For a while, her thoughts turn to Sovanna, replaying what she could and should have done to save her. There is no way of knowing if another path would have been better, but it's impossible to resist imagining a present where she is alive.

Fearless too cannot help but think of Laure, imagining her at the wheel, the look of concentration on her face. Had she known what was happening? Was there a flashing instant when she perceived the shattering glass and the world starting to tumble? Or did the crash occur too fast? Was her consciousness out there still, gliding down that road, driving infinitely toward the horizon? As he drives, she is everywhere, with him and around him. She occupies the exact same space as his body; he can feel her warmth in the raised hairs on his forearms.

Vasiliev appears to him farther along the road, sitting under the seven angry hoods of the Naga. Not long after their "death," he had been arrested by Cambodian police; Federenko, it transpired, could achieve something with those tapes. Nevertheless, within weeks he was free once again, remaining in Sihanoukville to supervise the building of a beach resort. A year after that, on a return trip to Russia, he was killed by a car bomb—a murder that remained unsolved.

Traoré appears farther along the road: seminaked on the massage table, patting it with his hand. He remains as untouchable as ever, a respected politician in his native land. The last Fearless heard, he had been dubbed an architect of peace for brokering new talks in the Sierra Leone Civil War, though it was impossible to imagine his deals had nothing to do with the massacre that preceded them: "Operation No Living Thing." For a while, Fearless had contemplated trying to ruin Traoré by following up on his threat to send the videotape to his son. "But who would win then?" Song had counseled him. "Not the boy. Not you. And certainly not me."

Fearless's vision of Federenko is a retrospective fantasy: he is bound to the wooden chair in Viktor's house on stilts, with Viktor stalking around him, clothes iron in hand. But like Traoré, Federenko had continued his ascent. For a year, he had slipped off everyone's radar before his signal reappeared even stronger and in Russia. He seemed free to travel the otchizna and inveigle himself into the "circle." In an act of posthumous revenge, he had sullied Fearless's name via the same newspapers that had covered Fearless's arrest in Cambodia. Fearless, not he, had made a career of fixing arms deals, stretching back to their first days in Bosnia and Chechnya. Fearless, not he, had established close links with the Islamists while enjoying unfettered access to their secret camps.

None of these lies meant much to Fearless save for the way they affected Luke who, according to Jimmy, had become obsessed with an ensuing legal battle; with the coroner recording an open verdict at the inquest, the life insurance company had refused to pay out, arguing that the case of an alleged arms dealer demanded much deeper investigation. As for Lucy and Conrad, their concerns lay elsewhere. Over the last year, Lucy's mental health had deteriorated. She was heavily medicated again, wandering the corridors of a psych ward.

Fearless knows all of this from Jimmy's letters. Jimmy sends him things constantly, including tributes and obituaries that Fearless ignores and stuffs into his bedside cabinet. The events of those momentous weeks had consumed Jimmy too. In each update, he would detail his continued investigations into Federenko, whose dealings were a web of extraordinary intricacy with one infuriating and perpetual feature: its creator, who one assumed would be at the center, was nowhere to be found. Many of Jimmy's discoveries made Fearless's past more discordant. For instance, the Bosanska Idealna Futura—the charity that had run the nursing home which had been burned to the ground—had been a front for terrorists exploiting the Islamic pillar of zakat to gather and divert funds to nefarious schemes. Luke and Jimmy came up with their own clever riposte: dispersing the money from the Samsonite suitcase through hundreds of microdonations to good and honest causes—a guerrilla rebalancing of scales that were otherwise rigged.

Jimmy, his career ruined by the hatchet job on J. D., now worked for a human rights NGO in Brighton, where, he wrote, he felt freer than ever: "In my old job I thought there was nothing higher than being pragmatic, that being an idealist was adolescent stuff. But those core beliefs—in justice, in fairness, in not giving an inch to evil—are a reality that none of us should *ever* let go. We tell ourselves they're not adult: that's the greatest fucking lie." Fearless agreed, but he wanted him to stop digging, throw down his spade, or, even better, use it to bury all their questions.

"How'd you know to be in Nairobi?"

Who had ultimately burned down the cottage?

Why did Laure visit his mother?

Was it better not to know?

He wondered about the phone call Federenko said he'd had with Laure. It could have been true; she was asking his advice. But even the innocuous now seemed clouded with doubt.

"No no no," Fearless mutters to himself, his hands on the wheel. He presses harder on the accelerator, driving on toward the shadow of the last ghost on the road, who is nonchalantly sticking his thumb out. He smiles to himself. These days, he sees Amos in the mirror: he has grown out his hair and styled it in similar short dreads. It isn't a question of disguise, but a matter of delight: of being free to be himself as he has never been before. In the summer, he even wears short sleeves in public. When he walks, he treads without watching his step. Let the world carry on, relentlessly Manichaean. Let it be. Knowing that Amos is out there, a fellow warrior, comforts him. Nothing has been heard of him, no record, no sighting. In idle moments, Fearless likes to fantasize about his life, the places he is wandering, his spirit carrying on.

On the beach at Étretat, Fearless heaves the clinker-built rowboat. Its wooden hull clatters over the pigeon-gray stones. It's quiet. Beachcombers in yellow anoraks dab dots of color along the shoreline and the sea lies still around the famous chalk needle. Beside it, the natural arch seems like the ruins of a giant cathedral, its great vault hollowed out by centuries of tide.

"Is this okay, Sothea?"

"It's just like you said—Thomas."

She hates calling him that, and he secretly agrees with her. It's strange to have a new name at a time—maybe the first time—when he would never choose to be anyone other than who he is.

"Hop in quick—I'll push us into the water."

Fearless has been here once before, with Laure, during their first year together. He remembers holding her hand and walking on the cliff top, the lush, mossy grass soft and springy beneath their feet. To have gone back to the U.K. would have been too risky for them now, but here at least is a place that he had shared with Laure, on the same water that she had seen from the other side of the Channel—due north lay Cuckmere and the white cliffs near their cottage. Fearless remembers pulling back the curtain from the bedroom window and the light falling upon her as she lay between the sheets, pools of sun upon the sea mirroring pockets in the cloud cover.

He pushes hard now and the bow of the boat lifts over the water and the cold sea rushes up to his knees and into his boots. Then he leaps inside and scrambles past Song and onto the thwart, setting the oars in the row-locks as quickly as he can, pulling hard before the next wave has a chance to ground them. This is the moment he and Song have talked about for eighteen months: the chance for them to give their dead the rites they should have had. "The rites of your unworlding," he whispers to himself.

Song gasps as a succession of waves bobs up beneath the boat and they plunge, rise up, and plunge down again, fronds of spray flashing, the hull rolling and pitching. But now they're out beyond the breakers, gliding clear, with a swell gently rising and fading beneath them as they coast farther and farther out, the shoreline receding. Song stretches her hand over the side, cupping the water and letting it fall. All the time, they say nothing, Fearless rowing on. With her other hand, she reaches for Sovanna's necklace at her breast, pressing the deep blue Tanzanite stone in her fist.

Then Fearless stops and lets the boat drift.

He swings the oars in and rests their blades in the ribs.

"I think it's time."

Song reaches behind her neck and unhooks the lobster claw clasp, letting the chain pool in her palm. At the same time, Fearless searches inside his coat pocket, bringing out the plastic letter *s* on its worn leather string and the engagement ring he had never been able to give.

For a moment, their eyes meet. When tears begin to well in Song's, he looks away. "Okay," he says. "I'll go first."

He reaches over the side and opens his palm, letting the ring and letter slip gently from his fingers. The ring sinks instantly; they can see it for the first few feet, a tiny silver fish diving away from the seabirds. The plastic letter drifts, floating close by for a moment before it is borne away on the crest of a wavelet. He tells himself he has to think of a future without Laure in it.

As Song raises her hand, tears run freely over her scars as she reaches out over the edge of the boat. She can't let go. She shakes her head. "For better or worse," she says, "this is the only thing I have left." It's so vast, this sea. And the sky's so vast. It seems to her that Sovanna will be lost in it forever.

"Then you keep it," he says. "It's okay by me."

"It's the only thing Sovanna ever gave to me."

Fearless looks up and takes a breath. "Oh," he says, "she gave you much more than that."

He is right. Sovanna gave her the truth. She was a diviner of it—past and present and future. She gave her the truth about their parents, understanding their human frailty. She had known the truth of Song's pregnancy when it was beyond her imagining. And she knew the truth of her own destiny—that her addiction would not be beaten.

At the beginning, in the dark days before the novice monk had pointed the way, Song had always hoped that the good people in the world outnumbered the bad. But Sovanna—and Viktor and Bun Thim and Amos—had taught her that no one is ever one thing. There are only good or bad choices and good and bad paths to follow, and you are only as good as the last choice you make. There was never an end that you could say that you attained—there was only the struggle, every hour, every day, of making a life as good as it could be. And, in that struggle, the person you should trust least and hold most to account is yourself.

Song raises her arm above her head and lets the necklace fly, its silver chain glinting as it arcs through the air. Then a splash—a spray of water like two leaves of long grass—and the sea is itself again, as if nothing ever happened.

Then, after a moment, the song rises inside her. She sings it to the waves and the birds and to Fearless, the spindrift on the breeze spritzing her face.

> *I look to the sky, the sky's so far.*
> *I look to the stars, the stars are as far.*
> *Water's waves crash and swirl.*
> *I reminisce. I feel a sadness.*
> *A sadness that makes my heart burst.*
> *I remember the hand you used to hold.*
> *I'll miss you. Our love has melted away.*
> *We will part; I'll miss you. Don't miss me, baby.*
> *All right my baby, my pretty baby.*
> *Karma is forcing us to part.*
> *This life and the next, my baby.*
> *I'll wish for you. Hopefully, I'll get what I wished for:*
> *That I'll meet you in every life after this.*

When she finishes and opens her eyes and looks at Fearless, she sees that look—the strange look Dara always had for her, with its mix of sadness and curiosity and hope.

It's only then that she truly understands: it's love given freely, with no thought of what it might receive in return. All along, she had been loved—by the children and also by Fearless—even in the time she had thought herself unlovable.

Without a thought, she leaps up and throws her arms around him, making him gasp, setting the boat rocking on the water. She screams out and they laugh and come apart to smile before he wipes her tears with his hand and they hold each other even harder. This is love—a continuous rhythm, like the waves in the wind, expanding and contracting with the things that befall them, the directions they choose, the weather of their emotions. It will not die.

For a while, they are buoyed up and down on the lilting waters. Their senses become one with the changes of wind and light. Each detail—the film of salt on the backs of their hands and cheeks, the way the light filters through the kapok of the clouds—seems imbued with a significance that in the past they searched for and had not been able to find. The gulls dip and swoop before losing hope and going elsewhere, and they are alone, the sky white and opaque around them.

When a shift in the wind drives a chill across their faces, dissipating the thin brume that clings to the water, Fearless lowers the oars and begins to row again. "Let's go home," he says. Back to Joseph and Paris, back to the new life they are trying to build together.

"You can relax," Song says. "There's no hurry, Fearless."

She calls him by his old name and he raises his eyebrows. He shakes his head and pulls even harder. The exertion gives him an excuse to grimace and hide his smile. "Fearless," he murmurs.

For the first time, it is true.

ACKNOWLEDGMENTS

Late nights and early mornings when the rest of the world slept. Illegible scribbles on the backs of shopping lists and tiny metro tickets that no longer exist. Writing this book was often a private process in stolen moments. But thanks to the support of so many, I was never alone.

To my readers, dear friends and sounding boards, I extend all my love and appreciation, with honorable mentions to Gavin Hollis, for his honest and wise insights, Glen Wright, for suffering my ramblings and conjectures, and Margaret Mistry, for an extraordinary friendship that has borne me unfailingly through everything life has thrown my way.

I am also deeply grateful to Millay Arts in Upstate New York, and the warm spirit of Monika Burczyk and Calliope Nicholas, who gave me the space, time, and support to be my best self. In Paris, I am indebted to Anna Segall, who kindly let me use her apartment during the pandemic so I could write peacefully during the *confinement*.

Of the hundreds of books, articles, and papers I devoured during the process of researching and writing this book, several made an indelible impression and merit special acknowledgment, not least Joe Sacco's *The Fixer*, Anna Politkovskaya's *A Dirty War*, Misha Glenny's *McMafia*, David E. Hoffman's *The Oligarchs: Wealth and Power in the New Russia*, Vadim Volkov's *Violent Entrepreneurs: The Use of Force in the Making of Russian Capitalism*, Douglas Farah's *Blood from Stones*, Andrew Feinstein's *The Shadow World: Inside the Global Arms Trade*, Peter Pomerantsev's *Nothing is True and Everything is Possible: The Surreal Heart of the New Russia*, and two books by Susan Sontag: *On Photography* and *Regarding the Pain of Others*. Above all, I remain utterly inspired by the entire corpus of Svetlana Alexievich's work and the masterpiece that is *Secondhand Time*.

I owe an enormous debt to numerous photojournalists who have shone a light on the darkest corners of the world and often paid for it with their lives. A complete list would run to many pages, but Tim Hetherington and Don McCullin have been particularly important to me. I salute you.

Working with Restless Books in the U.S. and Selkies House in the U.K. has been a privilege. My gratitude to Ilan Stavans, Lydia McOscar, my editors Nathan Rostron and Jennifer Alise Drew, who wrestled tirelessly with the fine details of the manuscript, and Rebecca Strong. The team at Tetragon was also vital: thanks to Alex Billington for Russian language advice and the attention given to font and ornament, and Sarah Terry for the precision proofreading. And respect to Choub Sok Chamreun, for correcting my rusty Khmer.

I will never have enough praise for my brilliant agent and friend, Anjali Singh, whose faith in me and unflagging commitment to this book brought it into the world. Having trekked a long road alone for years, I am honored to have you join me, nudging me along, clearing the dense brush, and sharing the reward of the view from the mountaintop.

Last, but always first, I want to thank those who share my daily life and often had to endure my absences in body and spirit: Rohini, Jo, Rokia, Noah, and Soizic, whose love lifted me up and carried me across the finish line.

ABOUT THE AUTHOR

PRAVEEN HERAT was born in London to Sri Lankan parents and educated at Oxford and the University of East Anglia. He lived in Phnom Penh, Cambodia, for several years, a period that marked him profoundly and prompted his research for what would become *Between This World and the Next*. Since 2010, he has lived in Paris.